RANGERS

Also by Mona Shepherd:

The Winterthur Chronicles: The Preserve

RANGERS

«««««««««««« · »»»»»»»»»»»»

«« ὃνό »»
( )

A NOVEL BY

MONA SHEPHERD

LIMNER BOOKS
- U.S.A. -

ISBN: 978-0-692-99326-2

LIMNER BOOKS U.S.A.

Available from Amazon.com and other retail outlets. Also available as e-book on Kindle and other devices.

Photography credits:

Front cover: ©Gelyngfjell, Dreamstime.com
www.dreamstime.com/royalty-free-stock-photo-smoky-mountains-national-park-image11261505
Fall colors in the Smoky Mountains National Park

Back cover: ©Pierre Leclerc, Dreamstime.com
www.dreamstime.com/royalty-free-stock-photo-grotto-falls-great-smoky-mountains-image27649598
Grotto Falls, Great Smoky Mountains National Park, North Carolina

With thanks to the men and women
of the National Park Service
for their dedication and service

~ NATIONAL PARK SERVICE ~
CENTENNIAL
1916-2016

"...WE HAVE BEEN COMPARED TO THE MILITARY FORCES BECAUSE OF OUR DEDICATION AND ESPRIT DE CORPS. IN A SENSE THIS IS TRUE. WE DO ACT AS GUARDIANS OF OUR COUNTRY'S LAND....

WE HAVE THE SPIRIT OF FIGHTERS, NOT AS A DE-STRUCTIVE FORCE, BUT AS A POWER FOR GOOD. WITH THIS SPIRIT EACH OF US IS AN INTEGRAL PART OF THE PRESERVATION OF THE MAGNIFICENT HERITAGE WE HAVE BEEN GIVEN, SO THAT CENTURIES FROM NOW PEOPLE OF OUR WORLD, OR PERHAPS OF OTHER WORLDS, MAY SEE AND UNDERSTAND WHAT IS UNIQUE ABOUT OUR EARTH, NEVER CHANGING, ETERNAL."

– HORACE M. ALBRIGHT
SECOND DIRECTOR
NATIONAL PARK SERVICE
1929–1933

. 1 .

Engulfed by a forest of green spires that pierced the sky, a road-worn Chevy Blazer wound its way along a ribbon of asphalt. The towering sequoias, along with the firs and ponderosa pines that skirted the road, were themselves dwarfed in this realm of granite giants stretching to the horizon. Titan sentinels El Capitan and Half Dome, luminous in the glow of dawn, guarded the Valley that had transformed many a visitor into poet, artist, and philosopher. Its sheer scale silenced the human intruder into insignificance even as it inspired.

Waters of the Merced rippling alongside, the vehicle with the National Park Service emblem continued its trek into the very heart of the park, the headquarters at Yosemite Village.

There was no denying it…it would be hard to leave this place. But it was the right thing to do.

Shane MacLeod glanced over at his daughter beside him on the front seat. The eleven-year-old was starting to look so like her mother, it made his throat ache at times. But it was her tight-lipped expression, the look in those blue eyes that fluctuated between imploring and resentment that captured his attention at present.

It's the right thing to do…. That had become his mantra these past two weeks. God knows they'd stayed on longer than they should have already, doggedly determined to maintain the routine, stay the course. But no matter how much he tried to deny it, the spark had gone out of him. He'd come to accept it. It was part of adjusting, part of…letting go.

Would he ever get it back? That drive deep down in his gut that got him up every morning, ready to take on life as a participant, not just a robot going through the motions?

Maybe it had something to do with age. Forty had come and gone and he'd ignored the jokes about mid-life crisis, but recently something had started to itch inside. Maybe that spark was waking back up, eager for new challenges, new vistas.

This could be the jumpstart he needed. Good for Marcie, too. She might not thank him now, but she would later, for taking charge, forcing them to look forward, not back anymore. At least he hoped so.

Here in early April, the park complex had the air of an isolated rustic settlement surrounded by pristine wilderness. The parking lot was virtually empty; warm-weather crowds would not descend upon them for another week or so. The Blazer approached the massive log and stone structure and rolled to a stop at the front steps.

MacLeod emerged, a lean, weathered figure in scuffed boots and the familiar gray-green uniform that marked him as an NPS ranger. He turned back to the child in the front seat. Something in that thin, elfin face and solemn eyes spoke of a calm adaptability beyond her years. But she was approaching that age of argument of late. She opened her mouth but he pre-empted her. "I've done a lot of thinkin' about this, Hon. The change of scenery'll do us good."

The little blond head dipped, the delicate chin rested on her chest. A telltale swallow. "If you say so."

There was as much resignation, as much guilt invoked in that reply as she could muster. The child turned to the window, craning her neck to look skyward, as if to catch a last glimpse of the wonders she would soon be forced to say good-bye to.

He reached across to give her shoulder a jostle, his smile worn but affectionate. "You'll see."

It's the right thing to do....

MacLeod trudged up the stone steps, his boot heels scraping loudly in the still morning air. Inside, the woman at the front counter looked up and acknowledged him with a warm smile.

"Good morning, Shane! Mr. Hayes is expecting you. Go right on back."

"Thanks, Meg." The ranger pushed his way through the gate and sauntered back to one of the offices. The half-open door revealed a large man at his desk, talking on the phone. He looked up and nodded, motioning his visitor to a chair. The nameplate on the massive old oak desk read *Superintendent William F. Hayes.*

"Okay...but tell them to call me as soon as it arrives...alright...bye." The head honcho of Yosemite Park hung up and settled back in his chair.

Park Security Ranger MacLeod came right to business. "You got something for me, Bill?"

"Yep." The man behind the desk began to hunt among the myriad stacks of papers before him, coming up with a manila envelope. He handed it across to the ranger. "Your transfer papers came in yesterday evening."

MacLeod opened the envelope and scanned its contents with no outward show of emotion. Bill Hayes leaned forward, hands clasped. "Congratulations—and good luck. You're gonna need it. The Smokies may be considered a plum assignment, but you'll have your hands full there—more than you might imagine."

MacLeod cocked an eyebrow. "They're full here. I just need a new set of problems." An amused look passed between the two men.

"Ah! Just remembered—" The Superintendent reached for another folder, marked *To Be Reviewed.* "Got something else here for you. Kind of a bonus. There's an opening for a backcountry Ranger, junior grade, in your new jurisdiction. As I recall, there's a friend of yours—name of Morgan?—you've been trying to push through the works for some time."

MacLeod shifted in his seat, the crinkle of a smile touching the corners of his flint eyes. "Ben's a good man. Just out of luck these past several years. Got overlooked—undeservedly, I think— then fell through the cracks. Like his file says, he got a couple of first-rate assignments as a seasonal his first two years out of school. Then funding got tight and he was dropped. He went into the Peace Corps and Vista after that, did a couple of tours, got some good experience under his belt."

"Where did you say he is now?"

"On a ranch in Wyoming, near Wind River Reservation, last I heard."

The Superintendent's eyes flicked up to meet the ranger's. "Peace Corps? Reservations? This friend of yours one of those bruised conscience types?" Hayes rubbed his balding head with a sigh.

MacLeod crooked a smile, if reserved. "I've known him for over twelve years, Bill. You won't find a better man for the job anywhere."

His colleague eyed him askance, but not in an unfriendly way. He leaned back and stretched with an expansive air. "Well…we'll run him through the mill and see what we get. Have him go back to the Smokies with you on that preliminary visit. We'll arrange an interview for him then."

The ranger gave a tight nod. "Thanks, Bill. You won't regret it."

"You're gonna be up to your neck with this assignment," the Supe said gruffly. "Figured you were entitled to bring along someone you could trust. Call it a going-away present." He swiveled in his chair, catching sight of the girl in the vehicle outside. "How's Marcie taking the idea of moving?"

"She's gettin' used to it, I think."

Hayes's eyes came up to meet his friend's directly. "I know it's been tough on you two since Becky passed away. If any of us can help out, let us know."

For the first time, the ranger's eyes faltered. "We'll be fine. Thanks. It's just time to move on, that's all."

The two men rose together. Hayes clasped the ranger's hand warmly. "Good luck, fella. Keep in touch." MacLeod turned and left the building without a backward glance.

Hayes ambled into the front office, dropping the application file onto his assistant's desk. She looked after the departing ranger with a twisted smile. "Not a mess-around kind of guy, is he?"

"Never was," the Superintendent mused. "Hey, process this one for me pronto, will ya, Meggie? Shane seems to think we've got us a live one here. Says we won't find a better backcountry man anywhere—" His gaze drifted out the window to watch the lanky cowboy-tough figure launch himself into the driver's seat of the Blazer, "—unless we're lookin' at him."

Hayes patted his expansive middle. "Man…wish I'd been in that good a shape at half my age."

The secretary joined him at the window. "Think he knows what he's getting in to?"

"He'll find out soon enough."

. 2 .

The cluster of Arapaho youths loitering outside Fort Washakie Trading Post looked on in fascination as a black VW Passat pulled up in front of the rustic establishment, dust billowing in its wake.

A tall, long-legged brunette emerged from the car, pausing to coolly assess her surroundings before striding into the store. Clad in designer jeans, work shirt with ski vest, cowboy boots, and sunglasses, she created a stir on the sleepy porch that looked to be the only gathering spot for miles around.

One old codger, ensconced in a frayed cane-back rocker, roused from his stupor to mutter to the grizzled fellow beside him, "Not from around these parts." His companion stared after her, nodding in agreement.

Inside, the young woman took off her sunglasses, taking a moment to let her eyes adjust to the darkness of the interior. Across the room, a man was wiping a beat-up oak counter that looked like it had been there since frontier days. The weathered fellow seemed perplexed what to make of this new arrival.

She sauntered over, not letting his skewed expression deter her, and plopped her elbows on the counter. One foot wagged at the base as she eyed him curiously. "Could you tell me the whereabouts of Ben Morgan?"

The proprietor/barkeep stepped from behind the counter, wiping his hands on his towel, and took a long look up and down her. "You must mean Ben *Jayhawk*." He nodded toward the rear of the post. "He's out back, helpin' unload the feed truck." The man jerked his chin at a small, dusky-skinned boy with wide eyes lingering near the door. "Go get Ben!"

The child jumped, startled, and scampered off. The young woman winced on his behalf.

A minute later, a dusty man with dark blond hair came through the back door, wiping his brow with the back of his arm. Sweat stains streaked his chambray shirt. He stopped, staring, and whipped the bandana off his forehead.

"What're *you* doing here?"

The long-limbed beauty pushed herself from the bar and strolled toward him with a crooked grin. Standing nearly at eye level with the man, who was every bit of six feet, she surveyed him head to toe. Her grin transformed into a smirk of amusement, though something tugged at her eyes.

"Hello, Boy."

The man eyed her warily.

A peal of mischievous laughter erupted from the woman. "Relax! I just decided to come up here and see if you were still happy."

Despite a twitch along one eyebrow, her companion answered, "I am," with a direct gaze back.

She cocked her head, taking in the outdoorsy man before her. There were a few more lines around those disarming green eyes than she remembered, but he looked, all in all, strong and sweaty and masculine and capable. She offered a wistful smile.

"The years look good on you, Cowboy."

His stance softened a bit. "They look good on you too, Andie." He shoved his hands in his pockets. "So…did you come here to cause trouble or what?"

She mimicked his stance but with a feminine little shrug. "Depends on you, I guess. Actually, I wanted to see this Native American princess of yours I heard about."

Morgan sighed and turned to go. "You're impossible, know that?"

7

She trotted after, jostling against him like a joyful long-legged puppy. "You always were the only one who could handle me!"

The two crossed the front porch and down the steps, passing the old men in rockers. One looked up with a squint. "Kin o' yers, Ben?"

Morgan looked back over his shoulder, distracted. "We-uh-grew up together." He threw another glance her way. "Guess you might as well come along for lunch."

Her eyebrows peaked in interest. "Where are we going?"

"Home!"

"Oh, goody!"

He led her to a dusty old Jeep, rolling his eyes as he swung open the creaky door for her then slammed it shut. Trudging around to the driver's side, he hopped in and started up the ancient contraption. It took off with a jerk and a whine of gears, accelerating up a rugged, worn-out road barely distinguishable as paved, dust billowing behind, snow-capped mountains ahead.

The Jeep pulled into the gravel drive of a modest ranch- hand cottage. A line of cottonwoods nestled alongside a small creek. Otherwise, the house stood amid a sea of grassland. A handful of similar houses were visible in the distance. One got the feeling these were people willing to live within yelling distance ready to lend a helping hand, but otherwise requiring an expanse of elbow room city folks could hardly imagine.

They emerged from the vehicle and she paused to stare about herself. Her companion walked on to the steps at the back of the house but stopped to look back with an air of suppressed impatience. She trotted to catch up and they went in the screen door together.

Finding herself in an old-fashioned farmhouse kitchen, she was caught off guard by the young woman who looked up from setting the table to greet them. High cheekbones like tiny Lady apples, doe eyes of a chestnut hue set in a finely tapered face of creamy bronze…a captivating mélange of heritage showed in that face.

Ben jerked a thumb over his shoulder. "I-uh-brought a visitor home for lunch. Old schoolmate. Hope you don't mind." He left the room and began washing at a basin in the little extension beyond, leaving both women to stare after him.

Andie came to herself and stepped forward, hand extended in greeting. "Hi, I'm Andie Carson—Ben and I used to be friends…back at Colorado State. I—uh—was in the area and thought I'd stop by to say hi."

The other young woman nodded slowly and shook her hand, bewildered but gracious. "I am Tawnee. Please…join us. I'll…I'll be right back." Gesturing shyly in the table's direction, she stepped to the screen door and onto the back stoop. Peering about, she yanked on a rope that hung from a rusty bell by the door. It clanged like an old schoolhouse bell. When the young woman returned, she passed by with a gentle smile.

Andie studied her in wonder. There was something otherworldly about her…almost mystical…graceful yet strong. And something very wise in those eyes. She got the distinct impression this Tawnee could read her every thought—a consideration that made Andie blush before she could stop it. It was clear what had attracted Ben. He had always wanted to meld with Nature. He appeared to have positively co-mingled with it, embodied in this serene young woman.

Ben re-entered the room. When Tawnee stepped out to the pantry, Andie turned to him. "She's beautiful." Her voice held a rueful tone she couldn't mask.

Ben met her eyes head-on once more. "I know."

Tawnee returned, gesturing them all to the table. The two broke from their exchange, he with the air of a man who'd said all he was going to on the matter. But she couldn't get over her fascination at this unlikely pairing.

Her eyes had hardly taken their fill when the screen door exploded open. A breathless young boy of seven or eight burst in upon them.

Ben grabbed the child up. "Whoa! Where have you been?"

"Ethan's! We—we built a tire swing!" the youngster exclaimed between puffs.

"Did your mother know you were there?" Ben cocked an eyebrow. The boy sagged against his father's arm and peered at him out of the tops of his eyes, on the verge of a pout. "I came as soon as she called."

Father and mother shared a glance over the child's head.

"Welll…all right this time, but next time you tell her beforehand, understand? Now go wash up—and don't wake Mary. She's taking a nap."

Ben released the boy and he scampered off.

Andie stared after him, hunger and ache competing for space in her heart. *Ben's child….* His stamp was definitely there, an interesting mix of Tawnee for good measure, evident in the tawny skin and tilt to the eyes. The blond hair came from the father, the hazel eyes, from the mother.

Ben caught her rapt expression. "His name is Jesse." A hint of self-consciousness was in his tone. But unmistakable pride as well.

Andie beamed, blinking back tears before they could start. "Good cowboy name." She turned to Tawnee. "Do you have others?"

"Mary Rose Bear," the young mother answered with her gentle smile. "We adopted her when she was two. She is almost four now."

"And Nathan is kind of a foster son. He's out with friends somewhere right now. He's almost fifteen," Ben put in.

"A teenager!" Andie exclaimed in mock horror.

Ben only grinned. "But not your ordinary teenager. He's pretty special."

Young Jesse rejoined them at the table and everyone chowed down like farmhands, which Andie realized was essentially what their lives were. At first no one spoke, busy digging in to the modest meal of cornbread, ham, and beans with carrots and onions. From the garden whose remnants she saw outside? The simple, homey aroma of a just-baked apple pie wafted over from the stovetop. No stilted city manners over this lunch, no niceties other than the basics of hospitality here.

"So…" she attempted, "I read up on the reservation here. Are you part of the Shoshone tribe, then, Tawnee?"

"Arapaho," Ben answered for her, mouth half-full. He swallowed. "It's a mix of the two tribes here, has been since the 1800's."

Ben finished his meal in record time and rose abruptly from the table as if anxious to be on the move again. The two women followed at a more leisurely pace. Andie stayed behind with Tawnee, following her to the sink with a load of dishes.

She opened her mouth to speak but her eye was caught by Ben. Over in the corner, as he talked on the phone, he gave her a curious signal, a subtle tug at his left ear, a slight frown, shake of the head, and a nod in Tawnee's direction. It took a moment but then it dawned on her what he was trying to convey. With a distracted nod back, she moved to the woman's other side. So…she was deaf in one ear? Unsure how to react to this, she tried to cover by handing her some glasses from the table.

"That was a wonderful lunch. It was really good of you to have me on such short notice." She glanced back up in Ben's direction. He had gone into the washroom, changed shirts, and was busying himself with a torn boot strap.

"I...guess I should be on my way...." She pulled her gaze away and tossed her hair back. "Thought I'd check out Yellowstone, maybe Grand Tetons before I head back to L.A."

Tawnee looked up from the sink, startled. "You've come such a long way! You should stay! Rest over. We would like that."

From the corner of her eye, Andie saw Ben's head jerk up in surprise. She laughed nervously. "I don't know.... Well...on one condition—that you let me pay for your hospitality. I mean, I could babysit or something, couldn't I?"

Husband and wife looked at each other, breaking out into laughter. Ben recovered first. "Where would we go?"

"Oh...guess you're right." Andie reddened, then broke into a grin. At least her goof had the effect of relaxing the atmosphere.

Ben visibly loosened up. "I've got a better idea. I'll get Rodney Deerfellow to introduce you to some horses this afternoon. That should keep you entertained for a while. There's not much out here to amuse a city girl but we'll see what we can come up with." He shot her the first genuine look of warmth since she'd arrived.

Andie couldn't hide her delight. "You remembered!"

He stepped past her and grabbed his jacket off the row of pegs by the door, pausing to plant a kiss on Tawnee's lips. "I'm going over that way now," he said over his shoulder. "You can come along."

As they headed out the door Andie caught the sidelong glance of amusement Tawnee cast Ben's way. He held to his stone face but did color a bit. She began to wonder just what they had in store for her....

*   *   *   *

In bed that night, Ben lay staring at the ceiling. Tawnee watched him quietly for a time, then snuggled against him, pensively caressing his chest. Soft and hollow against his shoulder her voice came, "You...were lovers?"

A frown flickered across Ben's brow and he craned his neck to peer down at her. "You could tell?"

"I could tell you were troubled."

He sighed, sat up, and glanced over his shoulder at her. "Sort of...a long time ago. We were...I guess you could say, college sweethearts." A grim smile played on his mouth. "More like sparring partners at times."

She digested this in silence.

"After college, we looked each other up a few times... like when I was between Peace Corps assignments. Once, when I was down on my luck, we ran into each other and she helped me out.... She's all right, really. I guess that's all there is to tell." He looked back at her again. "Sorry. She really threw me for a loop, showing up like that today."

Tawnee's voice in the darkness was a soothing balm, as always. "Don't be. It's all right."

He sat there a moment longer, shoulders slumped, before plopping back down beside her. She curled up against him and he threw an arm about her shoulders, irresistibly drawn. Pulling her close, he whispered against her neck, "There's nothing there now. It's more like some childhood friend come for a visit, not much more. I wouldn't go back to those days in a million years."

He could sense her mulling this over in the quiet.

"But she's still hurting. Perhaps this is part of her healing."

Ben threw her a strange glance. "You should be a shrink, know that? But then, you are already are, kind of, aren't you?"

13

Tawnee raised her face to meet his and placed two slender fingers against his lips. "You should not joke. I still have much to learn to be a true Healer. But…it works with you, does it not?"

He acknowledged the truth there with a twisted smile.

Quiet fell between them. But then Tawnee's voice came in the darkness again. "Why did you fix her up with Rodney?"

Ben grinned in the dark. "I figured—who's better at handling wild fillies? That's not all…tomorrow when Shane comes up, I can saddle him with her, as well."

"I thought Shane was coming up for a peaceful trail ride."

"That's true, but what he needs is a distraction. I figure, by the end of a trail ride with her, he'll either be furious or totally smitten. Either way, it should help him forget about Becky for a little while. If Andie Carson isn't a distraction, I don't know what is."

"You have a diabolical mind, don't you?"

Tawnee gave his ear a little nip and rolled away but welcomed his playful snuggle in answer.

* * * *

The next morning Andie and Ben Morgan walked side by side, silent as they approached the trading post where she had left her car the afternoon before. He squinted over at her. "Y'sure I can't talk you into that trail ride this morning?"

She shook her head, giving him a tight smile. "Mmmm…no thanks. I really need to be on my way back. I'm supposed to be back in the studio on Monday. Besides, my backside's still sore from yesterday!"

He shrugged. "Okay…suit yourself."

They continued on in silence until Andie spoke up again. "Tell me about Tawnee."

Hands shoved in his pockets, Ben stopped and turned to face her. "What do you mean?"

"I mean..." she cast about awkwardly, "how did she lose her hearing?"

Morgan nodded thoughtfully and resumed their progress toward the post. "Oh. That. She was in a childhood accident. Well...beating, actually. When we met, she was almost totally deaf, but she read lips so well that I didn't even know it at first. Some friends and I strong-armed a senator into finagling some surgery for her. Now she can hear pretty well out of her left ear."

"Wow...." Andie trudged alongside him, matching stride for stride, her eyes downcast. When she raised them, they bore a look of reassessment that bordered on admiration. "You've done well for yourself, Boy."

He looked about them with grim amusement...the dusty old buildings surrounded by old cars and machinery. "I doubt any of our old school chums would call it that."

She tossed her hair back with an air of impatience. "Then they're just stupid. You've got more integrity than any of them. Maybe not the trophy cars and big house but..." she shook her head, "at least you've got your head on straight." A sigh escaped her. "I'm still working on that."

Ben gave her a snort and a clap on the back that was more brotherly than anything else. "It'll come. You'll see."

They found themselves at her car, an awkwardness between them again.

"It was good seein' you again."

Andie looked down where he was scuffing his boot in the dirt like a self-conscious schoolboy and nodded with a twisted smile. "Yeah...you, too."

An awkward moment ensued where they seemed to be debating whether to share a good-bye kiss or hug or let well enough alone. Andie settled the stand-off, turning, tight-lipped, and sank into the front seat of the VW. But she looked up when Ben leaned in the window.

"Have a safe trip. Why don't you give us a call when you get in? Let us know you got home okay."

She yielded a reluctant nod. Ben straightened and shoved his hands back in his pockets. His boots started to scuff the dirt again but he stopped short. "You know…I still have that coat. I don't think I ever thanked you."

Andie fought back the sudden pang in her chest. "Don't mention it." She went to turn the key in the ignition but stopped, staring past Ben. "Who's that?"

He gave her a puzzled frown and turned. A lanky, tan, weathered figure complete with cowboy boots and hat emerged from a dusty Blazer across the parking lot. "That's my friend I was telling you about. Shane MacLeod, the ranger from Yosemite." He broke into a grin, wagging his head. "Look at that…you can take him outta Texas but you can't take the Texas out of him."

Ben turned back, gauging her expression. Andie rearranged her face, but not soon enough. He jerked his head, grinning. "Well, come on then. I'll introduce you."

A wave of anxiety welled up, surprising her. "No…that's okay. Maybe another time." She glanced past him once more, threw the car in reverse, and backed away.

Raising his arm in a bewildered wave, he turned away and headed for his friend.

Shane MacLeod looked on with mild interest after the car retreating into the distance. He acknowledged Ben's wave with his characteristic terse nod.

"Anything wrong?" he called out as Ben drew near.

Ben made a dismissive shrug. "Nah, just seein' off an old friend."

MacLeod's cocked eyebrow said he suspected more and Ben had to give. "Okay, okay…an old girlfriend…from college days. She just stopped by to say hello. "

The ranger grinned. "That was a dangerous-lookin' female there, friend. Your wife know you fooled around with that?"

Ben lowered his head and came up with a bashful grin. "No secrets."

"No net either, looks like." Shane shook his head but clapped him on the back. "So how things been treatin' you?"

Ben looked down to rub at the tear in his jeans. "Well enough, I guess." He squinted up at the older man, who stood there with a look that said he saw more than he was letting on. The two shared tight smiles, even as Shane lowered the gate on the Blazer and pulled out a large box, plopping it in Ben's arms.

"That one's got *your* name on it."

"Oooph! Who'd you rob this time? Sears?"

MacLeod chuckled. "Nah…just picked up some of those hard t' find things. And you know my sister. She can't resist buyin' kid stuff whenever there's an excuse."

Ben shook his head, trying to hold back a twisted smile, and changed the subject. "Hey, speaking of Andie back there…I was gonna fix you up with her on that trail ride—"

His friend lurched to a stop and shot him a dark look.

"Are you crazy!?"

He backed off with a sheepish laugh. "Okay! Okay! Enough about that. Come on let's get you settled in. We've got a lot of catching up to do."

Shane returned Ben's exuberance with a cryptic look. "Yeah, I've got somethin' to discuss with you, too."

"Really? What's that?"

17

"It'll wait."

Ben sighed in resignation. There was no budging Shane when he was dead set on keeping a secret. But as he headed for his Jeep to lead Shane out, he turned back. "Funny thing…Andie seemed to really perk up there when she first laid eyes on you, but when I offered to introduce you, it was like she got cold feet all of a sudden."

MacLeod nodded gamely. "Yeah…I have that effect on women sometimes."

Ben grimaced. "I don't know…she always was kinda unpredictable."

Wagging their heads at the vagaries of womankind, the two men continued on their way with no more comment on the matter.

* * * *

As the sun set behind the Teton Range that evening, Andie settled into her seat for the first leg of the journey back to Pasadena. A heavy sigh and she turned her attention away from the rugged beauty of Jackson, Wyoming outside the jet's windows.

She shook her head. *I could kick myself. But I could hardly have changed my mind again!*

Something in her wasn't quite ready to face a new onslaught on her psyche—not after all she'd gone through on this visit. *So drained….* Hardly the time to confront someone new.

Still…. How many times before had she balked instead of going after what she really wanted? Wasn't that what this trip proved beyond a doubt?

But for the first time in years, she'd seen what she wanted—standing outside the post at Fort Washakie, Wyoming of all places.

At least she had this….

Looking down at the crumpled note hastily scribbled earlier, she read again, a smile touching her lips:

> *SHANE MACLEOD*
> *YOSEMITE NATIONAL PARK*

.3.

Dolores Miller had been with the Park Service for thirty years, twenty-two of those while her late husband was an active member of the park's forces. As a result, she knew just about all there *was* to know about Yosemite's past and present—its geology, its flora and fauna, its history, as well as the dynamics of its personnel. She took it as her solemn duty to know these things—and Shane Mac-Leod was one of her personal favorites.

She'd been there to watch him mature from a skinny, greenhorn into a seasoned professional, now among the highest ranks of the ranger corps. She'd been witness to his personal tragedies, too—most notably the loss of his young wife to a car accident three years hence. Now she kept a protective eye over his goings-on, much to Shane's chagrin at times. This afternoon was no exception.

"I figured you ought to know," Shane was accosted as he came in the door of the Tuolomne Meadows ranger station, "some floozy was in here earlier asking after you—wanted to know your schedule and everything!"

A smile played at the corners of his mouth. "Yeah…I saw her at the amphitheater durin' my talk."

"Well, if you ask me, she had the look of one of those *obsession types*," Dolores huffed. "I think she's just plain got a thing for rangers—"

"A ranger groupie?" broke in another ranger. "Hey, next time she shows up, send her my way!"

Dolores shot the young fellow a perturbed look.

Shane only smiled, choosing not to elaborate on his mysterious visitor. He grabbed some trail maps on his way back out and playfully whopped his comrade's shoulder in passing. "Better leave this one to me, Junior. Might be more than you can handle."

Dolores looked after him in distress. "You be careful, now, hear?"

Shane poked his head back in long enough to give her a wink. "I'll watch myself."

*   *   *   *

The next morning dawned cool, clear, and bright—a good omen for the trail ride to come. On a day as beautiful as this, with the prospect of one of the more pleasant diversions in his routine before him, it was hard to let anything bother him, even the idea of an unpredictable female coming under his charge. Sure enough, there was that quirky woman he'd been warned about, standing in line with the rest of the visitors signed up for the overnight excursion. Besides, he told himself, there would be other rangers along to foist her onto, if need be. So he felt only a twinge as he stood alongside Rusty Calvert at the sign-up post.

His words had caught in his throat upon glimpsing that vaguely familiar but disturbing face in the crowd, the one with the dancing eyes. She looked like the kind that could break into mischief at the least opportune moment.

He braced himself as the young woman approached. A twitch in his brow was his only reaction to the brunette with the dark, glittery eyes and flushed cheeks.

She thrust her hand at him. "Hi! Andie Carson."

He extended his hand with the slightest of nods. "Ma'am. Shane MacLeod." A perfunctory clasp and he let go.

"I know—Ben told me, that is." She swallowed. "I'm—uh—writing a book on rangers and thought this would be a good place to start."

If Shane was inclined to doubt her, he didn't let it show. He nodded once, slowly. "Uh-huh." Their eyes locked a moment before hers faltered. For a fleeting instant, he was tempted to figure her out. *Strange one...all forward one moment, unsure the next.* He chased the thought from his mind and got back to business. "Ever been on a trail ride before? This one's a two-nighter."

That triggered a flash in the woman's eyes. "I can handle it." She crossed her arms, a flicker in her brow.

Shane chewed on his lip. Easy to bait, wasn't she? He looked to Rusty. The young ranger's eyes twinkled back at him. No help there. He turned back and gestured across the clearing in the pine grove. "All right, Ma'am. If you'll just take your gear over there to Brian, he'll help you saddle up."

With a jerk of her chin, the young woman picked up her REI backpack with its assortment of expensive-looking accessories and tried to make as clean an exit as possible. She stomped off to the next hapless ranger, leaving the two men to cast one last distracted glance her way.

. 4 .

The column of horseback riders plodded south along the famed John Muir Trail. The party grew quiet, their chattering hushed as they craned their necks in silent admiration of Cathedral Peak. Interspersed among the park visitors, three rangers and the camp cook plodded along on their trusty mounts, keeping a steady pace.

Shane looked over his shoulder, surveying the dozen or so riders behind him. Young Brian Woodrum, the rookie ranger, had found a couple of teenage girls to dazzle, he noticed, and Will, the bewhiskered cook, had attracted his usual string of fans among the youngest set. He started to turn back around when his eye fell upon the rider tenth in line. There she was again—the girl had a puppy-like air of enthusiasm, as though she'd never seen the outdoors before, which he found mildly irritating. Why was that? He shook his head and faced front.

A few minutes later, he found Rusty Calvert at his side. The junior ranger fell into pace with him agreeably. "This is different, having you along for the ride."

Shane nodded as they ambled along. "Yeah…thought I'd take the chance for one more trip along this trail before headin' out of here. Next month's gonna be too busy to think about such stuff."

"When are you leaving?"

"Late May, looks like."

"Oh, boy…just in time for the summer crush, huh? You like to jump into things headfirst, don't you?"

MacLeod grinned but offered no reply.

Rusty glanced over his shoulder down the line of riders. "That's your mystery woman?"

Shane emitted a low groan. "No mystery there, just some nutty ex-girlfriend of an old chum. I think he's behind all of this somewhere."

Calvert craned his neck for another viewing and came away with an appreciative look. "So…what do you know about her? Anything?"

"Nah. Says she's a writer. I thought Ben said she was a rock singer or somethin'." Shane shifted in his saddle. "No tellin' what kinda wild stuff Ben used to get into."

Rusty's eyebrows peaked in interest. "Yeah? So how wild is wild?" The younger ranger grinned wickedly. He dug his heels into his mount and surged to the front of the line, leaving Shane to glance once more, glumly, at that distracting female.

He sighed and gave the Appaloosa a kick, galloping to the column head after Calvert. That was the trouble with women like her. They had a way of messin' with your mind.

Becky had never been like that. No silly games, no temper tantrums. You always knew where you stood with her. Though perhaps time had managed to dull his memory a bit. He swallowed down the sudden lump in his throat. Three years now since that God-awful, rain-soaked November night but the wound was still fresh. Aggravatingly fresh.

He broke from his thoughts at the sight of two rangers on horseback coming towards them. From the looks on their faces, there was news to share. Shane spoke aside briefly to Brian Wood-rum, then signaled for Rusty to join him trailside.

Andie leaned forward in the saddle, squinting up the line of riders. Why had they stopped? She wriggled restlessly even as the sorrel pawed the ground, apparently of the same mind. Both were anxious to be on their way. She looked side to side from the trail.

There was a sign that read *Group Camp* to one side. She idly noticed a couple of people took the opportunity to dismount and head for the facilities there, their horses tied to a hitching post. Her attention then zeroed in on the group of rangers at trailside near the front of the line, heads together in conference. She arched an eyebrow. Something interesting was afoot. She could feel it. Or maybe it was just the image of those four men in their sharp uniforms, conveying a sense of secret danger under that calm façade they were so good at projecting. The hairs on the nape of her neck tingled. Whatever it was, she wanted in on it.

Sliding off her horse, she stepped over to tie the reins to a young redwood on the stream side. Behind her a high nasal voice came sharply, "What are you doing? We're not supposed to leave the trail!"

Andie turned back on the woman who had been gabbing all morning long about her family back in New York City. "Just hold your horses, will ya?" she barked back, then winced at the pun. Shaking her head in dismissal she made her way gingerly down to the streambed and followed a gravelly sandbar to a point just below the group of rangers. The bank was head high here, providing her coverage. She eased under the sheltering branches of a tilted cottonwood and held her breath.

"—so the only poaching so far has been west of Tenaya Canyon," Shane MacLeod was saying. "Camping at Sunrise should be safe enough for a group this size. We'll keep an eye out. In the meantime, you boys gonna keep up a steady patrol in the area?"

"You bet," came another voice.

Then Ranger Calvert's voice. "Think that's enough leeway?"

Shane's voice answered. "Should be. They won't venture far from an access road. Gives 'em a quick getaway. But we'll have a checkpoint at both ends of Tioga Road. They won't get out of the park."

Andie was so intent upon digesting this piece of news, she didn't realize the conference had broken up till she heard Rusty Calvert's voice boom out, "All right, everybody line up!"

She gasped and turned to hurry back to her horse. It was slower going then coming, she found to her despair. Maybe it was because she was in such a rush. The damp, heavy sand sucked at her boots, weighing her down. She headed for the stony river bottom itself, only to find it slippery, and lost her footing. She almost landed in the water but caught herself.

Horses were snickering, and reins jangled on the trail above, sounds of imminent departure. Any second now, one of the rangers would be trotting down the line to find her horse riderless and unattended. With a supreme effort, she slogged her way bankside, arms flailing for a cottonwood sapling to pull herself up. Her first attempt was unsuccessful and she got whipped in the face. Her second attempt, she fell backwards, seat first in the mud. In a real panic now, she jumped up, not bothering to brush herself off and grabbed this time for the reins, the horse's mane, anything she could get hold of. What she didn't count on was the horse stumbling. She didn't know something that big *could* stumble, brought down by one ill-placed yank. The sorrel whinnied in protest, sliding down the mudbank on its knees, barely missing her. Both landed with a *splat* in the streambed.

Brian Woodrum turned to look in the direction of all the commotion. Digging his heels into the buckskin, he cantered down the line of riders, scanning each till he came to a gap where the rider tenth in line should have been. Slide marks in the dirt led down to the steam. He coaxed his mount closer to the edge and peered over. Sure enough, there was Shane's mystery woman sprawled in the middle of the water. With her horse. A grin twitched at the corners of his mouth but he bit it back.

"You all right?" he called down.

The young woman pushed her hair out of her eyes and looked up forlornly. "I think so...."

The rookie ranger sat back in his saddle. Looked like just the kind of job he'd been waiting for. He dismounted. "Hold on. I'll give you a hand."

Andie looked up from her crouch beside Ranger Woodrum to see the big Appaloosa approach. She watched, spellbound, as the self-assured figure swung down from the saddle with ease. Her heart lurched and the warmth rose in her cheeks as MacLeod made his way down toward them. She prayed it didn't show. But then she looked down at herself. What did it matter if her face was turning six shades of pink? Didn't she looked enough of a fool already? And the poor horse! Had she injured it? She could see the charges now...*damage to property of a national park...was that a Federal offense?* She bit her lip, steeling herself for the barrage to come.

He was surprisingly calm. Kneeling alongside them, the senior ranger surveyed the sorrel's muddied forelegs. "What's the problem here?" He examined the animal, gently working the joints. The horse snickered but didn't fight his touch. "Just some bruising, looks like," he surmised. "Gonna need some rest, though." He looked up at his colleague. "You all go on. I can take care of this. We'll meet up with you by nightfall."

Young Woodrum looked disappointed but rose without argument. As he turned to go, Shane called after him, "Oh—have Will leave behind a couple of ice packs, would ya? Thanks." The young fellow nodded over his shoulder.

MacLeod rose to stretch and abruptly squinted, eyeing the track of footprints that led upstream. "Just what were you tryin' to do?" The steely-eyed ranger swung his gaze back on her.

Andie looked down, shifting from one leg to the other. "Oh...nothing. Just...looking around. Seemed like a good idea...at the time..." Her voice trailed off.

He cocked his head, assessing. "One of those *too curious for your own good* sorts, huh?"

She grimaced in answer.

A shout from the bank above interrupted. It was Rusty Calvert. "Shane! Here ya go." He lobbed two ice packs down to him. "Sure you'll be all right?"

"We'll be fine. Thanks." MacLeod waved him on.

Andie's stomach sank as she watched the line of horses disappear under the canopy of dark feathery branches. She was startled on top of that to find the ranger up close, surveying her.

"You get banged up any?"

She tried to sound dismissive. "Oh...no.... Just made a mess of myself, that's all. I'm just glad the horse is okay." She attempted to brush herself off but gave up. Her cheeks burned again, to her aggravation. Then she caught sight of her pack, half the contents spilled onto the rocks, and groaned.

"Oh, no...."

She trotted over to retrieve it all, but slipped in her hurry.

"OW!"

MacLeod looked up from tying an ice pack around the sorrel's foreleg. "What is it?"

Andie eased down onto a boulder with a grimace. "I think I sprained my ankle." She hung her head. *This is too much. Now I'm a certified klutz.*

He made his way over to her. As he squatted before her, she chanced a glance up. "Sorry...."

His lips thinned, but that glint in his steely eyes softened. "C'mere. Let's have a look at ya." With a surprisingly gentle touch, he felt along the joint. "So, does this qualify as a bad day for you or is this par for the course?"

She sputtered a laugh despite her chagrin. "I'm not usually this much of a mess. And I'm *really* sorry." With that stoic mug of his, it was hard to tell if he was kidding or not. She sniffed self-consciously but winced when he squeezed the tender spot on her foot.

The ranger sat back on his heel. "Yeah…looks like I'm gonna have to bind up the both of you. Might be better if we just camp here for the night."

"Here?"

"Here."

"Just like that?"

He rose, his solemn eyes decisive. "Just like that." Stepping off to the side, MacLeod used the radio on his belt to inform the trail party of their change in plans. They would be fine, he assured them, and had adequate supplies to make do until they rejoined.

That night, Andie eyed her taciturn rescuer over the flames of the campfire he had expertly built. He'd done all the things that duty demanded…secured a safe spot up from the streambed for them to rest, procured firewood, and made a passable cup of coffee, followed by crackers and soup from his K-rations. Even offered her a granola bar. But he'd been tight-lipped the whole time. She opened her mouth but hesitated, tugging the comforting warmth of her blanket about her shoulders before attempting again.

"I imagine you don't like me very much."

The ranger shifted his shoulders, his gaze flicking up to meet hers before returning to the fire. He took a long draw from his coffee cup. "Let's just say I don't cotton with being saddled with one of Ben's former…never mind."

After a long silence, Andie gave vent to a shaky sigh. "I see…." She reached, groaning, for her sleeping bag. With an angry flick of the wrists, she spread it out and rolled on it. "For your information," she snapped, "I've never been anyone's woman— or flame, for that matter." She turned away from him and lay down.

The ranger shot a glance her way. He looked about to say something but stopped. With a shrug, he settled back against the blanket-cushioned saddle and shut his eyes.

. 5 .

Morning in the Sierra Nevada....

A near spiritual experience...nestled beneath guardian giants of fir, incense cedar, and ponderosa pine...drawing in deep wafts of crisp air heavy with the scent of evergreen above, damp needle straw and peat below. Dawn's earliest rays float down in golden shunts, investing the groves with mystic beauty. Anything seems possible and everything is imbued with a splendor normally reserved for things not of this world.

Just such a morning Ranger MacLeod awoke to find himself in, devoid of the acrimony from the day before. The manifestation of a fresh start, incarnate. His eyes opened to witness the dew-sparkled bough overhanging where he lay. He forgot for a moment he wasn't alone.

A curious sound caught his ear and he rose on an elbow to peer about. He thought to glance in the direction of the woman's sleeping bag. It was empty.

His heart lurched. Then he spied her a few feet beyond the campsite. She was sitting on a fallen tree trunk, an expression of child-like delight on her face as she offered peanuts to a tiny but voracious chipmunk. The two made a winsome sight, he had to admit, giving in to a smile.

The tranquility of the morning was pierced by an ominous whistling noise, the sound of deadly force hurtling toward some hapless target. The nerve-tingling *whizzz* was followed by the sound of a heavy body falling into the underbrush.

In a flash, the ranger rolled out of his bag and was on his feet, crouching. His hand slid for the pistol on his thigh. Shane recognized the sound all too well. A power bow....

The woman had frozen in place, mouth ajar. The chipmunk was long gone, nuts scattered in its wake. Shane charged past her, crashing into the woods.

"What was that?" she called hoarsely.

He turned from his hunched position in the thicket to see her hobbling to join him. "Get down!" he barked and resumed his scan of their surroundings.

She obeyed without protest, wincing as she scrunched down beside him. "What is it? Hunters?" At least she whispered this time.

His gaze travelled to the body of the deer lying on the forest floor only a dozen feet away. It twitched once, twice, then lay still. His mouth firmed. "Poachers, looks like."

"*Here?* But that's—"

"Laws don't stop some people, Lady," he said tightly.

Andie opened her mouth to say something, but thought better of it. She chose instead to stare in the same direction that MacLeod was now studying through a pair of mini binoculars. Among the trees along the slope of the adjacent ridge line, there was movement.

When she looked back at her companion, he was checking the magazine of his Glock. A tingle of excitement coursed through her. "What are you going to do? Arrest them?"

MacLeod rose to a crouch, eyes still trained on the distant slope. "That's one of my options."

Her brow twitched in puzzlement. "What else?"

His lips thinned. "Gettin' shot in the process."

She looked up at him in renewed fascination as he rose.

"You stay here!" he snapped, startling her out of her admiration. The ranger proceeded to sneak down along the edge of the stream, using underbrush for cover, tread across with nary a splash, and hike stealthily up the slope.

Be careful, will ya? she fumed to herself.

Utter quiet followed, broken only by the sound of the wind in the branches high overhead. The sense of solitude closed in on her, beyond peace to something unnerving. She was totally alone out here. If something should happen to the ranger....

A manmade noise came from somewhere above and behind her right shoulder. Twisting to look though feathery needles, she saw a Jeep skid to a stop on the trail above where they had blithely ridden horseback the day before. A man in loose-fitting camouflage hopped out, carrying what looked like a long-range rifle. *Must be connected to the others....*

Holding her breath, she watched him step to the edge of the embankment, spy their campsite, and trot down to investigate. The sense of violation welled up in her, forced to watch as the man stomped about their site and gave a nasty snort—actually kicked and scattered their things about!—all while she struggled to maintain her silence. Even still, he could discover her any moment now. Her heart hammered in her ears. She blinked back an onslaught of dizziness. *Think!* What were her options? Where could she go? No way she could slip out of range, much less outrun him with her ankle.

Her focus was yanked from her own welfare when she saw the gunman jerk his chin up, eyes narrowed. Following his gaze, she almost gasped out loud. Shane was coming back down the slope, unaware of their visitor.

She watched in horror as the intruder lifted his rifle to his shoulder, taking cold aim at the ranger's chest. The outrage nearly took her breath away—but didn't stop her from surging to her feet.

"Hey you!"

The force she threw behind the cry surprised her. Her intention had been to call out then duck—quickly—but she wasn't quick enough. Andie barely saw the glint from the rifle as it changed its deadly aim.

The fire-burst of pain hit even as she was thrown backwards.

The back of her head banged against a boulder and everything spun into black....

At the far side of the streambed, MacLeod flinched and swirled to a crouch, scanning the area where they had camped. That unmistakable crack of a rifle chilled him to the bone. He thought he'd heard the woman call out. Was she in danger? Or was it a warning?

He made out, then, a mad scramble on the trail above. A man in camouflage ran to a mud-splattered Jeep and roared off in a flurry of gravel. Shane whipped up his Glock to take aim, but it was too far to chance firing. Slowly, he lowered his arm. Dread churned in the pit of his stomach. Something was wrong, bad wrong, back at the campsite.

He scrambled back across the stream and through the brush. There in the thicket lay the woman, her body crumpled against a tree....

Shane knelt, feeling her neck for a pulse. The young woman stirred, opening her eyes. She attempted to sit up but fell back.

"Wow...I got shot...." She let out a dazed laugh that was half groan. "Just like...in the movies...."

She tried to focus on the red stain spreading across her shoulder. But her head got wobbly. Her eyes looked dangerously close to rolling back.

"Just lie still," Shane ordered. He tore through his pack for first aid supplies, fumbling in his worry. He sorted out what could be useful and bent over the woman, making, first of all, a compress out of some gauze and an extra T-shirt from his pack. He drew out an airline bottle of Jack Daniels and eyed it—unorthodox maybe, but a tried and true pain-killer when nothing else was available. His Texan of a father still swore by it for everything from toothache to broken bones.

"You much of a drinker?" he asked over his shoulder.

"Huh? A…a little…" she mumbled.

"Then this shouldn't hurt ya." He held her head up and put the bottle to her lips. She flinched and sputtered, coughing. "Come on, just a swig or two. It'll make this go a lot easier, I guarantee."

The woman took a mouthful, screwed up her face and swallowed. She gasped, throwing him an incredulous look. He held firm. "It's all right. One more. Two if you can manage."

The second was easier. The third, she seemed to almost enjoy. Shane watched for signs of the whiskey's warmth beginning to filter through her body. It took effect faster than he expected. A drowsy smile twitched at the corners of her mouth and she raised her head unsteadily. "I got the Jeep's license plate… G…X…I…eight…one…eight…."

She hiccupped.

A partial…but close enough. Shane broke into a grin. "You're somethin' else, Lady, know that?"

"I know…." A woozy smile and she lay back, shutting her eyes. Her neck went slack.

His smile faded. His fingers scrambled for a pulse. She'd just fainted. He pulled out his phone and punched the number for HQ but all he got was static. Same with the nearest ranger station. Muttering a curse, he tossed the phone aside. They'd been lobbying for better ones the past couple of years but budgets just kept getting tighter. Deep in these mountains, even the best phones had trouble. For now, they were on their own.

He turned back. Time to get down to business here before that stupor wore off. The injury wasn't necessarily life-threatening, but if she went into shock, it could be. He'd seen city folks keel over and die from the nervous trauma of a wound that an outdoorsman could handle with ease. You never could tell with a tenderfoot.

He cut aside the sleeve of her T-shirt with first-aid scissors to see the wound. Surprise must have affected her assailant's aim, causing the bullet to deliver a glancing blow to her clavicle and shoulder. Still, it left a respectable gouge on her upper arm. Her fall backwards must have whammed her against the rock. He felt gently for a knot on the back of her head. Nothing sizeable. Probably just rattled her brain a bit.

Shane sat back on his haunches, studying her. She appeared to be holding her own. As long as he kept her calm, she'd likely be fine until other medical help arrived. But he still needed to clean that wound. At least there was no bullet to contend with. For that, he was grateful, but it was gonna be mighty uncomfortable when the medicine came in contact with that deep gouge. It was oozing now through the compress he'd fashioned. He dug through the first aid pack again and came up with a tiny bottle of hydrogen peroxide and antiseptic spray.

His charge opened her eyes at the commotion. "What…what are you going to do?" A trace of anxiety had crept into her voice.

Shane turned back from his rummaging but hesitated before his answer. If he didn't clean that wound soon, she risked getting a nasty infection out here in the woods. "This is gonna smart a bit…but it needs to be done." He eyed her for a reaction.

She strained to look into his face. He could swear she was gauging just how much she trusted him, a stranger, with her life. Whatever she saw must have satisfied her. She lay back with a nod and pressed her lips together.

But nothing could prepare her for what came next.

The bubbling peroxide was bad enough. She flinched and stiffened. "F-Feels like ants crawling all over me!" she managed through gritted teeth.

He nodded tightly and sat back on his heels, letting the cleanser do its job. Reaching for the first aid spray, he hesitated. This was the part he always hated. He took a deep breath and leaned over her, a hand against her good shoulder to keep her still.

The antiseptic made contact with her raw flesh. She let out a breathless scream and her eyes threw him a flash of horror before she blacked out.

Shane felt for the light, fast pulse at her neck. "Sorry 'bout that," he breathed and went about bandaging the wound as fast as he could. Afterward, he pulled a blanket over her and let her rest.

It was nearing twilight when Andie finally awoke—sore, drowsy, and ravenously hungry.

"So there you are."

She looked up to see Ranger MacLeod ambling toward her, a tin plate of beans and a steaming mug of coffee in his hands. Her nostrils drank in the comforting aroma as he knelt beside her. She blinked and looked about. It took a moment to reorient herself. The sound of other horses, other voices, made her turn, startled, to look past his shoulder. She felt like a bewildered, sleepy child.

The ranger smiled. "The group came back through about four o'clock and made camp across the way. By the way," he added, handing her the cup, "those poachers were caught just outside the gates—red-handed, thanks to you."

Andie managed a nod, still coming out of her daze. She took a pensive draught from the cup and flicked another glance in the direction of their fellow campers. There were a few curious stares her way. She squirmed, self-conscious, but the twinge in her arm broke her train of thought.

"Your wound there looks better," MacLeod said. "The redness has gone down and there's less swelling than I would've expected. We can airlift you out, though—"

"No!" She pulled back from her coffee with a frown, sloshing some on herself. "No need for that!"

She swiped at the droplets. The ranger handed her his napkin without a word. She took it reluctantly. "I'll be fine, thank you! I want to *ride* back!"

MacLeod shrugged and rose, turning away. "Suit yourself, Annie Oakley."

She paused from wiping to frown after him. "The name's *Andie!*"

MacLeod wagged his head as he ambled off to join the others.

She settled back in a huff to rest. Their exchange left her exhausted. She must have nodded off. When she next awoke, she felt anything but combative, her body wracked with shakes. MacLeod was already at her side.

"I'm s-sorry…" she chattered.

"It's okay. A little inflammation's set in, that's all." He pulled up more cover to combat the chills and found her some aspirin from his pack. "This should help."

"Th-Thanks." She took the tablets from his palm. A cup of water from the ranger and she settled back, lapsing into a stupor as she stared into the fire. The chills gradually subsided. Time became a floating thing, hovering somewhere over the jagged points of light that were flickering flames of the campfires.

Somewhere in it she must have dozed again, coming to with a jerk of the neck. She shook her head to clear it and stole a glance across the fire at MacLeod. He was leaning back against the Appaloosa's saddle, knees splayed as he whittled away at a twig. There was something comforting in the gesture. So classically Western. Eyeing those distinctly non-issue cowboy boots that emerged from his uniform pants legs, she idly wondered if he were one of those characters who slept with his boots on.

Then she noticed something else...he was left-handed. It somehow made him more human yet distinctive at the same time. She almost succumbed to a smile of contentment, but flicked a wary glance in the ranger's direction. Her voice, when it came, was on the weak side.

"Do you...do you think maybe...just for tonight...we could call a truce? Just for a little while?"

The ranger's eyes rose and locked on hers. The split second of surprise in them turned to a glint of warmth. Still, it took a moment for him to find a response.

"I don't see why not..." he offered with deliberation. He cast a thoughtful gaze at the fire. "The way I figure it, I probably owe my life t' you from this mornin'."

Andie's eyes flicked downward, warmth creeping into her cheeks. "I don't know about *that*." Her shrug turned into a wince.

The ranger hauled himself up, sauntered over and sat down beside her. In his eye was a look of reevaluation. "It took a lot of guts t' do what you did. Thanks."

He offered his hand, catching her off guard. Andie hesitated then shook it. MacLeod leaned back against a boulder, staring up at the stars visible between the branches of the looming evergreens overhead. Silence reigned between them for some time.

After a while, he said casually, "So you and Morgan used to be—"

"—pals," Andie finished for him. "We...hung around to-gether in college. Played basketball, hiked...skied some...stuff like that...."

The ranger cocked an eyebrow, leaning forward to stir the coals with a stick. "That's not what I heard." A devilish twinkle lit his eyes.

Her gaze jerked in his direction. "What exactly did Ben say?"

"Oh...Ben was the perfect gentleman...don't get me wrong. It was just kinda...obvious...from the way he spoke."

"Like what?"

MacLeod kept his eyes trained on the fire but the corners of his mouth twitched. "Mmmm...I think the phrase he used was *fooled around a lot*...somethin' like that." He blew out the glowing end of the twig and shoved it back into the fire.

Andie leaned back to consider this, her eyebrows going through so many contortions they began to ache. "That sounds about right," she concluded. "Sufficiently vague...I like that. Good ol' Ben...."

Shane wriggled tired shoulders, reflecting. "Yeah...he's a pretty good guy. I think a lot of him."

"Me too." The young woman returned absently.

His eyes caught hers, lingering a moment before blinking away to safety. He stretched with an over-sized yawn. "Well...it's sack-out time for me. If you're gonna be up for that ride tomorrow, better rest while you can." He rose, poured the rest of his coffee over the remaining embers, and turned away in the darkness, sil-houetted by the glow of other campfires.

"Goodnight," he heard her call softly after him. What he didn't catch was her eyes following his back before flicking up to look at the night sky, wide and staring.

40

*   *   *   *

Sometime later in the wee hours of the night he heard it, causing him to roll over and rise up. There it was again ever so faint—restive moans from the woman's direction.

Shane rose quietly and went to her. But, for a moment, he found himself kneeling there, just studying her. Without realizing it his gaze lingered…first on the sooty fringe of those eyelashes that formed such perfect crescents in slumber…up across the smooth expanse of brow to that sweep of dark russet that caressed her temples before cascading in a tumbled heap upon the sleeping bag.

He swallowed hard, holding back the reflex to reach out and grasp a fistful of those magnificent tresses…. The impulse startled him back on his heels, bringing him back to himself. A crinkle in her brow caught his attention and he scanned her. Reaching down hesitantly, he pulled back the cover to check her wound. The latest bandage still looked fresh.

Funny, he hadn't noticed before the unkempt nature of those brows. There was an almost child-like quality to them, a hint of wild abandon. This was no button-down gal…but definitely a city-slicker. Obviously taken with the outdoors but didn't have a lick of sense when it came to keeping herself alive in it. The kid was a real mess of paradoxes. He shook his head with a soft grin.

She stirred again. Another moan, more intense than before. There was an undeniable tug in his chest at the sound. He bent close, unsure what to do. Then like a blow from the dark it came, unexpected and cruel. She shifted with a frown, but seemed to find comfort against his arm, nestling there like a child. Her lips parted in sleep, ever so slightly, forming the name, more breath than utterance.

"Ben…."

Shane drew back with a frown of puzzled disbelief that felt…almost…like betrayal. With a dismissive shake of his head, he turned away and started to rise. Only himself to blame, letting his thoughts run away like that.

The soft touch of a hand on his arm startled him. Looking back over his shoulder, he found those dark, seductive eyes now awake and upon him, edged with sleep. The face tilted up to him was guileless.

"I'm so glad you're here…" she murmured before succumbing to slumber once more.

Shane sat back, soundly perplexed, letting her nestle against his arm undisturbed. He settled in for the duration, sliding into a blue funk of cosmic proportions.

The next morning, as the group packed for the return trip home, Andie was struck by the ranger's solicitous manner.

"Here, I'll help you with that." He took the saddle blanket from her without waiting for a response.

She stood back, grateful for once for the masculine assist. Hampered by her still-sore ankle and now one shoulder in a sling, the simplest tasks were daunting. But his change in tone caught her off guard.

Andie scanned her memory, sketchy as it was, of the night before. *Did I miss something?* She looked on as the lanky ranger hoisted the saddle with ease onto the back of the sorrel and secured it with a quick tug and a yank. There was that warm tingle in her cheeks again. Averting her eyes, she bit back a grin. Funny how she turned all awkward and strange whenever he came near. *Like some goofy schoolgirl….*

"Thanks," she said aloud. The ranger shot her a tight smile, a terse nod, and went about his tasks, checking on the other trail riders. Looking after him, a flood of admiration washed over her.

Maybe it had to do with the confident way he handled things, whether saddling a horse or making a campfire or handling a weapon. There really was a lot of the cowboy in him—it wasn't just appearances in his case. This grown-up crush showed no signs of abatement.

She *was* a little disappointed when Brian Woodrum showed up to assist her onto her horse. But later, on the ride back, she found MacLeod at her side. "How're ya doin'?"

"Not bad—as long as we don't hit any potholes."

He snorted a laugh. "You're out of luck there. I suppose you'll wanna go t' one of those LA plastic surgeons when you get home 'n have that fixed."

She cocked her head. "This? No way! I'm proud of it! Badge of honor!"

He appeared stunned for a moment, not knowing what to make of her, before delivering a nod that was downright philosophical.

"So it is."

He cantered off at that. She watched him get waylaid by the loud, nasal woman carping about not seeing any of the touted Yosemite sequoias along the trail. "Those are clustered in three groves in the park, ma'am," he answered patiently. "The Merced and Tuolomne Groves are located near Oak Flat, the west entrance to the park, and the Mariposa Grove is at the south entrance of the park. It's probably the easiest to get to. We'll be glad to get you a map if you stop by any visitor center."

Andie smiled to herself. At least she'd done her homework on that before coming. Her heart sank a little when the ranger rode on toward the front of the line. But her spirits leapt when he returned, giving the impression he was keeping tabs on her. At times they just plodded along, each lost in thought, now and again stealing sidelong glances at one another.

That night, at a farewell cook-out for the riders at the Visitor Activities barn, the two were caught in what looked like the quirky preliminaries of courtship. Perhaps they themselves did not see it as such, but the signs were unmistakable to others.

The young ranger couple, Russ and Judy Calvert, looked on in fascination. The eyes of the knockout from L.A. would go all funny and downcast in the firelight, then glance across at the weathered face of the ranger, only to dart away when he happened to look in her direction. After a while, MacLeod caught on and their eyes locked, once. Both looked away quickly.

Tin plate in hand, Rusty sauntered over and squatted alongside Shane, proceeding to polish off his beans and franks. He jerked his chin in the direction of the California woman, who was engaged in conversation with another visitor. "Looks like you've got yourself a fan there."

Something between a grimace and a wince crossed Shane's face. "Nah…that's crazy."

That just made Calvert nudge him. "Hey…remember ol' buddy, you're not married any more. It's been three years, man! Most people would figure you prime pickin's by now."

MacLeod looked down at his plate with a scowl. "Still *feel* married." Rising to his feet, he dusted off his pants. "I don't have time for this kind of foolishness."

He stalked off, away from the noise of the carefree crowd, the watchful eyes of the other rangers, and most of all, that confounding woman.

Judy Calvert joined her husband, looking after their friend with troubled eyes.

. 6 .

Fortunately for Shane, at least to his way of thinking, it was shaping up to be a very busy spring, leading into an even busier summer. He had no time to think about such nonsense as romantic pursuits, much less deal with them. First of all, he was helping to arrange Ben Morgan's initial interview with park personnel. Then he had to get his own affairs in order for the move cross-country to become the Smokies' new North District Chief.

At park headquarters on the Tennessee side of Great Smoky Mountains National Park, three men sat at a conference table in the briefing room, trading notes from the myriad folders before them.

Bill Hayes was among them. He handed off two of the application packets to the man on his left.

Smokies Superintendent Tom Jeffries leaned back in his chair and perused the contents. His relaxed manner contrasted with the take-charge demeanor of Hayes. Long-boned and spare with a bushy, sand-colored moustache, the Smokies Park Head had the look of a Tennessee mountain man himself.

"These two next on the agenda?"

"Yep. Shane MacLeod, one of my colleagues from Yosemite. Good man. Had a brush with bad luck when his wife was killed in a car accident couple of years back. Looking for a change of scenery, I think. Easy-going fella. Shouldn't cause waves with the crew."

"Look forward to meeting him." Jeffries's gaze glided to the second form in his hands. "Know anything about this other man?"

"Morgan?" Hayes stood to stretch out his back. "I'm not so sure about that one. Friend of MacLeod's, but they're as different as night and day. He's got impressive but what you'd call unorthodox work experience, little in the way of credentials with the Park Service, though he had internships at Glacier and Rocky Mountain and helped with the Yellowstone fires. His training was top-notch."

Jeffries eyebrows peaked with interest. "Colorado State grad, huh? I like the sound of those internships. What's he looking for?"

"MacLeod thinks he'd make a hell of a backcountry ranger, for starters, maybe ease him into Subdistrict status in the long-term, once he's proven himself. The guy was one of those who got the ax during the big budget crunch, so he's been out quite a while. The fella's moved around a lot. Had to haul him off a reservation in Wyoming to get him here."

Jeffries looked to the man at his left, a short, robust, silver-haired fellow. His name tag proclaimed him to be Hank Stone, Chief of Ranger Activities. "Sounds promising to me, Hank. What do you think?"

Stone took the form from him. "His reservation experience could certainly help relations with our Cherokee neighbors." He ran a finger down the page, pausing at one point. "Hey...the fella's roughed it from the Rockies to the Andes. Let's have a look at him."

"All right, let's get him in here and see what you think."

Hayes went to the door and poked his head out. "Are the next two here yet, Joyce?"

The young woman at the front desk looked up. "Yes, Sir. They just arrived."

"Good. Send them in."

Across the room, two men turned simultaneously from studying a giant wall map of the park. Shane MacLeod and Ben Morgan nodded when the secretary looked in their direction. Heading for the open door of the conference room, they were greeted by Bill Hayes. The Superintendent held out a massive hand to Shane. "Good to see you, old friend."

Shane shook it warmly. "Kinda surprised to see you here, Bill."

"Yeah…well…there've been so many retirements and transfers this year that things are jumbled up across the Service, nationwide. It's made a lot of people nervous, not knowing who they're going to be dealing with—so they asked some of us old-timers to pitch in, oversee the major slots being filled, kinda help ease the transitions."

Hayes turned to the younger man beside MacLeod. "And this must be Morgan." They shook hands and Hayes led both men to the table, gesturing for them to take a seat. "This is Tom Jeffries, Park Superintendent here, and Hank Stone, Chief of Ranger Activities."

Superintendent Hayes was brief in his allowance for the perfunctory handshakes. Sitting down, he got right to business. "At this point, gentlemen, your transfer requests and applications have already been looked over, so this is mostly a get-acquainted session…also an opportunity to…fill in any gaps—" his gaze flitted to Morgan "—that the forms might not have covered. So…I'll open the floor for questions on either side."

Superintendent Jeffries spoke briefly aside to Chief Stone then addressed Shane. "At this point I'd have to say the decision is yours, Ranger MacLeod. We've examined your file and like everything we see. Your references were all glowing. We'll be glad to welcome you aboard if this is what you're looking for."

Shane shifted in his chair and gave Jeffries a direct look with the hint of a smile. "Thanks. I like what I see here."

Superintendent Hayes looked from Jeffries to MacLeod. "Good, that's settled. Now, to move along, I have a few questions of my own for Morgan." He put on his glasses, flipped through the forms on his clipboard, and planted his gaze on the younger man.

"You've got a dossier that reads like an adventure novel, son. I don't think there was a man among us who read it without some degree of envy. However, as I think you realize, that's not all it takes to cut it in the Park Service. It requires a certain amount of teamwork and…stability…as well as adherence to a well-defined code of laws. Whether we agree with them or not, they have to be enforced. Your rather…colorful past leads me to wonder if there was any intentional reason why some parts of your application were left blank. For instance, this question twenty-two here…I take it you've never been accused of a felony or misdemeanor?"

Morgan blinked. "Accused or convicted, Sir?"

Shane gave Ben an arrested look.

Superintendent Hayes eyed him over his glasses. "Let's start with accused, shall we?"

Morgan looked thoughtful. "Well…there was that time with the senator from Montana…."

Hayes leaned forward. "Go on."

"A misunderstanding really." Ben shrugged. "They thought we'd kidnapped him until we explained we were just trying to get his attention."

"And the end result?"

"We got a half million dollar increase for Glacier put into the next Federal budget—no charges filed," Ben added as an after-thought.

Across the table, Hank Stone coughed. Tom Jeffries snorted a laugh.

"I see...anything else we should know about?" Superintendent Hayes's attention glided to Shane, who looked away, rubbing his jaw thoughtfully.

"Let me think...maybe that time a bunch of us borrowed an Arapaho artifact from the museum in Laramie. Don't know why they made such a fuss. It was just for a couple of days. My friends needed it for a ceremony. Funny thing was, we didn't even get caught till we were putting it back."

None of the other men in the room appeared to find that funny.

Ben leaned forward, meeting Hayes eye to eye. "You're welcome to investigate thoroughly. I have nothing to hide there."

Shane added his own gaze to Ben's, a dual challenge.

It was Hayes's turn to shift uncomfortably. He cleared his throat, frowning at the papers in his hands. "Yes...well...you can be assured that we will. –Any further questions for now, gentlemen?"

Chief Stone had a glint of amusement in his eyes. "I'd like to schedule a more in-depth discussion with both of you in my office this afternoon. Give you a better idea of our particular challenges here. Say...three o'clock?"

MacLeod and Morgan nodded readily.

"Then I suppose that concludes this meeting." Hayes rose and shook their hands. "Thank you, gentlemen."

Outside, the two friends trotted down the steps side by side.

"That went well," Morgan observed when they were clear away. "At least I think so. It's hard to tell with that Hayes fellow. Is he always that stiff?"

Shane frowned aside at his younger companion. "Just try t' keep your nose clean, will ya? I'm not always gonna be around t' keep ya outta trouble, hear?"

Ben flashed him a devilish grin as they walked on.

"What trouble?"

Over supper that night in Gatlinburg, the new North District Chief Designate Shane MacLeod and Superintendent Hayes talked again, this time alone. Both men looked more relaxed in the casual setting, but Hayes still had some business to bring up.

"I don't mind telling you, Shane…this new recruit of yours may go through but not without my misgivings. At best, you could call him a colorful misfit. At worst, he could prove to be a real pain in the ass. The impression I get is of a guy with a smooth tongue and hair-trigger response who could go renegade on you at no notice."

Shane shook his head with a smile. "Ben's not crazy. But I'll allow he *is* an independent thinker, with a lot of hard-core, practical experience under his belt. Whatever antics he used to get into are tempered by age. The guy's got a family now!" Shane eyed his old boss critically. "You know we could use someone with a fresh angle on things in the Park Service."

Hayes cocked an eyebrow. "You mean *you* could."

Shane gave an appreciative snort. "I won't deny that."

The Superintendent shifted in the booth, the cushioned seating groaning under his weight. "Well…Tom Jeffries had no problem with either of you, and ultimately it's his call. But I've recommended Morgan enter on a six-month probationary status. Jeffries agreed to that. Then we'll see…."

A frown flickered across Shane's brow but he nodded his acquiescence.

The next morning, he saw Ben off for his flight back to Wyoming and handed him his assignment packet, starting date the first of July. Now Shane had to wrap up his own preparations and return to Yosemite for the not-so-little task of packing up eleven years' worth of household memories and moving cross-country. In less than two weeks, he would be reporting, himself, two months ahead of Morgan. There was still much to do.

* * * *

That weekend in L.A. it was raining….

Andie Carson stood before the glass doors of her apartment in the Pasadena hills, staring down at the rain-soaked cityscape. The twinkling lights did nothing to lift her mood. It had been a nasty week, followed by a nastier Friday night's attempt to forget it all. The search for a so-called *meaningful existence* in this beehive of dream seekers and dream merchants had proved futile.

Small matter that she had risen in the ranks from office girl to designer's assistant extraordinaire—or that her weekend open mike sessions at Prisms with her spacey old roommate friends had resulted in a recording contract last year. Vicky had believed they could do it all along. But that whole lifestyle struck her as ludicrous now. She'd grown more and more disenchanted with the direction their music was going. Singing used to be just play, kicking around with Vic, Ben, and his guitar-addicted roommate Terry. Now it threatened to take over her life, playing only what other people told her to.

God...where did I get so off course? She gave a soft snort. *How far back do I have to go?*

This wasn't the life she'd envisioned. She was going to go off by herself after college, become an independent woman, stand on her own two feet, and wait for Ben to shake the wandering dust out of his shoes. He'd want to go live on a mountain top and she'd say yes because now she was ready and he was ready to stay put. Maybe they'd backpack around the world first.

But he'd taken a detour along the way...and she was left to invent a whole new future to head for.

She'd done the urban setting—the constant checks in the mirror at status parties, revamping, comparative analysis, psychoanalysis. It had drained the individualism out of her. How many layers would it take to peel to find her real self again? Responses to things now seemed robotic, triggered by someone else's opinion, someone else's agenda.

The outdoors pulled her once again, and the kind of people who spent their lives there. Not the hotdog skier, fanatic rock climber, or macho hunter she'd encountered trying to find a replacement for Ben...something quieter.

Right now she just needed to be....

"Face it. You haven't been the same since that trail ride," she muttered. Ironically, that was the happiest, most carefree, most alive she'd felt in ages—injuries and all! The happiest since.... That same old lump rose in her throat. Damn the boy! Why did he have to go and get responsible on her? *Get married of all things!* Their never-ending adolescence had stayed intact...playmates, friends with benefits...bouncing off each other, running together for comfort, allowing space when needed...until he'd gone and screwed it all up. *Fallen in love with someone else, mind you!* Without so much as a backward glance. Not even a clumsy, half-hearted note, to the one who'd been his twin in spirit.

Her fingernails scratched a dejected trail in the fogged window as a tear traced its path down her cheek. "How could you, Ben...."

It was going on eight years now...she'd been driving home after a Mexican dinner with friends in Venice Beach. Stopped at a red light in front of a dingy brick YMCA in mid-town L.A., she'd been shocked to spy Ben in a line of scruffy men waiting to get a cot for the night. He'd been quiet and sullen as she tugged him back to the car. His week's worth of beard was something she wasn't accustomed to, either. The sense of wounded pride emanating from him was palpable. She'd tried to make small talk as she drove along, but it was little use.

The night would prove to get more bizarre. Five traffic lights down, a brick hurled through the back window of her car, showering them both with glass.

"Get down!" Ben yelled, wrenched from his shell. He yanked her down across his lap, grabbed the wheel, and stretched to reach the gas pedal, flooring it. The Nissan shot through the—thankfully—open intersection. Their roles of rescuer and rescued abruptly reversed.

The adrenaline rush had a remarkable effect on Ben. The moment Andie turned the key to her apartment door and they stepped inside, Ben shoved her up against the wall. All the pent-up frustration, anger, relief and lust of the past year exploded from him.

This wasn't the Ben she knew. She couldn't fathom what must have happened to change him so. She wouldn't even try.

She only knew he was back and he needed her and that, enveloped in confusion and bruised ego as he was, he wouldn't let himself hurt her. They groped their way to her bed, resurrected old memories, and slept like the dead till morning.

He apologized profusely the next morning. She gave him a slap upside the head, but professed to be none the worse for wear, other than some minor bruises. Badges of healing, she dubbed them. He flinched when she called them that and tried to kiss them away.

They lapsed that weekend into their old routine...staying up late, watching movies, eating take-out. There was nothing worth venturing out for. Nothing worth breaking the spell. He would only say that he was between assignments and had no place to crash for the next couple weeks till word came through. Hopefully, he said, it would be in the States this time...maybe VISTA... maybe Wyoming...he could only guess. But he asked her to come.

It would be different this time...no jungles...no bugs...no mysterious rashes or fungus infections like that time she visited him in Venezuela.

And, once again, she told him she couldn't just up and leave everything. Not till things were more settled...whatever that meant. Nothing else was said.

She came home from work one afternoon to find he'd gone. On her pillow was a scribbled note that read: *Thanks for the save. I'll remember you in my estate.* A couple of twenties lay alongside.

Andie guessed it was most of what he had. No address. Nothing else.

But there was a crumbled up scrap of paper on the floor that must've fallen out of his pocket. She'd dialed the number on it and gotten hold of some guy in Yosemite National Park. He took the message and got back to her with the lead she wanted...Ben's forwarding address. She put Ben's money toward buying him a coat—Wyoming had ferocious winters, didn't it?—and sent it on.

She never heard from him again—only indirectly, when Terry Wyss called to say he'd gone to Ben's wedding. It had been an Arapaho ceremony....

Some guy in Yosemite....

A new image asserted itself in her mind's eye, sweeping the misery of the other away...safe-kept and startlingly vivid...a man swinging confidently into the saddle of a big Appaloosa, turning the animal onto a trail. The same rush washed over her as the first time she'd witnessed that image in the flesh. The lure of something authentic after spending years surrounded by people who hid behind facades.

She blinked. Why not? Maybe there *was* life...after death...from Ben....

Andie turned and stared at the phone, hugging herself in deliberation. Before she had a chance to lose her nerve, she snatched up her phone and googled *Yosemite National Park Headquarters*.

Punching in the number, it hit her...*what do I say?*

"Hello? Uh...Hi. I was wondering. Could you tell me how to get in touch with a particular ranger? His name is Shane Mac-Leod."

The voice on the other end was pleasant enough if a bit strained by her request. "I'm sorry, we don't give out staff numbers, but I can connect you with the station he was last assigned to—"

Last assigned?

"Um—yes, that would be okay, I guess." Her heart lurched. Had she lost her chance? Another voice came over the phone, that of a young woman, and she had to marshal her thoughts back to the business at hand.

"Tuolomne Meadows Station. Judy Calvert."

"Judy! Hi!" Andie gushed in relief at the familiar voice. "This...this is Andie Carson, I don't know if you remember me but—"

"Why yes, Andie! How's the arm?"

"Oh, much better, thanks. Listen...I...I was just checking to see if—" *If what?* "—if there was a way I could leave a message somehow for...for Shane MacLeod...you know...when he gets in or...or something." She paused to catch her breath, wondering if Judy could hear how fast her heart was thumping.

"Hold on a sec, Andie."

In the interim, she tried to catch her breath, slow that rabbit heart.

"Okay, I'm back," came Judy's cheerful voice. But her next words sounded carefully chosen. "Tell you what. I can't tell you much there…you see, he's in the process of transferring to Great Smoky Mountains National Park…in Tennessee. But I'm sure someone there could help you."

"Oh…" Another roadblock…but wait…it was a lead, wasn't it? She stirred from her funk. "Oh! Sure! Thank you!"

"You're welcome. Bye now. Gotta go."

Judy Calvert looked up from her desk to see her husband frowning at her from across the little office. He was shaking his head.

"Not smart," he muttered.

"Well why not, Russ?" she fumed. "She saved his life, for heaven's sake! It ought to be all right to give her a lead—technically I didn't give out any phone numbers!"

She turned back to her work but paused to eye her phone.

"Good luck, Hon," she whispered under her breath, "You're gonna need it. Right now, I don't think Shane MacLeod would recognize a good thing if it hit him in the face."

. 7 .

Shane flinched as a cascade of plastic cups and Tupperware rained down on him from the kitchen cabinets of his new ranger cabin. It seemed like he'd spent most of this rainy Saturday uncovering vestiges of the previous occupancy and assigning it all to the trash cans out back. There was enough stuff left behind to suggest they'd left in a rush. He stopped to peer about himself.

Maybe there was something about this rustic old place that made them want to leave in a hurry?

Kicking aside one more box of trash, the ranger commenced rummaging through his own boxes. He pulled out an old tin coffee pot, a couple of enamel speckle-ware mugs and a single pink bunny slipper. Oops…. With a fond smile, he set it down alongside the model horse and frayed jump rope unpacked earlier— evidence of a jumbled-up semi-bachelor existence led with a motherless daughter.

A knock on the door brought his head up with a frown.

Who in the world?

He glanced at his watch. It was nearly five.

Padding barefoot to the entry, he peered out the window, but it was fogged up. He opened the door warily. A hooded figure in a dripping yellow slicker stood there on the covered porch.

At first the face was hidden, but when the visitor slid the backpack off, the hood fell back.

"Hi," she ventured, biting her lip.

Shane just stood there, stunned. There was no mistaking that impertinent mouth…those witchy, lunatic eyes.

"Hi," he returned, finding his voice.

He stole a glance down at himself, eyeing the old black T-shirt and gray sweatpants that had become his off-duty uniform. His eyes flicked back up when she spoke again.

"I—uh—was in the neighborhood and thought I'd drop by. Heard about your new assignment here…." There was a forced breeziness in her voice. She swallowed hard.

Shane flicked a glance beyond her, noting the shiny black car with rental plates in the gravel drive, and broke into a grin despite himself. "Well, better come in and dry off before you catch pneumonia."

His visitor stepped in clutching her pack. Her eyes glistened as they took in the dark, cavernous interior. "Wow…looks like something from Teddy Roosevelt's era!" she burst out.

"Yeah…well…the plumbing is from *Franklin* Roosevelt's." He jerked his head toward the hall. "The bathroom's that way if you wanna change out of those wet clothes. I'll be in the kitchen unpacking."

"Thanks!" The young woman headed off. Shane made for the kitchen but stopped. He turned back with a puzzled frown. "You do somethin' to your hair?"

She reached up, self-consciously fingering a wavy, wet tendril. "You like it?"

Shane shrugged noncommittally and headed back to the kitchen. He leaned over yet another box, muttering, "Looks like a damn mermaid." The words sank in and he straightened to stare after the young woman. *Was that so bad?* Shaking his head to clear it, he resumed his labors.

Minutes later came the sound of a distinctly feminine yelp.

He peered through the pass-through to catch his visitor dashing into the hall. She spun around, caught sight of him and tugged the towel more securely about her.

"It—It's cold!" she sputtered.

"Told ya." He returned to unpacking, ignoring the fact that she stood there a moment longer, eyeing him balefully. With a mad swipe at her hair, she charged back into the shower, looking braced for combat.

Sometime later, his visitor appeared at the pass-through, her good mood restored. She looked on as Shane chopped up a pile of tomatoes, onions, and green peppers on the cutting board.

He glanced up. "Hungry?"

The woman leaned forward on her elbows. "Mmmm…uh-huh."

"I promised myself a steak tonight. There's plenty here for two," he said without looking up.

"That sounds wonderful!" She waltzed off into the cavernous den, giving in to a twirl in the dim light. Stopping to bask in the flickering glow emanating from the fireplace, she hugged herself.

Shane felt a smile tug at his mouth. "How's the arm?" he called out, returning to his chopping.

"Oh, it's doing fine," she called back over her shoulder. "Thanks." She hugged herself tighter and turned back to the hearth. "Great fire!"

"Ranger," he dead-panned.

She let loose with that tinkling bell of a laugh he remembered. "Right! —Where's your daughter? I was hoping to meet her."

He looked up abruptly. Alarm bells inexplicably started up in his head. "How did you—"

"Oh! Sorry…Judy Calvert told me about her, the night of the cookout."

"Oh." He wasn't sure what he thought of that but dismissed it with an inner shrug. Probably harmless. Still, Judy should have been more restrained giving out information like that. What was she doing, trying to play matchmaker? Dangerous business…. Yet here they were, three thousand miles from Yosemite.

Well…sounded like the thought of a kid involved didn't scare her away. Again…good or bad? He cleared his throat. Probably should say *something* else.

"She—uh—stayed behind to finish up the school year. My sister came down from Sacramento to stay with her. She'll come soon as school's out."

Lost in thought, Andie was startled to find MacLeod at her side minutes later with the grilling plate of steaks in his hand. "So…how d'you like yours?"

She broke from her reverie. "Huh? Oh! Well done, I guess."

"City slicker." The ranger knelt before the fire, placed the grilling pan on the grate, rose, and returned to the kitchen. He brought back a loaf of French bread on a wooden board and two goblets of Burgundy cradled deftly between his fingers.

"I was gonna have a beer but I guess you don't offer that when your guest is a lady. And a Californian."

She gave him a twisted smile from her perch on the stone hearth. "Times have changed. But then, I never really liked the stuff, myself."

He shrugged. "Guess I'm out of touch. Haven't been out on what you'd call a date in—oh—twelve years, I guess…." MacLeod stared into the fire and took a thoughtful swig from his glass.

Andie winced. "I'm sorry." Both went silent a moment.

Shane put his glass down and leaned forward on his knees. "Let's check those steaks. Hand me a plate, would ya?" Soon, they were chowing down.

Andie rolled her eyes in ecstasy. "This is incredible! What's this sauce?"

"Relleños. Something I picked up from my New Mexico grandmother. Navajo, actually."

"Really? It's wonderful!" Andie watched the flicker of fire-light dance along the planes of his face. Navajo? That was easy to believe, looking at him now. The lean, stony face looked as if it had been carved from the same hard-packed cliffs his ancestors called home. "So…what made you become a ranger?" she asked softly.

He looked up at her with a squint before turning back to the fire. Picking up the poker, he jabbed the logs a couple of times, sending a shower of sparks flying. He waited for them to settle before answering.

"I guess I just preferred the outdoor life over any kind of office job. Tried engineering for a while in college, didn't go for it…had a stint in the Navy but didn't wanna make a career out of that." He put down the poker and picked up his plate. Taking a bite of steak, he chewed on it awhile.

"It bothered me as a boy to see old wandering places disappear into developments…made me want to protect some places for the future, I guess." He chewed some more and swallowed. "As for the enforcement end of it, I just kinda fell into it. That was where they needed me when I signed up, although I've filled in at any job that needed doin' over the years—now Morgan, he'd probably claim I got into it because I like to boss people around."

Andie bit back a giggle. "Do you?"

"Naw…just him." He surrendered a laugh that wasn't much more than a sniff. Still, it was one of the first times she'd seen him truly relax around her.

"What about you?" he asked in turn. "How did you end up in Los Angeles?"

She sat back, resting her back against an old ottoman and grimaced. "I wasn't always like this."

"What do you mean?"

"I mean…clumsy City Slicker, as you call it."

He opened his mouth but she waved him off. "It's okay. I mean…if the shoe fits…. Funny thing is, I actually used to camp a lot, with my family…with—" She hesitated.

"Ben?"

She nodded. "After graduation, I went off to L.A., interned at the Pacific Design Center, eventually got hired by one of the designers who exhibited there. Thought it was a dream come true."

"But?"

"Oh, it *was* at first. Even that first couple of years, when I was little more than a glorified *gofer*. It was exciting, getting to help design big events…go to celebrity houses…dress up and rub elbows with the elite in the art world at cocktail receptions. But after a while, it all started to feel fake. At least I still had most of my weekends to myself. One of the girls I first roomed with in California got me to go with her to some open-mike clubs. One night we decided to go the circuit, try to get on stage at every one from Venice Beach to Malibu. By the third one, we had our act down. By the seventh one, in Malibu, we'd collected four cards from fellows who came up to us afterward."

"Sounds like a good time to be wary."

"Yeah…we thought so, too. But two of them we thought were legit. So we each called one. The one I called asked us to come into his studio…turned out he was in Century City! The next week, we were signed to a contract."

"Wow."

She lifted one shoulder, self-conscious. "Anyway…that's how I got detoured from Colorado nature girl to tinsel town torch singer."

"That's quite a detour."

Silence ensued as they enjoyed the rest of their meal. But before they had finished, Shane rose without a word and sauntered over to an old stereo. With a twisted smile, he rummaged through a box of CD's. "I think I've got something here you'll recognize." He slid the disc into its slot and a moment later, Andie's own vocals came over the speakers, accompanied by a backup band and another singer.

She sat up, wide-eyed. "Oh, no! Where did you get that?" she wailed.

The ranger grinned. "Ben sent it to me a few weeks back, after he heard we'd…run across each other. Didn't want me thinkin' you were just some 'front piece for a band' I think he put it."

She fanned burning cheeks. "So…what did you think?"

"Not bad," he allowed. "Energetic. Good unpackin' music. Probably good for…a lot of things." He scratched his jaw.

She cocked her head up at him. "Thanks. I think."

The urgent, primal backbeat of drums came to the forefront. Their eyes locked, a beat too long for comfort. She broke away.

Behind them, the song ended. Shane turned back to stop the player. "So how's that book comin'?"

"Book?" Her pulse quickened. "Oh…." She swallowed. "The…the book on rangers, you mean." Her eyes couldn't rise to meet his face.

Above her, his voice came, low, decisive, but with without judgment. "I didn't think so…."

His words hung in the air a moment before she could manage a retort. "That's not to say I won't still write it!" She looked up with a spark of defiance.

His eyes held hers fast. "So why are you really here?"

She was struck dumb. For a second, Andie considered jumping up to flee. But then she slowly laid down her plate and looked about the room, eyes glistening. Drawing herself up, she rested her chin on her knees, gaze gone inward.

"When I got back to L.A. I realized...I couldn't live like that anymore. It didn't make sense...nothing made sense anymore...." She lapsed into silence, sniffing.

MacLeod waited a respectable while before responding. Leaning back against the hearth, he balanced his goblet on his knee.

"So what makes sense to you now?"

She looked up into the rafters, eyes brimming over. She raised her arms as though to gather in the essence of the rugged old lodge. "*This*...all of this." She dropped her arms. Sniffing, she looked down, shaking her head. Abruptly, she surged to her feet, flailing her arms.

"Ohhh...I shouldn't even be here!"

The ranger reached up without a word, latched hold of her hand and tugged her back down. "Yes, you should."

She blinked back her tears, words tumbling forth. "Seems like I've been running from one thing to another, going through the motions but not getting anywhere...anywhere at all. Then I run into you and see something good...something strong and sure...no-nonsense. I *hate* nonsense...I'm sick of it." She squeezed her eyes shut and just let the tears roll, ending up with a shaky sigh. "Nothing like lettin' it all hang out."

He reached out a calloused finger to lift her chin and those dark eyes stared deep into hers. She snapped to attention and froze.

"Come here, Girl."

She leaned toward him tentatively, pulse quickening again. That calloused palm cupped her cheek. A tingle ran through her at the touch. Their lips connected. What seemed a small eternity later, they parted. She was scared to breathe.

MacLeod let out a sigh, "Let's get somethin' straight here. Is this all because Ben's married and you can't have him anymore?"

Eyes brimming, she took his lean, weathered face in her hands. "No, Silly…you've gone and made me fall in love with *you*!" She managed a crooked smile. "There was nothing I could do about it."

Shane gave a doubly long sigh this time and eyed the girl. What next? He had to think….

"I…better stir the fire some." He turned away and snatched up the poker, stabbing the coals with more energy than effectiveness. His mind raced through the dizzying array of possibilities looming here. Nothing helpful came to mind. There was no guidebook for this kind of thing. No protocol was covered in training sessions for dealing with female admirers turned amorous. Maybe someone like Brian Woodrum back at Yosemite would have no trouble whatsoever handling this…but it wasn't a situation he was used to finding himself in.

In fact, it had been so long since he'd had any kind of a personal life, it was hard to think of himself in those terms. It seemed almost…unprofessional. *God…have I dried up that much?*

But hang it all, he was startin' t' get feelings for the girl!

Something tightened like a fist in his stomach but he fought it down. Just nerves…. He took a steadying breath, turned, and promptly lost it.

The woman knelt there in seductive splendor, flannel shirt unbuttoned all the way. She'd also managed to slip off her jeans. Mercy…. *Must've stirred those coals longer than I thought.*

He swallowed hard, taking in the incredibly long legs, that tumbled cascade of russet hair and glittery dark eyes with the crazy light in them, staring back at him…half daring, half scared out of her wits.

Not to forget the creamy cleavage that beckoned. She was a bigger girl than Beck…statuesque, broad-shouldered, definitely well-endowed….

"Do I…do anything for you?" Her voice sounded more plaintive than alluring.

He broke into a shaky laugh. "Are you crazy?"

She stopped chewing on her lip long enough to form a trembling smile. "I think so…a little bit—" Shane knelt before her and pulled her to him. "—or maybe a lot…" she breathed, just before their lips made contact again, hardfast and sure.

Andie's hands slid up the front of his T-shirt, marveling at the unyielding chest beneath. Sinewy and spare…not an ounce extra on him. *Like a real cowboy….*

But something made her pause. He was several years older, there was a good bit of gray in his hair…he wasn't Ben, the insatiable one. *Is he up to—*

She gasped as a pair of strong hands handily lifted her up and laid her back against the sheepskin rug. "Nice move…" she purred and reached for him.

Those strong, safe hands slid under her shirt hesitantly, then more surely, gliding down to her thighs. She shivered and tugged at him.

He hovered over her, surveying her like a man come upon unexpected treasure and not quite sure what to do with it. His eyebrows twitched. "Why me…why here…why now?"

She reached up, fingertips brushing his temples. "You think too much."

A lop-sided grin worked at the corners of his mouth. "Prob'ly so...."

Shane resolved then and there to throw caution to the wind, determined to claim this prize in the most delightful ways imaginable—or die trying. He was surprised at the aggressive way he handled the girl. But somewhere back in his mind, a voice kept telling him this had to be a dream, so he might as well enjoy himself. He never felt so uninhibited in his life....

Andie could not have been more delighted with her cowboy-ranger turned into this lean, handsome creature hovering over her, the threat of possession enticing but not frightening. His expert touch surprised and pleased her. Even as he took charge, she felt secure that this was a man who would never hurt her. A twinge of pathos tugged at her heart, remembering he was once married.

Part of her couldn't believe what she'd set in motion. A dizzying sensation came over her, like wading midstream into raging waters, spun around, disoriented, too late for second thoughts... too late to turn back.

Swept up again with no thought save for the present, she fell asleep in his arms afterward, marveling at how he was softly furry in all the right places.

They awoke hours later, stirring almost at the same time. Rising up on their elbows, they stared about themselves, blinking. The fire in the hearth had burned down to glowing coals. A shared grin crossed both their faces as they looked one another's way, Andie's a little on the shy side. She was totally smitten....

Shane jumped to his feet and threw on his sweatpants. Grabbing a throw from the couch, he held it open wide. "Come on. It's not right t' make a lady guest sleep on the floor."

Andie rose with a twisted smile, letting him envelop her in the soft, fuzzy afghan, and trotted off happily with him. He escorted her down the hall, directing her to a rustic contraption of notched cedar posts, piled high with Navajo blankets. Just looking at that bed could ward off the chill of a rainy night in the mountains. She leaned against the doorframe with a sigh. It was too perfect....

Shane gave her a nudge from behind. "Go on git yerself in there before ya freeze somethin' pretty."

She ventured in but cast a glance over her shoulder, catching him in the act of giving her an appreciative once-over.

He grinned and turned away. "Be right back."

Shane left to check the house but soon returned, sliding in beside her under the thick covers. She greeted him with a snuggle then rolled to her side. Irresistibly drawn, he nestled up against her back and nuzzled her hair. Wrapped in his arms, safe and secure, she was soon asleep.

He lay there enjoying the sound of her soft regular breathing. Sleep would not come so easily for him yet. His brow furrowed. What in creation had come over him? Sex that good didn't come without a price—he'd been around long enough to realize that. He should know better. But when he gazed down at the brunette seductress drowsing alongside, he relaxed into a sheepish smile. There lay his reason for taking leave of his senses...a long-limbed, goofy free spirit with a wicked smile and eyes that beguiled him to distraction. That was what had gotten hold of him.

*   *   *   *

Andie took her time resurfacing from slumber when morning came, indulging in a tigress-like stretch and a delicious yawn. She hadn't slept like that in years. Sunbeams streamed through the slats of the shutters, making her blink. She made out MacLeod's form standing by the window, staring out with a steaming cup of coffee in his hands.

The ranger looked lost in thought. Already, he was dressed in his Park Service uniform. It made him look so official, so...distant. He turned and saw her.

" 'Mornin'."

Andie sat up hugging her knees and gave him a sleepy-shy smile in return. "Hi. You're up and about early."

His eyes flickered. "Yeah...well...duty calls. I told one of the fellas I wanted to ride along with him today, get a feel for the park. Didn't think I should up and change on him the last minute."

"No...of course." She raked a hand through her tumbled mane. The gesture was offhand, guileless but appeared to have an effect on him. He looked distracted, restless.

She frowned. "Is anything wrong?"

"Nope...just have t' report in, that's all."

She watched him cross the room to get his boots, come back and sit on the bed to put them on. "Something *is* wrong, isn't it?"

He looked over his shoulder at her, yielding a sigh. "I don't know, Andie. It's just...last night was so...unlike me."

She sat up, hugging her pillow. "I was afraid it was too good to be true," she muttered. Tears welled in her eyes. She swiped them away with the back of her hand. "I know I must've...come on a bit...strong last night. I'm sorry. I should go—"

Shane turned on her. "No! What I'm tryin' to figure out is how to ask you to *stay*!"

Andie looked on in confusion as he rose and began to pace. "I mean...I got my little girl comin' out here in a few days and...." He trailed off, shoving his hands in his pockets.

She looked up out of the tops of her eyes. "I never meant to cause you any trouble."

"I know," he groaned, "but Girl...you already have...."

She blinked even harder.

The ranger quickly sat down beside her. "What I mean is…you've gone and made me fall for you, too—hard. Sure, it's gonna throw things into a spin for a while, but…it can work itself out. If we want it bad enough, it will." He stroked her arm clumsily, a heartfelt gesture that only made her love him more.

She sniffed, attempting a smile. "You can count on me."

His hand brushed her cheek, lingered a moment, but dropped away. "I gotta go." He gathered up the rest of his gear.

"Can I go with you?" She winced even as she heard the words leave her mouth.

"What?" He turned back, plainly caught off guard.

"I—I'm sorry. It's just…that's part of what made me fall for you. I love what you do. I don't want to be in the way. I just want to be a part of it…learn all I can."

He stood there looking uncertain a moment, breaking into a reluctant grin. "You tryin' to seduce me again? Or just messin' with my mind my first day? —Tell you what, when I get back this afternoon, I'll take you out in that canoe 'round back. How's that sound?"

Her spirits soared at that. "Oh, I'd love that!" She bounded out of bed and padded after him to the front door, blanket trailing after. "Oh—and Shane—" she whispered.

He turned, leveling that steady gaze back at her. She melted against the doorframe. "I can be discreet." She bit her lip, suddenly in need of assurance again.

The ranger reached absently for his cap on the wall peg and cast a pensive squint her way. "Sounds like somethin' we need t' talk about." He brushed her cheek with the back of a weathered hand. All business again, he tossed on his cap and turned to go.

"You can reach me at that number by the phone if you need me," he called over his shoulder.

She followed him out onto the plank porch, marveling at the misty chill of the mountain morning. Gray-green wisps spiraled against the background of verdant green. Shutting her eyes, she took a deep breath, gathering it in.

He winked up at her from the bottom of the steps. "Don't go makin' yourself too discreet, now. I'm gonna want t' take you out and show you off soon."

Andie relaxed into a twisted smile and raised her arm to wave, causing the blanket to unravel from her shoulders. Gasping, she snatched it back, not quite in time to conceal some of her charms. Tugging the cover secure, she waved sheepishly.

Shane wagged his head, chuckling as he climbed into the park SUV and waved goodbye.

. 8 .

At the Cades Cove Visitor Center, speculation buzzed about the new District Chief. The staff clustered in the lobby, peering out at Shane as he talked to another ranger on the front walk.

"Have you met him yet?" one of them asked his companions.

"Yeah, he was at the staff meeting on Friday," the fellow at his elbow responded. "Seems like a nice enough sort, on the quiet side. Got the impression he knows his stuff, though. Hails from Yellowstone *and* Yosemite, I hear."

A young female ranger, whose badge read *Interpretive Division*, joined them to take a peek at the new top man. "Well! He certainly looks the part! A real Westerner."

Her colleague gave her a friendly jostle. "Look out! We got a buckaroo on our hands!"

Melba Davis, the District secretary, emerged from the back offices to catch the tail end of the conversation among the younger set. A woman of small stature but imposing girth, she drew herself up to her most commanding posture and cocked an eyebrow. "He happens to be a Navy veteran with a Purple Heart—and a widower besides, raising a daughter alone."

The jocular bunch grew serious at that.

One ranger shook his head. "That's gotta be tough."

The door opened and all talking ceased. In stepped the new Chief. Spare and sinewy, about six feet, with a weathered, rawbone face and graying hair, he epitomized the Old West hero in looks as well as carriage.

All hands returned to business as he sauntered up to the counter. A young blond ranger, whose name tag read *B. McIntyre,* glanced guardedly over his shoulder from the file cabinet, as though expecting the man to pull out a six-shooter, lay it on the counter, and ask to see the proprietor. In any case, he wasn't disappointed when the newcomer opened his mouth. Even the man's voice sounded the part—deep, quiet, and firm:

"Name's Shane MacLeod." He stuck out his hand to the young woman in uniform at the counter. "Understand you folks have an office waitin' to be filled."

"Susannah Corbin, Sir."

He cocked his head. "Like the cabin in the Cove?"

She grinned. "Yes sir, my family was among the original settlers."

The idea of descendants watching over the valley seemed to please him. "Nice."

She smiled brightly. "It's a pleasure to meet you, Chief. Come this way."

Shane came around to the other side of the counter, noticing out of the corner of his eye the older, portly woman on the phone who snapped to attention when he passed. She managed to look both flustered and disappointed in that brief second. He eyed her badge and made a mental note to speak to her later.

Down the hall, Susannah stopped by an open door. The room beyond was crammed with several desks and stacks of boxes with dates scrawled on them in black marker. Myriad jars of green water, racks of test tubes, assorted field guides, and capture nets filled the shelves. Three men looked up from their work as she introduced them.

"This is Rob Johnson, our aquatic biologist, and Zack Moore, with botany labs, and over there on the phone is Pat Arrowsmith, our raptor expert."

Shane nodded at each man in turn but his eyes lingered a moment on the last, a tall, barrel-chested man with jet black hair, piercing dark eyes, and aquiline nose, whom he guessed to be of Cherokee descent. Arrowsmith's imposing demeanor melted away when he smiled and nodded amiably.

Susannah continued down the hall. "Others will be in tomorrow. They're all anxious to meet you."

"Curious, too, I imagine," Shane responded.

His young companion gave an easy laugh. "Can't deny that—and here you are!"

Shane entered his new office, which had a window overlooking a panoramic view of the Cove meadow sheltered by a cluster of oaks that overhung the eaves. He cased it out, went behind the desk, and looked up. "You can tell 'em I plan to hold a meeting first thing in the morning, set everyone's mind to rest. I know they've had a lot of upheaval lately and they don't need more. We'll take it slow for the time being."

Susannah nodded readily. "They'll be glad to hear that, I'm sure. Is there anything else you'll be needing?"

"Not for now. I just planned to stop by before heading out on a patrol run." He paused to search through a couple of the drawers. "You got any of those patrol report forms handy?"

The young woman looked surprised. "Well, yes, sir, but—I mean—our District Chiefs don't usually—"

He stopped her with a glance up. "That's something you'll learn about me. I'll probably tend t' be out in the field more than you're used to. Besides, it gives me a chance to get familiar with the territory before things get jumpin' around here."

"Yessir, I'll get them for you." A smile of understanding passed between them.

Shane emerged from his office a few minutes later and reentered the front lobby. He nodded to the staff and was heading for the door when he hung on his heel. Catching sight of Melba

Davis at the counter, he turned back. No stranger to the subtleties of office interpersonal relations, he had sized up the Cove Center's pecking order at a glance. Show deference to the District Secretary and the rest would be easy.

The secretary's carriage and response to the new chief showed not only her respect for the position but a guarded affinity for the man as well. He shook hands with her and handed over a sheet of paper.

"Here's my itinerary for the day, Melba. Do you have my home phone number here yet?"

"Yes, sir," Melba returned crisply.

"Good. I'll be back around three and head home after that." With a nod, he turned to go, leaving the others to stare after him.

Susannah caught the look of admiration on Melba's face and couldn't help grinning. "I think you're really going to enjoy working with him."

Melba looked as though she'd been caught with her guard down and returned to shuffling her papers. "He seems like a nice enough sort," she allowed.

Susannah crossed her arms, nodding as she looked after the new Chief. "I like those boots...."

North District Chief MacLeod had been out on mounted patrol about an hour when he received his first call. He snatched up the radio at his belt. "MacLeod here."

The voice of the dispatch operator crackled in response. "We've got an APB out for a missing four-year-old white male. Wandered away from Cades Cove Campsite Five. Last seen forty minutes ago, wearing a red T-shirt and blue jeans. Name is Caleb Moore."

"I'm in the vicinity," Shane responded. "Tell 'em I'm on the Russell Field fork, heading north on Anthony Creek Trail. Over."

"Acknowledged. Will keep you posted. Over and out."

Shane picked his way carefully along the return trek to Cove Loop Road, keeping an eye groundward for clues.

Now and then, he pulled the Appaloosa to a stop but there was only the sound of a gentle breeze in the treetops and the occasional bird song.

"Caleb? Caleb!" he called out. There was no answer, but the snap of a twig and skittering among the leaves made him whirl to his left. It was only a pair of squirrels startled by his approach.

Further along, he spied something shiny on the path, stopped to dismount and knelt to investigate. He picked up what looked like a piece from a toy, the silver torso of a tiny robot. Shane rose, studying it, then tore his gaze away to scan the woods. Just the kind of thing a four-year-old might carry.

"Still warm…" he muttered. Hefting it in his palm, he reached for the walkie. "Sheree? This is Shane MacLeod. Can you get through to his parents? Ask if he owns one of those little robot toys, will ya? This one's silver and green, with a name stamped on it. Looks like…C-bot? Over."

"Be right back. Over." A couple of minutes later, she was back on the line, an excited edge to her voice.

"Affirmative, Chief!"

While waiting, Shane had noticed an overgrown side path he missed before. It appeared to lead down to the creek. He took a long breath, choosing his words with care. "Okay, I may be on t' something. Keep you posted. MacLeod out."

He tied the Appaloosa's reins to a hickory trunk and waded through the underbrush of the neglected trail. Now and again, he stopped to detect any unusual sounds. In the distance was the rush of water. If his mental map served him well, it was one of the tributaries of Abrams Creek. He hadn't seen much of it yet but read it had several treacherous spots. There was a tumble of giant boulders visible as he drew nearer the water, rock outcroppings with smoothed-out hollows where a child could have nestled to rest. Hopefully sans snakes.

Shane explored the most promising ones but all were empty.

He gauged the depth of the rippling waters on the other side of the rocks. His steps quickened downstream, passing in and out of underbrush near the bank.

Another group of boulders. This one had a tiny blue sneaker lying in it. Heart hammering in his ears, he scanned upstream and down. Surely the child didn't cross here. The water was much too fast.

His gaze swung skyward and he spied him....

The child was some thirty feet above, attempting to scrape and claw his way up the jagged embankment to his left. Great...just his luck. He had a future cliff-climber on his hands.

But not one yet. For every six inches of progress, he would slip back as much. How long had the little tyke been at it? And what possessed him to try such a thing? One thing for sure, he wouldn't last much longer. Under the matted mop of brown hair, the cherub face was scratched and smeared with mud. Clearly exhausted and liable to slip any second. He started to call out but thought better of it. *Don't startle him till I can get under him.*

Shane pushed through the rest of the tangled underbrush but a muffled snort brought him up short. He froze. The Smokies weren't losing any time introducing their hazards to him.

A wild boar stood there, snout quivering in the air, no more than thirty feet up the narrow, creekside path. Covered with black bristly hair and fearsome tusks, it held its ground, facing him down. Even as the breath caught in his throat, Shane tried to recall the briefing on them. An import to the park, they had escaped from a hunting preserve back in the 1920's, interbred with domestic pigs, and now infested the area...relentlessly uprooting acres of land as they foraged, competing with the native animal population for food when they weren't devouring them as well. One had been seen bringing down a small deer. It was odd to see one like this in the daytime. They tended to be nocturnal creatures. This one must've been disturbed from its resting place by the boy.

Park personnel were authorized to dispatch the wild hogs by trap or bullet if necessary. Still…it went against the grain to shoot an animal in the very park he was sworn to protect. How would that look on his first day? Only once had he been forced to shoot an animal before—a rabid coyote that had threatened backcountry hikers at Yosemite. He would hate to traumatize the child more than he was already.

The boar snorted again, pawing the ground, like a pint-sized bull ready to charge. Shane didn't relish a direct encounter. This one had powerful shoulders reaching thigh-high. It looked fast and poised in deadly earnest—protecting some young? Definitely a threat to both him and the boy.

Shane's hand drifted up to the hilt of his Glock, calculating… *Would one shot suffice?* The boar lowered its head, indicative of a charge. Shane's fingers twitched, spasm-like, middle finger curling about the trigger. He spied a scuff of dirt fly from the back hooves of the animal and waited no more. Yanking the Glock from its holster, he sighted on the bristly triangle between the beady eyes.

A flurry of feathers and noisome squawks caught both man and beast by surprise. A wild turkey, flushed from a laurel thicket, flapped with a frenzy into the space between them. Caught up short, the boar squealed its surprise and veered wildly off course, splashing across the streambed and galloping off into the woods like a renegade mini-rhinoceros.

It took a moment for the ranger to recover from his shock. But then he heard the boy cry out, followed by a frantic scraping against rock.

"Hold on, son! I'm coming!"

He trotted up to a position below the tyke. Judging from the trampled vegetation above, the child had tumbled from the top of the bluff, he saw now, rather than climbed up. The child sagged against the muddy, rock-studded cliff, gripping a tangle of vines, and began to whimper.

Shane took a moment to scan the embankment below the little boy. It might scrape him up a bit but nothing there that should really hurt him. The best route might be—

"Okay, Caleb. My name's Shane. I'm a ranger. Listen…you can let go now and slide down into my arms. I'm here to catch you. I promise. It might be a little bumpy, but I'll catch you. Understand?"

The tyke sniffed, and after a moment, nodded.

"Okay. I'll count to three and then you slide down to me. One…two…"

Little Caleb let go prematurely, either too glad to get off that cliff face or he hadn't learned his numbers yet. But Shane was ready for him. He landed with an *Oooomphh!* in the ranger's arms.

"Okay! You doin' alright? Anything hurt?" The boy buried his face against the ranger's shirtfront, sniffling, but shook his head. Shane brushed at a dirty worn spot on one knee of the little jeans. "Just a few bumps and bruises, eh? Nothin' you can't handle?"

He got a reluctant shake of the little head. "Good enough," he chuckled. "Alright, let's get you back t' your folks. Groping for his hip pocket, he pulled out the walkie but paused to eye his charge. "Your name *is* Caleb? Caleb Moore?"

The child nodded emphatically.

"In that case, I've got some people here who'd really like to talk with you." Shane pressed the button on the comm and held it to the child's mouth.

"Dadddyyyy!" he squawked.

Shane took it back. "MacLeod here. Caleb's been found. Repeat. Caleb is found. He's with me and appears unhurt. I'll be comin' up Anthony Creek Trail with him, on horseback."

The ranger slid the child to his feet but kept a firm grip on the little hand as they maneuvered their way back up the foot path. When they reached the spot where the Appaloosa was tethered, he eyed the boy. "Ever ridden a horse before?"

The child shook his head, thumb implanted firmly in his mouth as he stared wide-eyed up at the huge animal.

"Wanna give it a go?" Shane asked him. "I'll ride with you."

At the boy's nod, Shane hoisted him into the saddle and swung up behind him. He showed him how to hold onto the saddle horn, and gave the horse a gentle nudge with his boot heels, guiding it toward the campground.

When they emerged from the trailhead, they found a large crowd awaiting them. It rushed en masse to greet them. Young Caleb looked startled at the wave of strange faces coming at them so fast and burrowed his face into the ranger's jacket.

"It's all right, Scout." He slowed the Appaloosa to a stop and swung down. As he reached up for the boy, a couple burst through the throng to his side.

"I don't know how we can ever thank you!" the woman cried.

The father took his son from Shane's arms, swallowing back tears.

Shane gave them a self-conscious smile and a nod. "That's what we're here for, Ma'am." Fortunately, the parents turned away before they could catch his wince. Sometimes you just had to give in to a bad cliché. He hopped back on to lead the Appaloosa to the Cove stables.

The grateful parents headed back for their campsite, but not before Caleb whirled about to cast one last look over his dad's shoulder at the retreating figure of his rescuer. Thumb finally extracted, he found his voice. "Whozzat, Mama?"

His mother gave him a weary but fond smile.

"That, my dear, is a ranger."

. 9 .

Shane stepped in the front door of the lodge, arms laden with sacks of groceries picked up on the way back from work. The house was unlit and quiet. Frowning, he laid the bags down on the kitchen counter.

"Andie?"

There was no answer.

He walked back to the bedroom. No sign of her there, either. He retraced his steps back through the den to the other end of the house. There, in the small study he'd set up as a field office, he found her asleep on the daybed, wearing a faded Colorado State sweatshirt and shorts. She looked like a college coed sacked out after a heavy study session. Next to her were field guides, maps, and brochures extolling the virtues of the Great Smokies.

He slumped against the doorjamb with a soft grin. For a moment, he just stood there, staring down at her before stepping in to pull a blanket over her. He left to go through his groceries for supper fixings.

Mug of soup in hand, he plopped down on the couch in the den and reached for the newspaper, set to unwind. But when he perused the entertainment section, a jolt went through him. An article in the sidebar of the cover page snared his attention.

Accompanied by two photos, the caption read: *FOX ON THE RUN?* Shane's eyes narrowed as he took a closer look. Sure enough, it was Andie in both pictures—one, a stage shot with other singers; the other, showing her accompanied by a young man with a dark pony-tail as they ducked into a ritzy L.A. club.

He bolted upright, eyes racing through the article, comprehending little save for the last sentence: *Litigation against Ms. Carson is still pending.*

Shane laid the paper down and stared in the direction of his study and the young woman who lay sleeping there. His gaze swiveled to the fireplace and he took a steadying breath. He was still lost in thought later when soft footsteps made him jerk around. It was Andie.

She smiled sleepily and greeted him in a voice both drowsy and a little hoarse. "Hi! I'm sorry. I meant to be up and about when you got back."

Shane gave her a tight smile. "That's okay. I looked in on you earlier, figured you must still be pretty tired from your trip." His eyes flicked away to look about the room. "You've been busy. The place looks nice."

The young woman shrugged and joined him on the couch. "Just wanted to make myself useful. "How was your day?"

"Oh…nuthin' special." He shrugged, not meeting her eyes.

She cocked her head, frowning. "What is it?"

Shane leaned back and crossed his arms across his chest, jerking his chin at the newspaper on the table before them. "We need to talk."

Andie followed his gaze and picked the paper up with a puzzled expression. Scanning the article, her eyes widened the more she read. She shook her head in bewilderment.

Shane slumped in the cushions, hands shoved into his pockets. "What was I thinking? You don't take a city girl—a celebrity-type at that—and expect her to fit in here in the woods. I didn't know who I was dealing with. Sorry."

When he glanced up, he saw the stunned look on her face, a tear shimmering in one eye. It broke free to course down her cheek.

"Please don't give up on me, Shane. Not yet. I...I care for you too much."

He narrowed his eyes against the pain. "I care for you, too, but...I don't know what to think about all this...." Their gazes traveled together to rest on the offending paper.

"*I* don't know what to think about all this! Not the litigation business, anyway." She grimaced. "Maybe I did up and leave kinda quickly, but—"

"Exactly what circumstances did you leave under, Andrea?" His voice held that quiet authority he used on an errant daughter or careless rookie. She winced appropriately, he thought. And it took a couple of tries to get on track. Maybe now he would get something that approximated the truth. The *whole* truth. Her eyes held an earnestness he wanted to believe.

"When I returned to L.A...after that trail ride...."

He nodded and she continued, "I sat in my apartment for three solid days, just thinking about things. I didn't want to budge, didn't want to do anything. I was so sick of that life. Sick of turning over my life to someone else, someone else's schedule. I realized my life wasn't my own anymore. Nowhere near where I wanted it to be now. I wanted out, to start completely over."

"Ethan came by—that's the guy in the picture—and he reminded me we had an album to wrap up. The way I felt then, I didn't think I had it in me, but...I dragged myself into it."

Her hands twisted in her lap. "You see...the way I finally convinced myself to go through it was...to keep you in mind." She bit her lip.

Shane's eyes shot up, staring at her in disbelief. He shifted his shoulders uncomfortably. "I find that kinda hard to believe."

She sat up on her knees, giving him that wicked grin, if a touch wistful now. "Believe it, 'cause you're worth it, cowboy."

He chuckled uncomfortably. "You're crazy, know that, Girl?" He gathered her in, squeezing her against him but pulled back. "Are you still in trouble?"

She shook her head against his chest. "I don't see how. I finished the contract. I think he and Vic are just sore at me for steppin' out. Can't really blame them. I just had to get out of there to save my sanity. I know this sounds silly, but I had this fantasy of running to you and throwing myself at your feet to take me in. So much for women's lib! But I didn't want to bring you my problems—honest—just me, trying to start over. I'm so sorry…."

Shane gave a rueful snort. "Don't be. Gotta admit. I kinda liked your method. In any case, it worked."

She sniffed. "I didn't come her intending to mooch off you or anything. Tomorrow morning I'm scouting out some job prospects. I intend to carry my own weight."

Shane hushed her with a hand on her arm. "Don't feel you have to rush and do anything. You look like you could use some more restin' up first. Besides, possibly the best way you could help is keepin' an eye on Marcie when she comes. Summers are always tough, findin' a safe place for her while I'm at work. There are only so many camps, and my hours can get pretty unpredictable at times."

"I'd be honored." She blinked back the tears this time and decided to change the subject before he thought her a total basket case. Her eyes travelled to the offending headline once more. "By the way, I was careful to cover my tracks. I don't think they can find me, at least for some time."

Shane cast a dubious glance toward the paper. "Maybe not. Folks around here may not be likely to pay attention to that kind of thing. But it wouldn't surprise me if someone recognized you before long and made the connection."

"I'll keep a low profile...but...could that cause trouble for you?" He tugged on a stray strand of her hair. "It'd probably die down quick, anyway." A thought made him sit up. "But what about your place? Your stuff?" He caught the mad twinkle in her eyes. "Never mind. I don't want to know." His wariness softened into a twisted grin. "Let me guess. You gave it all away."

"What better way to start over?" she chirped.

Shane groaned and plopped back against the cushions.

She punched him playfully in the shoulder. "What's wrong?"

"Aw...nuthin'...just sounds like this other crazy friend of mine...name of Morgan? I seem to have this gift for linkin' up with you head cases."

The fool woman at his side only looked more delighted.

Her eyes crinkled into a warm smile. "I'm crazy about you, Cowboy."

Throwing an arm about her shoulders, he pulled her to him, planting a kiss on her brow. "What am I gonna do with you?"

Her warm hazel eyes took on the gleam of an impish ten-year-old. "Take me in your canoe?"

He sent her on her way with a well-placed swat.

That night, Shane padded softly from the bedroom where Andie lay sleeping to the den, where he plopped down on the sofa. He flipped on the light and, for a moment, just sat there, hand resting on the telephone. He stared into space, reliving the afternoon that had evolved into another night of abandon. The blame girl was intoxicating. Talk about frisky...what was she? Thirty-five going on nineteen? He shook his head to clear it and snatched up his phone with little regard to the clock alongside that read two a.m.

A groggy-sounding Ben Morgan answered on the other end. "H'lo?"

Shane plunged in without preface. "Listen, fella…that girl you shoved my way is really messin' up my mind."

There was a pause on the other end as Morgan tried to disengage from the land of dreams and focus on the here and now. "What? Who—oh…." He rose on an elbow, squinted at the alarm clock, and scratched his head. "I swear I didn't—"

Realization came to him and a sleepy grin spread from ear to ear. He laughed softly. "Good!"

Shane did not sound so delighted. "Yeah, but…what am I supposed to do about it?"

Ben chuckled again. "This is a switch! Me giving you advice?" He settled back, resting his head against the hand-carved headboard. "What do *you* think? Look, chum, you do whatever you want. You're free and clear now. You don't have to answer to anybody. Least of all me, if that's what you're thinking."

"Yeah…well…I guess I did kinda wonder, ya know, if she still…."

"The last time I saw Andie all she had eyes for was you."

There was a moment of silence. Shane let out a sigh. "This is gettin' scary, Bud. It's happenin' too fast. I need t' know…everything I can. Tell me I'm not makin' a mistake here."

Ben moved the phone to his other ear, gathering his thoughts. "She's there now, huh?"

"Since yesterday."

"Wow, worked on you pretty fast. Must've been quite a weekend."

Shane groaned in response, noncommittal in nature.

Ben gave it some thought. "Well…with Andie, what you see is what you get. She's a little Missouri girl deep down inside, spread her wings a little when she got to Colorado. But she's never been one for playing head games, always liked things simple and direct. But she's fun…a real guy's gal…kinda kooky, but just the right amount—*OW!*"

Shane gave his phone a funny look. "You okay?"

"Yeah…never mind…" came Morgan's disgruntled voice. In the background, Shane could make out his friend's muffled muttering and Tawnee's soft voice in response. He waited a respectful amount of time before continuing. "Okay, I know I gotta work this out myself. But this helped…I guess."

"Sure. Just…Shane…don't let your head do all the talking, okay? —You still there?"

"Uh…yeah. Andie just caught me."

"Let me talk to her."

She took the phone Shane handed her, voice a drowsy purr. "Hey, Boy…."

"Listen, Gal…don't go messin' up my friend there unless it's for real, hear?" Morgan ragged her.

Andie's smile twisted, on the verge of a snappy retort, but her eyes went moist when she looked over at Shane.

"I promise. Cross my heart. Look, buster, I gotta go."

She smiled conspiratorially at Shane.

"I know when to clear out," Ben laughed. "Take it easy, you two." He cradled the phone in his palm a second with a pensive look. The smile faded as he put it on the nightstand and lay back down. Arms behind his head, he stared into the darkness, unable to stop the flood of memories that came rushing back….

They'd met on a basketball court on a warm September evening early in their junior year back at Colorado State. He'd been staring at the same page in his Statistics book for an hour when he glanced out his window and spied a lanky brunette shooting hoops down on the court between the dorms. The fact that her dark po-nytail stuck out of a baseball cap emblazoned with the Baltimore Orioles logo only whetted his interest. Leaning back in his chair for a better look, he'd fallen flat on his back—or heels-over-head as his roommate Terry kidded him. Ben had scrambled to his feet and trotted down the stairs, basketball in tow. He approached the girl with what he hoped was a casual air.

"You're pretty good."

The Atalanta stopped, ball poised, and eyed him, arching one imperious brow. "You mean *for a girl* ?"

Ben wasn't daunted. "I didn't say that." She dribbled the ball in place three or four times, stopped and cocked her head at him warily. He gave her his best smile. "Come on. Help me out here."

She looked down with a little smile and resumed dribbling.

He shoved his hands in his pockets, cradling his ball with his elbow. "So…where are you from?"

"Missouri."

The mystery girl pivoted, executed an artful jump shot from twenty feet. She turned around and Ben realized his gaze was planted squarely on the front of that delightfully well-rounded T-shirt. "Show me," he blurted out. He felt himself blanch. "I mean…the *Show Me State*, right?"

She shook it off with a grin. "Show me yours and I'll show you mine." She turned and shot again. A picture-perfect bank shot. He followed suit, matching her.

They went on to be inseparable companions that year, a friendship based on love of baseball, tennis, Frisbee, the out-doors—not to mention a love of practical jokes. And always be-neath it, there was that playful flirtation making for a tantalizing tension between them. Pals with an edge….

Their one formal date came when he'd taken her to a spring dance. She'd made his jaw drop, all sleek and curvy in that slinky black gown with the tiny shoulder straps his fingers twitched to play with. But she'd played him for the sucker all evening. Whenever he got so much as remotely romantic, she'd thrown him off-balance with a joke or a goofy expression to ruin the moment—leaving him rattled but totally consumed with her the whole night. He resolved to wear down those defenses of hers the next camp-out they took.

And he'd tried, only to find out the girl just plain wasn't ready for the heavy stuff yet. Some minuscule part of his brain, mysteriously wise for its years, told him not to push for fear of losing something precious here. He backed off and bided his time. They continued, a cautious twosome, friends believing them to have crossed the threshold long before. Hadn't he been seen climbing the tree next to her dorm window one night? No one would ever believe he'd done it to tell her he made the baseball team.

Ironically, in the end, it was Andie who turned up the heat, the night before graduation. Something must have clicked inside her...fear of the unknown, maybe, or fear of time squandered, friendships about to be tossed to the four winds. Coaxing him back to her apartment with the line "Let's go make some memories," she'd set up a candlelight rendezvous for them there. Alternately silly and shy, they had come together, neither expecting the bond that would come with it.

"Definitely an E ticket..." had been Andie's pronouncement, drowsing afterward against his shoulder. When she handed him a bubblegum cigar, he eyed her quizzically.

She shrugged. "So, like, I don't smoke."

But for all her tenderness exposed, she still balked when the words tumbled out of his mouth: "You know, I think I lo—"

She stopped him cold with a hand over his mouth.

"Don't say it."

Later, as dawn streaked the sky, both awoke, still entwined. Andie whispered, "You know...I'm really going to miss you."

He had stirred awake. "Why miss me? Come with me!"

She rose up on an elbow, frowning as though she were giving the matter serious consideration for the first time.

"You mean to Glacier Park?"

"Or Costa Rica! I'll be volunteering there until my internship kicks in. Then you could come up to Glacier!"

"So I would just follow wherever you go? No way, buster! I'm not playing second fiddle to *any* man!"

He'd rolled onto his stomach and reached up to tweak her chin. "You could never be second fiddle to anyone."

She yanked on a strand of sun-streaked hair that hung in his eyes. "Don't go getting mushy on me again. Go back to sleep!"

Ben sighed at this good little Missouri Baptist turned mercurial nymph who'd condescended to join with him and settled back to slumber.

Ironic that her parents should choose that morning to show up unannounced. The fall-out from that confrontation continued to this day.

And even now, after all these years, she could still throw him a curve....

*   *   *   *

Over the course of the weeks to come, word slowly leaked out about the new District Chief's houseguest from California. And Shane, at forty-one, was getting his first reputation.

It began with isolated spottings of the two eating out together in Gatlinburg. Word came back that the new Chief didn't look so alone after all.

District Chief MacLeod and wildlife ranger Buck MacIntyre were returning from helping capture a nuisance bear. That was the name given to a bear that had become so accustomed to handouts or poorly stored garbage that they posed a threat to visitors' safety.

The two men had just settled back into the front seat of the vehicle. MacIntyre heaved a sigh as they watched the truck transporting the caged bear disappear down the road.

"That wasn't as hard as it is sometimes."

"Never a pleasant job, though, huh?" Shane returned.

"No, it isn't. Chances are those bears won't survive the year out. Even with relocation, they almost always fall victim to poachers or hunters if they wander off park territory. Some get hit by cars while trying to find their way home. The trick is to keep them from becoming a nuisance in the first place. It still hasn't sunk in to lots of people just how harmful it is to the bears to get 'em hooked on potato chips or leave granola wrappers lying around. It's no favor in the end."

Shane nodded.

A call came over the radio and Buck snatched up the transmitter. "MacIntyre here."

"Jeffries here. Just wonderin' how that bear hunt went."

Buck relaxed, grinning. "No problems, sir. The Resources guys have her now. They had to tranq mama bear but we were able to live-trap her cubs. They're in good hands, on the way to Cataloochee."

"Good work, fellas. Jeffries out."

Later that morning, it was Melba Davis's turn to be enlightened on the new Chief's enhanced personal life. As luck would have it, the district secretary was in the middle of one of her tirades when Andie walked in.

"Not that I think he would ever ask for it, but the poor man obviously has his hands full, and when that little girl of his arrives, it will only make things more difficult for him. They should—"

"Excuse me."

The secretary turned to see a tall, attractive brunette at the counter. Melba's mouth formed a perfunctory smile that was more a twitch than anything else. "How may I help you?"

"Hi, I'd like to see Shane MacLeod, please."

Melba assumed an on-guard stance. Behind her, Buck McIntyre looked up, eyeing the newcomer with interest.

"I'm sorry, District Chief MacLeod is a very busy man," the secretary said crisply. "I don't think he's available right now. Is this something I could help you with?"

The visitor cocked her head. "I really don't think he'd mind if I just popped in for a second and dropped this off. It won't take but a minute." She made for the hallway but was blocked by the short, stocky woman who threw her shoulders back.

"As I said before, the Chief is a very busy—"

Shane emerged from the hallway, his business face relaxing into a grin. "Hi! What brings *you* in?"

Andie turned from glaring at the little bulldog of a woman and waggled an envelope in his direction. "I noticed you left this behind. Thought you might need it."

He came around the counter and took the envelope from her.

Perusing its contents, he shook his head. "I've been lookin' all over for this. Thanks!"

She gave a self-conscious shrug. "Sure." She turned to go but Shane put a hand on her arm. "You wanna come on back?"

"Nah, I better not." She glanced in the secretary's direction. "I'm, uh, on my way somewhere. Catch you next time."

"Okay. See you later. –Hey, whatcha got there?"

Andie looked down at the batch of pamphlets sticking out of her shoulder bag. "Oh…just some…stuff."

"You got me curious now." He tugged them out and flipped through. "Smoky Mountain Field School, huh? *Appalachian Folklore…Wild Edibles…Mountain Stream Life…Mushroom Identification….* You buckin' for a ranger job?"

She shrugged with an embarrassed smile. "You never know!"

He gave her arm a gentle swat with the brochures before handing them back. "Have fun. Just don't eat anything before your guide does!"

She waggled a wave over her shoulder as she turned to go.

Outside, the brunette passed a couple of rangers on the sidewalk, giving them a merry wave. The two men looked after her, grinning.

Melba stood at the front counter, staring out the front doors with a befuddled expression. Susannah joined her alongside, eyes bright.

The older woman pursed her lips. "Who does she think she is? The new Morale Officer?"

"Works for me," Buck said behind her.

Melba shot him a withering look, but he shrugged it off.

"I tried to tell you earlier, Melba. The Chief may have his hands full, but not the way you thought."

Saturday dawned, soft and drowsy....

Shane and Andie drowsed contentedly into the late morning, sacked out in front of the stone fireplace. Happy as a clam, Andie nestled alongside her ranger, while Shane, oblivious to the world, snoozed on, arm draped over her side.

First to hear the soft click of the key in the front door, she struggled to emerge from her drugged-like state and rose up on an elbow. Her breath caught in her throat.

A woman stood in the foyer, looking as surprised as she was. There was movement behind her and the woman turned, whispering hurriedly, "Wait in the car. I'll be right with you."

Andie's voice rose, tremulous. "Shane...?"

He stirred. "Hmmm? What is it?"

The intruder cleared her throat.

94

Shane whipped around and sat up. He squinted, bringing into focus the person who stood in his entryway. A grim smile spread across his face.

"Hello, Livvie."

. 10 .

Shane turned, impassive, to the young woman who shared his sleeping bag. "Andie, I'd like you t' meet my sister, Olivia."

Unable to meet the other woman's eyes, Andie's response was a barely audible "Pleased to meet you."

"Hello," the newcomer returned with a droll smile, more evident in the eyes than in the mouth. Remarkably reminiscent of Shane's. So, too, was her gaze, direct but without judgment.

Just the same, Andie tugged on Shane's arm, whispering, "I think I'd like to excuse myself."

Shane nodded easily "Sure."

She stretched to reach a Navajo blanket on the couch and rose, carefully wrapping it about her. That accomplished, she trotted, shivering, back to the bedroom.

Olivia looked after her. "Poor kid…probably something Grandmother never expected her blanket to see." She swung back to eye Shane, hard put to hide her amusement. "Well! She certainly looks like the type who could do from zero to sixty in eight seconds flat!"

Shane glared up at her. "I don't care *what* you're thinkin'."

He stood up, arranging the sleeping bag about himself awkwardly. "Toss me those jeans, will ya?"

Livvie turned while he clad himself. "Relax, Big Brother. More power to you. In fact, I was beginning to worry."

Shane's glare softened and he relaxed his shoulders. "Where's Marcie?"

"Out in the car. I thought it best under the circumstances."

"We weren't expecting you till later."

"I get that." She bit back a wry smile and straightened her face. "Do you want me to take her back with me a while longer?"

Shane threw on his shirt and glanced up. " 'Course not! I want my girl with me!" At her shrug of resignation, he softened. "Thanks anyway."

Olivia nodded, agreeably enough. Shane noticed for the first time the box in her hand. "What's that?"

She held it out to him. "A housewarming gift. It's towels. Looks like you could use some extra."

He shared a tight grin with her. "Thanks."

His sister plopped her shoulder back down on the couch and looked around. "Well, here! Why don't I go start some coffee for us all?"

"Sounds good. I'll get Marcie." As Olivia headed for the kitchen, he padded, barefoot, out the door, still buttoning his cuffs.

Shane poked his head inside the car window. "Got yer head inside a book again, Mouse?"

The girl in the front seat looked up in surprise and threw her book aside. "Daddy!"

She sprang out of the car and into his arms, squeezing him tight. Shane returned in kind, clasping her shoulders to survey her from head to foot before pivoting her around for a view of her new home.

The girl's eyes took in the lodge, the lush shading trees over-head. "It *is* kinda pretty here," she allowed with a twisted smile. "Maybe this won't be so bad after all. Still…It's gonna take some getting used to."

He gave her shoulders a jostle. "I know…I know. Come on in. I'm havin' a late breakfast. You can have somethin' too if you want. There's somebody I want you to meet."

Shane steered the two of them toward the lodge. They went up the stone walk arm in arm, but Marcie stopped them midway. "Dad…why did I have to wait in the car? Where were you?"

He bit back a grimace. "I-uh-didn't hear Livvie come in at first." He led them up the steps and held the screen door open for her. Cocking her head in puzzlement, his daughter shrugged, and went in.

Shane passed by the kitchen and rapped his knuckles on the counter, meeting his sister's eyes. "Be back in a second."

He stepped back to his room and leaned against the doorjamb, watching Andie fret over final adjustments to herself. She stood frowning before the dresser mirror, tugging at her sweater and trying to finger-comb some order into her wayward tresses. Her expression gave the impression the prospects were dim.

"Hey, doll. You all right?"

She whirled in surprise, shoulders going into a slump. Walking up to her, he slid his arms around her waist. "Sorry 'bout that. This isn't the way I would've planned it, but Livvie seems to have taken it in stride. Now for Marcie."

"Yeah…" she sighed. Her eyes sought help, moving him to brush back a stray tendril. "Relax…. Come on, I want to show you off." He tugged at her hand but she pulled back.

"I was thinking…maybe I should come in, you know, separately at first, so we don't throw this couple thing at her all of a sudden."

Shane considered this and gave her a quick peck on the cheek. "Good idea. See ya in a minute then."

Andie nodded, gave his hand a final squeeze and turned back for one more look in the mirror. One more attempt to smooth out the unruly locks. Throwing her hands up in disgust, she plopped down onto the bed to wait.

Moments later, she paused outside the kitchen doorway, trying to assume a nonchalant air. It wasn't easy. She wasn't even sure, at the moment, whether she could remember what nonchalant looked like or might pass for it. Taking a deep breath, she stepped into the room, her eyes seeking Shane's for reassurance. He lifted his coffee cup to his lips and gave her a wink. Olivia was looking down with a soft, knowing smile as she poured orange juice into a glass.

Andie braced herself to look, then, in the direction of the little girl. At the moment, Marcie MacLeod was enjoying the singular pleasure of swiveling around on one of the barstools at dizzying speed.

"Mars," Shane called to her. The girl came to an abrupt halt with a smack of her palm against the countertop. When she looked up, Andie felt a jolt go through her.

The child was unquestionably Shane's...the same, thin, angular face with those high cheekbones from her Navajo ancestry...that pointed chin. The edges were softer, though, giving her an elfin appearance. She wasn't dark like her father but surprisingly fair. The cornflower blue eyes must have come from her mother, along with the honey-colored hair. It wasn't all sweetness and light, though. That determined-looking chin and tight little mouth predicted trouble. And that familiar no-nonsense look in the child's eyes was anything but comforting at the moment.

"I want you to meet a new friend of mine," Shane was saying. "Her name's Andie Carson."

The girl's gaze flicked to Andie and held there, surveying her. "Did you come with the house?"

Olivia snorted a laugh in the background. Even Andie gave a nervous laugh. It was left to Shane to find an answer to that.

"No...she—"

The child turned back to Andie. "Are you a ranger?"

"No." Andie managed a little smile. "But I think I'd like to be." She looked to Shane.

"Is my Dad teaching you?" the youngster pressed.

Andie shoved her hands in her pockets. "Well...I guess you could say he's been showing me the ropes." She looked up to find Olivia's amused eyes upon her and found herself relaxing into a genuine smile. It felt like the other woman had concluded she was okay and conveyed her acceptance all in that brief instant. The whole atmosphere seemed to change, flooding her with a sense of warmth. She was more herself now, ready to take an active part in this familiarization process.

"Oh! I made some blueberry muffins last night. How about some with those Cheerios?"

Marcie looked up from her bowl, mouth dripping milk. Giving her chin a swipe, she nodded with enthusiasm.

As Andie went to get the muffins, Shane settled down onto a barstool with a sigh. That little piece of business was over, at least. But, he realized, it was only the beginning.

Olivia, bless her, was the one to steer the situation into safe waters as they all sat down to eat. "So, where are you from, Andie?"

"Missouri, originally, Jefferson City. When I was in high school, my father got transferred to Boulder. I went to Colorado State and got a job in L.A. after that. Spent the last dozen or so years there, with a short stint in Georgetown, outside D.C."

Olivia rested her chin in her hand, interest piqued. "So…a California girl…." Livvie's glance at Shane said volumes. He took a sip from his cup, maintaining a neutral expression.

Andie looked down, taking a bite out of her muffin. Olivia offered her a refill on her coffee. "Shane probably told you we grew up hopping from one Air Force base to another…San Antonio, Edwards, Sacramento—"

"My granddad was a test pilot! He trained lots of astronauts!" Marcie chimed in.

"How wonderful!"

Olivia laughed. "I'm not so sure Mom would agree with that assessment. She hated Edwards."

Shane nodded in agreement. "Yeah…she preferred Albuquerque. We stayed there with her relatives while Dad was in Guam one summer."

Olivia turned back to Andie. "So where did you and Shane meet?"

Andie bit back a smile. It was fascinating, seeing Shane in this new light. All kinds of questions bubbled up inside her, but for safety's sake, she moved on. "I guess you could say Wyoming. We kind of met in passing there." She looked up to see Shane's eyes upon her. "Turns out we have a mutual friend—"

"Don't tell me! Not by any chance a rascal named Ben Morgan? Or does he call himself Jayhawk now?" Olivia cocked an eyebrow at her brother.

Andie perked up, "You know him?"

"Oh, yes." Olivia groaned. "Our family's known Ben for years. Ever since he straggled home with Shane like some stray pup from that crazy trip to Mexico."

Andie looked to Shane but he chose to deflect it. He snatched a muffin from the basket on the counter. "You were quite taken with him, as I recall."

"Who wasn't?" Livvie smiled ruefully in Andie's direction. "A stray, skinny, but very cute pup. What a charmer! But then you probably knew that. Way out in left field, though."

Shane leaned back with a soft grin. "Different drummer, that's all."

Marcie plopped her chin in her hands, frowning at all this grown-up talk. "So when did you decide to become a ranger?"

Andie smiled down at her cup. "I didn't really decide that but…after a trail ride at Yosemite that your dad led, I went back to Los Angeles and discovered I didn't want to live there anymore. Too crowded…too noisy…too dirty. Mean, too…." She trailed off, glancing up at the other two adults self-consciously.

Olivia cast a knowing look Shane's way. "Another burn-out of western civilization?"

Andie's eyes faltered. "Maybe…anyhow…Shane was nice enough to let me stay here a while till I figure things out."

Olivia hid a smile behind her coffee cup but said nothing.

Shane ignored her and turned to his daughter. "Andie's gonna be spending the summer here with us. Think you can handle that?"

The ten-year-old regarded Andie a moment. "Sure." She didn't exactly smile but there was an air of decisiveness about her.

Shane put down his cup. "Good. She's gonna be our guest so we want to make her feel at home."

"Make that *working* guest." Andie blushed. "I want to make myself useful around here. She picked up the empty plates, joining Olivia at the sink.

Shane looked over at her with a little smile. She'd handled herself well. He looked then to his daughter, who was nodding with apparent satisfaction. She seemed to be accepting the situation okay, on the surface at least. He wondered, though, what might really be going on in that busy little head of hers.

The afternoon was taken up with exchanging family news and rest for the travelers. That night, Shane took them all out to eat at a popular old mountainside inn that overlooked Gatlinburg. The next morning, the newcomers were given a grand tour of the park, with the requisite first stop at Sugarlands Visitor Center for souvenirs. Marcie was given a toy otter as a welcome home present and Olivia was unable to pass up buying her boys back home some nature books. Even Andie couldn't resist an oversized Smokies T-shirt for sleeping in. She and Shane shared a secret smile. From there, it was on to Cades Cove for a picnic lunch along the pastoral eleven-mile loop.

The next morning, they took the winding road along Newfound Gap to Cherokee at the opposite end of the park, and on to Asheville Regional Airport for Olivia's flight back to Sacramento.

Olivia took advantage of the chance to speak alone with Shane in the security check line. She looked over at young Marcie and Andie who were peering out at the runway together. "I'm still trying to figure out how to tell Chuck when I get home that my reserved big brother snared himself a California knockout. He may find it hard to believe, but she's probably just what you need."

"And what's that?"

"Something different. A little bit *wild*." She nudged his shoulder. "Definitely not a paint-by-the-numbers kind of gal you've got there. Sure you can handle the two of them?"

Shane appeared undaunted as he followed her gaze. "I'll have 'em eatin' out of my hand in no time."

Olivia cast him a dubious look. "*Right.* But what about—?"

Shane issued a sigh that was somewhere between embarrassed and exasperated. "We'll be careful. I promise."

"Okayyy...." She gave him a peck on the cheek. "Well, then, take care."

"Call us when you get in!" he said, backing away. She waved over her shoulder. Shane turned to regard the two unpredictable females now under his charge. A sense of vulnerability started to settle over him but he shook it off. He hung on his heel a second, then walked over to join them.

His face must have betrayed his thoughts. Andie cocked her head with an impish smile. "What's wrong? Afraid we're going to gang up on you or something?"

He threw her a strange look as he put his arms around Marcie's shoulders and steered the three of them out. "Funny, Livvie said somethin' about that."

Andie stuffed her hands in the pockets of her sweater and swaggered playfully at his side. "Oh, really? What did you say to her?"

"That I'd have both of you under my thumb in no time flat."

She paused as he opened the Blazer door for her. "And here I was gonna say how you were safe with your fan club. Right Marcie?"

The little girl in the back seat nodded vigorously. "Right!"

Shane turned away with a twisted grin. "Fat chance...."

The ride back was quiet, everyone tired out from the whirlwind visit. Andie turned to admire the sunset, layers of mauve, orange, and champagne with fingers of deep indigo creeping into the sky from the east. The black ribbon of highway scooped and curved above valleys that looked like great cauldrons of mist. Each ridgeline was rimmed with feathery spires of spruce, fir, and hemlock, punctuated by craggy manmade cliffs where machines had cut a mountain in half, exposing its granite heart. In the gathering darkness, the glow of dials on the Blazer's dash offered comfort, a compass point against the wildness beyond the windows and tidy confines of the interstate.

Andie nestled back in her seat, ready for home and hearth. Each of them, she sensed, was eager to get on with the comfort of routine. The child in back was quiet for so long that Andie had begun to think she'd dozed off, but then the girl's voice piped up from the backseat.

"Daddy, when are we going to get the puppy?"

Shane peered in the rearview mirror, his face registering a blank. "What puppy?"

"The one you said we could get after we moved."

Shane shifted in his seat. "Oh. That one." He looked to Andie for sympathy. She crinkled her eyes in response.

"Uh…let's get settled in good first, Baby," he responded. "Then we'll see."

A soft whine emanated from the backseat.

"Mars…."

A soft sigh from Marcie was the only reply. Andie bit her lip, trying not to smile, and turned back to the window. As much as she enjoyed witnessing these chinks in Shane's armor, it seemed best to keep her thoughts to herself.

The three lounged on the floor before the fireplace that night, playing a game of Battleship. Shane turned to Andie with exasperation. "Look at that. Four ships down and she's gunnin' to blow me out of the water."

Pajama-clad Marcie peered up slyly. "Would that be your submarine?"

Shane cocked an eyebrow. "I think you know."

With a triumphant grin, his daughter finished him off. "D-three."

Shane sighed and extended his hand. "Congratulations." Marcie clasped it and pumped vigorously. "Good game."

They picked up the pieces together. Marcie stood and he handed the box up to her. "Yeah...my Dad gave her that game for Christmas and promptly regretted it. She wiped him out on the first try."

Andie cast a dubious look up at the girl. "Is this the grandfather who was the test pilot?"

An impish grin spread across Marcie's face. "I'm going to be a pilot, too—on an aircraft carrier."

Shane rose with a groan and went to retrieve his glass from the mantle. "Not if I can help it." He turned back to face his adventurous offspring. "Is that before or after you explore the Amazon?"

Marcie considered this. "Before, I think...no...after...I don't know."

"Come here, you." Shane gathered her in for a quick embrace, adding a scalp rub and a kiss before sending her on her way with a pat on the behind. "Off to bed for you. I'll be there in a minute."

He turned from looking after her to see the glow in Andie's eyes. It enveloped him with warmth yet he couldn't help a twinge of discomfiture as well. This whole thing of learning to mesh public and private life, family life, and a new love life came hard for him. It was enough to give a fella a nervous rash. Thank heaven Andie was proving to have a good head on her shoulders.

On the way home that afternoon, he noted gratefully her sense of the situation. Riding beside him in the front seat of the Blazer, she refrained from any displays of affection that might unsettle the little girl in back. Yet when he looked her way, there was always that flash of smiling eyes in return. With all the tumult of a family reunion, she must have had her difficult moments, but she breezed through them, save for that unfortunate introduction. The sting from that was starting to fade, he hoped. With a twinge of guilt he noticed the tiredness in her eyes, though she spoke up brightly.

"She's a handful, isn't she!"

"Yeah, her own version of Lewis and Clark. Think you can handle her tomorrow while I'm gone?"

"Oh, sure. We'll be fine. Don't worry."

Shane shrugged. "Maybe you can find some girl stuff to do together, I don't know."

Andie stretched, screwing up her face. "Just one problem with that. I was never very good at girl stuff."

Shane considered her a moment. "In that case, you two should get along just fine." He threw an arm about her shoulders and pulled her to him for a quick kiss before walking off to see his daughter to bed.

When he returned, he found Andie standing on the back deck. She was gazing down through the trees at the moonlit lake beyond.

He joined her there and she looked up with a smile.

"It's so beautiful here," she said softly.

"You're beautiful." The look on her face was so wistful, he couldn't help slipping an arm around her, resting his cheek against the silky, dark hair. "It feels so right having you here. Say you'll stay."

She nuzzled back. "There's no place else I want to be, believe me." His arms slid down, tightening around her. Gently, she pulled away, though one palm rested against his chest. "I guess we should say goodnight."

Shane sighed. "Yeah...guess so."

They stepped back from one another reluctantly. Andie dug her hands into her pockets. "Can I fix you breakfast in the morning or something? I feel like a freeloader here."

"Nah, that's okay. Don't worry 'bout it. You two sleep in. I'm used to stumblin' around on my own in the mornin', anyhow."

"Well...okay. Goodnight then." She headed for the little study at the opposite end of the house from the other bedrooms, leaving Shane to look after her.

In bed later, he rolled to the center, reaching by habit to the pillow beside him. Sensing keenly the absence of his soft, warm companion of late, he rolled away with the air of a man deprived.

Andie had just slipped her sleep shirt over her head when a soft knock sounded on her door. She found Shane there with a twisted smile, holding a bathrobe out to her. "You left this in the closet. Thought you might need it in the mornin'."

"Thanks." Andie smiled back tightly and took it. He remained, leaning against the doorframe, looking as though there was something else on his mind. Andie's heart began a slow hammer. She dared to meet his eyes, reading the message there.

He gave her a rueful grin. "This is really hard."

She came up to him, laying a hand on his chest. "I know...."

He tossed the robe about her shoulders and drew her to him possessively. She didn't object. He pulled back and cocked his head. "She's asleep." Her smile transformed into a pirate's grin of conspiracy. "Okayyy...."

They leaned into another kiss. Shane fingered the neckline of her nightshirt and slowly tugged it aside, kissing her shoulder. Her breath quickened as his lips explored other territory...her temple...her neck....

"No!"

Shane swung around. There stood Marcie, angry tears on her face.

"You're not my mother!" The girl stamped her foot, convulsing into angry sobs.

Andie's heart jumped. She could feel his as well, racing furiously, even as he let go of her gently and turned to his daughter.

"Marcie...."

Shane stepped toward her but the child only screamed again.

"N-No! Go away! I...I hate you!" She turned and ran down the hall.

"Marcie!" He turned eyes of consternation back at Andie. She wrapped her arms about herself to stop her own shaking. "Go!" she said hoarsely.

With a dazed nod, he swung about and left.

He found the child crumpled up on her bed, tears spilling onto her pillow. He eased down on the bed's edge and reached out to lay a hand on her side. She jerked from his touch.

"Marcia Kim, look at me."

The girl froze. After a moment, she rolled over to face him, brushing back the wetness from her lashes and stared up at him warily.

Shane didn't know what to say. His mind was a jumble of emotions—shock, bewilderment, anger, frustration, and heartache. How could he have caused his child such pain? But how could he explain his feelings to her...feelings an adult might readily understand, but to a child of ten might seem only betrayal. He swallowed and plunged in.

"I'm sorry this happened this way, Mars. We wanted to let you know more gradual-like. But you might as well know now...I think I love her, Baby."

Her little face started to cloud up again. Shane steeled himself, though his insides were churning. "And there's nothing wrong with that," he stressed. "It doesn't mean things change between us..." he paused to swallow, "or the way I felt about your mom...understand?" He tried to peer into her face.

She eyed him through the curtain of hair hiding her face, but he could tell she was still far from convinced. Shane leaned back, clasped a knee, and prepared himself to try again. Beyond the panes of the old lodge's windows, a breeze gently swayed the pines. Stars winked between the undulating branches. He tried to focus on the serenity outside while summoning the courage to continue.

"It's like…when you lose your best friend. It's been really tough without your mom. It's hard to live that way, day in, day out, but I thought that was the only choice I had. Then I met Andie and she made me feel not so alone."

"But you have *me*," his child pleaded.

"I know, Honey—thank God for that." He reached up to stroke her hair. "It's just that…grown-ups need each other's company, too. Men and women need each other. It's different. You'll understand better when you're older—just the way children need the company of other children. You wouldn't want to have to be around grown-ups all the time, would you?"

Shane let this sink in for a minute. Marcie Kim gave in to a shake of her head and bowed it. He could see the little fringe of lashes flutter against her cheek. One small finger traced the stitching on her quilt thoughtfully. "It…it hurt to see you lonely."

Shane swallowed down the sudden lump in his throat. The two eyed one another cautiously.

"She *does* seem nice," she allowed.

"So…still hate me?"

She flung herself into his arms. "I could never hate you, Daddy! I'm sorry!"

Shane released a weary smile of relief—and gratitude—at his daughter, settling himself across the bed. "That's okay. I understand. –But give Andie a chance, Mars." He paused to consider a moment. "I think I oughta tell you something. Remember how Andie said we met on that trail ride back in Yosemite?"

The girl nodded.

"Well, what she didn't say was…she saved my life that day."

Her eyes went round, mouth flopping open. "How?"

"We ran across some poachers. One tried to ambush me from behind. I would've been shot in the back if she hadn't yelled out and distracted them. She ended up takin' a bullet intended for me, for her trouble." He winced at the memory.

Tears welled up in his little girl's eyes. "Ohhh, Daddy...." She let out a shuddery sigh and fell into his arms.

Shane rubbed his cheek against her soft hair. "So you see, she really is okay."

"*Okay?* She rocks!"

Shane snorted a soft laugh. His daughter's sheepish grin was replaced by a frown of concern. "She thinks I'm really awful now, huh?"

He stroked her cheek. "No...but I think, between the two of us, we shook her up pretty bad. And I think you do owe her an apology."

Marcie Kim nodded reluctantly. Shane stood her up before him, kissed her forehead, and turned her in the direction of the door. She headed there but stopped in the doorway, looking back. He urged her on with a jerk of the head. "Go on."

Marcie paused just outside the study turned guestroom. There was the woman sitting on the edge of the bed, hugging herself, with a forlorn look on her face.

The girl cleared her throat. "Hi."

When Andie looked up, Marcie could tell she'd been crying. She approached, twisting her hands before her. The woman braved a smile. Marcie took heart and sat down a little ways from her. Every bit her father's child, she took the bull by the horns.

"Please don't cry. I hate it when grown-ups cry. It's worse than having them yell at you."

Andie blinked back tears, sniffing, and cocked her head at her curiously. Marcie pressed her hands between her knees and looked at the floor.

"I'm ...sorry I acted that way. Dad explained things to me. It's just...I still miss my Mom sometimes." She stiffened her chin. The woman's hand stole over hers. She willed herself to be still though she wouldn't raise her eyes when Andie spoke.

"Of course you do! I'm sorry, too, Marcie. Believe me, I don't mean to replace your Mom. I just want to be friends with you and your Dad."

Marcie shot her a direct look, a squint she'd picked up from her father. With an intensity beyond her years, she asked point-blank, "Do you love him?"

Andie smiled through brimming eyes. "I'm crazy about him. I think he might just be the most wonderful man in the world!"

Marcie beamed, unable to help herself. "Me, too."

A tentative glance passed between them. Andie breathed a sigh. "Well...since it looks like we're on the same side here...does that mean I can give you a hug?"

A reluctant grin broke free from the girl. "I guess so." She leaned into the outstretched arms, letting herself be gathered up against the unfamiliar breast. It didn't feel so bad. In fact, there was something achingly familiar about it. Was that how her mother had felt? It was going on four years now. She couldn't conjure up that feeling. Aunt Livvie's hugs helped fill the void, but this new pair of arms, they would take some getting used to. Maybe she could handle it if the hugs didn't come too often. At least this Andie person didn't seem to be one of those grabby types. She had the sense to ask first.

From the doorway, Shane cleared his throat. "So...you two friends again?"

The two looked up in surprise. Both nodded back at him.

He entered and reached a hand down to Marcie. "All right, then, back to bed with you, young lady. I don't know about you, but I need my sleep. You two can visit more tomorrow."

As he grasped his daughter's hand, his eyes met Andie's. Leaning over he gave her a quick smack on the lips. "G'night."

This time, Marcie didn't flinch, though she seemed somewhere between mesmerized and embarrassed by it all.

Back in her room, Marcie climbed into her bed and plopped down onto her pillow. Her dad leaned across to pull up the quilt and brushed her forehead with a kiss before turning to go. Her fingers clutched his in the dark, holding him there just a bit longer.

"So are you going to get married?"

Her father hesitated, but only for a moment. "First I have to ask her...and hope she doesn't turn me down!"

Marcie sprang up in her bed. "She wouldn't do that, would she?"

Shane squeezed her hand. "Well...maybe with your help, we can make sure."

. 11 .

The next morning, bright and early, found Shane pulling up in his truck at the Cades Cove Stables. He parked by the corral, got out, and strode into the barn. Shortly, he reappeared, leading the Appaloosa that had been his trusty companion for many years in the Park Service. The horse belonged to a breed known for its stamina, agility, and sensible, easy temperament, not unlike the man who rode him. Shane tied his trusty mount to a post and went to procure a saddle. As he hoisted it into place over the Park Service blanket, a voice came from behind him.

"Hello there!"

He turned with a frown that relaxed only slightly when he saw who approached. The man's face was not familiar but he wore the collar of a minister. Shane gave him a curt nod.

"Mornin'."

The man maintained his affable air as he stopped and held out a large hand. "John Matthews, the Methodist chapel in the Cove. I was told I might find you here. Just had a spirited conversation with your daughter. Quite a spunky young lady you've raised there."

Shane jerked his chin as he adjusted the straps on the horse's underbelly. "She's had to be."

The pastor looked down at his feet. "So I understand....

Well! I just wanted to extend a personal welcome to our new District Chief. I make it my business to read up on the new personnel coming into the park and I read the news release about you with a great deal of interest. You've quite an illustrious past on you. Let's see…." The pastor squinted skyward as he searched his memory. "Distinguished service record as a Navy helicopter pilot…Purple Heart…service awards at Yellowstone and Yosemite Parks…." He paused, chin resting on his expansive chest as his voice became a gravelly whisper. "Had your share of hard knocks, as well…disabled for a year from a helicopter crash…losing your wife to that dreadful car accident three years ago…and left to raise that precious young daughter on your own…."

Shane turned and leveled his warning squint at the man, the one that said *back off*. "You got a direction here Reverend? I got a busy morning ahead."

The minister smiled at the ground again. "Just wanted to pass along my recognition and admiration, good sir—and extend an offer of help in getting settled, should you need any."

Shane shook his head and swung into the saddle. "Thanks. None needed."

The pastor shielded his eyes from the morning sun as he squinted up at him. "I couldn't help but notice you have another young lady staying with you as well—"

"That's my business. Now, if you'll excuse me, I have a patrol to run." Shane turned the big Appaloosa toward the Cove Road and headed off, perturbed at the lump in his throat he found himself having to swallow.

The minister stared after the ranger. "That's all right, my friend. I know a wall thrown up when I see one…but I enjoy a challenge."

Back at the lodge, Andie was scowling as she scraped the remnants of another set of blackened discs off a griddle. As luck would have it that was when Marcie MacLeod bounded in, wrinkling up her nose.

"What's that smell?"

"What do you think it is?" Andie snapped, scrubbing harder. She felt an immediate twinge of guilt at her outburst, half expecting the child to scurry for cover. Instead, the girl slid into place at the counter and rested her chin in hands, casually surveying the kitchen. "Looks familiar." She shrugged. "Why don't cha just relax and do what yer good at?"

Andie whirled about, staring at her. The child had mimicked the exact cadence of Shane's speech. She wagged the pancake turner at her precocious companion. "You're your father's child, all right. Now what am I gonna do with you?" She crossed her arms before her.

The girl gave her an impish, Shane-like smile. "So…what're you good at?"

Andie looked about them. "Obviously not this, I'm afraid. I've probably made pancakes a total of two times in my entire life. But I do make a pretty mean Denver omelet, if I do say so myself."

Marcie hopped off the stool. "I'm easy. So…how do you make it?" She joined Andie at the fridge, poking her head in alongside. Soon, they were working together, Marcie cracking eggs with enthusiasm while Andie chopped the peppers, tomatoes, ham.

"There aren't any mushrooms so we'll just have to rough it," Andie said.

Her young companion wrinkled her nose. "Suits me. I don't like them anyway."

"What? I thought all good little ranger kids ate nuts and berries and mushrooms, all that natural stuff."

"Not me."

Andie poured the egg mixture onto the skillet. "Next you'll be telling me you don't like the outdoors—or animals either."

Marcie climbed onto the kitchen stool beside her. "Oh, no…I like animals a lot…and camping…and guns, too."

Andie stopped what she was doing to stare at the elfin-faced moppet. "You're serious?"

The girl nodded matter-of-factly.

"You're not telling me you've actually handled—"

The child's innocent eyes brightened as she spoke. "Uh-huh. Daddy helped me fire his Colt into a dirt bank a couple of times, just to get the feel of it. And his .22 at a firing range. I got a marksmanship award at camp last summer…BB gun, that is."

"I see…." Andie turned back, just in time to save the omelet from scorching. Her brow furrowed as she flipped it over with the turners. This wilderness family stuff might be more than she'd bargained for. What was next? Snakes for pets? Bears in the backyard? She swallowed. Now *that* was a distinct possibility around here….

"Andie—"

"Huh?"

"It's starting to get brown around th' edges."

Andie looked down at the skillet. "Oh!"

She scooped up the omelet and plopped it onto the platter…a bit crusty, but nonetheless, a golden masterpiece. They shared a smile of triumph.

"Want some cheese grated on it?" she ventured.

"Pile it on!" the child said with glee.

Andie picked up both plates, heading for the table, but paused, eyeing the view outside the sliding glass doors. "Want to eat out on the deck?"

"Sure!"

From their rustic perch out back, they enjoyed the antics of two chipmunks. The pair got brave enough to scamper along the rail, eyeing the breakfast plates with interest. After the meal, Andie squinted down through the trees at the lake beyond. "You like canoeing?"

Marcie's eyes sparkled in answer. "You bet!"

"Do you think your Dad would mind?"

"No—as long as I wear a life jacket and don't go alone—and stay near the bank."

"Don't worry about that. I'm still learning, myself. He's been giving me lessons, but I'm pretty comfortable in this area."

Andie rose from the picnic table gathering up the plates. "Okay, let me put these away. You know where the life jackets are?"

"Yep."

"Good. Oh—and grab your boots, too. I'll join you at the bank."

Moments later, they rejoined. Andie balanced the canoe for Marcie to get in, then hopped in herself. With a wobbly start, they were off. After several attempts, they got their rhythm down, settling into a pattern of smooth, synchronized strokes. Hugging the bank, they headed westward, the morning sun warming their backs.

The sun was an hour higher in the sky when they tugged the canoe back up the bank at home. Marcie straightened, staring up the slope in the direction of the driveway.

"Who's that?"

Andie straightened, brushing the hair out of her eyes. Her breath burst from her. Eyes narrowing, she watched the figure emerge from a red convertible that looked out of place here in the woods.

"Why don't you go on inside, Marcie. I'll be right there," she said without looking back. The girl hesitated but trudged toward the back deck with one more curious squint at the visitor.

Scowling, Andie went to meet their unwelcome guest.

She stopped before him in the gravel driveway, hands on hips. "What are you doing here, Ethan?"

The lanky young man with shaggy black hair removed his sunglasses, taking in his surroundings, and Andie, with amusement. "Don't we look the backwoods bit?"

Andie set her shoulders. "I don't know why you're here, but you're spoiling a perfectly nice day—so why don't you just hop back in your little toy there and leave?" She waved derisively at the flamboyant sports car and turned to go.

"Oh, I think you know perfectly well why I'm here, Babe," he said behind her. "You and I have a little unfinished business to discuss."

Andie turned back. "I'm at a loss for what that could be. I tied up everything neatly when I left. I don't have anything else to say to you." She pivoted on her heel and marched up to the front door, unlocked it and went in, locking it behind her. In the entryway, she let out a sigh and looked down at her hands. She tried to shake off the trembling and went into the kitchen, snatching up one of the breakfast pans and scrubbing vigorously.

"You won't get rid of me that easily."

Andie whirled around. There stood Ethan Stang—as he liked to call himself. "How did you—?" Her gaze travelled to the patio door, still ajar from earlier. Her shoulders sagged, then braced again, outrage surging. "I told you before, I have nothing to say to you. *Now get out!*" She flung an arm in the direction of the door, meaning business.

Stang leaned against the counter, crossing his arms. "Still taking your medicine?"

Her expression faltered a second before settling back into a scowl. "I don't need it now that I'm away from people like you." Seeing him now, she wondered how she'd ever found him even remotely attractive. Another world...another time.... One, it appeared, that wasn't content to let her go.

In the hall, Marcie listened to the commotion coming from the kitchen, then, stepping softly into her father's room, picked up the phone from the nightstand and punched in a number.

"Dad? —Yeah, it's me. I think you should come home. There's this man bothering Andie. —No, they're just fussin' in the kitchen right now...o-okay...bye." Doing her father's bidding, she sneaked out the front door and waited for him outside....

The NPS Blazer tore into the driveway, scattering gravel. Shane sprang from it and headed straight for the front door. Marcie came running to him and he grabbed her up in his arms.

"Are you okay?"

His daughter nodded, anxious to tell her tale. "They're still in there arguing. She keeps tellin' him to leave but he just keeps following her around and won't leave her alone. I think they used to know each other."

Shane straightened, peering at the house. "Okay...you go sit in the truck and stay there till I call you, hear?"

Marcie nodded shakily and headed there, stopping at the truck's door to watch her father enter the house.

Shane strode to the front door. Fingering the Glock at his belt, he unsnapped the holster but left the gun sheathed as he went inside. From the dark entryway, he could see the two combatants faced off in the den, in front of the fireplace.

"Is there a problem here?" he asked quietly. Andie and the intruder turned in surprise. Shane fixed his gaze on the shaggy young man. It was the same guy who was in that newspaper photo with Andie. His eyebrow twitched but he gave no other sign of recognition. He kept his voice flat.

"I understand she wants you to leave."

The young man looked exasperated. "Name's Ethan Stang. You've probably heard of me. I'm just an old friend come to check up on her. We were worried about her running off like that. It wasn't like her." He paused to look about them. "*This* isn't like her. I don't think you know who you're dealing with here."

Shane crossed his arms, looking from Andie to the stranger. "I think I know who she is now. The lady wants to be left alone. I suggest you leave."

The young man narrowed his eyes, noting the holster at Shane's side and burst out laughing. "So this is what you left us for? The Marlboro man? Give me a break!"

Shane stood steady, he and the intruder staring one another down. Out of the corner of his eye, he saw Andie take a step back towards the mantle.

"I'm not going to tell you again, Ethan. *Get out.*"

He and Stang turned in surprise. Andie was holding a pistol, poised in earnest at Stang's chest. With a jolt, Shane recognized the old .45 in her hands. His eyes flitted to the mantel. Sure enough. It was the one he kept in a tin box for protection at home—the ivory-handled Colt his father had handed down to him. He silently cursed himself for not removing it before the girls joined him.

Marcie bounded in.

Shane lunged, shoving the child behind him. "I told you to wait outside!" he barked. The girl peered around him, eyes grown large.

"I said *get out*," Andie repeated. "These are good people. You're not gonna mess up their lives the way you did mine, understand? You had me so confused I didn't know what to think. Couldn't even trust myself." Her voice began to shake. "Well. That's over now. I'm not sick any more…just sick of you and your kind." She cocked the hammer.

The young man stared down the gun barrel, licking lips gone pale. His attempt at a sneer was more like a sick smile. Just the same, he backed up. "That thing's probably not even loaded."

"Wanna gamble?" She stretched out her arms, aiming pointblank at his sternum.

"Andie...." Shane's voice was calm, but its solemn tone added weight to the situation. Stang backed away more, half-stumbling over a stool on his way out. Andie followed, pistol leveled until they were both out the front door. Grimacing, she pressed the trigger. A bullet sang, spitting gravel at his feet.

Stang flinched and vaulted into the convertible. The engine came to life with a roar and he yanked the gearshift into reverse. Backing what seemed a safe distance, he stopped to yell, *"You're disturbed, know that?"*

"You bet I am!" Andie shouted back and followed up with another bullet. This one ricocheted with a *zing* nearly taking out a headlight. The convertible roared back another twenty feet onto the road. Stang stopped for a parting shot of his own.

"You're crazy, too!"

"No! I *used* to be crazy!" Andie yelled back. "I'm not crazy anymore!"

Chest heaving, she watched their unwelcome visitor disappear in a flurry of gravel. When he was out of sight, her shoulders sagged. She looked drained to the core.

Shane quietly retrieved the pistol that dangled from her hand. "I think you better let me take this." He hefted the weapon and studied her. Marcie leaned into her father's side, staring up at Andie with a look of profound admiration.

But she could only stare, dazed, at both of them. "I'm sorry. I just...couldn't let him hurt...either of you."

She turned and staggered into the house. Shane turned to Marcie, giving her a nudge. "Why don't you play out back awhile, Mars."

"Again?" The little girl twisted her mouth, but her father's cocked eyebrow sent her on her way.

Shane found Andie sprawled on the sofa, arm flung across her face. He eased down beside her. "You alright?"

"I guess so..." she returned in a nasal voice. Shane smiled faintly and pulled her arm out of the way. She kept her eyes shut tight as if afraid to face him.

"You're a pretty dangerous woman." His tone didn't reveal whether he was put out or amused.

She peered up out of one eye. "Are you going to arrest me?"

"*Arrest* you?"

She grimaced. "You know...for disturbing the peace or brandishing a weapon...something like that?"

Shane leaned back against the cushions and chewed on his lip a moment. "I don't think this situation's even in the book...though there is an ordinance against visitors discharging a firearm in the park. But this was my gun. I shouldn't have left it out like that. And from the looks of him, you had a right to be disturbed. Nah...long as you promise not to let it ever happen again, I'll just issue a warnin' this time." He stroked her leg pensively.

"I promise. Thanks. If...If there's a fine or something, I'll gladly pay it."

"I'm sure we can work somethin' out." His mouth twitched as he gave her a hand to sit up. She promptly plopped her chin into her hand and sighed. "Seems like I bring trouble wherever I go...."

Shane stretched out, boot heels digging into the rug, and crossed his arms. "I wouldn't say that. You just...lead a more colorful life than the typical person. Somehow, I can't see you in a routine job."

She glanced up at him with a wince. "Meaning?"

"Meaning…Lady, I think you'd make waves no matter where you were." He reached from behind to ruffle up her hair. She stretched out alongside him. He draped his arm around her shoulders and they sat quietly.

"So…who was that? 'Nother old boyfriend?" Shane broke the silence with.

Her eyes flew open. "No! Just…someone I used to work with. A musician. Fancies himself a rock star."

Shane got up and walked over to the patio doors, peering out at his daughter swinging on an old monkey swing in the backyard. "Well…I better get back to work."

"Shane?"

He turned in the half-light.

She was resting her chin on the couch back. "Thanks for putting up with me. I'll make it up to you."

Once again he felt himself coming under the spell of those eyes. How did they go from wistful to seductive so fast? He nodded, mouth twisting.

"I know."

The week that followed settled into the routine, offering a respite from the upheaval of days past. Saturday morning came and Shane determined he should spend his free day with his daughter, re-establishing the link weakened by their three-week separation. The two stood by the old two-tone Blazer, loading it down with fishing gear.

Marcie looked back toward the house. Andie was visible, just inside the patio door, doing her morning stretches. The faint throb of rock music was audible. Marcie knew the old stereo was cranked up inside, the way Andie liked it when she was doing work around the house or exercising. "Things sure are different with Andie," she observed.

Her father straightened and followed her gaze. "Yeah…she's a lot different from yer mom. But it's prob'ly better that way, don't you think?"

Marcie hung on the truck door, resting her cheek against it. "I guess…. Did you know she let me carry a lizard into the house other day and didn't freak out? Mom would never have let me to that. She took a long hike with me yesterday, too, and she asked me to tell her about Mom. We looked for animal tracks and found a raccoon in a tree. And she didn't once ask me about dolls."

"What dolls?"

Her eyes twinkled. "Exactly! –And you know what else? She said next week we could visit the Cove stables—if we cleared it with you first. She'll even ride with me. Mom would never—"

"I know." Her father's eyes held amusement tinged with something else.

She hung her head, then squinted up at him. "Sorry."

"It's okay. Sounds like you figured it out for yourself. Well, get in, pardner! Those trout are gonna get tired of waitin'!"

Marcie grinned and hopped up into the big front seat of the Blazer, settling in with a wiggle.

Back at the lodge, Andie rose from a lotus position and dusted off her hands. "Time to get to work!" she said under her breath. With a bounce in her step, she headed off for the master bedroom, barefoot. There were a couple of boxes there Shane hadn't gotten around to unpacking yet. Maybe he'd like it if she did that for him. This seemed like as good a time as any.

She sat down on the bed's edge and pulled a box closer. Yanking off the plastic tape, she unfolded the top and peeked in.

Just a bunch of paper wadding, some nondescript white cardboard boxes, and some three ring binders. Nothing interesting at first glance. But what looked like a scrapbook wedged in the side of the box caught her eye. She pulled it out and put it on the quilt beside her.

A laminated newspaper clipping fell out and she picked it up. It was from the *Sacramento Bee*, dated nearly 20 years prior. *Son of Mather Head Returns Home* the heading said. She took in the article with hungry eyes:

Navy Lieutenant Shane Scott MacLeod, son of Mather AFB second-in-command Colonel Mike MacLeod, arrived home today after a two-month convalescence at the Naval Hospital in Honolulu.

The 22-year-old helicopter co-pilot, assigned to the aircraft carrier Nimitz, sustained serious injuries in a crash during a classified mission. He was the lone survivor of the four-man medical rescue crew.

Medical reports made public indicated that the junior officer was treated for multiple broken bones, contusions, and a concussion. After weeks of bed confinement the young man has begun a daunting regimen of physical therapy. It was conjectured early on that he might not walk again, but his progress surprised everyone when he advanced to the use of crutches. Upon his arrival at Mather, Lieutenant MacLeod was awarded the Purple Heart by Assistant Secretary of the Navy William Hart and California Senator Benson Hughes.

While his father was quoted as saying the family would take it one day at a time, it is clear that this determined young man is eager to return to normal life, stateside.

Andie let out her breath, realizing she'd held it the whole time she was reading. With an air of reverence, she laid the article down on the bed and picked up the scrapbook, opening it with care. Page after page of mementos…it seemed unlike Shane to put together such a carefully constructed trip down memory lane. He'd shared almost nothing of his military experience. An occasional stiff shrug in the morning or after a long day, but she had no reason to connect it to old wounds. Perhaps she should have asked more…if she'd known what to ask.

For all that had happened to them, they'd really only known each other two months. There hadn't been time for a lot of stuff to come out. Seemed like they spent most of that time dealing with her past instead of his. And here he was trying to adjust to a new assignment. A lump swelled in her throat.

She flipped to the front page of the book. Sure enough, it was inscribed by the giver:

For Shane with love—
For your children and your children's children's children.
Love, Mom

The lump in her throat grew bigger. There was so much here….

Snapshots of a preschooler holding his baby sister's hand in front of an adobe house—Albuquerque?

A bemused seven-year-old in a cowboy hat licking a finger-full of icing from a birthday cake….

A gangly teenager posing with his dad in front of a fighter jet….

High school track awards….

His whole life was laid out here.

A separate section chronicled Park Service years…articles on a fire at Yellowstone…an avalanche at Yosemite…a search and rescue operation at Kings Canyon…a citation for his two years' service in the U.S. Park Police Aviation Unit at Yellowstone…a crash course on Shane.

She laid the binder aside, rubbing its well-worn cover pensively. Her gaze slid back to the box. With a sigh, she reached in to retrieve two small cardboard boxes. Opening the larger one, she froze....

A wedding photograph...a couple standing inside the wooden archway of the Ahwahnee Hotel, Yosemite...flanked by wedding guests. Shane had a spark in his eye and a twisted grin as if the camera had just missed him in a joke aside. Then she saw the culprit...Ben, just behind the bride's left shoulder. The errant groomsman had wrapped half of himself around a pillar. His right hand trailed behind the voluminous wedding dress, threatening mischief.

A laugh escaped her. Typical Ben....

They all looked so young and carefree, not knowing the trials to come their way. Bracing, she dared for the first time to study the bride's face. So this was Becky...the shadow hanging over them now had a face. It didn't help that she had the face of an angel. Blond, twinkling blue eyes, heart-shaped face, a happy-shy smile....

Andie's eyes brimmed with tears. She shut the case and laid it on top of the scrapbook, brushing away the wetness on her cheek with the back of her hand. *Didn't know what I was getting into here, did I?*

Still, one more box beckoned to her...a small leather case with brass trim. She picked it up cautiously and pried it open. A medal, Shane's Purple Heart, glinted up at her. Something tightened in her chest.

All these images of a past perfect life...an honorable life, well-spent...all before she'd come along.

What have I ever done to compare with this?

She stared at the medal, transfixed, then sniffed and laid it gently on the bed....

The blue and gray Blazer pulled up into the gravel driveway, Marcie bounding out and running into the house. Shane emerged more sedately from the vehicle, going around back to retrieve fishing gear from the cargo compartment. In civilian garb for a change, he looked relaxed, even mellow, from their morning of teasing brown trout out of a mountain river.

His expression changed, however, when Marcie burst back out of the house and came running up to him, breathless.

"She's gone!"

Shane straightened, giving her a hard stare. "What d'ya mean *gone*?

"She's not here! Come see." His daughter tugged on his arm. He let her pull him into the lodge, leaving hard-won trout behind in the ice chest.

Shane walked back through the darkened hallway to the bedroom. Frown flickering across his brow, he opened the closet. All of her things were missing. On the nightstand, he spied a folded piece of paper. He sat down slowly on the bed's edge and opened it, reading:

I'm sorry Shane,

The more I've thought about it since Ethan came, the more I'm convinced this is the right thing to do. I don't want to mess up your lives any more than I already have. You deserve so much better.

Love always,
Andie

An envelope was attached to the note with a paper clip. Inside, he found a check made out to him...for five thousand dollars.

She'd scribbled on the flap:

Please put this away for Marcie—I'm good for it.

Shane dropped the note to his knee and stared out the window, mouth twisting. His eyes narrowed the more he thought, barely aware of Marcie coming in to sit down beside him. She snatched the note from his hand and read silently.

She groaned. "I don't understand! Everything was fine this morning." She leaned into her father, gazing up at the furrows in the weathered cheeks.

Shane shook his head. " 'Nother one of her doggone mood swings." He surged to his feet. "Dang fool woman! It's not her place t' say what's best for us—her either for that matter!"

Wavering on his heel a moment, he snatched up his phone and punched in *McGhee Tyson Airport-Flight Information*.

Five minutes later he burst out the front door, Marcie in tow. The little girl headed for the nearest vehicle, the green and white Park SUV.

Shane glanced over his shoulder from the door of the trusty old Blazer. "Nope, this one. This is *personal*."

He hopped in, waited just long enough for the child to get safely in, and slammed the Blazer in reverse, heading out with a flurry of gravel.

* * * *

Shane traversed the concourse at a clip, Marcie trotting to keep up. At his abrupt stop, his daughter bumped smack into him. He ignored it as he studied the screen, double-checking the gate numbers. Continuing at a brisk pace, he slowed to a stop four gates later.

Across the way sat a familiar figure, her back to them. She appeared to be reading a magazine. Hands shoved into the pockets of his old fishing jacket, he sauntered over, planting himself before the seated woman.

Andie looked up with a start. She was wearing sunglasses, but it was apparent that she had been crying in the recent past.

"You got somethin' t' say t' me face to face?" he challenged.

Her chin jerked up. A shiver and she looked away. In the background, the first boarding call for the flight to D.C. was announced. She rose with deliberation, dipping to grab the straps of her carry-on bag.

"Please Shane...don't make this any harder. I've gone through that already." Her voice was hoarse.

"Yeah? Well *I* haven't." He blocked her way.

A tear trickled from beneath the sunglasses, running down her cheek. "I...I don't belong here after all."

"How the hell can you find that out if you don't stay put long enough?"

She swallowed but stepped past him. Head bowed, she made for the exit.

"You know, Lady, you got the nerve of a fighter pilot but none of th' control t' go with it! That's a downright fatal combination!" he called after her.

Andie froze, cheeks reddening. Several people in the lobby looked up in their direction. A shift in her shoulder and she turned on him.

"Well, you've got the *control* part down pat, don't you!"

Shane stiffened. Marcie winced at his side.

He and Andie stared each other down.

Final boarding for Flight 327 to Dulles International, the speakers interjected.

She hesitated.

Just long enough.

131

Shane strode over, took the bag from her, and pulled her to him for a quick, fierce kiss.

"You want control...you'll get control."

She took hold of his head and kissed him back, hard.

A smattering of applause broke out among the onlookers. Shane ignored it but Marcie broke into a wide grin, throwing a thumbs-up at the boarding agent, who gave her one back.

Out in the parking lot, Shane opened the door for Andie, keeping a wary eye on her.

"Just one thing. Why were you headed t' D.C.?"

She looked up at him under long eyelashes, gone suddenly demure. "I...used to have some friends there."

Shane's eyes narrowed to slits. "Like who?"

She gave the slightest grimace. "There was this ballplayer...a short-stop...in Baltimore—"

"Never mind. I don't want to know." He swung her door shut and tramped around to the driver's side with a weary wag of the head.

Back in the Smokies that night, Andie stood on the deck, staring up at the full moon as it rose above the pines. Shane joined her, resting his elbows on the rail alongside. He squinted into the dark woods beyond and ventured a sidelong glance her way.

"It's just a box, Andie. A box of another life. Stuff I shouldn't forget...but tucked away so I can get on with life. At least I was hopin' to."

She bowed her head but said nothing.

"I hope you see now where you belong is here, with us." His mouth twisted. "Guess I'm just gonna have t' make an honest woman out of you."

Andie came out of her daze. "What?"

Shane turned around and crossed his arms, leaning against the rail. "Well…I figure if you try to seduce me one more time when I'm in uniform, I'm gonna have to arrest you. Let's cut out this foolishness and go ahead with it."

Andie turned, copying his stance, and cocked an eyebrow at him. "Go ahead with what?"

Shane had the look of a man about to squirm. "You know."

Her expression changed to one of exasperation. "No…you're going to have to ask me, Shane MacLeod, or forget it." She turned to go but he reached out, reining her in.

"Alright!" He slid his hands down to grip hers with an awkward little waggle. "I wanna marry you, Andie."

She shook her hands free and re-crossed her arms.

"*Will* you marry me, Andrea Carson?"

She leaned into him, encircling him with her arms. "There now, that wasn't so hard, was it?"

They stood nose to nose. He eyed her, up close and exasperated.

"*Well?*"

She gave him her pirate's grin. "Uh-huh." She kissed him.

Shane's hands slid up her back and held her to it, sneaking in a little slap on her backside.

A voice startled them from their embrace. "Can I go on the honeymoon?"

Shane broke off and spied Marcie peeking out her bedroom window.

"Not a chance!" he laughed.

. 12 .

Visitors at the Smokies' Sugarlands Center looked on in curiosity as a dusty Jeep with Wyoming plates pulled up and parked in front of the building. A tall, tan, blond man in jeans, denim shirt, and cowboy boots hopped out. Pulling out a faded red bandana, he wiped his forehead and the back of his neck in the July heat. A smile spread across his face as he cased out the scene before him. He turned back to poke his head inside the vehicle.

The dark-haired young woman in the front seat wrinkled her delicate features. "So many people..." she breathed.

He reached in and brushed her cheek. "Relax! It'll be all right. Why don't you guys wait for me in the Visitor Center? You'll be more comfortable there. Get some drinks. I'll check in at Headquarters and be right back. It shouldn't take long."

The young woman nodded and turned to the back seat. Two tousled little heads, one blond, one dark, popped up to peer about.

"Is this it, Dad?" the bigger child, a boy, asked.

"This is it." The blond man gave him a tight smile and ruffled his hair. The boy's sleepy eyes grew large as he took in his surroundings with new interest. The young father turned to go.

"Ben...."

He turned back. His wife held out a comb to him with a gentle smile.

"Oh. Yeah. Okay." With a sheepish grin, he took it, running a couple of swipes through his windblown hair.

He took leave of his family and sauntered down the sidewalk, taking a path that led off to a sturdy stone building labeled *Park Headquarters*. As he drew nearer, anxiety gnawed at his gut, the first since getting news of this assignment. He paused at the flagstone steps to wipe his hands on his jeans before approaching the door. Taking a deep breath, he took hold of the handle and went inside.

The rush of cool air was welcome. The lobby was dark, paneled, but devoid of furniture or people. His boots scraped on the hardwood floor as he looked about in wonder. To his left, a wall of old portraits and photographs of men prominent in the early days of the Park Service stared down upon him. Some of these were men he had admired since his college days...names like Horace Kephart, Stephen Mather, John Muir.... His gaze came to rest on a long counter which ran the length of the opposite wall. A bell rested on it, with a sign that read *Ring for Service.* He walked over and eyed it a moment, considering, but decided against it. Spying a door in the hall to his right, he approached it and stuck his head through the partial opening.

A generously-sized office lay beyond, with a band of schoolroom style windows running along the back wall. Hemlocks crowded the outside view, much as the profusion of gray metal government-issue filing cabinets and side tables crowded the interior. Stacks of manila folders and boxes of soft-bound documents on the floor testified to a never-ending workload. A silver-haired woman sat there at a desk, going through mail. Despite her swamped surroundings, she looked up with a pleasant smile.

"Can I help you?"

Ben cleared his throat. "Uh—hi. I was told to report for work here. Guess I should head for the Superintendent's office?"

The woman cocked her head, assessing him. "That depends. Are you seasonal, Job Corps, or permanent?"

"Um—ranger."

"Oh." The woman blinked, studying him anew. "What division?"

"I...don't know that yet."

"Well...never mind. They're all in a meeting right now, anyway, down the hall...the Superintendent, the Division Chiefs, and that new North District Chief, too...so if it's one of them you need, you'll have to wait. Why don't you go on down to that fourth door on your right and have a seat. That's the Superintendent's front office. Someone there can get you started, I'm sure."

With a nod of thanks, Ben proceeded down the hall. But as he neared the Supe's door, his attention was drawn to a meeting room on his left, full of some thirty NPS personnel. Most were in the familiar gray-green Park Service uniform with its signature arrowhead patch on the sleeve. Some were sitting, others standing, in what appeared to be an informal briefing session. Before he realized it, he was standing in the doorway.

Several of the men standing along the back wall looked up in his direction. One of them was Shane. With a terse nod, he signaled Ben to join them. Ben resisted the impulse to break into a wide grin. It was hard to hide his delight. *Finally*...to be in a room full of his peers after so many years!

He made his way as unobtrusively as possible to Shane's side, assuming the same stance, one the mirror image of the other. Inclining his head toward Shane, he whispered, "What's up?"

"Division shake-up, lots of reassignments," Shane whispered back without shifting his gaze. "Came down this mornin'. We're all waitin' to get our new staff lists."

Ben settled back to digest this, stomach doing a flip-flop. A stapled handout was passed to Shane. Around them, the room erupted in muttering as people clustered to look over theirs. As the ranger flipped through it, Ben ventured a peek, swallowing. "So...what does it say?"

Shane continued to read. His eyes crinkled with amusement as he handed the list over to him. "Welcome to the wonderful world of Law Enforcement."

"What?" Ben took the proffered handout, skimming down the list of names till he came to his own:

MORGAN, BENJAMIN JAY. . . .VISITOR PROTECTION
                    NORTH DISTRICT
                    CADES COVE

He looked up at Shane in consternation. "But...I was supposed to go into Wildlife Management...wasn't I?"

Shane cocked an eyebrow and shrugged. "Sorry."

Ben scanned the sheet for the name of the District Heads. Maybe he could take up his case with one of them...but discovered he was to be under the supervision of none other than one *S. S. MACLEOD.* He squinted up at his friend. "You have something to do with this?"

Shane shook his head. "Not really. There were slots that needed filling. Resource Management and Visitor Services were full, Enforcement/Protection Division needed beefing up. I just tried to steer your assignment to a Subdistrict I thought you'd like." He paused to regard him. "You still want it?"

"Well sure! I mean—hell, Shane I've been waiting fifteen years for this! It's...it's a privilege. I'm glad to be serving alongsi—uh—under you." Ben stuck out his hand.

Shane eyed him askance before taking hold of it. "You sure?"

"Oh yeah. I'm sure."

The ranger smiled grimly. "Welcome aboard then. We'll see what you think after a few weeks at it. It's good to see you can be philosophical about it. Who knows, maybe you can switch over to Resource Management eventually—or you might even come to like this branch." He took the handout from Ben, flipped over a couple of pages and gave it back, pointing to the heading *JOB DESCRIPTIONS.*

Ben read silently. "Backcountry patrol, huh?"

"Yep."

"And I'd be on some search and rescue teams as well…."

He looked up to meet Shane's amused eyes as they headed out of the room together. A lanky, uniformed man with a sandy mustache approached, prompting Shane to stop.

"Tom, here's Ben Morgan, just arrived."

"Ah! Good to see you again." The man held out his hand. "Welcome aboard."

Still engrossed in the assignment sheets, Ben forgot to glance up. "Uh…hi. Thanks." He resumed his scanning until Shane gave him a meaningful nudge.

"Ben…Tom Jeffries is the Park Superintendent. Remember?"

He came out of his other world. "Huh? Oh! Sorry! Pleasure to be here!" He took Jeffries' hand and pumped it.

The Superintendent chuckled, flicking a glance at Shane. "I understand you were hoping to go into wildlife management, Ben. Sorry 'bout the switch. Just be glad we didn't let Pamela get hold of you." He shared a grin with Shane. Even as he spoke, a small, square-shouldered woman with bobbed hair approached them. She planted herself in front of the new recruit and thrust her hand at him.

"Pamela Lyons. You must be the new soldier on the block. Morgan, isn't it? Hear they want to make a trail cop out of you. Too bad. We could use someone like you over in Public Relations. Well, if they don't treat you right, come next door and we'll fix you up. Gotta go. Nice meeting you." Giving him an appreciative scan, the woman pivoted on her heel and plowed her way through the crowd.

Ben stared after, speechless. Jeffries leaned in. "Don't let her snow you. She's always like that. A real fireball. Pamela practically got the two divisions in a bidding war. Word is they're looking for a new poster ranger over there." The Smokies' Superintendent walked away, chuckling, and joined another group.

Shane clapped Ben on the back. "Come on, let's introduce you to some of the more regular folks around here."

"Take him on in there to meet Joyce and Peg," Jeffries called after them. "Tell 'em your packet is on my desk, ready to go. Buck should be by, too."

Later, the two friends headed back up the path toward the Visitor Center. Shane stopped in his tracks upon sight of the Jeep relic he recognized all too well.

"You hauled your family cross-country in that?"

Ben shrugged. "It wasn't so bad."

A crooked grin spread across Shane's face. "Tawnee still speakin' to you?"

"Last time I checked." Ben grinned back. "So, when do I report in—tomorrow morning?"

"Well…it's kinda complicated at the moment." Shane rubbed his jaw. "Trouble is, they got their timing off. See, if you're goin' into Enforcement, you're supposed to take this six-week course in Georgia at the Federal Law Enforcement Training Center down there. We call it *FLETC* for short. Anyway, the next session doesn't start up for a couple of weeks, so, in the meantime, they don't know exactly what to do with you."

Shane continued walking. "I figure you can hang around at the District office and Subdistrict offices, make some runs with me or Cal Evans, and we'll pass you around to Resource Management—that's what they call the wildlife division here. Also you can spend some time with Visitor Services to familiarize yourself with their operations. We'll keep you busy." He paused to look past Ben's shoulder. "Speaking of…here come Buck MacIntyre. He's in Resource Management."

A blond-haired ranger with an earnest, boyish face and solemn eyes approached, Shane signaling him to join them. "Buck, this is Ben Morgan. He'll be joining us in Enforcement at the Cove."

The young fellow reached across to shake hands. "Been hearing about you. Welcome to the Smokies."

Ben clasped his hand and eyed him. "Virginia?"

MacIntyre broke into an amiable grin. "Blacksburg. You're good."

"It's that *oot* and *aboot* thing that gives you away—I've had some friends from Virginia."

Shane broke in. "I think Ben would actually prefer to be over in Resources with you guys."

"Really?" Buck turned back to Ben. "Anytime you wanna drop over, it's fine with us."

"Thanks."

Buck's gaze traveled to the heap Ben was leaning against. "Hey, let me know when your stuff comes in and I'll be glad to help you move in."

"Thanks, but this is everything, actually. We'll manage."

The young Virginian looked in search of an adequate response. Ben had to hand it to him, though. The guy tried hard to mask his shock. "Oh…you guys like to travel light, huh?"

Shane reached over to jostle Buck's shoulder. "MacIntyre's our resident diplomat. Not to worry Buck, Ben's kind of starting over here, you could say."

The fair-haired ranger smiled bashfully and tried to move on. "Y'know, these folks are gonna need some supplies to get by on until they get settled in. Those Subdistrict houses don't come with much in the way of extras."

"Yeah, I was thinkin' about that. Maybe we should check into one of those cabins at Little Creek or Elkmont for the time being. They're equipped with the basics at least." He turned to Ben. "Some new housing is almost finished in the Cove itself. I'll see if I can claim one of those for you."

Buck hefted the case he was holding. "I'd better be on my way. The lab's waiting on these test samples."

Shane nudged Ben. "I'll get back to you with an answer this afternoon. Why don't you head on over to my place? Let Tawnee and the kids have a chance to rest and shower if they want. We can grill out tonight. I should be able to dig up some keys for a cabin by then. Gotta run over to Cosby now." He turned to go, calling back over his shoulder, "I'll let Andie know you're on the way. She's excited to see you all."

Later that afternoon, the old Jeep turned into the gravel drive that bore the sign *District Chief's Residence*. Ben cut the engine and hopped out. He ambled to the front door, taking in the lush, shady green of the secluded lawn, the fragrant carpet of sun-warmed pine straw underfoot...a far cry from the wide-open, windswept range of Wyoming with its ever-present backdrop of jagged snow-capped peaks on the horizon.

It would take some adjustment. He might even admit to a touch of claustrophobia in the thick of all this verdant growth. And the mountains here seemed to close in on a person. Still there was a certain serenity, an older kind of majesty. Here and there, a swath of open ground would burst open from a leaf-canopied tunnel of trees, pretty enough to take his breath away. He'd seen one this morning on his drive over, at a place called Oconaluftee.

There was no answer to his knock on the rustic front door. Ben ventured a peek in the window but all he could make out was darkness. Nonplused, he decided to look around back.

Rounding the corner, he stopped in his tracks, struck by the scene before him.

There sat Andie on an old tree stump, dressed in cargo pants and a faded T-shirt, grappling with a tiny rabbit on her lap. She was trying to give it something from a medicine dropper, unaware of his presence. Ben enjoyed the chance to watch her absorbed in her patient ministrations. This was not the same brash young woman who'd sauntered into the Fort Washakie trading post a couple of months back and turned every head in the place. This one had an air of peace and contentment about her.

At a glance, he might have mistaken her for someone else, but then she raised her head. Those familiar mischievous eyes caught sight of him—and took hold of him. The sparkle of delight that lit up her face knocked him off guard. It took a moment to think of what to say. He put on his old teasing grin and walked over.

"Now who could this be?" He planted himself before her, hands shoved into his pockets. "So...you've finally found your niche...a rodent nurse."

That elicited a quick frown. "Rabbits are not rodents! They're *lagomorphs*, I'll have you know. Marcie and I looked it up." She stood and plopped the little ball of fur into Ben's hands.

He had to wrestle for a firm handle, the wiggly little creature finding a secure hold on his shirtfront and settling down. He cradled it with one hand. "I stand corrected. Where'd this little guy come from?"

Andie reached over to stroke its fur. "I guess you could say he's a consolation prize for Marcie. She saw a cottontail get caught by a fox a couple of weeks ago and was really upset over it. We saw a litter of these at the farmer's market in Asheville other day and well…."

Ben smiled down at her. "Poor Shane, having to put up with you soft-hearted females."

"And you don't?" Andie shot him a knowing smile.

She had him there. He looked away, lifting his chin to savor the evergreen-scented breeze. It *was* beautiful here…that sense of contentment settled over him as well. He turned back to her. "So…you and Shane, huh? Am I to blame or thank for this?"

"Don't flatter yourself." She headed leisurely up the slope towards the deck, tossing her hair as she went. "When did you get in?" she called over her shoulder.

He caught up with her in four strides. " 'Bout noon. We spent the night in Cherokee, drove over and had lunch in Gatlinburg, then stopped by Headquarters."

"Sounds like you took time to explore. Let me guess…" she put a finger to her chin. "Knowing you, it probably involved a trail…to one of the falls, I'll bet. Which one?"

He grinned. "Mingo Falls. Hey, it was right there on the way." Their eyes met but Andie broke away quickly, he noticed.

She turned her face to the breeze. "Seen Shane yet?"

"Yeah, ran into him during a staff meeting. There was all kinds of shuffling going on. I ended up being assigned to the Law Enforcement division."

Andie choked back a laugh. "Now that's a paradox!"

"All right, you…." He handed the rabbit back to her. "Here, take back your…whatever you called it." He brushed off his hands, looking over her shoulder as she eased her tiny patient into its makeshift hutch, a laundry basket with a soft towel inside and a screen on top anchored down by a brick.

"Better bring that in at night. Something's liable to come out of those woods and make him a midnight snack."

Andie stood, grimacing. "I know that! We bring him in whenever we're not around to keep an eye out. He has a corner in the laundry room."

Ben cocked an eyebrow. "How's it going to get along with that Collie pup Marcie told me about?"

She sighed. "That's on hold for a while. Shane's going to help us build a hutch soon anyway."

"Sounds like you've thought of everything, ranger woman."

He backed off, laughing, as she shoved past, a half-hearted punch to his middle. Picking up an old tin sprinkler can, she carried it to a spigot on the back of the house.

He looked around the yard. "So where's my brilliant and beautiful niece?"

Andie turned off the water and straightened, giving him a quizzical look. "You mean Marcie? She's at a junior ranger camp. Shane thought it would be good for her to meet other kids. I wasn't aware you'd been adopted—Uncle." She bumped his arm on her way to the deck where a patch of Shasta daisies awaited her attention.

"Sure, we all go way back." He tugged at his chin. "Let's see, that would make you and me...?"

"Brother and sisterly-like," she said with a withering glance.

He smiled down at his feet. She had him there. He nodded toward the front yard. "So why don't you take a break and come see the tribe?"

She straightened from her watering. "They came with you? Why didn't you say so!" She absently brushed her fingers on the back of her jeans and followed him up the slope to the front yard.

Ben paused for her to catch up, eyeing her hip pockets as she passed. Sure enough, black loamy streaks ran down both of them.

She caught his look and frowned. "What?"

"Oh...nothing...." He chewed his lip but his eyes couldn't help crinkling.

That only made her brows lower more. "Give."

"Oh, it's just...you've managed to smear dirt all over the seat of your pants. I'd brush if off for you but then you'd probably just think I was getting fresh. Can't have that, can we?"

She looked up at him uncertainly. "No...we can't. And here I thought you'd changed." She sighed, walking on to the Jeep. Ben hung on his heel, wondering at himself and the moment. He looked up sharply, though, when his two children burst from the Jeep, full of pent-up energy from being cooped up for days. They made a mad dash for the house.

Ben joined Tawnee and Andie, looking from one to the other. "What did you say?"

Andie looked up guilelessly. "Just the magic word—popsicles!"

*   *   *   *

The lights from the windows of the old ranger lodge shone into the wee hours that night, like a lantern set deep within a forest of black velvet. Inside, old friends reminisced, traded jokes, and celebrated the chance to finally work alongside each other. The cluster of adults gathered around the hearth while the children played with the baby rabbit.

Ben clinked glasses with Shane. "I guess I'd have to say this is all a dream come true. Took long enough!"

"Yeah, well, I did have to stick my neck out on this one a bit," the veteran ranger allowed.

Ben looked up with a grin but his eyes were solemn. "Hope I'll be up to your expectations."

"You better be." Shane cocked an eyebrow but chuckled as he gave Ben's shoulder a jostle.

. 13 .

National Park Service Ranger Morgan stood before the full-length mirror, fidgeting as he took one more look at his new uniform. It felt stiff, foreign, after all the years of going about in worn jeans and work shirts on the range. He frowned and straightened his posture.

"Not big enough in the shoulders for you?"

He turned, startled. Tawnee looked in from the doorway, a mixture of amusement and admiration in her eyes. Ben's shoulder's relaxed. "No...just feels strange, that's all." He met her eyes and broke into a sheepish grin. "Feels kinda special, too, gotta admit."

"You look special." She came up to him and draped her arms around his neck. He delivered a lingering kiss to her lips.

Tawnee's hand slid down to rest over his heart. "Promise you'll be careful out there today."

He reached up to caress the tumble of dark hair. "I promise."

She pulled away, tugging on his hands. "Come, you need to get your breakfast before Shane gets here. It's waiting."

Ben let go with reluctance and followed her into the cabin's cozy kitchen. But he'd barely gotten down a couple of biscuits with his coffee before a truck horn sounded out front. He bounded up, grabbed his gear, and charged out the door.

Out in the Park Service vehicle, Shane looked on in amusement as Ben did an about-face and met Tawnee at the screen door, giving her a quick kiss before trotting out to join him. As the rookie ranger climbed in alongside him, Shane shook his head.

"Same ol', same ol'...."

Morgan looked up distractedly as he found a place to wedge in his backpack. "Huh?"

"Nuthin'. Anybody ever say you were born under a lucky star?"

Ben looked genuinely puzzled. "Sure never felt that way."

"More than you know…." Shane sighed as he turned onto the main road. It was vintage Morgan this morning…running late, making up for it like an errant schoolboy…undisciplined, incapable of toeing the line but hanging on to that engaging mystique that kept others from getting mad at him, at least for long. Some might call it charisma. Shane settled for calling it *born lucky*. It seemed no matter what kind of scrape the fellow got himself into, he always managed to work his way out. Maybe…just maybe…the guy's luck would hold long enough this time for him to be given permanent status.

Shane marshaled his thoughts back to work. Retrieving some papers off the back seat, he plopped them into Ben's lap. "Here's the schedule I worked out for you for the next ten days, till you're due at FLETC."

Ben scanned the three-page list with the attendant booklets. "Kinda intense…."

"Well, like FLETC, it's designed t' be an accelerated course, get ya up to speed fast." Shane backed up the drive, flicking a glance his way. "I know you can be one of the best—if you put your mind to it."

Ben nodded. Enough said.

The rookie ranger settled back to take in the scenery, his eyes gleaming like a kid embarking on high adventure. "So where are we headed first?"

Shane's tone was matter-in-fact. "First, I gotta stop by Sugarlands, pick up some forms, then head over to the Wear Cove area. There's an old fella there whose property borders on park land. He, or somebody, has been crossing over the line and chopping down trees. Personally, I think the old character's got some kinda secret business goin' on, maybe a still, but I don't have any hard evidence. At this point, I don't want to get him in trouble, just give him a friendly warning."

Beside him, Ben smiled. "Doesn't sound like the hard-nosed commander I expected."

Shane threw him a look sideways. "You know me better than that."

The truck pulled up in front of the Sugarlands Visitor Center. On this summer morning, it was living up to its reputation of being the National Park Service's most heavily visited center. The place was already filling up at this early hour, the latest tricked-out SUV's alongside cars with tarps lassoed to their roofs, vans plastered with vacation stickers, a bicycling group…people were milling about all over the grounds.

Ben took it all in, realizing that soon all these people would be under his care. Shane hopped out, walked up to a door marked *Backcountry Permits*, and disappeared inside. Ben got out a moment later and strolled up to the front of the building just to look around.

He was feeling a bit full of himself this first day of official status. Catching furtive glances of some children sitting on a rock wall, he imagined them to be looks of awe. He casually made his way over to them, a little self-conscious but ready to put his best foot forward in the name of public relations. Giving them what he thought was a winning smile, he called out, "Hi, kids! Where are you from?"

The urchins squinted up at him and burst into snickering.

The oldest, a girl of about twelve, sneered, "Who're you? Dudley Do-Right?" They scampered off, giggling up a storm.

Ben stared after them with a befuddled look that settled into a scowl, about to mutter something under his breath when Shane's voice came from behind him.

"Let's go!"

He shook his head to clear it and joined Shane in the SUV.

The Park Service vehicle bearing Shane and Ben pulled off the boundary road onto a gravel drive that was little more than an overgrown path. At the far end of it sat a dilapidated old home-stead tucked in a hollow. The place looked as though it had been there since the Civil War.

Ben watched, intrigued, as Shane pulled the truck to a slow stop while still some distance away. Knowing Shane had a rationale for everything he did, Ben figured this action to be some sort of precaution or local custom.

Shane cut the engine and pulled the keys. "Just open your door and step out slow," he muttered.

That was when Ben started to worry.

Shane went first, Ben following his example to the slightest detail as if his life might hinge upon it. The senior ranger shut his door and ambled up toward the house.

When Ben closed his own door and made to follow, he was met with the *zing* of a gunshot. He crouched for cover, peering around the front fender to check on Shane...but was confounded by the sight of his partner standing there unhurt and unalarmed.

Shane stared back with a twisted grin.

"What th—?" Ben was more angry than afraid now. He straightened up—and was met by another echoing blast. This time, he flinched but didn't flee, suspecting some kind of strange introduction ritual was going on here. He glared at Shane for an explanation.

"It's all right. That's all there'll be."

Mollified somewhat by Shane's easy response, Ben edged up to join him, keeping a wary eye on the windows of the old place. "You wanna tell me what that was all about?"

"Don't worry. If he hadn't a liked your looks, he wouldn't have missed."

Ben squinted up at the sagging, weather-worn porch with its ominous, dark windows. All was quiet now save for the drone of locusts in the hot, still, morning air.

"Just how old a character are we talking about here?"

Shane shrugged. " 'Bout eighty, I guess."

"That's what I was afraid of."

Ben's muttering trailed off as he followed Shane toward the front steps. Ranger MacLeod planted himself squarely before the front door and belted out, "Hendrickson! Get yer butt out here, you old coot!"

Ben almost jumped out of his skin. A flick of the lace curtains in one window grabbed his attention. He froze, straining to make out the faint sounds of movement inside.

A ghostly figure appeared behind the old screen door, gradually becoming visible. It was a girl—or woman, barely, from the looks of her—tall, slender-hipped in an oversized shift of some printed gauze-like material that hung below her knees. Long, fair hair framed a child-like face. Her feet were bare, Ben noticed. And she was unarmed. Not their shooter?

Shane was plainly caught off guard. "Sorry, Ma'am. I was lookin' for someone else."

The girl called back over her shoulder into the far reaches of the house, "Granddeddy! There's some lawmen here t' see ya!"

The sound of shuffling on the plank floor inside was audible before an old man's voice bellowed out, "Hell, I know that child! What'd ya think I was shootin' at? Th' moon? Now go on, invite 'em in and be off with ya."

The girl appeared used to such carrying on. She pushed the door open wide, a look of resignation on her face. Not meeting their eyes, she turned away and languidly left the room without another word.

Ben found his gaze following her a moment before turning his attention back to their volatile host. The squint the old man fixed on him bordered on malicious. Wondering if he'd gone and committed another mountain taboo, Ben looked to Shane for help.

The old mountain man shuffled across the creaking floor, cane tapping. He headed for a faded, overstuffed chair and eased himself down into it.

"Careful what you stare at," Shane whispered aside.

"Got that." Ben swallowed.

Shane turned back to the old man. "I guess you know why we're here."

Hendrickson stamped his cane on the plank floor. "Humphh! Dadblasted gub-ment types tellin' people what they can and can't do!"

"It's a national park, Wiley! Somebody's got to protect it. Otherwise, there'd be nothin' left for people to come see," Shane said evenly.

The creases in the old man's jowls grew deeper. He leaned forward, chin resting on his cane. "Too many blame people comin' 'round here anyhow, pokin' their noses where they oughtn't...cloggin' up the roads. I was here first! My people was here, first! Eighteen thirty th' first ones come here!" He pounded his cane for emphasis.

Shane approached and hunched down alongside the chair.

He kept his voice low, conciliatory. "Well...y'know, Wiley...there're kids walled up in those concrete jungles who've never had a chance to see a mountain till they come here. This place is for people like them just as much as it is for people like you. Hell, if it weren't for the park bein' here, you know what you could end up with? Some chemical plant or logger on your back doorstep. And your water 'round here is kept safe by the park's Watershed Protection Act. It's a constant battle for us as it is."

Shane paused, shifting. "Now all I'm tryin' to do here is maintain a good neighbor policy 'cause that's what we are. Neighbors. And friends, I hope." The ranger lowered his voice to a conspiratorial whisper. "So...just between you and me...you don't go cuttin' park trees and I won't let on what you used that last batch of logs for. And anytime you need firewood for a good reason, you let me know and I'll see that you get it, hear?" Shane sat back on his heels. "Now what do you say to that?"

The old codger squirmed but eventually nodded.

Ben spoke up from the corner, nodding at a dulcimer that hung on the wall. "Do you play?"

The old man whirled around to glare at him. *"Who the hell are you?"*

Ben was rendered speechless.

Shane answered for him. "This is Ben Morgan. He'll be helpin' patrol the park. And probably lookin' in on you from time to time."

From the corner, Ben mouthed *I will?* He recovered before Hendrickson turned those fierce pale blue eyes on him again.

150

Coming back to the subject at hand, he gestured at the instrument. "So...*does* anyone around here still play this?"

His none-to-gracious host settled back in the tattered easy chair with a disgruntled "Yes...."

Ben studied the dulcimer in more detail. "Those are Cherokee symbols carved on it, aren't they?"

The old man turned, giving him a wary look of reassessment. "How'd you know that?"

Ben relaxed enough to smile. "My wife's part Arapaho. I've learned to notice these things."

Hendrickson leaned back in his chair, gone into another world. "Those were put there by my grandmother. She was full-blooded Cherokee...." The mountain man turned another hard glare in Ben's direction. This time, the rookie ranger didn't flinch, returning stare for stare. Still, he was jarred when the old man burst out, "Rachel! You invited these fellas t' lunch yet or what?"

Shane headed for the door with polite haste. "Uh-thanks. We need to be on our way." He nodded to the young woman standing by the old harvest table. "Ma'am."

Ben followed, nodding as well.

He let loose a sigh of relief once they reached the safe confines of the park Blazer.

Shane started up the engine. "I can tell what you're thinkin'. Stop it."

Ben broke from his reverie. "What?"

"I know you," Shane shook his head wearily. "You're already startin' up some new crusade in your head, aren't you? Forget it, Ben. There's hundreds more just like 'em up and down these mountains. You can't take on all the hard luck cases in the world."

"You saw her, Shane...." Ben stared out the window. "That place is falling down around them...it's got to be an icebox in the winter. And I'll bet you anything she dropped out of school to look after him."

Shane's mouth firmed. "Okay! I saw her. I also saw those antlers over the door. They didn't look all that old."

"Well...maybe it was hunted off park land."

"I doubt it. And you and I both know it's not deer season. Someone's been doin' some illegal huntin' and I don't think it was either of them. Some of those plants dryin' under the eaves are on the endangered list, too. Old-timers use 'em for all kinds of cures. Impossible to tell where they got them."

Ben glanced sideways. "You think something fishy's going on?"

Shane shrugged, staring at the road ahead. "Maybe. Trouble is, his kind are dyin' out too. And they don't cotton to the new ways. It's hard to blame 'em. There are a lot of these folks, poor as dirt but sittin' on a gold mine—their land. Lot of 'em refuse to budge off the old homeplace, but it's gettin' impossible to survive. It would break their hearts to see it parceled into small lots or turned into some resort complex for rich folks. Their best alternative is to have the park buy their land, if and when the funds are available. At least then the land would remain undisturbed till they pass on—although that caused a lot of hard feelings among their heirs back in the twenties and thirties when the park was created. It was a boon for some, an unforgivable exodus to others."

Ben eyed him from the side. "Wasn't there a grandfather clause set up, though?"

"Yeah...a number of the older folks were allowed to stay on and live out their lives on their homesteads after the park formed, mostly in the Cades Cove area. There's no one left in it now. Their children and grandchildren return for Old Timers' Day every year. No one's left to remember the old days, though.

"As for these border neighbors like old Hendrickson, there's the possibility of gettin' a land trust agreement with one of those land conservancy groups. They're eager to buy land adjacent to parks, keep it off limits to development, protect the watershed, patches of endangered plants, and so forth. Wiley could stay on till his death that way, still farm, and have some cash for creature comforts as long as he didn't develop it or cut down existing trees."

"What about the girl?" Ben asked quietly.

Shane nodded thoughtfully. "Yeah...once her grandfather dies, she'll have to leave, most likely. Even if she were allowed to inherit, there's no way she could handle the place alone. Her best bet's to get some more school, learn a trade to support herself."

Ben shook his head. "They're as endangered a species as those fir trees I keep hearing about."

"That they are...."

Both men settled back, riding in silence until Shane spotted a familiar figure up ahead. A ranger was sitting astride a big bay at the side of the road. Shane slowed to a stop and leaned across to call out the window, "Cal! What's up?"

The barrel-chested black man in a crisp NPS uniform leaned from the saddle to peer in. "Howdy, Shane! Just heading back to the stables. What you up to?"

Shane jerked his head toward Ben. "Showin' the new recruit around. This is Ben Morgan. Ben, meet Cal Evans the Cajun Cowboy, from down New Orleans way."

"Ponchatoula, to be exact."

Ben peered up at the big man. "They have cowboys down there?"

"My daddy was a farmer. Ponchatoula's the strawberry capital of the world. That's what we made our livin' by—that and sugar cane—and a little horse-racin' on the side!" he cackled and reached down a muscle-cabled arm to shake Ben's hand. "Nice t' meet cha, Ben."

The rookie ranger hesitated at the size of the hand about to engulf him, but was reassured by the man's easy grin. "Likewise," he returned.

"You two should have a lot to talk about. Cal's our horseback patrol trailmaster," Shane said, looking on. "Ben here just arrived from Wyoming, Cal. He worked on a ranch there for, what, four years?" He glanced at Ben, who nodded.

Cal Evan sat back in his saddle with a look of assessment. The well-worn leather creaked and the bay shivered, pawing the ground restlessly. The rider, nonetheless, appeared in no hurry.

"Well, what do you know? It'll be good to have another experienced hand around. Why don't you come over to the Cove stables when this character gets through with you? I'll show you around."

Interest sparked in Ben's eyes. "I'd like that." Shane started the truck rolling again and waved. "See ya around...."

Shane turned back to Ben as they rode along. "Hey, where's that Palomino of yours? You didn't sell him, did you?"

Ben bolted upright. "Are you kidding? Rodney Deerfellow's bringing him in for me, soon as a trailer's available. He should be here late this week or early next."

Shane's eyes crinkled. "Knowing you and that horse, you must trust Deerfellow a lot."

"Yeah...well...we go way back. It was Rod who gave him to us as a wedding present. Kind of a tradition in those parts. Wrangled him, himself. Figured I couldn't leave him in better hands—what's this?" he broke off, frowning.

Ahead, in a wide spot on the shoulder, a woman flagged them down, arms waving frantically. Shane pulled over and both rangers sprang out and the woman rushed up to them. Her clothes were dripping wet and hair clung to her face. She wiped the wet locks out of her eyes and struggled to catch her breath. Her knees started to buckle and Shane took her by the arms.

"What is it?"

"Our—our little girl! She slipped on some rocks at the base of the falls. We—we were taking pictures," the woman gasped. "She grabbed onto a rock in the river. My husband's trying to reach her. Please hurry!"

"Where is she now?" Shane pressed. Glancing up, he saw that Ben was already by the railing, peering down through the trees to where the Little River rippled and churned below. He pointed to something.

Shane let go of her and hurried back to the truck, flipping down the tailgate, and hauled out a coil of rope, a couple of life jackets, and a first aid kit. He glanced up in time to see Ben vault over the railing. The woman looked ready to follow. Shane slammed the door shut, slung the rope over his shoulder, and trotted over, gripping her by the arm. "Stay on the path. Meet us down there."

He swung around to get a bead on Ben's whereabouts. There he was, tearing down the slope like a teenager. Shane muttered under his breath and skidded down after him.

By the time they reached the bank, they saw the situation had worsened. Both father and child were now midstream in the river, clinging to separate boulders. The current swirled about them. In the woods beyond, a crevice in the mountainside harbored a cascade that tumbled down a jagged path. The father pushed away from his rock and let the current carry him to his daughter, arm outstretched for her.

The little girl let go with one hand to reach for him but lost her tenuous grip on the slippery boulder. With a terrified wail, she washed out of reach.

Shane took in the situation at a glance. The foamy current was sweeping her toward a treacherous stretch of water pitted with depressions he knew lay downstream.

Ben didn't break his run at the water's edge, flinging himself into the swirling eddies. Shane yelled to him and flung out one end of the rope. Ben caught it midair, threw it around his waist, and knotted it on his belt.

On the bank, the veteran ranger braced himself to pull as hard as necessary. He inched sideways to an old sycamore and wound a length of the rope around its trunk to use as a winch.

By now, Ben was nearing midstream below the child. Her squeals of struggle could barely be heard over the rush of water. He thrashed his way against the waist-high water, hit a depression, and disappeared beneath the water.

Shane lurched forward, heart in his throat.

Ben resurfaced, sputtering, and shook his head to clear it. A second later and he might well have missed the child as her arm flailed past him helplessly.

He lunged crosscurrent, grasping for a hold on the slippery little limbs—fingers, arms, hair—anything he could latch on to. A tiny hand closed around his wrist and elation surged through him.

155

He reached for the rest of her. But as he did, the water spun them both around. They collided hard into each other. The blow, coupled with the fury of the murky waters, stunned him. Despair enveloped him. He realized the surge might carry them both off. But Ben was not about to let go of his prize. He bobbed and burst clear to the surface, caught a glimpse of rock looming ahead and saw his chance.

He fought to swing around, shielding the child from impact against the boulders. Ben's back banged against the unrelenting granite. He grunted in pain but forced himself to press against it as hard as he could. Using it as a brace, he inched to his feet, trying to ignore the stabs of pain radiating down his back. The rope wrapped around his chest grated raw into his skin. Gulping and spitting, he found his footing and slogged to the bank, child hugged to his chest. He dared a glance down at her. The little girl lay limp, the tiny pearlescent eyelids shut tight, rosebud mouth slack. Something tightened in his chest. He thought of Mary Rose Bear.

His distraction cost him. He stumbled and sank to his shoulders beneath the water's surface. His head spun, his teeth chattered from the cold…limbs sluggish…lost his sense of direction. The pull of the current took over….

On the bank, Shane scowled and gave a tentative yank on the line. The rope pulled free, shooting out of the water. He slung a section of it around his waist, double-looping and clamping it to the utility hook on his belt. He charged into the swirling water, just below the terraced cascades where Ben was sliding, child held fast in his arms.

Bracing himself against a boulder, Shane reached out to halt their wild ride. He grabbed only a fistful of Ben's shirt on his first try but got a more substantial hold the second try, hauling Ben onto the giant flat rock beside him. Ben lay there panting, struggling to catch his breath as he handed the child over to Shane.

He carried her to the bank, laying her down gently on a grassy spot beneath the sycamore. The girl's mother and father sank to their knees beside him. Shane rolled her onto her stomach, turned her head to one side and rubbed her back. Water dribbled from her mouth. He rolled her back over and started mouth-to-mouth resuscitation.

Three breaths.

No response.

Beside him, the mother began to moan. Shane tried to block the sound out of his mind and tried again.

Three more breaths.

No response.

Ben staggered up and sank alongside, dragging a half-folded blanket. Dripping and shaky, he draped it across her chest.

Shane stopped to catch his breath and looked up. The rangers' eyes locked.

"Again," Ben urged, hoarse.

Shane bent over once more, placing his mouth over the child's nose and mouth, and gently blew. He stopped and put his ear next to her mouth, listening.

Nothing.

The parents sagged against one another, the woman sobbing.

Then…a gentle hissing, deep down.

It grew into a gurgling.

Water erupted from the child's mouth. A spasm jerked her upright and she broke into a fit of coughing. Just as abruptly, she froze, staring up at them all, eyes wide in fright. Shane braced for her to go into convulsions or fall back unconscious.

He was about to roll her back on her stomach when the little girl spied her mother. The child burst into a wail, reaching for her. The woman grabbed her up, tears streaming down her cheeks. Shane sat back on his heels, took a couple of steadying breaths, and broke into a weary smile.

He thought to turn around and check on Ben. Morgan had risen quietly and stolen away to retrieve his gear. Bent over and still coughing, Ben sniffed and glanced up.

Shane put a hand on his partner's back and leaned down to peer into his face. "You all right?" At Ben's nod, he straightened back up. "Good. Thought I was gonna have to resuscitate you next. Not something I looked forward to."

Ben rose with a smile but stopped upon seeing Shane's face. The veteran ranger flicked him a tight glance but looked away without another word as they were surrounded by a crowd of admiring spectators.

Back in the truck, Shane sat for a long time just staring out the windshield. Finally, he spoke, low but edged with fury.

"Don't *ever* do that again."

Ben looked up in shock. "Wh—? What do you mean?"

"Tearin' off like that, throwin' yourself into a situation. *Follow procedure.*"

Ben made a dismissive sound in his throat. "Don't go preaching *procedure* in my face. You know I don't operate that way."

Shane turned on him, the grip on Ben's arm like a vice. "I'm not talkin' words on a page here. In this job, you follow the ground rules or you're out. You can get yourself killed along with the rest of your team when you don't. That rope wasn't secured right. Y'don't slip knot a tie line when lives are at stake. You double-knot and fasten it to that hook on your belt. That's what it's there for. And you get a life jacket on yourself first.

Got it?" Shane let go of his arm and sat back.

Ben sagged in his seat, mulling this over.

"It worked out, didn't it?"

"You were lucky—and you had help."

"Damn good help..." Ben muttered.

Shane flashed a glare his way, not about to be buttered up. "Maybe." He turned his gaze out the windshield again. "Why do you think I had you assigned to my district?"

"Because I'm good?"

"No...so I could keep an eye on you!"

The younger man looked properly subdued as he sat back.

Shane sighed. "Look...I wasn't gonna tell you this but...Hayes had you put on probationary status as a condition for your hiring. I had nothing to do with it."

Ben's head jerked up, his eyes narrowing. "I guess I shouldn't be surprised. For how long?"

Shane shifted in his seat. "Six months. Then they'll see."

Ben stared into his lap, silent a moment. The fight had gone out of him, though whether from the fatigue of the rescue or the bruise to his ego, it was impossible to tell."

"Andie know about this?" he asked quietly.

A rueful smile touched Shane's mouth. "You know she has a way of findin' out everything that goes on—and you can figure she had a few choice words of her own—but she knew well as I there was nothin' to be done about it. You're just gonna have t' toe the line for a while. I know that's not your style but..." he shrugged and started up the engine. "Come on, let's get you home to change."

They rode in silence till Shane tossed gruffly aside, "What you did back there…it was gutsy but foolhardy. I don't take well to riskin' good men. Don't like puttin' any of my men at risk if it can be avoided."

"You make a good commander," Ben said quietly.

Shane wagged his head. "I just don't take this position lightly."

The two men's eyes met, both men recalling another time, another park, where Shane's capacity for good leadership had come into play. Twin avalanches at Yosemite had pulled in rescue teams from all over California. A rookie team staffed with volunteers had nearly gotten killed when the team commander jeopardized the men's safety in favor of a quicker route to one of the sites. Shane had gotten wind of it, charged over to the team's base camp and taken over, in the interim dispatching patrols to haul in two scouting parties at risk. Ben was one of the scouts brought in, half-frozen, having refused to abandon his partner, who'd busted a kneecap….

The radio's beep cut across their thoughts. Shane snatched up the comm.

"MacLeod here."

"Chief? Susannah here. We've just gotten report of a hiker with a possible broken leg on Meigs Mountain Trail, near the intersect with Jakes Creek Trail. One of his friends came to us here at the Elkmont Amphitheater in the middle of a workshop. Are you handy?"

"I'll meet you in five minutes," Shane answered without hesitation. He flicked a glance at Ben's wet uniform. "You okay?"

Ben nodded. A reluctant smile twitched at the corners of his mouth. "You call the shots."

Shane gave him a tight smile in return. "For the time being, yeah."

At the entrance to the Elkmont Campground, they were met by a young woman in an NPS uniform who trotted over to them. She had a sun-freckled, fresh-faced look about her, and the sandy-haired braid that emerged from beneath her ranger hat made her look very young. Shane did quick work with introductions and with a brisk nod, Susannah Corbin came right to business.

"This is the boy's friend, Allan Jenkins. He'll take you to him. Another friend stayed behind."

Once again, Shane pulled down the tailgate on the Blazer. "Is he on a slope or flat land?"

"Flat...now," Alan answered with a grimace. "He tried to cut short on a switchback. Ended up slipping to the trail below. Landed bad." The boy licked his lips. "We—We think the break's just above his ankle."

Shane continued to fish through his gear. "What age?" he tossed over his shoulder.

"Nineteen." The young fellow hovered at Shane's elbow. "Want me to carry something?"

Shane emerged from the storage compartment with a backpack and a couple of telescoping stretcher poles. He looked from the boy to Ben, noting that he had his pack on, ready to go.

"No thanks, I think we've got it." Shane nodded and they were on their way.

Still recovering from his last ordeal, Ben found the going uphill tough. It took them half an hour at a clipped pace to reach the downed hiker. He looked on as Shane knelt and, with an air of calm efficiency, felt along the hiker's injured leg. The teenager winced, eyeing the ranger apprehensively. Shane glanced up.

"What's your name?"

"Tim...Mayfield." The boy didn't meet the ranger's eyes straight-on. He seemed embarrassed by the whole situation, even through the haze of pain.

Shane sat back on his heels. "Well, congratulations, Tim. You've got a broken bone there all right. Fibula, looks like, just above the ankle."

"How bad is it?"

Shane was matter-of-fact. "Better there than the upper leg. Still, you won't be hikin' or playin' ball for a while. Maybe catch up on your readin'." The boy groaned as Shane turned to Ben. "Hand me that leg constraint sleeve, will ya?"

Allan, standing over them, gave a nervous laugh. "Tim never was one much for books."

The other boy joined in. "Oh, I bet we can dig up some magazines he'd be more than happy to look at."

Ben, hunched down beside Shane, looked up with a twisted grin. But he was more intent at the moment absorbing Shane's reassuring manner. Mastering that, he guessed, was the larger part of the job. He helped Shane slide the casing into place and fasten it snugly. Ben pulled over the carrier then, at the ready.

Shane studied their patient. "Lookin' kinda green, son. Better lay your head back." The boy complied as the ranger finished up. "Feelin' nauseous is common with a break. Nothin' to be ashamed of. Just try t' relax and let us do the work. We'll have you out of here in no time."

Shane turned to Ben. "Ready?"

Ben nodded and the two of them carefully lifted the boy onto the stretcher. Together, they maneuvered their way back down the trail, the boy's friends following close behind.

The two rangers shielded their eyes against the sun, watching the US Park Police helicopter lift off that would carry the injured hiker to Knoxville. University Hospital there was a frequent recipient of overzealous park visitors. By air, it was less than thirty minutes away. When the chopper disappeared from sight, the two rangers headed back to their truck.

"I learned a lot back there," Ben said as they got in.

Shane nodded absently as he started up the engine. "Yeah...there's a lot *to* learn, not all of it from books. Like that sleeve business...you don't necessarily want to tell them, at a time like that, it's to keep th' broken bone from rupturing an artery. It's especially a danger when it's th' upper leg, a broken femur. You just go about your business as much as possible without alarming 'em more than they already are. Sometimes th' calm part's harder to learn than th' medical knowledge. How much first aid training have you had?"

"Just the basics, really. I learned CPR in the Peace Corps and there were those Life Guard courses back in college—but something tells me you've got a lot more in mind for me."

"Well...I'd like to see you reach the EMT level—Emergency Medical Technician. In my opinion, all the Enforcement Division rangers should have that amount of training."

"Is that your level?"

Shane nodded. "In this park, we have three levels of first aid personnel. There are what they call First Responders, who have general first aid knowledge, CPR, and so forth—that much is required. Then you've got the EMT's, on a par with ambulance personnel, and at the top is the Park Medic. We have only one so far for the entire park. We're working on getting another so there's at least one per district. The Medic has the training to administer drugs, do the heavy-duty stuff.

"We also have an Emergency Services Coordinator. He arranges the training sessions, reviews performance, and handles the reports for major incidents in the park. I'm sure you'll be meeting him after our two incidents today."

Shane stretched to retrieve an item from the backseat floorboard. "In the meantime, here's a little homework...."

"A little?" Ben hefted the dictionary-sized volume that was handed over to him.

"A refresher course—before you take the real thing."

Ben flipped through the book. "Kinda old school, isn't it?"

"An oldie but a goodie."

"You got anything I could use to prepare for this FLETC business, also?"

Shane gave a little smile of satisfaction. "I might be able to dig something up." His nose wrinkled. "But first, let's get you home to change. You're beginnin' to smell like a wet coyote."

Ben sniffed his sleeve. "More like muskrat, I think."

An hour later found them standing in the middle of traffic backup, helping another ranger direct cars around the scene of a five-car fender bender.

"It started out a Bambi Jam," the other ranger explained. "One driver spotted the deer and stopped too sudden, then the four behind plowed into each other. Happens way too often."

Shane looked at his watch. "It's one o'clock. Come on, let's catch some lunch. Then I'll hand you off to Buck MacIntyre. He's the wildlife ranger you met other day. He can bring you up to date on what you need to know in that department. I think you'll enjoy that."

After spending all morning in the park, the teeming shops and restaurants on the streets of Gatlinburg were an onslaught on Ben's senses.

On the one hand, the town had the air of a tightly contained Bavarian village, sheltered on all sides by mountains that rose abruptly behind the hotels and tourist attractions.

On the other hand, it was part carnival, part artist haven. Bunched cheek-by-jowl were art galleries, pancake houses, T-shirt shops, rock shops, mountain crafts, and museums of the odd, interspersed with lodgings quaint, showy, or nondescript to fit the budget. The sidewalks were thronged with window shoppers being drawn into a particular establishment by its aroma.

The place smelled like a carnival as well…grilled steak competing with cotton candy, fudge, taffy, and funnel cakes.

Ben looked on in a daze as the truck crawled through traffic.

Shane followed his thoughts. "Yep…sooner or later all of these people make it over to the park and come under our jurisdiction."

Shane turned off the main drag into a tiny alley of a side street Ben knew he wouldn't have noticed. They parked there and walked through the gravel parking lot into an establishment that looked like a log cabin and smelled wonderfully of barbecue. As they were led to a window booth, Ben couldn't help noticing the deference paid to their uniforms as they passed other tables.

One middle-aged, balding man looked up, startled from his plate of ribs. Ben wondered if he had a guilty conscience or had simply parked illegally. A shaggy-haired young man in dingy coveralls took a draft from his beer and averted his eyes. Ben pegged him for having his share of run-ins with the law already.

A group of pre-teen girls stared at them and giggled behind their hands while the little boy in the next booth gazed solemnly over his sucker. The rookie ranger had a hard time resisting some self-conscious glances over his shoulder.

"Relax," Shane admonished as they slid into their seats. "People always think we're sheriffs or highway patrolmen at first. Ya get used to it."

"What'll it be, fellas?"

They glanced up at the waitress, a friendly-looking sort with a breezy manner and lots of red hair.

"I'll have the whole pig," Ben said wistfully.

The waitress threw a knowing look Shane's way. "Wearin' out another rookie?"

Shane grinned in answer and handed the menu back to her. "I'll have the chopped plate and iced tea, please."

"Make that two," Ben followed up.

The waitress left with a wink and a gentle whack to Ben's shoulder. "Don't worry, Honey, first two weeks are the toughest. You're in open season. After that, you get in the groove."

Ben rested his elbows wearily on the table. "The people are pretty nice about here—except when they're tryin' to kill you."

Shane chuckled. "You ain't seen nuthin' yet."

* * * *

Ben stood alongside Buck MacIntyre on the banks of the Little River, peering past the wildlife ranger's shoulder as he pointed upstream.

"There goes one now!" Buck whispered. A sleek brown mammal emerged from a thicket of mountain laurel, paused on the sandy, rock-strewn bank to sniff the air, and slipped into the water without a splash. It glided silently across the stream, submerged, and reappeared on the other side, a rainbow trout in its mouth.

Ben laughed out loud before he could stop himself. "Some catch! That's gotta be the first otter I've seen in the wild."

"There're close to sixty of these little guys in the park right now. We brought in ten last year and another ten just this spring. Half of them had babies soon after release."

They turned from the bank and made their way back up toward the roadside where Buck's vehicle was parked.

"What's the survival rate running for the young?" Ben asked.

"Depends on the area. Little River seems to be doing better than over in Cataloochee. There are fewer large predators here…also a smaller population of raccoons, beavers, and muskrats to compete with for food. So if it's close to ninety percent here and fifty percent over there, I guess you could say it rounds out to a seventy percent survival rate."

"Not too bad. What do they have, four pups in a litter?"

"Two or three is most common. We hope that we'll be able to approach their population back in the mid 1800's."

"How'd you get hold of those figures?"

"Oh, it's estimation, really. But there are some trappers' ledgers, fur-traders' exchange receipts from back then…plus settlers' personal accounts written down in journals, stuff like that we use to extrapolate from."

The two men paused to take one more look down the tree-canopied stretch of shallow water. Ben shook his head. "I wish I was as good a fisherman as those little guys."

"You like to fish?"

"Oh, yeah. Haven't had much chance lately."

MacIntyre warmed to the subject. "I can show you a couple places 'round here. Next time we both get some time off, I'll take you to Cherokee or Cataloochee Creek, if you want. I go every two or three weeks during the summer and early fall."

"I'd like that." Ben smiled, shoving his hands in his pockets. The two of them ambled up the embankment. McIntyre had one of those sincere faces that probably got him kidded a lot but Ben sensed a depth of thought beneath. The impression he got from their afternoon tramp in the woods was that of a man eager to understand and accept others, tempered by a native bashfulness.

They continued up a grassy slope toward the park vehicle.

"So what steered you into this line of work?" Buck asked.

"Well…I guess you could say I was a delinquent Boy Scout. Nothing but baseball and backpacking appealed to me. Ran off at sixteen and moved in with my best friend's family. They kinda turned me around. Terry's dad was a scout leader and a coach for the high school baseball team when he wasn't at his hardware store. I ended up going to college where Terry did."

"Where was that?"

"Colorado State."

Buck looked impressed. "Really? That's known as Ranger U. around here! So you knew then you wanted to be a ranger?"

"Not till sophomore year. Got steered into Conservation Studies. After that I was hooked. Had a blast as a summer intern at Rocky Mountain and that clinched it."

"Did you get assigned there after graduation?"

Ben shook his head ruefully. "No such luck. Got a stint as a summer seasonal at Glacier, though. After that, a round of budget cuts slashed programs and I had to look elsewhere. About that time I ran into Shane down in Mexico."

Buck stopped. "In Mexico?"

"Long story. Some other time," Ben tossed over his shoulder. He waited for the other ranger to catch up. "Anyway, he recommended the Peace Corps. Got in a little travel and some useful experience like surveying, reforesting, construction work, digging water wells…. How about you? Where'd you go?"

"Virginia Tech. I've got a lot of family up there. One of my uncles used to be a ranger at Shenandoah. I decided I'd rather go into his line of work than my father's."

"What's that?"

"Apple orchard. Goes way back. You have any idea how sick of apples you can get after twenty-two years? Coulda been worse, I guess. My mom's family in South Carolina wanted me to carry on their business since I was the only grandson."

"That being—?"

"Car dealership. Goes way back, too."

The two outdoorsmen groaned together.

Another park truck drove up alongside. Shane called out the window, "You two finished playin' yet?"

MacIntyre grinned, Ben noted, already used to Shane's dry humor. He held his hand out. "Thanks for the tour, Buck."

"Anytime."

. 14 .

The next morning, Shane picked up Ben again. But this time, they headed in a different direction.

Ben shifted in his seat, eager for what his second day might hold.

"Where're we going today?"

"I'm taking you with me to Cades Cove, your assigned district. They've been pesterin' me at the office to get you down there so they can get a look at you."

"So that will be my base of operations?" Ben asked.

"Yep, your home base...."

They rounded a curve in the road.

The Cove spread out before them in all directions...miles of soft, golden-green pasture as far as the eye could see...sheltered on all sides by the great slumbering ridges of the Smokies. The mountains presided over the Cove with an ancient dignity, wrapped in mystery with their shawl of blue-white mist.

The broad expanse of meadow, in particular, caught Ben's eye. Amid the lush grass dotted with wildflowers, a dozen horses of as many varieties grazed peacefully, their backs glinting in the morning sun.

The SUV slowed, the senior ranger content just to sit there, enjoying the look of rapture on Ben's face.

"Think you can handle this?"

Ben broke into a slow grin. "I think so...."

At the Cades Cove Visitor Center, several people looked up as the two rangers walked in. Susannah Corbin was the first to greet them, followed by two other rangers who emerged from the back offices. Shane excused himself and went behind the counter to fill in a logbook.

Cal Evans passed by and gave Ben a friendly whack on the shoulder. "I hear Shane took you out and tried t' get you killed yesterday but didn't have any luck."

"Yeah…guess I'll just have t' go out today and try again," Shane said without looking up.

Ben threw him an uneasy look. Evan's booming laugh didn't help much. He turned to find himself staring across the counter into the unsmiling face of a stocky, silver-haired woman.

"You must be Ranger Morgan," she said in a voice worthy of a grade school principal.

Ben held out his hand. "Call me Ben. And you are?"

"Melba Davis."

The corners of his mouth twitched. "Melba?"

"Melba," she stated with an unwavering gaze.

"You mean, like in—"

"Melba." The woman's lips thinned.

Ben eyed the hardening visage of the woman and conceded with a slow nod of comprehension. "Melba."

The woman remained stone-faced save for two cold blinks of the eyes. A crisp sigh and she continued, "Now that we have that settled, Ranger Morgan…when are we to expect you to report for duty?"

Ben eyed her askance. "I—uh—thought I already had. I was on patrol with Shane all day yesterday, when I wasn't with Buck MacIntyre over in Elkmont." He felt like an errant schoolboy having to explain his absence. Frankly, it chafed. As soon as the woman turned to retrieve some papers, he made a snarling face at her back. Susannah looked up, catching him, and their faces melted into grins of conspiracy.

When Melba turned back, Ben feigned rubbing a stiff neck. The older woman looked suspiciously from the female ranger to him and cleared her throat. "I understand this is your first assignment. Aren't you a little…older than the average rookie?"

Ben eyed her sourly. "So I've been told."

She cleared her throat. "In any case...I've discovered some discrepancies in your file that warrant immediate attention. Among them the matter of this incomplete physician's release form."

Ben squinted at the form she thrust at him across the counter.

"You are to report for a complete medical exam," she continued, "and have all necessary papers properly signed before the end of the week. I hope the importance of this is clear?"

Ben nodded solemnly. "Yes, ma'am." He turned to go.

"Oh...and Ranger Morgan...the regulation belt for the Park Service uniform is black leather, not...cowboy wear. This is not the Wild West." She eyed the hand-tooled belt with its distinctive silver buckle.

Ben took a startled look down at his waist. "Oh! That!" His cheeks flushed. "The other one's still drying out. I took a dunk yesterday. Had to change."

"She peered at him over her glasses. "A *dunk*? On your first day? I assume it was in the line of duty?"

"Absolutely." Ben chose not to elaborate.

"Very well." The jerk of her chin gave the impression of dismissal.

Ben took a steadying breath and tried to escape again, this time bumping into the District Chief, who clasped his shoulder.

"Whoa there! –Come on, got a message just in from John Gage over in Chilhowee. Bear problem. Need t' look into it right away." The two exited together.

One of the seasonal help, a college girl, looked after them.

"Talk about your tall, blond, and handsome...."

Melba pursed her lips. "Too handsome if you ask me."

Out on the sidewalk, Morgan turned back, caught them staring after him, and gave an impish grin, waving back.

Melba crossed her arms. "Land's sakes, that man's smile would make an angel blush." Getting no response, she looked at the younger women. Both were still gazing out the window.

Out at the truck, Ben paused by the door. "Just one thing."

Shane looked over the roof at him. "What?"

170

"Don't leave me alone with that woman again!"

"Melba?" Shane shook his head. "Hey…with that legendary charm of yours, you'll have her sidlin' up to you inside of a week."

Across the parking area, three men in a black Land Rover watched as the rangers got into their vehicle.

"That's him?" asked the man in the front passenger seat. He looked as though he had stepped out of the pages of Esquire magazine…sleek black hair, aquiline nose, and designer sunglasses.

"Yep, that's him." A husky man in cheap polyester and oversized shades leaned forward from the back seat. This one had the appearance of a local trying to mimic the look of the other man but failing by a long shot. "I saw him come in t'other day. Rickety Jeep with Wyoming plates. One of them rainbow families…all shades of skin, ya know? And dirt poor. I sweet-talked one of them front desk gals and she told me he's the new backcountry ranger in the Cove."

"Hmmm…yes…." The well-dressed man shifted discreetly away from the speaker. He had yet to get used to the reek of fried pork rinds, something called ramps, and—what did they call them? Oh, yes…hushpuppies. He coughed delicately and cleared his throat. "What did you say his name was?"

"Morgan" was the answer from the backseat. The husky one squirmed and leaned forward. "Ain't this kinda risky?"

The man in front smiled serenely. "Not at all. What could be safer than having a ranger guard our operation?"

* * * *

John Gage, it turned out, was a bear of a man, himself.

Ben tried not to wince when the man's paw engulfed his hand to shake it. The red-whiskered giant looked like a Viking. He found himself hoping they'd always find themselves on the same side of an issue. It took a while for his attention to shift from the man to the matter at hand.

171

"What do you make of it?" Shane was asking. He knelt along-side the carcass of a full-grown black bear that lay in the truck bed of Gage's pickup.

Big John rested his arms over the sides of the truck bed and wagged his head. "Damndest thing I ever saw. Wasn't any ordinary hunter did this. One shot through the skull and nuthin' taken, 'cept that slit in the side."

Ben reached out to sink his hand into the thick black fur and ruffled it, surprised at the lump in his throat. He forced it down with a swallow. Even after all these years, it still got to him when an animal's life was taken without good cause. "Such a waste..." he murmured. Glancing up, he caught both men's gazes upon him a second before they turned back to each other.

Shane squinted up at the big ranger. "You got any cult activity around here?"

Gage made a disparaging sound in his throat. "That's California stuff, ain't it? Although..." he rubbed his chin, "Some of that West Coast stuff's been creepin' into Asheville." He shrugged. "Coulda been some freaky high school prank."

Ben eyed the eight-inch slash on the right side of the animal's abdomen, something tickling at the back of his mind.

"Gall bladder...."

The other rangers looked up. "What?"

"It's valuable in Asian markets," Ben explained.

John Gage made a face. "What the hell for?"

"Some kind of medicine...maybe an aphrodisiac...don't know for sure. Just remember reading about it somewhere," Ben muttered.

"Sorry I asked." Gage turned back to Shane.

District Chief MacLeod rose with a sigh. "Looks like we got us some poachers with sophisticated tastes, fellas."

Gage frowned. "What do you want me t' do with it?"

Shane hopped down from the truck bed. All three men surveyed the large carcass silently a moment. Disposal was no easy matter, nor was preservation. It was, after all, evidence in a crime.

"Take any pictures yet?"

"Yep…took six on the site before moving it and three more close-ups here," Gage answered. "Oh—we got the spot marked on a trail map inside. I'll get it for you." He turned and lumbered over to the small cabin station.

"Thanks, John," Shane called after him. "Tell you what, let's keep it here in the shed till this afternoon. I'd like for Buck to get a look at it and be aware of the situation, too. In the meantime, I can call the boys at the State Fish and Game for advice, contact Customs, too, and find out if there's some protocol to follow here." He turned to Ben. "Let's see if we can find a tarp around here somewhere. It's gonna take all of us to move this guy…."

Half an hour later, they had managed to haul the bear's carcass from the back of the pickup into the small storage building behind the Chilhowee ranger station. Even with the use of a plywood ramp and the tarp, it was still hard to drag the two hundred-plus pound animal without disturbing it any more than necessary.

Ben straightened, rubbing the ache out of his back, and wiped sweat from his brow with the back of his hand. John Gage straightened as well, giving him a look of assessment. The big man stretched out his hand again. "Thanks for the assist, Morgan. Glad you came along."

Ben braced himself but took the hand. To his surprise, his fingers endured the crushing and still worked. Heading back to the park truck, he was surprised to find Gage following him. When they stopped alongside the vehicle, big John clamped him around the shoulders. This time, Ben couldn't hold in a wince. He eyed Shane on the other side of the Blazer, safely out of reach of the giant's cheerful camaraderie. John's booming voice followed as Ben made for the passenger door with purpose.

"Shane! You told Morgan here about Friday yet?"

Ben's eyes darted to Shane and narrowed.

Shane had a mysterious smile on his face. "Not yet. Forgot to tell him."

"See ya there, rookie!" Gage laughed and waved goodbye.

"No big deal," Shane said casually as he shoved the gear in reverse. "Just some routine rescue practice." He looked over his shoulder to back the truck up.

Ben sat back in his seat with a sense of foreboding. "Where exactly is this practice session?"

Shane bit back a smile as he pulled onto the main road. "Just some cliffs."

The next morning before work, Ben pulled his Jeep off Highway 321 near Cosby and traversed the sweeping gravel driveway leading up to an elegant old country home. The white frame two-story with its gingerbread trim and generous veranda sheltered by maple trees was not what he expected a doctor's office to look like. But sure enough, there was the shingle hanging from the lamppost. One arrow directed him to *Emergencies* around back, the other to *Reception* at a side entrance.

Opting for the latter, he parked, got out, and walked up the steps to the veranda, approaching a door with an oval window. He hesitated, then rang the door buzzer. No answer. Maybe you were just supposed to go in? He tested the doorknob. It turned easily and he stepped in, finding himself in a small parlor...dark green walls, polished oak floor, and Victorian chairs with wine-colored cushions. A carved mahogany fireplace with a marble mantle dominated one wall.

Ben's brow puckered. The place was quiet save for the ticking of a grandfather clock in the far corner. He felt like an intruder in someone's home.

There was a white paneled door to his right. He went over and pushed on the brass plate. It swung open, exposing what looked like a converted farmhouse kitchen, all white, with a black linoleum floor and glass doors on all cabinets. Glass bottles, metal canisters, bandage rolls, and assorted other medical supplies showed inside. An old farmstead table stood in the middle of the room and along the wall to his left was a conventional examination table, the first standard piece of equipment he'd seen in the place.

Spying a cluster of framed diplomas on the far wall, he walked over and was giving them a look when a voice came behind him.

"What can I do for you, young man?"

Ben whirled about to see a tall, spare, dignified woman in a lab coat. Her white hair, drawn up in a bun and her onyx earrings gave the impression of a genteel aunt rather than a physician. Still, her sudden appearance caused him to step back. "I'm—uh—here to see Dr. Alston…ranger physical."

The woman's eyes gave him a brisk once-over. "I am Doctor Alston. Do you have any of your records with you?"

"This is all I have." Ben handed her a manila envelope full of papers.

She pulled a delicate pair of glasses out of her coat pocket and laid the packet down on the examination table. One by one she studied the ragged slips of paper.

"When was your last physical?" she asked over her shoulder.

Ben shrugged. "Maybe five years ago…."

She turned and eyed him over her glasses.

"Maybe more like seven…or eight…." he mumbled.

The doctor pursed her lips, frowning at the tattered forms.

"Okay, Soldier, drop your pants. You're overdue two booster shots."

* * * *

That afternoon, Ben pulled up in front of the park headquarters. Shane, walking over from the adjacent visitor center, paused on the sidewalk to meet him. Ben emerged stiffly from the Jeep.

"I see Doc Lillian got hold of you," he observed with a wry smile.

Ben grimaced and rubbed a spot just above his back hip pocket. "Yeah…but you know…somehow, by the end of the visit, I think I actually liked her. She's an interesting character, isn't she?"

Shane nodded. "She tell you her husband was a ranger here? It was many years back now. Her family moved down to Asheville from Boston when she was still a teenager. She and Frank Alston met then. He's a legend around here, I understand."

The two of them passed another ranger, who was kneeling beside the walkway and engaged in a lively conversation with an elderly visitor.

"But ma'am, it really is against the law to dig up these plants. It's another form of vandalism, same as cutting down a tree or poaching. Some of these you have bagged in here are on the endangered list."

The ranger looked up hopelessly. "Back me up on this one, Chief."

The petite octogenarian brightened upon sight of Shane. "Why, hello again, Warden!" she greeted in a British accent.

"Ma'am." Shane bent down to study the contents of the brightly-colored tote bag. "He's right, you know. These are gonna have to be confiscated, Agnes. And this is absolutely your last warning. Understand?"

She nodded blithely. "All right, Warden."

Shane rose, meeting Ben's amused eyes. They walked on. Behind them could be heard the ranger's offer to help her to her car, minus the booty. Shane wagged his head. "She knows exactly what she's doing. That was ginseng and bloodroot in those bags. Both fetch a high price on the commercial market. I have a feeling we'll meet again. And there will be a stiff fine for Miss Agnes."

He paused at the fork in the sidewalk and fished into his pocket. "Listen, I'm gonna be tied up in meetings the rest of the morning, looks like, but I did get a vehicle cleared in your name. The garage is down there. Just show 'em some ID. They're expecting you. Then you can take yourself over to the Cove Station. Cal Evans will meet you there. He'll take you on a backcountry patrol. He's also got directions for the rescue practice session Friday morning. I'll check in with you later this afternoon at the Cove Center," Shane winked, "so you can have some alone time with Melba."

Ben's head jerked up.

"Just kiddin'."

Ben glowered. "Don't scare me like that."

"Sorry, couldn't resist. Actually, there are some manuals there for you to read. They should be under the counter. Susannah will know. You can find yourself a quiet corner and nobody will bother you." Shane clapped him on the shoulder. "Catch ya later."

Ben nodded and headed off for the garage, separated from the Headquarters building by a short winding path canopied by mountain maples. As he rounded the corner of the garage, a voice came from behind him.

"Excuse me. Ranger Morgan?"

Ben turned to find a dapper, European-looking man in tailored khakis and a polo shirt. The visitor smiled, white teeth against a perfect tan.

"I was wondering if I might have a word with you...."

* * * *

Friday morning...rescue practice at the Cliffs of Little River....

Ben discovered they'd saved the best for last in this, his introductory week on the job. Best, that is, if you enjoyed heights and the singular thrill of being wrenched over the edge into nothingness by a couple of fellows you'd met only minutes before. It took more trust than he could muster on the spot, and an ample suspension of reality to let himself be outfitted for his first descent by a kid who looked barely out of school.

Maybe back in college he would have tackled this sort of thing with a show of bravado, hiding his sweaty palms, but it had been a long time since he'd taken on any mountain climbing. That Chimney Tops hike he'd taken midweek with Shane satisfied his desire for heights for a while. How time changed things....

Unable to put it off any longer, he stepped forward through the woods, its tangled undergrowth of honeysuckle and wild grapevines snagging in the tread of his boot. Two men stood before him, perched on the rocky ledge to assist his descent.

With a scowl, he surveyed the broad expanse of river valley that lay a hundred feet below. At least it was a pretty place to die.... Maybe not the rugged beauty of his western mountains but it had its appeal. Wear Cove they called it...a pastoral community of neat, white farmhouses, faded red barns, and cattle grazing in what looked like, from way up here, an ocean pasture of green waves. Beyond slumbered the Smokies, curls of early morning mist entwined with the treetops.

Someone tugged at the harness encircling his chest, waist, and groin, checking its security.

"I *have* done this before," he grumbled. He turned and found himself staring into the eyes of another fresh-faced kid. The boy ranger hooked on the cable ad stepped back with a contrite, "Yes, sir!"

Ben opened his mouth to say something but let it go. Assuming the ready stance, he took a deep breath and let it out. At the *Go* signal, he abruptly reversed to face the cliff and pushed off, making sure to focus only six to eight feet below himself.

He swung out from the cliff face about four feet, knees loosely bent, and came to a bouncing stop, boots skittering against the rock. Some gravel dislodged, clattering down. He grimaced, feeling rather than seeing the stares up at him from the team below.

"Make your own rockslide, why don't ya," Ben muttered to himself. He attempted more spring in his next push-off and managed a more solid contact, sans gravel. But when he attempted to make up lost time, he winched out too much slack and grimaced as he was yanked down the cliff face some fifteen feet farther— and faster—than he intended to go.

He tried to cut short his groan of pain before attracting attention to his plight, but no such luck. The rangers monitoring progress at the base of the cliff looked up, Shane now among them.

"All right up there?" he called up.

A pause and Ben's frustrated voice travelled down to them. "Yeah...I'm fine."

He made it down the rest of the way without further incident, and was bent over, disengaging himself from the harness when John Gage lumbered by. The Paul Bunyan of the ranger corps almost sent him sprawling with a friendly whack on the back. "Happens to all of us now and then, chum."

Ben rose, stretched out his back, and brushed himself off. Another ranger, laden down with equipment, passed by with a rueful expression. "You think this was fun…next month some of us get to do it from a helicopter…."

Sore and weary, Ben pulled into his driveway that evening with a grateful sigh. Eyeing the dark windows of the little cabin, he decided to go around back. No one was in the screened porch either. He wandered down to the streambed that ran along the back edge of the yard. A figure reclined there in midstream on a broad, flat, sun-warmed river rock.

Her eyes closed, Tawnee basked contentedly in the late afternoon sun. Seeing her lying there, so peaceful, made his cares and soreness float away on the breeze. A smile spread over his face.

The water's gurgling masked his approach. He squatted, pulled a catkin loose, and reached over to tickle her cheek.

Startled, she rose on her elbows, shielding her eyes from the sun. The pucker between her brows relaxed into her gentle smile. She patted the flat boulder beside her.

Ben made his way over and stretched out on his stomach with a groan.

She surveyed the length of him. "Are you all right?"

He rolled over and leaned back on his elbows. "Yeah…had a little run-in with a rope during the rappelling exercise. That on top of the doc playing darts with my backside." He shifted with feeling. "All in all, a good week for a masochist. But…nothing you can't remedy." He grinned up at her. Tawnee's look of concern melted into a knowing smile.

He looked around. "Where're the kids?"

"Andie took them with her and Marcie to a children's program at the campground."

179

"Good girl." He stared downstream, taking in the peace and quiet. After a while, he asked. "Happy?"

She rolled onto her stomach alongside him, hands fiddling idly with a stem of buttercup. "It's beginning to feel like it could be home."

He noted the cautious optimism in her voice and gave her a lop-sided smile, knowing it had been a small death for her to move so far away from her homeland, her people. But she knew as well as he that their future had been a limited one there. They needed to take this risk.

For now, he would be content with her answer.

She turned, chin dipped to rest on her shoulder, and looked at him out of the tops of those lovely soft-fringed eyes. "And you?"

Ben raised his eyebrows. "Oh, this is gonna be great—if I can survive the next six weeks."

. 15 .

Andie stepped out that afternoon to plant some chrysanthemums by the front steps, a sort of pre-wedding compulsion. In the same vein as mothers-to-be getting that nesting urge, cleaning house from top to bottom the last weeks before giving birth, she'd been seized with the desire to get things just so before their wedding weekend commenced.

She was happily absorbed in her digging when she became aware of a car pulling up the gravel driveway. It came right up to the walkway and stopped. The window rolled down and a friendly male voice called out, "Hello, Beautiful! You must be the future Mrs. MacLeod!"

With a twisted smile and a ready retort on her tongue, Andie rose to view her accoster. The fellow who sat there smiling up at her looked to be somewhere between Shane and Ben in age. Something in his face said this was the kind of guy who sneaked out of his own bar mitzvah as a boy. The unruly brown hair and mischievous blue eyes told her who this was.

"And you must be Phillip Stevens." She brushed off a dirt-caked hand and extended it. "Shane said to be on the lookout for a big gust of wind from the West Coast."

Her visitor got out of the car and took her hand. His other hand rested over his heart. "Does this mean I can't come in? I promise to behave myself."

Andie cocked her head at his wistful look. "Oh, I suppose it's okay. Shane says I'm a sure cure for puffed heads, anyhow."

She led him up the steps and opened the door. "Come on in. Don't mind the buckets and mops. I scared Shane off good with my cleaning fit...."

That night the ranger lodge was once again the scene of old friends coming together to talk about the past and celebrate the future as the MacLeod household held its own quiet version of a wedding eve party. The majority of the celebrants, including the groom, appeared relaxed and jovial, but there was one notable exception....

"Looks like she's got a case of the pre-wedding jitters, buddy," Cal Evans noted as he nudged past Shane in the kitchen doorway. Both men cast a look in the direction of the bride-to-be who kept peeking out the window at the waning twilight.

Shane wagged his head. "She's afraid Ben's not gonna make it in. He was due to finish the FLETC course today and wasn't sure if he'd make it back up here tonight or tomorrow. I told her not to worry. Ben always cuts things close."

Later, Shane lay in bed staring off into the darkness. His mind wandered, keeping him from sleep. He thought first of Andie, worn out from her preparations for the big day ahead. She'd finally fallen asleep on his shoulder, listening to him and Phillip drone on into the wee hours about youthful escapades.

His thoughts then turned to Ben, slogging through that hot, humid, hellish obstacle course down in Georgia alongside guys nearly half his age, straining his heart out to make good on a dream deferred.

And then there was Phillip, now snoring on the couch in his rumpled Armani suit.

They'd all come a long way since meeting that day, by accident, along a desert highway fifteen years ago....

He and Phillip, his old college friend from Cal Poly, had taken off for Mexico on a last-ditch effort at a bachelor fling. Shane was to marry his college sweetheart later that summer. They were headed for one of the small coastal towns along the Gulf of California where, presumably, they could afford to lodge. Twenty miles over the border, however, their plans went bust when a tire blew on Shane's old Jeep. That might not have been such a problem if Phillip hadn't chucked the tire jack to make room for his camera tripod. Added to that, the first passers-by on the scene turned out to be a low-rider Chevy with three teenagers. The three pulled over on the dusty shoulder, hopped out over the sides, and swaggered toward them, looking over the situation.

"Nice Jeep," one of them sneered. He was presumably the leader, a stocky, muscular fellow with wavy black hair down to his shoulders and a black leather bolero over a bare chest. There was a long scar just above his navel and a nick over his left eye.

Shane was eyeing the skull and crossbones tattoo on the fellow's arm when another vehicle sped by—the familiar, somehow comforting putter of an old VW bug. Shane's heart sank a notch as it flew by. But then, in the distance, he saw it turn around and head back toward them.

The face-off came to a standstill as all five watched the newcomer pull over and park on the adjacent shoulder. Shane's heart sank another notch when the occupant emerged...tall, slender, blond-haired...probably one of those SoCal surfer kids, he surmised. Not much meat on him. Hardly a scare to these guys. But to his surprise, the young fellow had reached back into his car, pulled out a jack and a tire iron, and sauntered over to them, a loose confidence in his gait.

"Trouble?" he called out amicably.

Shane swore there was a smile in the mischievous blue eyes but took it for show.

"Yeah...damn jack broke," he called back. He threw a glance Phillip's way. Damned if he was gonna admit they'd been stupid enough to leave it behind!

As the boy came up to them, he casually pitched the tire iron underhand to Shane. "See if this fits."

Shane snagged it midair and swung it loosely at his side. Their eyes met for a split second and he shared the ghost of a smile with the kid. "Thanks."

One of the Mexican trio pointed at the newcomer's feet. "Hey, that's Santos's knife!" All eyes went to the onyx-handled blade sticking out of the tan cowboy boots. A ripple of unrest went through the low-rider set. One of them peered sideways at the blond boy. "Where'd you get that?" he asked in a voice gone hoarse.

Shane saw something click in the boy's eyes. The young fellow raised his right leg and pulled the eight-inch blade from its sheath. He held it up, letting the sun glint off its polished planes. Cocking an eyebrow, he deadpanned, "Santos didn't need it anymore."

Phillip gave Shane a look that said *What now?* When they looked back, the Mexican contingent was backstepping its way to the Chevy. Reaching the safety of its side, they vaulted in, and roared off in a cloud of dust.

Shane turned to their young rescuer. "Thanks."

The boy shrugged. "Just thought I'd even the odds."

"So who's this Santos guy?" Phillip asked, caution in his voice.

The blond head shook side to side. "Damned if I know. I just found this in an alley. Looked like something that could come in handy."

Shane wiped the sweat from his forehead with the back of his hand and broke into a chuckle. "All right, come on. We've got a tire to change, remember?" He jostled Phillip as he passed by.

Stevens stayed rooted to his spot, staring in disbelief at their new acquaintance. "That bluff could've cost us our lives!"

The boy, kneeling with Shane beside the flat tire, looked up with a frown. "It worked, didn't it?"

"That's the way they're supposed to work, Phillip," Shane admonished, then grunted as he wrenched off a lug nut. They made quick work of the tire change, but just as they were spinning on the last lug nut, they heard an ominous noise.

All three looked up, watching in dismay as the little VW started rolling faster and faster away from them. Down the sloping shoulder it sped, then veered off, rolled over, and tumbled down the steep embankment.

The three ran to the edge and looked down, wincing as the Bug tumbled over and over, landing, finally, in a heap at the bottom of the dry ravine.

For a moment, no one spoke. A cloud of dust rose toward them then slowly settled back down. After a space, the blond boy said quietly, "Oh well…easy come, easy go."

"I admire your attitude," Phillip said with reverence.

Hands dug into his back pockets, Shane rocked back on his heels, deliberating over the situation. "Looks like yer stuck with us. Why don't cha go salvage what's left?"

The boy broke from his daze.

"Uh…yeah…thanks."

Shane and Phillip looked on as their new friend scampered down the slope, scrambling the last twenty feet to reach the pile of rubble that used to be his car.

"Need some help?" Phillip called down half-heartedly.

"No thanks, I got it!" the boy yelled up to them, then wriggled his lanky frame around the jammed door on the driver's side. A sleeping bag and backpack came flying out before the boy emerged and proceeded to the back. There, he peeled off the license plate from what was left of the back bumper.

"Might save some trouble later!" he hollered up, grinning. Shane nodded his head ruefully. Beside him, Phillip called down, "Hey, you might want to scrape off the serial number on the front left dash, too!"

The kid gave Phillip a salute from the ravine. A couple of minutes later, he rejoined them by the Jeep.

Shane took a last look down at the abandoned wreck before they turned away. "Parkin' brake ever give out before?"

"Didn't have one."

The two older Americans eyed each other.

"That…that woulda cost extra," the boy muttered as they piled into the Jeep.

Shane rolled his eyes, popping the Jeep into gear. They lurched onto the highway, continuing their trek south

"What's your name?" he asked after a while, eyeing the rear-view mirror.

"Ben Morgan." The boy stuck out his hand gamely. Shane twisted 'round to shake it, introducing himself. Phillip did likewise.

"So where're you headed?" Shane called back over the buffet of the wind.

The answer came back, jostled by the rough road.

"Oh...anywhere's fine...."

Shane broke from his thoughts, smiling. That answer seemed to sum up Ben's approach to life in general. The consummate drifter. That first evening revealed another facet to him that would prove definitive....

By the time they reached the coastal village of Bahia Kino that night, they were hot, dusty, tired, hungry, and familiar enough to lob jokes each other's way.

Ben, it turned out, was a seasonal ranger, right out of college, who'd just been let go due to cutbacks. He'd spoken little of this beyond the basics, but Shane could see that he took the loss deeply, judging from his eagerness to look for happiness in the bottom of a beer bottle.

And there was something else eating at him, Shane gathered. It became evident when a carved wooden keychain fell out of Ben's pocket.

Phillip had picked it up, eyeing the letters etched into the back. "BJM, Ext.?"

Face reddening, Ben reached for it. "Just an old girlfriend's art project."

Phillip waved it out of reach. "I've seen *Esq.* after a name, but what's *Ext.?*

"Extension?" Shane offered with a grin. He leaned back in his chair and signaled to the waitress for a menu.

Ben made another swipe for the keychain but Stevens waved it out of reach. "Give," he pressed.

Ben leaned forward, eyes narrowing. He seemed to be gauging the situation. Shane began to wonder if he needed to step in to prevent bloodshed. But the boy gave in with a sigh.

"All right...it stands for *Extraordinaire*."

Phillip exchanged looks with Shane. "He must be really good at something."

Shane shrugged, keeping a straight face.

Phillip presented the wooden bauble on his open palm. Ben snatched it back with a glower.

"Oh...one more thing."

Ben leveled hot eyes on Phillip. "What?"

"The AC on the back?"

"Her initials...." He mumbled and looked away.

Shane said nothing till Phillip left the table for the men's room, then nudged Ben's boot with his own. "*Old* girlfriend?"

The boy's eyes came up to meet his and held a moment.

"Rather not talk about it."

Shane nodded in tacit agreement as Phillip rejoined them, just as the entertainment for the evening came in. If it was distraction the kid wanted, he'd come to the right place, Shane thought. The little cantina proved an excellent choice. The food was good, the drinks better—and then the band started up. Front and center was the most seductive little Mexican bombshell the three Americans had ever seen.

Their attention was glued to the temptress in the spotlight as she crooned, slithered, and beckoned mercilessly to all there. Phillip, his upper lip perspiring from more than the heat, leaned aside to Ben. "What do you think she's saying?"

"Something about *I want you, body and soul,*" Ben translated without moving his gaze.

"Ohh man...." Phillip slid back in his seat, jaw dropping in earnest. "So who do you think she means?" he groaned.

Shane fielded this one. "I think all of us." He scanned the crowd and took a last swig from his Dos Equis. But it became increasingly obvious who the torch singer was directing her words to...the blue-eyed, blond American boy in their midst. One more glance the kid's way and Shane rose, nudging Phillip's shoulder. "Keep an eye on Junior here till I get back."

Stevens nodded distractedly, hardly noticing he'd left the room. When Shane returned, it was apparent Ben's evening was not going to end with the last song. The young woman sashayed by the table on her way out, dropping a scarf into his lap. Young Morgan had swallowed hard, looked after her, then down at his lap...then bolted to his feet. Only Shane's iron grip on his wrist held him back. The boy stared at what was being slipped into his palm.

"I don't care what she says—use it!" Shane whispered.

Ben nodded numbly. "S-Sure. See ya...." He headed off, looking less the youngster and more the determined man on a mission.

Shane looked after him, heaved a sigh, and turned to Phillip.

"Come on, let's go. I think that's all the excitement for the evening."

"What just happened?"

Shane gave another jerk of his head and rose.

Phillip followed but started whining the second they were out the door, arms flailing in frustration. "How'd he do it? He just sat there and got the girl!"

Shane shrugged philosophically and headed off in the direction of their beachfront lodging down the street. "Some guys have just got it."

He and Phillip passed a restful if uneventful night at the Playa de la Conchas, falling into their beds after a stroll on the beach.

By lunch the next day, their young friend still hadn't rejoined them and they began to worry. Asking around with the adequate number of pesos eventually procured the information they sought.

The girl had a beach house outside of town. It was easy enough to find. The catch was, it was more like a villa. They could hardly believe their eyes, surveying the pink stucco walls with its lush, tropical courtyard.

"You thinkin' what I'm thinkin'?" Shane asked.

Phillip nodded. "Little Arielle's got herself a sugar daddy. And odds are, he could show up any minute. We better find Morgan fast."

They parked up the beach a ways, skulked their way through the gardens, and vaulted onto the veranda. Keeping low and hugging the wall, they took turns raising their heads to peek into windows. On the fourth try, they hit pay dirt.

"Bingo! Holy—you gotta see this!" Phillip exclaimed under his breath.

Shane yanked him down, glowering to mask his discomfort. "Come on! Let's do this and get out of here!"

"But...I don't think...we should...interrupt right now," Stevens managed with an awkward smile.

A thud sounded from within. Shane flinched in reflex, rising to peer in. He froze, eyebrows twitching, before slinking out of view.

They eyed one another.

"Do we just wait them out?" Phillip asked.

"I don't know." Shane felt a headache coming on. He wasn't used to feeling indecisive.

"Next question—do we *really* have to be doing this?" Phillip pressed.

Shane swore under his breath, mind awhirl, but finally came to a conclusion. "Yeah...yeah we do. He helped us out of a serious jam yesterday. He even lost his car because of us, remember?"

"I think he would've lost that car eventually anyway if you ask—"

"Shhh!" Shane interrupted him.

"What is it?"

Shane inched toward the balcony wall and peered over from the balcony. Sure enough, the little seductress had company. And it looked like El Hombre himself. A white Mercedes had pulled up into the circular drive at the front of the house. A barrel-chested guy in a pastel suit got out, followed by two beefy bodyguards. All wore dark sunglasses and slicked-back hair.

"Classic..." Phillip groaned.

Shane shoved his hand over his friend's mouth, still watching, then turned back, all business. "Listen good...I'll get the Jeep and meet you right below the veranda wall on the other side. You do whatever it takes to get Morgan's attention. Haul him out of there yourself if you have to. Hurry!"

The two scurried in separate directions. What happened next became the fabric of their collective lore for years to come....

As Shane sprinted back for his Jeep, Phillip tried to roust Ben from his stupor. Details became blurred, sketchy, even embellished over the years, but went something like this—

Phillip summoned up the courage to duck into the lovers' window and fire off his warning. *"Psst! Morgan!* Come on! Get outta there fast!"

Ben, it was said, raised a groggy head and looked at him in disbelief at first. But the little senorita caught on fast. This scenario was not new to her, Phillip guessed. She unwound herself from the covers on the floor, grabbed her robe, and ran to the door, listening. Heavy footsteps were audible, coming up the stairs.

The girl trotted to where Ben lay sprawled on the floor, and began alternately tugging and pummeling him with her fists, spouting off in rapid-fire Spanish.

Ben seemed to get the picture finally—so when Phillip cried out, *"Dive, Morgan! Dive!"* Ben did exactly that.

When Shane pulled up in the Jeep, he caught sight of Ben, clad only in a sheet, exploding headfirst out a window and tucking in as he hit the roof of the veranda below. The young Romeo proceeded to roll off the tile roof, landing with a thud in the back of the Jeep. He lay there, stunned, as Shane roared off. Bullets sprayed the air behind them. The subsequent two-hour run to the border was a record that had not, to their knowledge, been broken.

Down the road, Shane took time to squint in the rearview mirror. "Has he moved?"

Phillip turned to study the figure lying in the back compartment, prodding it with two fingers. "Hey Morgan! Wake up!"

No response. He swiveled back, meeting Shane's eyes. Phillip swallowed.

Shane surveyed the road behind them. No sign of pursuit—yet. But how long would that last? They couldn't risk taking time to pull over.

"Take the wheel!" he ordered. Wriggling out from under the steering column, he somehow managed to switch places with Stevens, maneuvering his skinny frame into the backseat as the Jeep sped on under Phillip's lead foot. In the cramped confines of the back, he squeezed in beside the boy.

"Come on, Morgan. You playin' possum or what?" Shane attempted to roll him over. That, at least, elicited a low groan. The kid stirred and turned his head, face scrunching up into a grimace. He shifted and Shane saw the welt on his temple. Shane winced, putting a hand behind the boy's neck to support him. "You okay, Bud?"

Ben made an unintelligible sound, nonetheless verifying he could hear and comprehend. Shane moved his hand then—and saw blood. Startled, he pulled the boy onto his back. Ben gave a sharp moan and tried to roll back into a fetal position.

Shane held him still and pulled down the sheet. "They nicked ya, huh?" he muttered.

"Little problem, guys!" Phillip yelled from the front seat. "We're coming up on the border in less than an hour. How're we gonna explain *him*?"

"Turn east!" Shane shouted back.

"What?"

"Forget Nogales…take the next road east. Head for New Mexico."

"*New Mexico?* Why?" Phillip yelled back.

"Anybody followin' us will be less likely t' look for us there. They'll be expectin' us t' head west."

"You think you got this all figured out, don't you?" Stevens cracked.

"This thing's got California plates, doesn't it?" Shane yelled back over the wind.

Phillip simmered down after that. "So what comes next? Where're you takin' us?"

"Las Cruces. I have relatives there." Shane shouted back against the wind.

Phillip screwed up his face. "But what about the border police?"

Shane looked down at the boy sprawled across his lap. "He's closer t' your size, I think. Lend him a T-shirt and some of your cut-offs. I'll bandage up this graze and lose the sheet."

Stevens stared into the rearview mirror, far from happy. "All right…but he's not getting any of my underwear! What about his head?"

"He can wear my ball cap," Shane offered.

Phillip peeked once more at the semi-conscious Ben. "We'll pass him off as your half-wit brother. He looks more like you anyway."

Ben attempted a goofy grin up at him.

"Thanks a lot…" Shane muttered.

His estimation of the boy edged up several notches though when they reached the border station. In hundred degree heat with a knot on the head and a bullet graze in the side…battling nausea as well, the kid had held it together. When they were ordered out of the Jeep for an inspection of the interior, Morgan stood along-side them without complaint. As to Ben looking green around the gills, Shane made his excuses for him.

"Montezuma's Revenge," he said to the station guard with a grimace. That seemed to suffice. They got back into the States without further incident. And only then did Shane give Ben back the wallet he'd confiscated the night before. Not only had it kept him from losing all his money, it served to keep his identity safe from the Mexican hit squad once hot on their trail.

Like he'd said before…the kid was lucky…with a little help from his friends….

Phillip had had enough, and took a flight home to San Diego. But Shane, after accepting the airline tickets his father insisted upon—with an affectionate "Get your tail back here!"—sold off his old Jeep and flew home to Sacramento, Ben in tow. Morgan proceeded to charm the whole MacLeod clan. There was some-thing downright Texan about Morgan's footloose attitude, his fa-ther declared. Little sister Olivia admitted to a crush on him, though she was practically engaged herself. But his mom, despite admitting Morgan's charm, stated flatly, "That one's got trouble written all over him."

Shane bought that Blazer he'd had his eye on and the two new friends, inveterate explorers both, checked out Old Sacramento, toured the Gold Rush towns of Sutter Creek and Angels Camp, and ventured on to camp at Mount Lassen. Shane then found the guy begging to come along when he reported to his new post at Yosemite. Against his better judgment, he let him tag along.

Too bad that funding wasn't available there to offer him a place but word came down that Glacier, up in Montana, would be short-staffed in the fall and winter and needed a seasonal. In the meantime, Ben hung around doing odd jobs, long enough for the wedding that August, held at the Ahwanee Lodge....

Shane thought briefly of that day and forced himself to move on. A new life started tomorrow. A stretch and a yawn and he thought to check his watch. What was he thinking? He'd better get some sleep. He was, after all, getting married in a little under fifteen hours. Rolling to his side, he tried to settle down, but soon rose with a frown. Swinging his legs over the side of the bed, he padded, barefoot, through the dark house...to the other end of the lodge, and the study where Andie had been sleeping since Marcie's arrival.

Treading softly, he stepped in and stared down at her for several moments. Brunette angel at rest...no doubts there. He bent down, brushing her temple with a kiss. Andie stirred and smiled sleepily up at him. She looked absolutely delicious.

Her brow crinkled. "What is it?"

He smiled sheepishly and shrugged. "Oh...nuthin'...."

Andie cocked an eyebrow and lifted the covers in welcome.

"Well...since you asked...." He slid in alongside her. "I won't tell if you won't."

Andie snuggled close with a drowsy smile. "Hush up, Cowboy. I need my beauty sleep. I'm gettin' married tomorrow!"

He pulled her close and soon both were fast asleep.

. 16 .

Inside the tiny robe room of the chapel on Lake Cheoah, Andie fidgeted with a flowered comb in her hair. An un-bride-like frown of frustration stared back at her from the mirror. Beside her, Olivia calmly retrieved the comb and pinned it in place, between Andie's intermittent jerks aside to peek out the window.

"Where is he?" she fumed.

"I'm sure he'll be here. Relax!" Livvie soothed.

Down at the lakeside, Shane was a picture of calm amid the frenzied activity around him. He knew he had the basics covered. Anything beyond that was someone else's problem. He'd said as much earlier to numerous individuals attempting to complicate his life this day. He turned to Cal Evans, who had just returned from checking on the bride's progress.

"How is she?"

"Still up in the air." Cal took his stand beside him and crossed his arms, beginning to show some concern himself.

"He'll make it," Shane assured him.

Indoors, Andie was still frowning into the mirror, giving her dress an impatient tug, when she caught the reflection of a man standing in the doorway, grinning. She turned with a cry—and proceeded to pummel his chest with her fists.

Ben only laughed as he fended off her blows. "I said I'd make it, didn't I?"

She stopped pounding long enough to sag against him. The last few days had drained her physically and emotionally. One fist rested against his heart.

"What took you so long?" she demanded.

Ben looked taken aback. "I just got in two hours ago!"

"Two hours? You could've called!"

"Hey, I took time to clean up! After driving six hours in this heat, you wouldn't have wanted me to come the way I was!"

She pulled apart from him with a sigh. Truth was, he looked—and smelled—wonderful. There was something terribly reassuring about his presence.

"I'm so glad you're here."

"I wasn't about to miss this."

The two melded into a quick, fierce hug. He pulled back to survey her. "You look great."

"Shut up." She sniffed, wiping at makeup that threatened to run. Stepping to the door, she peered down toward the lake. "O-Okay…they're waiting on us, I think."

Ben offered his arm gallantly. She looped her arm through his and they stepped out, pausing in the doorway before descending the steps and embarking on the path to the lake. A sizeable crowd had now gathered, a sea of faces looking their way. She recognized Rusty and Judy Calvert from Yosemite…and smiled to see Olivia surrounded by her husband and three boys.

Andie looked down, self-conscious, before glancing up at her handsome escort. "I guess I should, you know, thank you…for steering me in his direction. He's…the best thing that ever happened to me."

Ben looked over with that familiar grin that could melt stone. "I gave you to the best man I could."

Their eyes locked a moment before each looked resolutely away, saved by the sound of dulcimer music wafting up to them on the September breeze.

To the strains of *Ash Grove*, a plaintive old Welsh song played for generations in these mountains, the two wound their way down through the pines in the late afternoon sun.

Andie saw Shane turn and catch sight of her, a light come into his eyes. She threw him a big smile, delighted to see he'd opted to wear his ranger uniform, as she'd hoped.

She looked reminiscent of some early 1900's adventuress, herself, in her handkerchief-collared blouse and floral skirt of pale blue and old rose with graceful, flat sandals. Palms sweaty, she twisted her grip on the bouquet of asters, coneflowers, lilies, and garden roses. Ben, true to form, shunned either suit or uniform, going with khakis and an open-collar white shirt. A loose bolo tie sporting a silver bear set off with turquoise was his only surrender to ornament.

The two groups merged, Ben handing off Andie to Shane, then taking his place behind the groom.

The sun was just beginning to gild the treetops as the brief ceremony came to a close. The Reverend John Matthews closed the Methodist book of service and clasped it to his chest with a satisfied smile. "I now pronounce you man and wife. You may kiss the bride."

Shane hesitated, but only for a second. Andie coaxed him with a teasing smile and they locked lips. His hand sneaked up to clutch her at the waist, holding her to it. Behind them, Ben found himself staring and pulled his eyes away, forcing a grin.

As the new couple turned to face their well-wishers, Shane gave a thumbs-up, keeping a lock on Andie's waist. Ben whistled, leading the crowd in a round of applause. Then, leisurely, the line of guests worked their way up to the rustic lodge reception hall on the hill.

Inside, the guests milled about the buffet table, dispersing into small groups. Phillip Stevens looked up from his drink and spied Ben, sauntering over. "So…the Colorado Kid finally grew up." He held his hand out and Ben shook it, breaking into a twisted grin.

"Hello, Phillip." Jesse Morgan ran up at that moment and tugged on his father's sleeve. Ben leaned over as his son whispered something excitedly into his ear.

196

"All right, but don't go wandering off."

The boy scampered off and Stevens looked after him. "Yours?"

Ben nodded. "Jess. Going on eight."

Phillip shook his head in disbelief. "What's it been? Twelve years? Fifteen?"

"Something like that. How 'bout you? Got a family yet?"

"Nope...no...not me. Still playing the field." He took a swig. "Haven't found the right woman yet."

Ben eyed him. "My guess is you've found a couple dozen by now."

Stevens snorted and raised his glass to his lips, covering a sneer. "Look who's talking."

A flicker of impatience crossed Ben's brow. "That was another time, another person."

"I don't know, old ways die hard. Speaking of interesting women...that new Mrs. MacLeod is something else, isn't she?"

"Too good for the likes of you," Ben said flatly.

Phillip's eyes narrowed as they viewed the newlyweds. "Hey...isn't it our place to cause trouble or something?"

Ben cocked an eyebrow. "What did you have in mind?"

Phillip looked around, his gaze coming to settle on one corner of the room. "Follow me...."

Shane looked up to eye the two warily as they walked past, headed, he noted, for the jukebox. He was none too keen on the idea of dancing in front of a bunch of folks. In fact, if he had his way, he'd pay his respects to the guests and slip off with Andie as soon as possible.

But when the first words of the old love song started up:

Wise men say...only fools rush in....

he was caught by surprise. His eyes found Andie's across the room, seeking him out as well. She sashayed over and they met in the middle of the hall, both wearing twisted smiles at the way they'd been manipulated, nonetheless enjoying the moment. He took her in hand, looped her around the waist, and with a pivot of the heel, swung into a slow, easy rhythm with the music.

Shane looked past Andie's shoulder, levelling a gaze at his two friends. Ben looked far from worried. Phillip waved blithely back.

When the song ended, Shane thought to retreat, but then

Hold me, hold me...never let me go until you've told me...

came over the speakers and he pulled Andie back tight. She laughed in delight, the light in her eyes dancing. The rascals had somehow dug into his past, rooting out old favorites. Which was alright until the next one....

The operatic opening strains of *Cara Mia* burst forth. Shane's head jerked up. He looked truly dangerous now. Glaring, he made his way over to the two miscreants.

"Your favorite song from Mexico. How could we forget?" Phillip grinned, eyes glittering.

Shane flicked a glance that encompassed Ben, who shrugged. "Hey, all I remember is you hauling it for the border to this song, a lot of sand and wind in my face."

That didn't lighten Shane's scowl. "You're both dead."

"Excuse me..." Phillip brushed aside merrily and waltzed over to Andie, commandeering her for the next dance. She was still giggling too hard at Shane's flushed face to say no, allowing herself to be swept back onto the dance floor by her husband's inebriated but strangely endearing friend.

Shane planted himself next to Ben, who, at the moment, was doing a pretty convincing job of holding up the wall while he nursed his drink. "I thought the best man was supposed to dance with her next."

Ben shrugged. "Nah...that's all right."

Shane's gaze traveled from him to the couple on the dance floor. He took a sip from the champagne flute and let it settle. "Strange how her parents didn't show up."

Ben shook his head. "Not surprised. Last I heard, they hadn't spoken since the day we graduated from college."

Shane's sidelong glance said volumes. "I assume that had something to do with you?"

Ben looked down at his shoes and glanced back up. "Maybe so."

Shane wagged his head. "I don't want to know." He promptly changed the subject. "So…did you pass FLETC or what?"

Ben knocked back the last of his drink. "You think I'd have the guts to show up if I didn't?" His grin was a weary one.

Shane met his eyes squarely, but softened it with a faint smile. "Sounds like we got us another little ceremony to perform, then, before taking off this evening. Cal can witness for you."

Ben nodded distractedly. Over the jukebox, to his chagrin, came another oldie but goodie he recognized all too well, the Vogues' *You're the One*. Memories from a college dance-a-thon came flooding back. And there was Andie, standing in the sea of guests, eyeing him back, a wistful look on her face. She jangled a hand out to him. He hesitated, then lay his glass aside, crossing to her.

She drew him close, whispering in his ear. "Come on, boy, let's show 'em how it's done. For old times' sake." She kicked off her shoes.

Ben came to himself, taking the situation in hand, and the two treated their audience to an artful fandango, clear they were accustomed to each other's moves.

Ben slid his hand down her back and loosened up, staring into the glowing face of his dance partner. The summer of outdoor life suited her. There was an unaccustomed smattering of freckles across her nose and her dark hair glinted auburn now. A tan line shone golden against the plunging V-neck of her eyelet blouse. Idly, he found himself wondering to what extent the sun had kissed other regions…but didn't let his thoughts dwell too long there.

When he swung in close, he noticed her eyes held the glittery look of a six-year-old too bubbly to contain herself. "Happy? Or too much champagne?" He smiled down indulgently.

Her smile in return was exuberant. "Oh, *very* happy…and very much in love."

He gave her a twirl out and back to his clasp, staring past her shoulder. "With Shane I hope."

"With Shane…with you…with life in general right now, I guess…." She sounded almost too exultant.

His smile twisted. "Know what you need?"

"What?" she panted. Those spirited eyes locked onto his, threatening his resistance to the core.

With effort, he broke free and spun her back to Shane, where she collapsed, giddy, into her new husband's arms.

"Better hold on to this one. She's dangerous," Ben handed her off with and headed away.

Shane caught the feverish light in Andie's eyes. "I think it's time to take you home, Girl. But first…." He nodded to Cal Evans nearby. "Grab your family. Ben's too. I'm not leavin' town till this is seen to…."

By the soft glow of candlelight in the old log chapel, District Chief Shane MacLeod gave newly-fledged ranger Benjamin Jay Morgan his oath of commission as a law enforcement and public protection officer in the National Park Service.

Ben stood before his friend and mentor, right hand raised, and repeated the oath after him. In their midst stood the new wife of Chief MacLeod, holding a small candelabra. Tawnee Morgan stood solemnly at her husband's side, a faraway look in those topaz eyes as she held a sleeping little girl.

Outside the window, a young boy with those same eyes looked on intently. His fair hair and the quizzical frown on his face echoed the features of the man inside now shaking the District Chief's hand.

"Come on, Jess!" whispered his companion, a tall, slender black boy who looked to be a couple of years older.

"Just a second, Ty!"

Jesse Morgan took one last look, satisfying himself the proceedings were over, and stole away with his friend once more.

* * * *

It took a family of raccoons foraging at the garbage cans, clanging lids, and squeals from a couple of attendees to finally break the party up in the old hall. By then, the moon was high, past time for the honeymooners to hit the road.

Their guests followed them outside to the new Blazer parked there. Its sleek black finish was now festooned with camouflage net, stuffed animals, streamers, and balloons, plus the requisite tin cans tied to the bumper, bearing the label *SPAM.*

Shane stared in disbelief. Buck MacIntyre, Jesse Morgan, and Ty Evans, rose slowly from the side of the truck, their faces smeared with grease. Ben shrugged at Shane's side. "Couldn't be everywhere at once…had to delegate."

Shane shook his head. "We're gettin' outta here. Where's that daughter of mine?"

Marcie appeared, pushing her way through the crowd. Mysteriously, she had grease on her face, too. Nonetheless, he pulled her close to his side. "You be good for the Morgans, now, hear?" he whispered into her hair.

She nodded wistfully, holding on a second before letting go. Ben tugged her to him and tousled her hair. The crowd threw rice as the newlyweds got in and drove off into the moonlit night. Ben slid an arm around Tawnee's waist and joined the others in waving good-bye.

Cal Evans chuckled. "Happy trails, cowboy."

Everyone watched until the Blazer disappeared over the hill, then leisurely dispersed. Cal turned to joke with Ben but he was nowhere in sight. Puzzled, he went searching….

* * * *

Shane glanced over at his California girl turned Smokies bride. "Barbecue and cheap champagne…probably not the reception you ever pictured having."

Her eyes still sparkled though now there was a hint of weary contentment in them. "Are you kidding? It was perfect! I couldn't have imagined having more fun."

"Sorry about those raccoons crashin' the party."

She giggled. "Appropriate, don't you think?" Nestling her head against his shoulder, she closed her eyes, napping as they drove into the sheltering embrace of the dark mountains that loomed ahead.

* * * *

Cal discovered Ben on the deck of the reception lodge, over-looking the lake. He seemed to be contemplating the starry sky overhead. Regarding him silently a moment, Cal stepped forward. "Mind if I join you?"

Morgan looked up in surprise. There was a furrow in his brow Cal wasn't used to seeing.

"Not at all." The response was civil but tight.

Cal noticed that the ranger's eyes quickly wandered else-where.

"You okay?"

The flicker of a frown crossed Ben's face. "Yeah. I'm fine." He turned back to stare at the lake through the trees.

Cal did likewise, for a moment. His voice then came, low but clear in the night air, "So…you two used to be an item, huh?"

Morgan's face turned sharply, half lit by the glow from the windows of the hall where people were starting to pull down the decorations, and gather up chairs. Cal sensed the melancholy there.

Ben said nothing at first, then sighed, turning away. "That was a long time ago."

"Not long enough maybe?"

Ben's face jerked toward him again, a retort there bitten off.

Instead, he shoved his hands in his pockets and brushed by him. "It's okay. Really. See ya 'round."

The reception hall was still brightly lit, though empty of guests now. Ben ambled inside and, just for a moment, stood in the middle of the cavernous lodge. With its stout, roughhewn walls and those massive beams high overhead, the old place held a reassuring ambience. Some things didn't change…. He soaked up the quiet as snatches of memory from the evening flooded through him.

A noise outside brought him out of his reverie. He turned, making out the figure of Phillip Stevens on the front porch. Leaning on the rail a bit heavily, it appeared. A rueful smile touched Ben's lips. He shook his head and headed out to join him.

Phillip didn't look up at his approach, just started in morosely, "You know what coming here, seeing you guys has convinced me to do?"

Ben was game, ready to focus on something…anything…else. "What?"

"That I should chuck it all and be what I wanted to be, all along."

Ben cocked his head, intrigued but wary. "What's that?"

"A professional photographer."

"Oh good…I was afraid you were going to say *ranger*."

"*Right.* You know I don't like to get that dirty."

Ben snorted. "Then do it."

Phillip wagged his head sorrowfully. "I'm a *dentist*. How did *that* happen?"

He had nothing to offer there.

"Think my patients could manage without me?"

"I'm sure."

Phillip looked up sharply. Ben just shrugged. Phillip dismissed it with the ghost of a smile. "You're right, of course. You know…I think I'll always be unhappy till I do…."

Ben held his peace for a respectful silence before venturing, "Maybe you wouldn't drink as much then."

Stevens didn't haul off and tear into him, as he half expected, just nodded glumly.

"Sorry 'bout bringing up that story about the triplets from Truckee…."

Ben sighed. "That's gonna take some explaining. Maybe we can just pass it off as you being so drunk you were confused."

"Maybe so…." Phillip grimaced. "Were there any women I *didn't* hit on tonight?"

"I don't think you missed any. Not even the bride."

The fellow at least had the sense to groan, rubbing his face. "The last thing I should've done was hit on her…or your wife…."

Ben's eyebrows arched skyward. "You hit on my wife?" He considered this long enough just to scare Stevens a little bit.

"I guess I can let that go this time."

Phillip wagged his head. "I feel really miserable about that…but you know, she is a beautiful woman…and I was base drunk. You're a champ. I mean…if it'd been my wife, I prob'ly woulda slugged me…I mean—"

"Don't push it, Phillip."

Stevens wasn't done with his wallowing.

"I made a total fool of myself, didn't I? I don't see how I can face any of those people again. And sweet little Tawnee—"

"You're pushin' it, Stevens."

"—she's so…sweet…you know…so kind…so gentle. She didn't make a fuss at all. And you know, she's got that little wild doe look in her eyes and the most exquisite li'l—"

"*Phil*—"

Phillip paused in his rambling long enough to look up—just in time to see the fist that made contact with his face. It sent him sprawling backwards—and almost over the rail, if Ben hadn't followed up with a snatch at his lapel in time to catch him.

There was a warning glint in Ben's eyes.

"*I know.*"

Both men settled back unsurely. Phillip felt along his cheekbone then patted half-heartedly at his rumpled suit.

Ben turned to walk off.

"Thanks. I feel much better now…" Phillip mumbled behind him. The guy sounded genuinely repentant.

Ben stopped in his tracks. "You're welcome." The echo of a growl was still in his voice. He turned back and was treated to the sight of his friend settling unsteadily onto a bench, massaging his sore jaw.

"God help me...."

Ben broke into a chuckle. "God help you." He walked back to him and jostled his shoulder. "Come on. I'll drive you back."

. 17 .

Carefully scheduled between the Labor Day weekend and the crush of the fall season, Shane had allotted no more than ten days for their honeymoon, but strove to cram as much into that time as possible. Keeping Andie in suspense, he drove them over the mountains to the Inn at Biltmore for the night. The next morning at breakfast downstairs, along with tickets for a Biltmore tour that day, he surprised her with some tickets for a cruise to the Bahamas.

Andie was speechless at first.

"Is this a good kind of speechless?" he asked, concerned that perhaps he'd miscalculated.

She sputtered a laugh. "Most definitely! It's just so...."

"Not like me?"

"Not what I would have seen coming!"

He reached across the table to squeeze her hand. "Never let it be said I can't show a girl a good time."

"Just one thing." She chewed her lip.

He felt a thud in the pit of his stomach. "What's that?"

Her mischievous eyes crinkled. "You know this means I'm going to have to buy a new swimsuit!"

With a chuckle of relief, he leaned back in his chair.

"I think we can manage that."

The next evening, as they leaned on the rails of the Norwegian liner, taking in the ocean breeze and a gorgeous magenta and orange sunset, Andie brushed a strand of windswept hair from her face and turned to her new husband, a look of wonder in her eyes. It was still hard to believe they were here...that she was seeing the ranger...the man...out of his element.

"Shane MacLeod, I do believe you're reinventing yourself."
He slipped an arm around her waist, tugging her to him.
"You helped."

*   *   *   *

Despite Shane's concerns, the North District did not fall apart in his absence.

The 'tween season lull of September picked up come the first of October, when those in search of fall foliage descended upon the park like a storm. This was an older crowd in general, especially during the week. Weekends brought in families and hikers, lured by the crisp nights and crystal blue skies that made for the best in camping and nature treks.

The rangers found fewer injuries to tend now than in the summer, but more intense traffic snarls. They joked about contracting a full-time mechanic for the park, there were so many fender benders and minor car problems to oversee.

Ben admitted he had yet to figure out how to maintain Park Service demeanor during a tire change when the girl kept flirting with him and her boyfriend stood over him with a tire iron in his hand.

With Marcie now at school in Townsend, Andie took advantage of her free mornings to take up nature photography, an interest she had always kept in her back pocket. Inspired by some of the artists ensconced in the Gatlinburg area, she considered trying her hand at framed works and notecards. Pottery also beckoned. Though she could never hope to reach the craftsmanship of those in the area, it still looked like loads of fun, and would get her out there meeting the locals. Now she felt ready.

For the MacLeod household, autumn meant cookouts on the deck and canoe rides on the lake when Shane could grab time off. Weekends were often his busiest times, though the ranger ranks tried to spell one another.

After an Indian summer and a brilliant fall, winter hit with a vengeance. The thinned ranks of the ranger staff, minus their seasonal help, found it was all they could handle, keeping up with the workload Mother Nature handed them.

Shane was right. Winter was not a time to kick back as some presumed. The work that eased up from the decrease in visitors was offset by the natural pitfalls of the season. There were roads and trails to clear after ice storms, roads to barricade, stuck vehicles to free, daily checks of building conditions as well as keeping an eye on the various animal populations. Avalanches and mudslides in the higher elevations, floods in the lower regions, and periods of high wind all served to worsen the routine hardships.

Signs of the winter's severity were evident everywhere in the park....

The sign at the Cherokee entrance was covered with a cap of snow nearly a foot high. Personnel struggled to keep clear the walkway to Sugarlands Visitor Center on the Gatlinburg side. The mountain village itself was a winter mecca for tourists and honeymooners, and Sugarlands was the most heavily visited center in the National Park Service, but even it had to close some days.

Cal Evans and Ben Morgan struggled to free the horses at Cades Cove Stables from their snowbound barn and spread out plenty of hay. Buck MacIntyre spent a backbreaking afternoon trying to free a young deer caught in the forked trunk of a snow-clad tree, knee-deep himself. Ben, lending a hand to a local relief mission spearheaded by Reverend Matthews, was stunned by the number of normally self-sufficient mountain families who showed up at his Christmas train, in hopes of food, clothing, and perhaps a toy for their little ones.

And though generally a hardy crew, the rangers were susceptible to the same winter illnesses and accidents as other people. One icy morning, while carrying firewood, Shane himself slipped, banging face-first into the side of the lodge....

At the Cades Cove Center, everyone looked up in surprise when the door opened on this cold, reclusive day. Shane trudged in, stopping to stamp his boots on the mat. When he turned around, the big white bandage covering the bridge of his nose became visible. Melba, Susannah, and Buck tried their best not to stare but found it impossible.

"Don't ask," Shane growled. He ambled stiffly over to the counter and began to flip through some papers. Buck broke into a coughing fit. Shane glanced up, giving him a bleak look.

"Go home."

Buck looked from his desk, sniffing, his nose red, eyes watering. "I won't argue," he rasped.

The District Chief sighed, noting the hushed emptiness of the office, and turned to Susannah. "Wasn't Morgan supposed to report this morning?"

"I...heard he got the mumps, sir."

"The—?" Incredulity was replaced by an odd compulsion to laugh. He restrained himself, though a slow smile crossed his face as he wagged his head.

"Apparently, he caught them from one of the mountain children last week...you know...at the train?" she explained delicately.

The door opened then and who should walk in this time but Ben himself. He turned from hanging up his parka on a wall peg to witness all the stares in his direction. Shifting his shoulders and making his way to his desk, he winced, but his scowl was dangerous. "Don't ask. It wasn't mumps. Just felt like it."

The others returned to their work, trying to hide their smiles. Buck, however, couldn't resist. Spreading his lunch out on his desk, he unwrapped a sandwich and looked up innocently.

"Want a pickle?"

Ben issued a low groan, clutching the still swollen glands under his jaw. Buck was unprepared for the paper wad hurled at his head a second later, ducking but not in time.

Shane passed them on his way out, pausing at the door to grin. "You kids try to behave yourselves while I'm gone, hear?" Grimacing, he yanked the door open, venturing back out into the blustery, flurry-ridden air.

Reverend Matthews paused a moment at the door of the District Ranger's lodge before knocking. He was not normally given to peering in the windows of his parishioners, but this young woman had captured his curiosity for some time now.

He could see her through the windowpanes of the door. She sat cross-legged on a mat on the hardwood floor, in the midst of what looked like Yoga exercises. The incongruous throb of rock music was audible to the outside. He smiled to himself. Time to get to know the Smokies' newest free spirit.

There was a child-like vitality behind those dancing eyes of the new Mrs. MacLeod—and a wounded innocence, he sensed, beneath that breezy, sometimes feisty front. Not one to be trifled with, nor one to suffer subterfuge, from him or anyone else, he'd observed. She could give as well as she got. So why had she withdrawn to the seclusion of a ranger's cabin deep in the mountains of Tennessee? Was she hiding from something? An intriguing question....

And beneath this hermit existence, she had been withholding her talents from the world. His ear captured the sound of her clear alto, free of affectation. How well it expressed the buoyant energy he'd come to associate with her. True, her music tastes tended toward the more primal music of youth, but perhaps she could be swayed—

After all, it was a minister's job—wasn't it?—to draw out the hidden strengths of those under his care and nudge them gently onto the right path. He certainly had his work cut out for him. It was a tough bunch to nurture, this new set.

There was MacLeod himself, a hard nut to crack, though he understood him better now...a straightforward man though one who preferred his feelings under wraps. But it was becoming evident where his vulnerabilities lay. MacLeod was the strong, silent, duty-bound hero of the group. He could deal with such.

Then there was that Morgan chap, an iconoclast if he'd ever met one, but one with heart. The fellow had already made his presence felt in the Cove community. A hardworking, headstrong self-determinist with lady-killer looks, he seemed inextricably linked to trouble—but more often than not, tied to some greater good. It

210

spoke well of MacLeod that he had the insight to cut the young fellow some slack now and then.

Morgan might be bound by nature not to make an easy peace with any man of the cloth, but John Matthews respected his style nonetheless. Definitely a complicated crusader there.

While there were many other psyches to plumb among his flock, each weighing upon his mind these days, these three new-comers intrigued him the most. Certainly, they had brought with them a new dynamic to the region.

But he wasn't about to get anywhere on his mission just stand-ing here. "Knock and the door shall be opened unto you—but first you have to knock."

The door, indeed, opened at his request. There she stood, with that mixture of warmth and wariness in her eyes.

"Hello, Rev! What brings you out this way?"

He took off his rain hat. "Mrs. MacLeod, I hope you'll pardon the intrusion. I…have a proposition for you."

Eyebrows raised quizzically, she ushered him in….

The weekend before Christmas, the weather cleared up, a be-nevolent gesture on nature's part. Deftly swept away were the snow clouds that had plagued the mountains for weeks on end. Left behind was a dazzling display of sunlight on glistening white meadows and evergreen boughs bejeweled with crystalline pen-dants.

The ranger families took advantage of the good fortune by summoning up an impromptu holiday party to raise spirits weighed down by the demands of the past weeks. Everyone was eager to dig out and venture forth on this bright Sunday morning.

Reverend Matthews issued a special invitation to all the Cove families, with the promise of a "most satisfying and memorable gathering in store for all."

Even the habitual absentee, Ranger Morgan, showed up with his young family on this "fine new day of Creation" as the minster pronounced in his hearty greeting. And for once, the restless trailblazer sat in the pews without his customary expression of be-mused skepticism. Even he seemed at peace with the world this morning.

"And now, if you will refer to your program, you'll see we have a treat in store for us." John Matthews looked down upon his congregation with satisfaction. He'd just finished his homily with-out detecting a single head nodding, an accomplishment in itself, not to mention what was to come.

His eye caught Andie MacLeod's, caught the dip of her head in response. She took her cue, rising to leave her husband's side. The ranger's eyebrows flickered but he kept any questions to him-self.

John Matthews met her on the stairway behind the choir loft. Her cheeks were flushed and she was chewing her lip. "You have a way about you, don't you?" she whispered. He smiled and wrapped an arm about her shoulders for a quick squeeze. "You have a gift! Share it!"

Andie took a deep breath and sneaked a peek at her audience before stepping out. She walked, unannounced, down past the altar and took her place, front and center. For one paralyzing instant, her mind went blank. She could only focus on the hammering in her chest that threatened to become audible. It had been so long....

Swallowing hard, she glanced over her shoulder at John Mat-thews. He smiled encouragement from the doorway. She turned back to face the congregation, hands folded before her, and shut her eyes.

Softly, she began to sing, a capella:

> *Hark the herald angels sing,*
> *Glory to the newborn King.*
> *Peace on Earth and mercy mild,*
> *God and sinners reconciled...*

Her eyes fluttered open and she found herself staring at the rafters. Her gaze dropped and went by instinct to Shane. She sensed the shakiness in her neck, her voice as well, but drew strength from the warmth in those steady eyes. He sat ramrod straight, attention fixed upon her. Beside him, Marcie's mouth hung open. Others, she saw, had straightened, also. Taking a deep breath, she launched into the second verse, gaining nerve:

> *Mild he lays his glory by*
> *Born that man no more may die,*
> *Born to raise the sons of Earth,*
> *Born to give them second birth...*

Her gaze fell upon Ben, catching his twisted grin, the teasing yet pleased spark in his eyes as he crossed his arms and leaned back. A smile twitched at the corners of her mouth. She was hitting her stride—

The reverend nodded to Melba Davis, perched upon her accustomed seat at the organ. With a little bounce, she swung into action, accompanying Andie as she broke into the third verse, reaching the crescendo:

> *Hail the heav'n-born Prince of Peace,*
> *Hail the Son of righteousness...*

Andie caught sight of the minister maneuvering to the back of the church, quietly opening the doors. He put a finger to his lips as a huddle of children entered hesitantly. Dressed in faded but neatly laundered clothes, hair slicked back or tied with sprightly bows, they stuck together as one, staring with eyes large in wonder and maybe a little fright.

With a gentle prod, he sent them on their way. The children made their way toward Andie. Her gaze flew to the reverend midst her singing:

> *Light and life to all he brings,*
> *Ris'n with healing in his wings...*

213

The congregation stood and voices joined hers as the children began to gather about her.

> *Christ the highest heaven adore*
> *Christ the everlasting Lord*
> *Come desire of nations come*
> *Fix in us thy humble home*
>
> *Come desire of nations come,*
> *Fix in us thy hum-ble...home...*

At the back of the church, John Matthews crossed his arms and allowed himself a sigh of satisfaction as the congregation broke into applause. Young Mrs. MacLeod looked in his direction with a wondering smile. He nodded back. *Well done.*

With one orchestrated maneuver, he had paved the way for her place in the community, ranger and Cove families alike. Hopefully, it would allow all these new neighbors to relax around one another.

Despite the flush of triumph on her face, their songstress looked all too glad to be off the hook. She took her seat as he gathered the children about him, calling forth all the other children in the congregation. Sitting down on the steps among them, he regaled them with a Christmas tale, one they could relate to, about a family long ago and their Christmas in the Cove.

Afterward, each child was presented with a big Christmas cookie in the shape of a star and a wrapped gift.

The congregation rose for the benediction:

> "The Lord bless you and keep you;
> The Lord make his face shine upon you
> and be gracious to you;
> The Lord look upon you with favor
> and grant you peace."

To the strains of another familiar carol, everyone filed out.

Shane sneaked an arm about Andie's waist. "You're full of surprises, aren't you?"

She smiled in answer, caught up in the Cove scene spread before them in all directions as they paused on the church steps. The majestic slumbering giants sheltered this little valley of peace, wrapped in mist. She succumbed to a sigh. How perfectly it fit the words of the carol—

> *Angels we have heard on high,*
> *Sweetly singing o'er the plain,*
> *And the mountains in reply,*
> *Echoing their joyous strain…*

How far away L.A. seemed….

"Mrs. MacLeod?"

Andie broke from her musing. "Yes?"

Reverend Matthews was smiling down at her. "We want to thank you again for sharing that lovely voice with us this morning. I believe we had a few herald angels of our own present today." The minister turned to shake Shane's hand.

The taciturn ranger gave a twisted smile in answer, tugging his bride closer. "Maybe so." He glanced down at her. She flicked a smile but her attention was drawn elsewhere.

Across the way, Melba Davis stumbled in the loose, icy gravel. She had been staring over her shoulder a little too long in Andie's direction. Andie bit back a smile. With a flustered look, the woman whirled about and charged onward, which only compounded her problem. A steady hand took hold of her arm.

"You okay?"

Melba looked up to find herself staring into the smiling green eyes of Ranger Morgan.

"Yes. Fine, thank you!" she returned crisply and extricated herself from his grasp. Gathering herself up, she proceeded to lurch and slip onward to her car.

* * * *

At the MacLeod lodge that afternoon, everyone was either inside, curled up by the fire, or outside, burning off the bountiful holiday buffet. Seated at the hearth, Rachel Hendrickson played the dulcimer beneath the attentive gaze of Buck MacIntyre. Andie walked by with a little smile, carrying a tray of cups to the kitchen.

She laid the tray down next to the sink where Tawnee Morgan was washing dishes. Andie looked on as Tawnee handed a dish to Cal Evans to dry. "It's nice to see a man who knows when to pitch in," she observed.

Cal chuckled. "Nita's got me trained. If I don't, I catch heck." He winked as his wife walked in with another empty tray.

The ranger nodded toward the living room. "Nice piece of work there. How'd you manage that?"

Andie followed his gaze to where the bashful ranger hovered, spellbound, over the delicate dulcimer enchantress.

"Yes it was, wasn't it?" She put her hands on her hips. "I heard about her from Shane and Ben. I think Shane softened up ol' Wiley with something to let her come. Probably a bottle of Jack Daniels, but he's not talking. The rest I figure you just leave to chemistry, eh?"

Cal nodded appreciatively.

Andie turned to the window, breaking into a smile. Outside, a snowball fight had broken out. Jesse Morgan, Ty Evans, Marcie MacLeod, and little Mary Rose Bear had all ganged up on Ben. He lay in the snow where they'd tackled him. Adding insult to injury, Mary toddled over and sweetly tossed a snowball in her father's face. Ben howled for mercy.

"One guess who the biggest kid is out there."

Tawnee nodded ruefully, handing off a tray for Andie to dry. "That was beautiful this morning. You do have a gift."

Andie shrugged, cheeks warming. "I don't know any-more...."

Tawnee paused in rinsing to look up at her quizzically.

"What gifts are, I mean," Andie added, self-conscious all of a sudden. Absently, she stroked the tray with her towel. "Seems like...sometimes talents get in the way of other things, you know? Kind of like...distract you from what you should have been doing

216

all along...." With a start, she realized her eyes had drifted in Ben's direction. She yanked her gaze away. After a discreet pause, she glanced up at Tawnee, who seemed focused on the sudsy sink as if nothing untoward had happened. Maybe it hadn't.

She turned abruptly and reached for the coffeepot. "I better see if anybody needs another cup before we wash this." She headed for the den.

The clang of the pot hitting the floor made Tawnee whirl around.

Andie had sagged against the doorjamb and was sliding to the floor, coffee pooling on the floor beside her. Tawnee rushed over, kneeling at her side. Cal Evans was the first to join them.

"What happened? Did she slip?"

"I...I'm sorry. I made such a mess," Andie groaned. "I just...got so dizzy...all of a sudden." Her head started to loll and she braced herself against the doorjamb, closing her eyes. Lillian Alston was the next one at her side.

"Don't worry about that now, Girl," the doctor snapped. She examined her hands and arms. "Did you burn yourself?"

Andie drowsily shook her head.

"Good." Doctor Alston proceeded to check her pulse and lifted her chin, staring into her eyes with a tiny flashlight. "Alright. Let's get you to bed." She looked up to see John Gage towering over them.

"I'll take her," he offered.

Cal rose with a frown. "I'll get Shane."

As big John cut a path through the crowd with Andie in his arms, the other guests stopped to look on, murmuring. Cal shoved his way through to the patio doors and stepped out on the deck, bellowing for Shane.

Seconds later, it was Ben, not Shane, who burst in breathlessly. *"What is it?"*

Cal's steady eyes took hold of his. "It's Andie. She took sick all of th' sudden. Where the hell is Shane?"

Ben swallowed, catching his breath. "He took a call. Car stuck up on Little River Road. I'll find him."

Cal nodded solemnly, sending him on his way with a clap on the back.

Half an hour later, two park vehicles appeared in the snow-covered driveway. Both rangers burst out of their vehicles, tramping to the door, where Cal met them. Shane rushed by without a word, tight-faced. Ben close behind, was detained by a firm hand against the front of his parka.

"She's his concern now," Cal whispered.

Ben's eyes narrowed for a moment before his shoulders relaxed with effort and he nodded in compliance.

Down the hall, Shane almost bumped into Doc Lillian at the bedroom door. She stepped aside with a droll expression.

"Congratulations."

Shane stood rooted to the spot in confusion.

"It's perfectly all right to go in!" She laughed, shooing him in.

He stepped in as though into an unfamiliar room. Andie was sitting up, cross-legged in bed, rubbing her head. Tawnee rose from the chair nearby and passed by with a little smile of her own.

He approached the bed. "Andie?" A flustered frown flickered across his brow. "Will somebody tell me what's goin' on?"

She raised a face still trying to decide how to arrange itself. Her eyes were the give-away, ready to brim over. She bit her lip then attempted to smile. The tears spilled over.

"I'm pregnant!"

Shane blinked once, twice, then swallowed. His mouth opened but no words came out. Perching on the bed's edge, he tried again. "Don't kid me here, Girl. I'm too old for this sort of thing."

She sniffed, letting loose a nervous laugh. "Apparently not!" She nuzzled against the calloused hand that cupped her cheek. "No joke."

"No joke..." Shane echoed, staring deep into her eyes.

She scrunched up her face. "I…guess I kinda suspected it…a few days ago…but I thought it might just be nerves…or something going around…." She shrugged. "Guess not!"

Shane considered this. His gaze travelled to the window, eventually coming back to her. "Well…how do you feel about it?"

She studied him out of the tops of her eyes. "How do *you* feel about it?"

He sat back, brows twitching. "Okay, I guess. You?"

That elicited a sniff out of her, followed by an uncertain frown. "It…doesn't mess things up too much?"

Shane chewed on his lip a moment, venturing a soft snort. "Can't see how it would."

Her smile came out crooked. "Sorry. I know I'm acting like a child about the whole thing. It's just…I can't picture myself a mother yet. It's kinda scary."

He pulled her close and nuzzled her hair. "It's not so bad. I think everybody feels that way at first. At least you've got a veteran along for the ride."

Marcie burst in the door.

"Daddy!"

Shane whirled around, catching his daughter as she fell into his arms. "Looks like I was about to forget somebody, wasn't I!"

The murmuring in the hall reached to the other end of the house for those who had remained. Buck MacIntyre stepped onto the deck and cupped his hands to his mouth.

"She's pregnant!"

The crowd gathered down by the lake looked up with one accord. A round of applause and cheers rose to greet him.

Inside, Shane made his way through those gathered along the hall and into the den. The sea of faces parted for a second and he caught a glimpse of Ben by the mantle. Morgan raised his glass, mouthing a silent "Congratulations." Shane acknowledged with a nod. He opened his mouth, feeling the need to say something more but was distracted by others come to pump his hand and pound him on the back. The moment passed.

But as the last of the guests were leaving, Ben sneaked back to the master bedroom to give his regards.

Andie rose up on her elbows, seeing him linger in the darkened doorway. "Scare you off?"

"I just...thought you might be asleep."

She sat up the rest of the way. "Don't just stand there giving me your *nice* smile." She swallowed the sudden lump in her throat.

Ben ambled in as though not quite sure what distance he should observe. For a moment, neither spoke, both with eyes cast on the floor, on the bed, anywhere but each other. Andie summoned up the nerve first.

"Surprised?"

Standing there with his hands in his pockets, Ben finally looked up, with the ghost of a smile.

"No...just surprised he took this long—" He warded off the pillow she *almost* threw at him. She considered it a moment longer before plunking it back down with a sigh. "This is kinda overwhelming, y'know?"

Ben sank down onto the bed's edge and reached out, tugging on a stray strand of her hair. "Hey now...that's not the way I brought you up, is it?" he said in a brotherly tone. "Just another one of life's little adventures it throws your way...one ya gotta meet head-on. It's your turn to grow up, that's all."

She raised her eyebrows, though she liked his little speech. "Excuse me? Didn't I teach you a thing or two?"

Ben rose and leaned over to plant a kiss, a lingering one, on her forehead. "Oh yeah...never to take anything for granted," his voice came, uncommonly soft.

Andie's eyes flicked to the doorway, causing Ben to turn as well.

Shane was leaning on the doorjamb, looking on. He didn't look disturbed. Rather, he wore somewhat of a lop-sided smile, as though he had intruded upon something precious in the way of a friendship, and knew it. Perhaps he saw the exchange as their making peace with one another. Andie hoped so, at least.

220

Ben made his way to the door. "I gotta be going. Take it easy." The two men's eyes met. Andie held her breath. But there was only warmth in Shane's eyes, the genuine kind.

"I'll walk ya out."

The two made their way to the door. Out on the porch, Shane dug his hands in his pockets. "Gotta admit, it *is* kinda hard t' picture her a mom."

Ben turned back from the bottom step, his grin reassuring. "Oh, I don't know. She may not make your garden variety mom but…with a rock 'n' roll mama who can make the prettiest hook shot you ever saw, the kid'll be all right."

. 18 .

Buck MacIntyre had been crazy about animals since he was a small boy. On his thirteenth birthday, upon being presented with the traditional squirrel gun Virginia farm boys were given as a rite of passage, he had quietly asked his dad if he could exchange it for a pair of binoculars and a pup tent.

One morning soon after, he became so engrossed studying a red-tailed hawk with his new lenses that he fell down the front porch steps, breaking an arm. His parents knew then their only son wasn't destined for the family farm. Fortunately, his older sister had a boyfriend who made for a good prospect in that direction.

The MacIntyres started setting aside funds from timber sales, a portion of the apple orchard yield, and proceeds from his mom's apple jelly making—all earmarked for college.

He started out up the road at Mountain Empire Community College and transferred with a scholarship to Virginia Tech. He gave them a solid return on their investment, graduating with honors from VT's College of Forestry and Wildlife Resources. Internships and early assignments took him to Jefferson National Forest, Cumberland Falls, and Cloudland Canyon near Chattanooga.

In his twelve years as a wildlife biologist in one capacity or another, he hadn't lost his boyish enthusiasm for the outdoors.

This morning he was at it again, up with the first rays of dawn. After downing a quick breakfast of Grapenuts on his deck, he headed out with his backpack slung over his shoulder—the goal, to catch a glimpse of the newest otter family this fine spring morning along a tributary of the Little River.

But this morning he came upon an unexpected form of fauna....

Buck stuffed the remains of his lunch—half an apple and an extra granola bar—into his pack and started to rise from his streamside spot. A flash of white upstream caught his eye. He groped at his waist for binoculars and whipped them up, scanning the area.

All was placid on the water, as well as the banks to either side. No sign of life...other than the bluejay that swooped overhead, squawking at him. He lowered the binocs and shook his head. Whatever it was, he missed it.

The rustle of branches behind him made Buck whirl around.

From the leafy shadows, a girl emerged...tall, lanky, hair like sunshine spilling to her waist. The sweet, wild scent of honeysuckle came with her.

He took a step backwards, knees gone wobbly. That mountain girl...Rachel was it? Her dulcimer music had held him spellbound at the MacLeod's party months ago. His ear still longed to recapture the magic her fingers had spun on that humble stringed instrument.

Buck swallowed, his eyes taking in the curve of her cheek in profile. That corn silk cascade falling to her waist had been indelibly stamped in his memory.

"H-Hi!" he stammered.

The girl blinked, took a wavering step backward.

"It-It's okay! Don't be scared. We met before...last Christmas. Do you remember?"

It wasn't clear at first whether she recognized him or not. Her eyes traveled up and down his uniform, resting on the NPS insignia. She seemed to be considering something, perhaps whether the uniform made him friend or foe. Eventually, her posture relaxed. A nod came, slowly. Her gaze then went to the instruments laid out on the boulder beside his pack, her eyes widening in interest.

"What cha doin'?" she asked in a child-like voice.

Buck's cheeks flushed warm. A shy grin twitched at the corners of his mouth. "I—uh—was just finishing up a field study on a new pair of otters we brought into the park last fall. They just had pups, turns out. Wanted to see how they were getting along."

He nodded at the basket she grasped at her side. "Looks like you've been busy yourself."

She looked down at the collection of wild greens she'd gathered and back up at him in alarm. "Got these over t'other prong o' the spring branch. Not from the park! Honest!"

Buck eyed her solemnly. "It's okay. I believe you."

The girl's wide eyes gradually relaxed. Her attention was drawn to his pack again. She seemed intrigued by the field guides stuck in the outer pocket. "Guess you had a lot of schoolin', huh?" She chewed her lip.

Buck shrugged as he reached for his pack. "A fair amount. I went to Virginia Tech, took Wildlife Studies there. Ever hear of it?"

She dipped one cheek to her shoulder and shook her head shyly. Her gaze wavered. "Naw…I hadn't been too far aways from here." Her chin jerked up. "But I been t' Asheville oncet a while back…the Farmers' Market…an' Jones…Jonesboro, I think it was…." She frowned but then her face brightened. "They tell me my fam'ly took me t' Knoxville when I was real little. They got a zoo there…an' a liberry…. I'd like t' visit it sometime…." This last she said with an air of confession and looked down, as if awaiting reprimand.

Buck nodded, storing this bit of information away for future use. He started packing away his things. "I better be on my way." He straightened, "You're pretty far from home, aren't you—Wear Cove, isn't it?"

The girl nodded.

"I'd be glad to give you a lift." Buck cocked his head but tried not to look as though he was giving her a once-over. He'd heard enough about mountain customs to know the way you looked at a woman could get you married or shot on the spot, at least in the old days. In remote corners of the Appalachians, old attitudes lingered.

She looked taken aback by his offer. But just when he began to think he'd blundered, he saw the eagerness that came into her eyes. She looked down, shielding the look, torn, he suspected, between her own wishes and custom. Control? After a moment, she raised her chin. "I'd like that."

Buck heaved a sigh of relief. "Great. Just follow me. My truck's parked up on the road."

The girl was quiet as they rode along, focused on the passing scenery. Buck found himself stealing glances her way and searched for something to say.

"If you don't mind me asking...what...I mean...how do your folks manage so far from things? How do you make a living?"

She shrugged. "Off the land mostly...got our own garden...sell some corn n' t'maters in th' summer, trade eggs fer stuff in Townsend at the gen'ral store. This lady from Gatlinburg brings by scraps fer me to make inta quilts she sells fer me...sometimes my baskets."

"At Arrowmont?"

That spark lit her eyes again. "You heard of it?"

"Oh, yes. They're well known for showcasing mountain crafts. Good place."

She yielded a little smile of pride at that.

"Oh—an' Cousin Stoke, he brings by stuff when we need it, too."

"Is he a farmer, too?"

"Naw...he sez he's got this new job but don't tell us much. Somethin' 'bout...foreign in-vest-mints?"

"I see...." Buck nodded congenially but his brow puckered at that one. He grew quiet but more questions kept knocking around in his head. He hoped they wouldn't scare her off.

"So how'd you come to be living with your grandfather?"

Rachel fastened her gaze on the dashboard. "My ma died when I was born," she said without emotion. "Ever since, I lived with them—he an' Granny—till she died few years back. Now Grandpa needs me to watch out for him."

"I'm sure you're a great help to him." He paused, wondering whether to forge ahead. "How 'bout your Dad?"

"He lit out before I was born. Heard he died drunk in a car wreck."

Buck grimaced. "Sorry. That's a lot to handle."

But the girl just shrugged it off, apparently untouched by these long-ago events.

"It's just around that bend." Rachel pointed up ahead to a field of broom straw bordered by a fence row of cedars.

"Okay…." Buck's thoughts went into high gear. "I was wondering…" he started, and found his mouth dry. "Would you— uh—be interested in bringing that dulcimer of yours to play at Old Timers' Day? I could take you."

The girl turned back from staring out the window. Eyes the color of wisteria held him in thrall. "I…I'd have to ask." Her voice was tentative but her face glowed at the prospect.

Buck pulled into the deep-rutted dirt path that led to the old farmstead, the park truck's suspension squeaking and groaning as they were jostled all the way to within sight of the place. He made out the figure of a stooped old man stumping to the rail of the front porch to peer out. Remembering Ben Morgan's warning, Buck stopped while still some distance from the house. He pulled the door lever and started to get out but the girl put a light hand on his arm.

"Maybe I should get out first."

Buck nodded tightly. "Good idea."

He watched her get out and stroll to the porch steps before he opened the driver's side door and emerged. He gave a tentative wave to the old man. No wave back. He lowered his arm, feeling foolish, and turned to get back in. But from the corner of his eye, he caught a glimpse of Hendrickson giving Rachel careful scrutiny then squinting out his way. Buck froze in place, awaiting the barrage.

Old Hendrickson's face screwed up to match his squint. He spat sideways into the yard and cocked his head. "What's yer name, ranger fella?"

"MacIntyre, sir," Buck called up to him.

"Scotch, huh?" The old man continued to survey him.

"Virginia Scot." Buck braved a grin.

226

Hendrickson uttered a summary *hmmph* and turned to stalk into the cabin. Rachel chanced a peek and a shy smile Buck's way before following her grandfather inside.

Audience over, Buck shrugged to himself and hopped back in the truck.

* * * *

At the Cades Cove Center, District Chief MacLeod answered his phone to find a testy Bill Hayes on the other end.

"I was just clearing up some old business and came across Ben Morgan's file," said the new Assistant Director of the National Park Service. "I see it's been ten months since I set that six-month probationary period."

Shane leaned back in his chair. "Yeah, I guess that did slip by a little. There've been no problems to report and, frankly, it's been too busy around here to worry with it."

"That's not exactly what I hear. There've been some complaints."

"What complaints?" Shane looked up as Cal Evans entered the office and locked eyes with him. "All right, so he took some time to chop wood...they were park neighbors. It was good PR.... Yeah, I heard about that, too. He was huntin' up bats and gloves for the Cherokee High baseball team—he doesn't disappear more than once every month or two." Cal turned from the file cabinet and grinned back at him.

Shane rolled his eyes. "Okay...I'll talk to him. Another six-month probation? Fine. You'll see all this worry's unwarranted. Some things just come with the territory, Bill. Like I said, you don't get a good backcountry man without some quirks.... All right...talk to you later." He hung up, muttering, "Ever since moving up t' DC, Bill has turned into a real hardass."

"Maybe he's feelin' th' pressure, himself. –Say, I hear the Rev wore you down. When's that young 'un of yours gettin' baptized?"

Shane looked up. "Huh? Oh...Sunday, eleven-thirty."

Cal saluted him with a map. "We'll be there."

* * * *

Inside Cades Cove Methodist Church, a small gathering stood before the congregation at the wooden baptismal font. Andie carefully handed off a bundle wrapped in a trailing white blanket to John Matthews. Shane stood at attention alongside, a hand resting on big sister Marcie's shoulder. Across the font, Ben and Tawnee Morgan faced them.

John Matthews settled the infant into the crook of his arm and proceeded to dab the child's forehead with drops of water.

"Adam Shane MacLeod, I baptize you in the name of the Father, the Son, and the Holy Spirit."

Tiny knotted fists emerged from the blanket, boxing the air, but there was no crying, only soft coos. The minister handed the baby boy back to his mother and was turning back to his congregation when, out of the corner of his eye, he caught a glimpse of movement. Ben Morgan was tying a strange-looking concoction of leather thong, beadwork, stone, and feathers onto the child's tiny ankle. The young mother did not appear perturbed in the least, casting a grin in the direction of the roguish fellow.

Matthews threw him a look, only to be met by a schoolboy grin in answer. The ranger resumed his pose, hands folded before him in perfect respect. Still, it was enough to make the minister stumble over his next line.

"Please…Please be seated."

As the group at the font headed back to the pews, John Matthews turned aside from the sea of faces and squeezed the arm of the ranger, whispering, "I'd like a word with you later, please."

Back in his seat, Shane sighed in relief. Ceremonies always made him uncomfortable. While he might appear calm and collected on the outside, he was more than happy to remove himself from the center of attention. He glanced over at the tiny boy with his wisps of dark hair. Soulful eyes the color of blue denim peeked back at him from his mother's shoulder. The ranger stretched an arm out along the pew behind Andie, relaxing for the first time this morning. Time to muse over all the changes wrought in such a short time. He still found it hard to believe the baby was here. His son....

Wild and woolly was an apt description for the night his son came into the world. A thunderstorm had kept their guests late that Saturday evening. Ben and Tawnee, with their children, had brought by supper and stayed to visit, only to end up spending the night due to the storm that blew in. Shane had done a final check on their guests, sacked out on couches and sleeping bags, then gone to join Andie.

Her moans awakened him in the middle of the night. Adam, it turned out, was not content to wait for his due date, a week later, to make his appearance. As luck would have it, the electricity had gone out and the phone call to Doc Lillian was barely audible. She would be delayed by flooded roads, she had told him, but would be there as quick as she could.

Shane almost dropped the phone when he turned to see the look on Tawnee's face. An experienced midwife back at Wind River Reservation, she recognized the signs of advanced labor. Her tight expression told him this baby would not wait.

For once in his life, Shane was content to let someone else take the lead, numbly following her directions. They helped Andie to a half-sitting position. Shane took his place behind her, letting her lean against him for support. Everyone was so wrapped up in their work, Shane didn't even mind that Ben was there in the middle of it all, at Tawnee's beck and call. In fact, it took his stronger fingers to grasp and pull little Adam's head and shoulders out when the baby boy seemed stuck.

There was a collective gasp of relief when the newborn lay squirming in the nest of sheets. Tawnee snatched him up, wiping his face, and gave him a pat on the back. The child uttered his first lusty cry.

They were almost too absorbed in the new arrival—all, that is, save Ben, who looked up to see Andie's eyes roll back right before she collapsed.

It still bothered Shane that he had been totally useless at that critical moment. Maybe flashbacks from another time, another scare caused him to freeze. He wasn't sure. Thank God, Ben kept his head. He rushed to Andie's side, checked her pulse, and was starting to give resuscitation when she came around. She had only fainted.

Doc Lillian appeared in the doorway just as Ben was removing his lips from Andie's mouth. "About time you showed up!" he snapped. Shane, still dazed, had trouble tearing his gaze away.

After a couple of days' observation at the hospital in Maryville, Andie and little Adam came home, and the household, as much as could be expected, returned to routine. Marcie had been a big help, as had the tightknit community of ranger families. And gradually, he was getting used to the idea that he had a son and namesake. Andie had insisted upon making the boy's middle name Shane.

As they filed out of the church, John Matthews shook Shane's hand heartily. "One of my smoother baptisms, I must say," the reverend confessed. "How's our Chief holding up?"

Shane shook his head in wonder. "Just goes t'show, you never know where a year will take you."

* * * *

At the Old Timers' Day celebration the next weekend, Shane paused by the split rail fence on the grounds of the Gregg-Cable house, quenching his thirst with a cup of fresh-squeezed cider from the antique apple-press one of the locals always hauled out for the occasion. His watchful gaze travelled over the crowd enjoying the festivities. Smoke billowed from a shed where John Gage was putting on a show as village blacksmith. A cluster of wide-eyed children stood before him, hands over their ears at the mighty clang each time he pounded his hammer, Thor-like against the massive anvil. Red sparks flew from the molten iron bars, making the children jump back then gather in to admire the poker he had fashioned.

An odd assortment of aromas wafted on the breeze...wood smoke mingled with the tang of apple mash, lye from the laundry kettles, hay, along with the smell of barn animals, cooking oil from corncakes frying in the millhouse, and the sweetness of sorghum molasses being stirred in vats with long-handled paddles.

Melba appeared at his elbow, staring off in the direction of the old house itself. A cluster of the younger rangers had gathered on its front porch. Among them was Buck, leaning against a post as he stood guard over young Rachel Hendrickson. She sat on the steps, attired in a simple pink and white calico dress like her ancestors might have worn, charming visitors with her dulcimer music. Her repertory of lively dance music and poignant mountain ballads added another stamp of authenticity to the setting.

Ben was there, as well, sitting a few steps below Andie, trying his hand at juggling some apples, with intermittent success. Buck looked on, shaking his head dolefully, but Andie seemed delighted with Morgan's efforts.

Shane's eyes glided easily over the scene and went to others.

But Melba, appearing at his side, couldn't contain herself. "I know it's not my place…but I'd watch those two if I were you," she whispered sharply.

Shane relaxed into an indulgent smile. "It's all right…they're old friends." He walked away, in the direction of the blacksmith's shed, leaving Melba to cast a troubled look after him.

Back at the steps of the Gregg-Cable House, there was nothing but good-natured smiles as Buck took up Ben's challenge and tried *his* hand at juggling those apples…executing a remarkable performance. He even garnered a smattering of applause from passers-by. It wasn't every day that park visitors were treated to the sight of a uniformed ranger juggling.

Feeling a bit foolish, Buck gave a curt bow and retired with a quick toss back to Morgan. He shrugged, self-conscious, as he sat down beside Rachel, muttering, "Twenty years on an apple farm…you come up with just about everything there is to do with apples."

"Including some nature never intended?" Morgan, sprawled on the wooden steps, threw a devilish grin up his way.

Buck eyed him sourly. The guy had a way of unsettling him at times, but he found himself liking Morgan despite that. Maybe because he was so comfortable in his skin, not trying to be anything else, consequences be hanged. Buck wished he could be more like that.

He turned his attention back to Rachel. She had put her dulcimer aside and was now weaving a basket of dried honeysuckle vines. Beside her, another basket held dried herbs. Some he recognized, others he wasn't so sure of. Rachel, though, had a name and use for each of them, he knew.

The girl had a reputation for more than herb healer in these parts, he'd learned, thanks to John Gage. Just last week, he'd been talked into joining some of the fellows at a local watering hole on the way home. The conversation turned to rumors of Buck hanging around the Hendrickson place, much to his discomfiture.

"I'd be careful if I were you, Buck," John advised him with a wink and a bear-sized arm around his shoulders. "Word is that girl sees things." Buck barely suppressed choking on Gage's beer-laced breath. He swallowed and tried to come up with a polite reply.

"That's okay. I had a grandmother who used to see things."

Morgan had taken a swig from his bottle and fixed him with a knowing look. "That was different."

"No! I mean really!" Buck insisted. "That kind of stuff doesn't spook me. Not everything can be explained away, just like that." His gaze traveled around the table, registering the four doleful expressions cast his way. There was a collective shrug all 'round.

"Suit yerself, pardner," John dismissed him with.

Buck decided to try his hand at delving into this facet of the Cove girl who'd snared his heart. It was impossible to imagine her with any kind of dark side. He waited for Morgan to clear out. When he and Andie MacLeod left to join their spouses, Buck turned to the young mountain woman.

"Uh...Rachel?"

She looked up from her basket weaving, fixing those lavender eyes on him. "Yes?"

Again, he almost forgot what he was going to say. That seemed to happen every time she planted that gaze on him. He didn't know quite how to work into this, so he dove right in, the way she did things, herself.

"Do you ever…like…see things?"

One fair eyebrow peaked on that smooth brow. She went back to her weaving. "People been talkin, huh." It was more statement than question.

Buck squirmed on the step. "Well…a bit. I was just curious that's all. I had a grandmother—"

"Does it bother you?" She followed her question with a side-long glance, not quite meeting his eyes.

He bent to look into her face. "Not at all."

She said nothing.

Silence settled over them. From past experience, he knew it wasn't necessarily a bad thing. Sometimes there would be great spans of silence in a mountain conversation, only to be picked up where it left off like nothing had happened. A different culture, different sense of time. Sometimes it was just to let an idea settle in good so a person really knew what they thought about it…the luxury to contemplate…keeping a hurry-up world at bay.

Buck rested his elbows against the sun-warmed slats of the old porch and let his gaze glide over the shade-dappled crowd under the canopy of oaks, trees that had been saplings when the area was still frontier. After a time, he asked, "What's it like?"

Rachel showed no confusion as to what he meant. Her fingers continued their nimble movement. "Oh…I just feels stirred up a mite sometimes. Don't always know what direction it's comin' from. I might have to stop and look about. It comes to me d'rectly. But sometimes it takes days b'fore I figger out what the commotion's about."

Her hands lay still a moment on her lap of calico as she looked out across the sea of strangers. "People's got auras, y'know."

She chanced a look up at him and he nodded solemnly. "I've…heard something to that effect." He cocked his head, intent upon her. "Do you see…or feel these…all the time…or just some of the time?"

She shrugged and went back to her work. "It's kinda like you can ignore it, see through it sometimes, and concentrate on what the person's sayin'. And if all's well with 'em, it's not distractin'."

"I see…. Do you think you could show me how it works…a little?"

Her eyes narrowed. "It ain't no parlor game."

"I didn't mean—!" Something squeezed around his heart.

She put a hand out, resting on his arm, a soft light come into her eyes. "It's all right. I know. It's just…sometimes…people gets kinda strange about it and I get touchy. I know you don't mean no harm. That's what I sensed about you, early on, Buck Mac-Intyre…." She smiled down at her lap, pink creeping into her cheeks. "There's naught but good intenshuns in yer aura. It's all healthy colors."

He stared, entranced. She drew her hand away but fixed a smile on him. "All right. I'll give it a try for ya."

Buck sat up gingerly and scanned the surrounding pockets of visitors and Smokies personnel. "I don't know…maybe somebody we both know…." His eye fell on Morgan. "Okay, like Ben Morgan over there, say…."

Rachel drew back with a shivery laugh. "That man's dangerous!"

Buck settled back, disgruntled. "I coulda told you that." Women seemed to find that attractive in a man regardless of what they said to the contrary. *Dangerous-looking* was not a label ever attributed to him.

Rachel laughed, pearl droplets in a gurgling stream. Another of those sidelong glances. "No…I don't mean like that. Nothin' t' be jealous for. More a…sad kind of trouble…like no peace." A wistful look crossed her face. "He's restless…tugged on the in-side…by sumthin'…."

Buck shook his head. "Looks happy to me." He turned his attention to the pair standing beside Morgan. "What about the MacLeods there? They seem different as night and day, but real happy together."

Rachel studied them with a squint. Buck noticed she extended her hand discreetly, palm outstretched. The gesture reminded him of pictures he'd seen of people water-witching.

She cocked her head with a little smile. "Nothin' but goodness in that man, real calm waters. Nothin' much ruffles him, does it? But that Miss Andie…. She's real friendly and all…but she's confusin' t' me. There's a good spirit there…the colors are good around her…but there's lotsa spikes."

"Spikes?"

"Little shoots of strong color, like flames spurtin' out in the middle of the flow. Signals a restless spirit. Not as peaceful as she lets on."

Buck smiled. "Where'd you learn all this stuff?"

"I been seein' stuff since I was little. Didn't make no sense of it till I was older. My granny she taught me t' *'terpret the signs*, she called it, like her granny taught her.

"So it runs in your family."

"Uh-huh. Seems t' skip generations, tho'."

Buck settled back to digest this. What would it be like to live with someone like that? She gave him a few more readings on people passing by—just general stuff, she insisted, nothing personal—then he saw her expression change when her eye fell on Tawnee Morgan.

The delicately-boned young woman was holding Mary Rose Bear on her hip. The little girl looked too big for her to carry now. Nonetheless, Tawnee was smiling serenely up at her husband, as usual. You got the impression she worshipped the ground he walked on. Buck found himself hoping, for her sake, he was worth it.

But it was Rachel who concerned him at the moment. She wavered, looking like all her energy had drained away.

He reached out a hand to steady her. "Are you okay?"

She blinked out of her daze and straightened. "I—I guess I'm just tired, that's all. All this commotion…the crowd."

"Sorry. I imagine you're not too used to it, are you? Want me to take you home?"

She nodded, eyes pleading.

"Well sure. My truck's just back of the house. Are you up to the walk?"

Rachel nodded again and he stood, offering his hand. She gathered up her things and with a wan smile, took hold of it.

Once they were down the road a way, she seemed better. Whatever had troubled her, the dark cloud had lightened from her face and her shoulders no longer sagged. She leaned back in the passenger seat, relaxed now, and gave him a smile.

"I want t' thank you. I had a really nice time t'day."

Warmth flooded his cheeks. "I'm glad you could make it. From the look of things, you got some new customers, too." He eyed the supply basket in the floorboard, laden with strips of memo paper bearing names and phone numbers for baskets to come. "I think you've got your work cut out for you. Can you handle it all?"

She wriggled back in her seat with a little smile of satisfaction. "Oh, yeah. I ain't afraid of a little hard work."

They pulled into the winding two-track that led to the Hendrickson place. Buck didn't hesitate pulling up close this time. They were expected. The late afternoon sun flinted off the peak of the tin roof though mountain shadows intruded. Half the front porch was already cast in darkness. Buck waited for Rachel to go up the steps and open the door before he turned the truck around for the journey home to Elkmont Station.

Rachel watched from the window as the park truck disappeared around the bend, a smile dancing at the corners of her mouth.

A hand grabbed hold of her arm, causing her to gasp. She whipped around, peering into the shadows for her accoster. The glaring face of her cousin emerged from the darkness.

"Stoke! What you think yer doin'?"

"Whatcha think *yer* doin', 'sortin' with them rangers?" he snarled back.

She pulled her arm away, rubbing it, and tried to match his angry look with one of her own, though she knew it came out no more than a pout. "I gotta right t' see who I want!"

"Sez who?"

"Sez me!" She stuck her chin out.

He grabbed it in two bruising fingers. She fought not to wince.

"Don't give yerself airs, Gal. They're just fillin' yer head with nonsense. Probably just usin' you t' keep an eye on us. That's th' way them Feds are. Always spyin' on people."

Rachel struggled to keep her chin from trembling when he let go. "No they ain't!"

Stoke wagged his head. "Yeah they is. Stay away from 'em. Now go on in there and git me some supper. I got business t' tend to."

She eyed him sidelong, still frowning. In his old jeans and dirty boots he hardly looked dressed for any kind of meeting. She paused in the doorway. "Where you goin'?"

"None o' yer business, missy. Now go on."

Rachel went into the kitchen but paused to rest her back against the doorframe when he was out of sight. Reaching into her basket, she picked up one of the apples from the festival and took a long, thoughtful bite. One corner of her mouth screwed up and her eyes narrowed. Blamed if she was gonna *Skip to my Lou* every time he said *Jump*. The time for that was over. Cousin Stoke was in for a rude awakenin'.

She took her sweet time sashaying past her grandfather into the kitchen. The old man looked after her wonderingly.

A small act of rebellion in itself, but a start.

. 19 .

This summer was proving to be a true test of Ben's endurance on the job. As any ranger would admit, the high traffic months could make or break an unseasoned man and make a veteran contemplate early retirement some days. Two incidents particularly tried his mettle.

The first one started out as a routine patrol one evening over the Fourth of July holiday. Shane invited him along to patrol the route from Tremont to Sugarlands to Chimney Tops along Newfound Gap Road, a distance of about twenty-five miles. On the first leg, their one encounter was with a family fixing a flat tire at the Laurel Falls Trail parking lot. After seeing them on their way, the rangers continued their run. All was quiet, problem-wise, along Newfound Gap Road, punctuated only by a deer bounding across the road ahead of them and a lone coyote trotting down the gravel shoulder.

On the return trip they spied the car—a late-model family van lying at the foot of a slope, half hidden by woods. They pulled over and got out. Ben started to go down the slope but Shane put a hand on his arm. "Wreck most likely, but stay alert," he advised, unsnapping his holster.

Ben did likewise, frowning. "We couldn't have missed *this* earlier."

"Probably just happened." Shining a flashlight down into the woods, they could now see that the vehicle's front end was smashed against the broad trunk of a hemlock. Steam spewed from under the buckled hood.

Shane took an extra moment to call in the wreck, grabbed the first aid pack, and started down the slope behind Ben, carrying the rolled up stretcher.

Halfway down the hill, a weird feeling made Ben halt. Maybe it was the eerie quiet, with only the hiss of the radiator's last gasps. Even the tree frogs had stopped their ratchety chorus in the night woods.

There was death down there. He could feel it.

He held back Shane with a hand against his shirtfront.

"What?" the senior ranger barked.

Ben searched for the right way to say it fast. "Wait here a second. Let me go first."

His train of thought must have clicked in Shane's head as well. "It's okay. I got past that a long time ago. I had to."

Ben hesitated, then let go, giving a tight nod.

"But thanks for the thought." Shane pushed past him toward the wrecked minivan.

But what met their eyes was more than anyone could become inured to, no matter how often encountered. In the front seat, a man and a woman were slumped forward. The lower halves of their bodies disappeared under the crumpled dash in a grisly conglomerate of metal, plastic, and blood. Ben swallowed back a surge of nausea.

Both rangers knew at a glance the front passengers were dead but checked for a pulse anyway. There was none.

In the back were two children in safety seats. The force of the impact had caused the back compartment to twist sideways, partially exposing it to the outside. The safety seats hung loose from their straps. One tilted toward the open door, the other rested against the front passenger seat. Neither child looked to be bleeding. A quick hand to the neck of each proved they were alive, presumably knocked unconscious.

"Those safety seats are amazing."

Ben's voice was jarring in the grim silence. He could hear Shane's labored breathing and eyed him across the backseat. Regardless of what he might say, this had to conjure up ghosts of Becky's fate. Four years wasn't long enough for some memories to fade. They lay in wait, just below the surface. The tension in Shane was palpable.

Before Ben could say anything, one of the children, a little blond girl of about four, began to stir. Her eyes fluttered open, caught sight of the rangers, and widened in fear. "Mom-myy!" she wailed. Ben watched Shane swallow back his grief of the past to deal with this present one.

"Come on, Hon—no—don't look there—" His voice cracked as the child strained against her straps, wiggling to see up front, to see why her mother wasn't responding to her distress.

"Come with me, Baby," Shane said in measured tones. "We're gonna help you out of here. Can you move okay? Anything hurtin'?"

Twenty minutes later, they had both children up at the park vehicle, being looked over by ambulance personnel.

"No, we don't have a place to take them. We've had so many calls this evening, no one except the dispatcher is in. You could try Knoxville or Asheville. Where did you say they were from?" the driver asked.

"Rome, Georgia," Shane answered, kneeling to brush back the little girl's blond bangs. She, unfortunately, was old enough to know something terrible had happened, though she couldn't fathom its scope yet. Her wrenching cries had softened to whimpers now, as long as Shane stayed close to her side. He seemed to be her compass point amid the stupefying confusion of lights, sirens, and strangers.

The sandy-haired cherub in Ben's arms, a boy of one or so, squirmed but seemed more fascinated than scared by the same bustle of activity.

The two rangers' eyes met. Shane reached across the little girl to snatch his personal cell phone from the dash. Tears glistened in his eyes. "Andie...I got a situation here. I need your help, Hon."

Ben chewed his lip and looked away, blinking hard himself.

A moment of stunned silence on the other end was followed by Andie's voice over the speaker, sounding full but loud and clear: "You got me, pardner."

* * * *

The second incident occurred on a particularly quiet Sunday when the Morgans and MacLeods had a rare chance to gather for lunch on the MacLeods' deck. As the other adults brought out the fixin's for ice cream sundaes, Ben was in the middle of relating a tall tale to the children.

"…so the first thing I know, I roll over in my sleeping bag and there's this big hairy face in my face—"

Marcie gasped. Jesse, resting his chin on the table, gazed transfixed at his father, eyes glittering in shivery delight. "What'd you do then, Dad?"

The phone rang inside. Shane rose to answer it. Ben's voice faded behind him—

"I thought he was a bear at first. Before I had time to think, I shot out of the bag and onto my feet, and there I was, staring at this weird old guy with a beard down to his waist and a knife at his belt. Had to be this long…." Ben held up both hands, measuring some eighteen inches apart.

Shane shook his head, grinning, and turned his attention to his caller. "Yeah, Hank, what's up?" His brow furrowed. "Which camp were they from?" He turned away from his guests. "Okay…yeah…we'll be right over."

Shane hung up and turned to the group on the deck. Ben caught the look on Shane's face and rose abruptly.

Tawnee took the interruption in stride but Andie stood up with a frown, tossing her napkin aside in frustration. "That's the third time this week!" She followed the others into the entryway.

Shane was already retrieving gear from the closet, handing some off to Ben. Andie leaned against the doorjamb and crossed her arms. "What is it this time?"

"Couple of scouts missing from Mount LeConte."

She grimaced. Everyone knew that was rugged country. No telling what they might find when they got there. Marcie wriggled her way in among the grownups, casting a solemn look up at her father.

"When will you be back?"

Shane reached down to stroke his daughter's hair. "When they're found, Hon." He leaned across and delivered a quick smack to Andie's lips. "See ya when I can."

Behind him, Ben gave Tawnee a quick kiss as well, a solemn wink Andie's way, and followed Shane out.

Shane and Ben pulled up alongside several other park vehicles at the Chimney Tops rest area. They hopped out and trotted over to join the huddle of other rangers. Two scout leaders were there also.

The Scoutmaster looked up with a frown as they approached. Ben looked down and realized neither he nor Shane had taken time to change into uniform but came as they were—Shane in a black T-shirt and hiking pants that looked military issue, Ben in faded jeans and an orange T-shirt with *COLORADO* emblazoned across it. Well, they were here to do a job, not win a contest. Their heavy-duty hiking boots were on, proving they meant business.

When the scoutleader spied the NPS insignia on their caps, his frown relaxed.

Hank Stone, Smokies' Chief of Ranger Activities, did the introductions. "Mr. Allen, this is North District Chief MacLeod and Ranger Ben Morgan, one of our backcountry experts."

The men shook hands hurriedly. Shane got immediately to business. "You got a list of th' particulars?"

Stone handed over the standard questionnaire for Search and Rescue. Shane scanned it.

"Ages fourteen and sixteen, huh? What's their level of experience?"

"Dan's the older and more experienced of the two, as you might expect. Close to four years' backpacking experience, a year of rappelling and rock-climbing—"

Ben and Shane flicked a glance each other's way.

"Pete's the younger. Less experienced. Probably only a year of trail skills. Just started indoor rock wall practice."

With a tight nod, Shane turned to the map spread out on the truck hood, tracing the marked trails with his finger. "Okay...

John's already on the Bulls Head Trail...Gil from Greenbrier Station is on the Brushy Mountain Trail...and you say you've got Michaela coming up the Boulevard Trail.... Ben, you cover the Alum Cave Trail, you're familiar with that. The rest of us can fan out along Gap Road and the AT."

Shane glanced up at Hank Stone. "You got that copter called up?"

"They're on their way."

Shane nodded to Ben. He slung his pack onto his shoulders and headed off. Behind him, Hank Stone called out, "All right, everyone to your stations. Keep those channels open."

Ben paused for a breather at a point where the trail leveled off, took a swig from his water bottle, and looked back over the way he'd come. From here, a sweeping panorama of forested ridgeline spread before him. Ahead rose the hundred-foot overhang of Alum Cave, towering over the footpath. It always made him a little uneasy to pass under the slant of that massive hunk of rock. It was like standing beneath the prow of a colossal ocean liner. Heaving a sigh, he let his eyes travel uneasily up its sides one more time before plodding on.

He hadn't gone very far when a sound from above captured his attention. Shielding his eyes, he squinted upwards, then took out his binoculars for a second look. The tip of a white tennis shoe protruded over a jagged ledge on the bluffs...some eighty feet above him. The words formed soundlessly on his lips. "My God...."

He swallowed. Should he reach for his radio or call up to them first? He decided to scramble up the path for a closer look. Trouble was, he could only see that one shoe. And it wasn't moving. Not wanting to make matters worse by startling whoever was up there, he took a deep breath, cupped his hands to his mouth, and in a measured voice, called up:

"*Don't...move.* I'm a ranger. We'll get you down. Don't do anything till we give you the go-head. Understood?"

A muffled, shaky response drifted down to him. "Y-Yes."

Ben cupped his hands to his mouth again. "Are you Dan or Pete?"

"Pete...."

Ben sagged against the rock face to think this over. Pete was the less experienced of the two. There was nothing to indicate the other boy's presence. He was almost afraid to ask the next question.

"Is Dan with you?"

The same boy's voice drifted down to him again. "Yes."

"Are either of you hurt?"

"Dan...Dan's got a broken leg, f'sure. He hit his head, too."

"How about you?"

"I-I'm mostly scraped up...but my ankle hurts, somethin' fierce."

Ben chewed his lip, considering the next course of action. Someone had to get up there and get a handle on things so the rest knew what to bring. And that someone appeared to be him. No way around it. "All right," he called up. "Hang in there, Pete. I'm on my way up to you. More help's on the way." He twisted around for his radio.

Thirty minutes later, an entire squad of rescue personnel had converged on the scene from every direction including above. The rescue helicopter maneuvered its way over the top of the bluff for an overview as another half dozen men, rangers and Scout personnel, stood below, watching from the dusty, gravel-strewn lip of Alum Cave.

Another ranger appeared at the top of the cliff face, signaling his readiness with a wave. On the ground, Hank Stone gave a nod and the ranger began to rappel to the ledge of rock where Ben now huddled alongside the two boys.

He had worked his way up to the boys utilizing his old rock climbing skills from college, making a zigzag ascent along one corner of the bluff. Once he had reached the ledge, the situation didn't improve much. There was little room for maneuvering on this precarious perch.

Pete, the less injured one, crouched, hugging the rock face, his eyes shut tight. *Got my work cut out for me there*, Ben surmised. He tried to get a better look at the other boy but was wary of any movement that might make the eroding edges crumble further.

Above, scuff marks in the rock and matted grass showed the path of their fall from the top of the cliff. The edge must have given way beneath them. Ben knew there were no official trails up there. The area was dotted with signs marking the area off-limits. Chain-link fence reinforced the warning in places as well, but even those didn't stop the foolhardy.

"How'd you guys get up there, anyway?" he muttered. Young Pete stole a glance at his cohort but said nothing.

"I take it this wasn't your idea."

The boy shook his head, not meeting the ranger's eyes. "I'm not so good with heights."

"I gathered."

The other boy stirred and looked up sharply.

"Be quiet, you little weasel! We wouldn't be in this mess if you'd—"

"Stop callin' me that!" Pete shot back. "You're always pushin' people around. I'm never gonna let you talk me inta anything again!"

At the base of the cliff, Shane was trying along with everyone else to get a better view of the situation, gauging the stability of the ledge…its weight load…even as the sounds of an argument drifted down to them. His squint turned to a scowl. "What's goin' on up there?" he bellowed out. The scoutmaster alongside threw him a worried look.

Up on the ledge, Ben's carefully cultivated professional manner was evaporating. "Guys! Enough!"

He took a deep breath, hoping to regain his composure. Jake Willis, one of the Oconaluftee rangers, landed on the ledge, suspended by cables. He handed off two harnesses, one tethered to the top of the cliff. Ben took that one and fastened it around his waist, between his legs, and across his chest. He turned to the less-injured young scout. "Now Pete, I know you don't know me very well but…I'm gonna ask you to trust me on this. Think you can do that?"

The boy eyed him, considering. "You seem…pretty good…at your job." Still, he swallowed.

"I do my best." Ben ventured a smile. "You can count on it." That seemed to have an effect. Ben inched closer and stretched out his right arm toward the boy. Pete was having trouble letting go of his precious grasp on the scrub spruce jutting out of the rock face. After a couple of shaky attempts, he flung one arm out.

Ben scooted up alongside. "Good…good…." Bracing his left foot against the rock face, he slung the shoulder harness over the boy's head and under one arm. "Okay…now I need your other arm," he directed in a soothing voice.

The sound of the helicopter's rotors reverberating against the cliff face caused Pete to clamp his eyes shut. His right hand seized up on the flimsy tree trunk. Ben bit back the urge to bark at his charge. That wouldn't help now. He lowered his voice, for the boy's ears only. "You've got to trust me, Pete."

The boy's grasp slid reluctantly along the tiny, gnarled trunk. With a shredding sound, his hand came free, clutching a fistful of sweaty needles. Ben swiveled to balance himself. Jake crouched nearby, ready to assist.

The copter lowered into position, a third ranger suspended from it. He swung in close, perching long enough to hook up young Pete with Ben's help. With a tight hold on his charge and some well-chosen words of encouragement, the ranger signaled the okay for them to be lowered to the ground.

Ben and Jake watched their descent until satisfied that both were safely back on terra firma. Once the two below disconnected, the helicopter rose to rejoin the remaining trio on the ledge.

Now to deal with the irascible half of the pair. The boy had spent much of the time scowling at his fellow scout, at Ben, and now at Jake as well. Dan had batted away Ben's earlier attempts to examine his condition, giving in only to the bandana Ben handed him to put on his head. From the looks of that twisted leg, though, it was, at the very least, dislocated. The kid had to be in a lot of pain, but resisted any attempt to attend him.

Jake and Ben looked at each other, both wondering how they were going to manage getting this one into the litter now swinging alongside the ledge. Jake stood to grab hold and pull it closer. Ben inched toward the scout.

What happened next was not clear to those watching below.

"Quiet!" Shane barked amid the rumblings. All eyes were trained on the rock ledge two-thirds up the cliff. There appeared to be an altercation. The teenager's arms could be seen flailing, batting off the two rangers attempting to secure him into the litter. Rock began to crumble. Fist-sized chunks rattled down the cliff face, trailing dust. There was an outcry—a desperate lunge by one of the rangers—reaching for the boy as the front of the ledge gave way.

The scout fell with it, plummeting in a sickening hurtle to the valley floor below. A matter of seconds. Young Pete's cry of horror was followed by stunned silence....

Four rescuers scrambled down to where Dan had fallen. They knelt in the high grass. In a matter of heartbeats, they looked up, shaking their heads soberly. The helicopter veered off to find a place to land, its mission cruelly curtailed.

Shane's gaze swiveled back up the cliff to check out the rangers still on the ledge. The two were hanging precariously. Jake had reclaimed a toehold, steadying himself against the bluff and what was left of the ledge. Shane then saw, with a jolt, that half of Ben's harness had come loose, jostled during the breakaway. Scrapes on the cliff face betrayed the drop he'd taken. Ben had nearly followed the boy to his own death.

Shane steadied himself, exhaling sharply. They had nearly lost four in this incident. Two of them rangers.

"Get those men down from there! Now!"

* * * *

The front door of the lodge opened to a darkened house.

Shane and Ben trudged in, dropped their packs from their shoulders, and stretched their backs in tandem. In the semi-darkness Ben plopped down on an ottoman, staring moodily into space. Frustration and anger smoldered just beneath the surface.

Shane went on to the kitchen. He eyed Ben impassively from the pass-through, then pulled a couple of canned sodas from the fridge. Ambling back into the dark den, he lobbed a can Ben's way and went out on the deck. He stared down through the pines to where moonlight glinted in wavelets on the lake.

He heard steps behind him and turned to see Morgan there, sagging against the doorjamb. His friend took a swig from the can and looked up into the starry night with a jagged sigh.

"This job sucks, know that?"

The ghost of a grin flitted across Shane's face. "Yeah…it can. But other times…you can't beat it for the world."

He lifted his chin, listening to the muffled hoot of a barred owl on the soft breeze, and noted the ring around the moon. Rain was on its way. Tomorrow it would wash away all sign of what had happened today. No one would have reason to know, save those who were there. Nature believed in moving on. They had to, too.

He could feel Ben's eyes staring at his back, knew the look he would find if he turned. He'd seen that look many times before…had worn it himself a few times. Hungry for reassurance….

"You did your job," he said without turning. "The best you could. No one could've done more."

It sounded like a litany to ward off nightmares in the dark, a mantra against the boogey-man of self-doubt.

Ben grimaced. "Didn't do that kid much good, did it?" He crunched up the can in his fist and turned to go.

"You saved one, too," Shane said after him. "Don't ever forget that."

Ben paused to heed his words before continuing inside. Shane walked him to the door. "Go on home. Get some rest. I don't want to see your mangy mug before noon, hear?"

Ben nodded stiffly and went out into the night.

*   *   *   *

Debriefing session over, the afternoon meeting at Headquarters disbanded. The past two hours had been spent poring over the sequence of events at Alum Cave Bluffs in minute detail. Even with no blame laid at the foot of any ranger, everyone in the meeting shared a fervent desire to prevent such a calamity from ever repeating itself.

Flanked by John Gage and another ranger, Shane and Ben emerged, heads bent together as they proceeded down the hall. Outside, the two paused by their vehicles.

Ben shook his head. "I still can't figure what made the boy so combative. That was more than a teenager rebelling or being embarrassed. He had to have been in too much pain for that to matter."

Shane scratched his jaw. "Well, you gotta realize, with millions of people comin' into the park, some of 'em are gonna bring their problems with them. Turns out in this case, he was off some meds."

The two drew quiet a moment, mulling that over.

"Thought you oughta know," Shane ventured, "I put your name in for a commendation."

Ben made a wry face. "Why?"

"Oh...I just thought, after all the hard times some of 'em gave you, it'd feel good to see 'em have to eat their words."

"Gee thanks...I think."

The radios on both trucks blared out a call: *Ranger requests assistance, Elkmont Campground....*

"I'll take this one." Ben ducked into his Jeep and reached for the comm.

Shane tossed him a wave and swung into the driver seat of the Blazer alongside. Starting up the engine, he looked across with a nod. "See ya 'round."

*   *   *   *

Shane slowed his truck and peered across the field at the old Carter Shields cabin. Two figures sat on the bowed plank steps… one an elderly man, the other a sassy-looking brunette in jeans. Unless he was gravely mistaken, there was only one person in these parts with a mahogany head of hair like that. He smiled to himself, stopped the engine and got out, walking leisurely up the worn path to join them.

Andie sat there across from a lanky, white-haired gentleman with a face grown kindly and eyes that spoke mischief. Baby Adam dozed on a blanket on the covered porch.

As Shane trudged up the rise to meet them, he was struck by the tranquility of the scene. The sun glinted off that heart-stopping cascade of russet. He found it hard to believe he could lay claim to such a woman, much less that she'd sought *him* out.

Thoughts of the night before came to him, when he had stumbled to bed and found those soft welcoming arms and drowsy smile waiting for him…wiping all the heaviness of the day away.

He blinked himself back to the present. Back to business.

Resting a foot on the porch, he eyed his wife.

"You get around, don't you?"

The old gentleman squinted up at him. "This your doll baby?"

"Which one?"

"The pretty one, fool!"

"I guess I'll claim her."

The old man wagged his head. "Rats! All the good ones are taken!"

They all shared a laugh. Shane reached across the steps to shake hands. "How ya doin', Harv?"

The old fellow returned with a hardy if bony clasp. " 'Bout as well as can be expected, I suppose."

Andie looked on, eyes beaming. "Harvey was just filling me in on some local legends. He's got me hooked now. I may take some of those mountain lore classes at Tremont."

"If any man knows those stories, Harv should. You were rangerin' 'round here fifty years ago, weren't you?"

"Still would be, if they let me!" the old fellow huffed. The spark of pride in those fierce eyes was followed by a wistful wag of his head.

Shane considered him a moment and glanced at his watch. "Tell you what. I've got a little time to kill." He eased himself down onto the steps alongside the two of them. "Why don't you fill me in on this old place?"

On the other side of the park, Ben was trying to make sense of the request just come over his radio.

"Now wait a minute. You said you needed *what?*"

The static-laced voice of Buck MacIntyre came over the line. "*I said*...a small saw and an extra pair of hands. Maybe a crowbar, too. Y'got any of those?"

"Well, yeah, I got 'em. Hold on, I'll be there in five minutes."

Ben turned the NPS Jeep off the main road and onto a gravel path. "What now?" he muttered.

Shortly, he was pulled up to Campsite Number Ten per Buck's instructions. He got out, went to the back of the Jeep, and rummaged through the back compartment for the requested items. As he approached the small group of people gathered around one of the wood slat bins that normally stored firewood, he could swear he heard howls coming from it.

One of the men kneeling at the bin saw him approaching and stood with a worried frown. Ben got his first good look at the situation. He struggled not to laugh out loud. A child of about eight— a boy, he presumed from the clothing—lay sprawled on the ground, his head encased in the confines of the woodbin. The spacing between the slats must've been enough to allow him to maneuver in but not out of the bin. To make matters worse, his head apparently wasn't in there alone. Some kind of small animal was scrambling about inside, scratching at the slats, and howling. A beagle pup, Ben judged, from the baying. All of this was punctuated by the boy's yelps—

"Ow! Down, Sammy! No! Stop! Ow!"

A man came forward with a sheepish face. "My son's new puppy crawled in there, you see...he tried to coax it back out. We had no idea..." he trailed off helplessly.

Ben looked over at Buck, his eyes twinkling. "Relax, we'll have him out in no time." Ben knelt alongside his fellow ranger, handing him the crowbar. Buck glanced up at the father hovering over them. "Uh—sir—could you hold your son still? That would be helpful."

The man knelt to do so but cast an anxious look Ben's way, eyeing the saw the ranger laid beside him.

"Just a backup," Ben reassured him, with a smile that was perhaps too enthusiastic. Unconventional methods aside, the boy was freed in a matter of seconds with the right tools at hand...though not without a splintering *CRACK* as the slat came loose. The child whimpered—and froze.

Ben bent down to peer in his face. "It's alright. You can come out now. You've still got all your body parts."

The boy turned his head gingerly and peered up at him with big brown eyes. "Oh." The puppy beat him in escape, however, wriggling past, tail wagging in his young master's face.

"Alright, you!" Buck snatched the pup up, helped the boy to his feet, and dusted him off. A round of contrite thank-you's and the rangers were on their way back to their respective vehicles.

"You know," Ben mused aloud, "we could've been done even sooner if I'd brought along that new chainsaw—"

Buck shot him an uneasy look, edging away from him.

"Just kidding!" Ben laughed and reached out to jab him. "Hey, have you noticed how these types of calls keep coming to you?" his voice trailed off, followed by Buck's soft reply.

"Yeah...I've noticed that...."

. 20 .

Buck thought about Ben's words a couple weeks later as he took a wildlife count along the Metcalf Bottoms Trail. At times, it didn't seem his Division got the respect it deserved. Maybe they weren't the flashier *big guns* of the Enforcement Branch or Back-country Patrol—the glory boys, search and rescues, who got in the papers—but Wildlife Resources had its share of tough jobs, too. Even in a park this big, roles frequently blurred, with a tight staff and tighter funds. One morning, he might be helping band a red-tail hawk with a radio transmitter; that afternoon, responding to a campground disturbance in his home territory of Elkmont; the next night, on surveillance with John Gage to catch elk hunters.

In his ten years as a ranger, he'd fought forest fires, delivered babies, rescued flood victims, taught unruly cub scouts, and hauled in unsavory characters on poaching charges—aside from performing his primary duties as a field biologist.

There had been no obvious signs of poaching lately, at least not since that bear business a year ago…but there had been a marked decrease in several small mammal sightings lately. That worried him.

Either the poachers were getting smarter, neater with their handiwork, or he was slipping. Who knew what kind of high tech equipment they had at their disposal these days?

It was hard to know for sure in a park of half a million acres, surrounded by three National Forests. Maybe all that was going on was migration or a naturally occurring cycle. He needed to check in with the boys at Pisgah, Nantahala, and Cherokee as well as the meteorologists in Knoxville to chart any weather patterns that might have a bearing on things.

Of immediate concern was his otter population. The last two outings, he'd failed to see any....

Buck paused to rest against a rough-hewn cedar pole that served for a rail at one of the creek crossings beyond Little Greenbrier School. He frowned at the patrol sheet in his hand. Four squirrels, two blue-striped skinks, a couple of chipmunks, a blue jay, and one downy woodpecker. Not much for an entire morning's outing. On such a quiet morning, his trained eyes would have normally spotted several deer, a napping raccoon in a hollow tree trunk, maybe even some of those otters rumored to have moved into the area. He eyed a length of the Little Brier Gap Trail, considering this.

At least the hike was pretty…leaves had started to turn along the trail, tulip poplars among the first, dropping yellow leaves onto the path. Fall was his favorite time of year and while it meant ramped up workloads for many of the rangers, especially around Sugarlands, Cades Cove, and the campgrounds, he appreciated the chance to get off the beaten path by himself like this.

His ear detected something and he froze, cocking his head to catch the sound again. There it was. He tried to zero in on the direction the distinctive chittering and grumbling was coming from.

No mistaking—it was one of his otters…maybe two. But this was not the accustomed playful chitters or wrestling growls he knew them to make. This was more urgent…frantic.

Buck flung the backpack onto his shoulders and skittered off trail, scrambling over lichen-covered boulders toward the sound. He came to a stop and tried to slow his breathing, straining to make out the faintest sound.

This time a rustling, scratching sound caught his ear, accompanied by a low *rowl*…then panting. Buck verified the direction and charged upslope through a thicket of rhododendron and mountain laurel. A small wild turkey exploded out of the bushes, a flurry of squeaky protest. His heart jammed into his throat. He staggered back then pushed forward, wading through the shoulder-high tangle of vegetation.

When he cleared the sprawling patch, he saw it.

A wire cage...contents, one juvenile otter.

Outrage surged in him, coupled with relief. At least it was a live trap. Whoever laid it wanted the animal unhurt—or at least its coat unmarred—he thought grimly.

An adult otter, presumably a parent, sprawled on its side, clawing with frustration at the crate's metal frame. Buck approached cautiously. He found himself trying to imitate some of the chittering noise he'd heard them make in more playful surroundings. Not that he'd pass for a huge otter, but just maybe it would put them more at ease—that is, if he wasn't signaling fight language by mistake. You could never be sure of the subtleties when it came to animal communication.

The big otter backed away with a low grumble. Nonetheless, Buck did not read it as poised for attack. He lapsed into human tongue as he drew near the cage and knelt before it. "Hey now, little fellow...don't worry. We'll get you free in no time."

He slid his pack from his shoulders and peeled open the side pocket that held his Swiss Army knife. "I was wondering when this would come in handy next." The primary blade made quick work of sawing through the tough leather sinew that held the trap in place. Curious choice for stake cords...it told him that whoever set this up was likely a deer hunter. The really serious ones, not in it just for trophy heads, prided themselves on using every part of the animal possible, like their forebears. Someone who had roots in the area, perhaps. Cherokee or white? Others borrowed those skills, learning them in survival camps that had been springing up in the area more and more lately.

Buck's darker thoughts were wiped away when he peered in at the forlorn-looking pup. It had backed itself into the far corner of the cage. He couldn't help but smile. Something about the playful, bewhiskered critters had won his heart early on. They were now one of his research specialties in the park, along with deer and the groundhog meadowland communities.

He sat back on his haunches, scanning the woods with a frown. "What are you doing all the way up here anyway? Somebody entice you with some fish? Wish you could tell me who's responsible for this." He proceeded with his work but couldn't shake the feeling he was being watched. The hairs on the back of his neck prickled.

Slowly, he lifted up the wire box and backed out of the way. The otter pup continued to cower there, bobbing its head up and down as it eyed him.

Buck cocked his head. "Well, what are you waiting for? Scram!"

A rustle in the brush behind made Buck whirl around—but not in time to catch more than a blur of his assailant. He was tackled to the ground, hard, and rolled onto his stomach. A glimpse of black hood was all he made out before a fist slammed into the side of his face, his head ringing from the blow. Relentless pummeling followed, the taste of blood filling his mouth.

Buck struggled to flip onto his back and face this attack head-on, searching for something, *anything*, to push against. He brought his knee up…a shallow jab…but with enough force to make his attacker roll off with an *Oomph!* Buck scrambled to his knees. The woods spun around him as he fought to keep his balance.

A flicker of movement brought his head around. The young otter wavered at the cage opening. Buck flung out his arms.

"Git!" he forced through swelling lips.

That distraction cost him dearly. A wall of muscled force struck him sideways, knocking him back to the ground. He winced as jagged pebbles bit through the lightweight khaki of his uniform. The two rolled together through the thicket of laurel, rhododendron, and fern, kicking up dirt and leaves.

Fingers fumbled at his side. Buck realized the guy was going for his gun. Show over if he got hold of *that*. He wriggled to his left side, trying to get a hand free even as he felt the Glock slide out of its holster, heard it scrape against the dirt. Pedaling madly, he scooted ninety degrees, trying to get his shoe in range.

He was suddenly aware they'd hit rock. The next second, he found his head suspended backwards over thin air. He caught the dizzying glimpse of a craggy drop into the green blur of a ravine. What he took for an outcrop of boulders proved to be a ledge that hung out over nothing. His assailant didn't let up. Strong hands yanked Buck by the shoulders, poised to ram the back of his skull into the granite beneath.

His feet sought to dig in, then backpedal against the unyielding rock. He tried to slip out from under the guy's hold, but it caused him to pivot closer to the edge. But at least it gave him something to work with. His foot found the loose gun and he kicked as hard as he could, sending it flying over the edge.

Even as he did so, Buck grappled for a hold on the black hood. It started to give way. Stout fingers, in return, pressed into his face, obstructing his view, mashing craters into his flesh. Resolutely, he held on, feeling tufts of hair come loose from the edges of the hood. His fingers closed in on a patch and he tugged with all his might. He might go down, but not without taking a piece of his killer with him…maybe enough to incriminate.

His attacker grunted in pain. The grip on him loosened for an instant. Buck used it to shove with his heels, sliding backwards…to the edge—

Before he could summon effort from his bruised backbone to roll away, the guy scrambled to his feet and lunged toward him. But halfway, he stopped, straightening with a deep-gutted guffaw. Buck had heard less beastly sounds come out of a bear. Something in MacIntyre's Virginia mountain blood wasn't going to let go without getting a final blow in. Teeth clenched against the agony of battered bones, he forced a leg up once more and kicked out with all his remaining strength, aiming, he hoped, for his assailant's kneecap. He caught a blur of the thick body staggering back. Buck used the momentum to roll over as well.

But the ledge was not solid where he landed. A muffled crunch, and cracks spread out in every direction. The section beneath him gave way. Buck scrambled for a hold as the rock began to tilt, slanting him feet first. He slid on his belly six feet down, taking chunks from the cliff face with him. His battered fingers trailed across a tangle of roots and clamped on for dear life.

The sound of heavy breathing came from above. Squinting past the dirt, sweat, and blood, Buck made out the form of his combatant peering down, hands on knees. The crook of a sneer was visible beneath the skewed head covering. A wheezy chuckle issued forth. "What cha hanging 'round down there for? Come on back up and we'll settle this with a friendly knife fight, eh?"

He hauled out a hunting knife that looked like it could gut a bear in one swipe, flaunting its deadly glint in a ray of sunlight.

Buck didn't answer, gauging through the haze of pain what his options were. He strained to look over his shoulder at the drop below. No comfort there.

No ledge to break his fall. No soft landing in sight. Fifty feet…maybe more….

Not so bad, he told himself. Over soon…might even survive the fall. Only some broken ribs…a leg…to show for it. Could survive the night till help came. Better than having his stomach unzipped by the likes of Jethro up there….

"What's the matter, ranger? Thought you fellers were tougher than that!" the taunt floated down from above.

Roots ripped loose beneath Buck's tenuous grasp. He sought purchase on the moss-covered rocks jutting out of the cliff side. Still wet from morning dew, they afforded an even flimsier hold. Finger joint by finger joint, his precious grip failed. Time to let go. Buck knew it. Still…it was hard to give up the fight….

Having uttered only a handful of oaths in his entire life, Buck considered this an appropriate time.

"Oh, Hell…" he groaned, forcing fingers to let go…feeling his weight succumb to gravity.

A silly old saying of his father's came to mind: *It's not the fall that hurts ya, it's th' hittin' bott—*

A thud that made his head ring ended the thought. A split second of nausea…followed by inky black….

A scuff of dirt skittered down, landing on his back. From the ledge above came a muttered, "I'll be damned. Good riddance."

The hooded assailant spied the ranger's radio in the dirt where they'd scuffled. Going over, he picked it up, considering it a moment, then gave a snort, dropping the radio to the ground. Smashing it with a heavy boot, he kicked it into the brush and stomped away.

* * * *

Shane looked up from his desk, frowning at the interruption. The look on Susannah's face said something serious was up.

"What is it, Susie?"

"We've got a missing ranger, sir."

Shane tossed his pen aside and stood, knuckles pressed white into the desk. "Who?"

She bit her lip. "Buck. He was supposed to meet Pat Arrowsmith at one for a talk at Elkmont Amphitheater. An hour later, Pat started checking around. Bobby Dickerson called in, said he found Buck's vehicle at the Metcalf Bottoms trailhead but no sign of him. It's…not like Buck to not check in."

Shane saw her trying to blink back the concern in her eyes. She was particularly fond of Buck. They all were. It was unthinkable that something should happen to such a nice guy. The advice Bill Hayes had given him years ago during an avalanche rescue came to mind: "When the troops start to crumble, keep 'em too busy to feel!"

Shane came around the deck and took her by the shoulders. "Tell Sheree to get hold of Cal, John, Ben, and Pat. Tell 'em to meet me at MacIntyre's truck—and make sure the police in Townsend are notified to be on the lookout for anything suspicious. Put Sugarlands in the loop, too. We'll get to the bottom of this." Shane swiveled to snatch the keys off his desk and gave her a reassuring swat to the shoulder on his way out.

Buck drifted into a fuzzy consciousness he mistook for another dream at first. Funny thing was, he couldn't really remember dreaming at all…just snatches of black punctuated by the sensation of falling. Muscle jerks…the kind just before sleep overtakes weary muscles.

Another spasm, this time followed by a stab of pain that forced the breath out of him. The sound of his own gasp brought him 'round. Several more seconds and his eyes remembered to open. Squint, that is. Focusing was another matter. Out of the question. He tried to raise his head. It wobbled and fell back. Was his neck broken? *If it was, I couldn't move…could I?*

His thoughts went round and round like they were on a carousel. *Did I? Didn't I?* Right now, he didn't trust his brain to know what was real.

It was easy to just lie there in the cool shady cushion of fern. But his body began to shake. Shock? *Gotta move...take stock....*

He tried to sit up. Another stab of pain, this one squeezing his rib cage, laid him back, panting.

Memory came slow to him. *Must've taken a bad fall.* No...that wasn't like him.... What...? His hand twitched, the skin of his palm prickling. His left arm obeyed his summons, albeit wobbly. He brought his hand close to his face, squinting at the fuzzy mass matted in his sweaty, swollen fingers. Looked like...bear fur? The ache in his finger joints echoed earlier strain. Nerve endings carried remembrance with them. His teeth clamped down as images flooded back. Whoever it was...they hadn't gotten rid of him yet.

Grim satisfaction gave him the impetus to face rising again. Braced this time against the pain, he met it head on and pressed through. Every muscle in his back and arms screamed at the insult. To Buck's surprise, the stabbing pain ebbed once he was upright, leaning on his right arm. Just a faint throbbing. Maybe no broken ribs after all. A miracle, to say the least. Something had to be broken in that fall. He just hadn't found it yet.

Buck gingerly waggled his ankles, found them sore but sound. He stared down at the dirt-caked, bloodied tears in his pants legs, tried flexing his knees, one at a time. Resistant but mobile. But the numbness in his left elbow told him not to attempt anything there. With a grunt, he rolled to his right side, pushed with his right leg, and got himself almost vertical, leaning heavily against a dirt bank covered with last year's leaves. Gradually, his left leg got the idea and followed its companion. He saw then it was a dry creek bed he'd been lying in. Pausing for a breather, he eyed the course before him. *Follow stream down the mountain...gotta come to something....*

Mountain-bred instinct took over. A couple gulps of air in anticipation of the pain to come and he shoved off, staggering his way down the ravine.

Fire coursed through his leg, followed by a numbing ache…. Buck stared down in shock at the fang marks in his calf. After all he'd been through, now this….

Mammals might be his specialty, but he knew his reptiles. It was a copperhead that had gotten hold of him. He saw it slither off into the thicket.

A brief respite was all he'd been seeking, just a minute's rest, dropping onto the boulder that held warmth from the sun's passage earlier. It offered comfort to his grinding joints. But that was too much to ask. Luck was determined to run out on him after all. His brain told his hand to reach in his pocket for his knife, but the hand only lay there in his lap, trembling. He tried to stand, take a step. The ground rushed up at him. Strange sparks of light swam before his eyes. His sense of time, distance, depth perception were rapidly deteriorating.

Buck knew the signs. In a second of clarity, he thought he spied a clearing beyond the trees…what looked like an open field. He headed toward it….

Rachel Hendrickson looked up from watering the scuppernong trellis at the back of their yard.

"Grandpa! Look!"

She pointed to a figure staggering through the far end of the fallow field. Her grandfather rose from his rocker, shuffled over to the porch railing, and peered out. "It's one of them ranger fellas."

Rachel squinted, bringing the person into sharper focus. A man…dressed in that mossy green uniform she'd come to recognize as Park Service people. Sure enough, a ranger…. He appeared sick…or hurt. Absently, her fingers let go of the hoe. It plopped into the cool, wet grass. Recognition made her heart skip a beat.

"Buck!"

She broke into a run.

The ranger had not crossed much ground before she met up with him. Save for the glint of sun off his hair and the uniform, she might not have recognized him. She threw an arm around to steady him. His body sagged against her, threatening to unbalance them both. No sign of recognition in his battered, dirt-smudged face. Rachel led him to the back steps where her grandfather waited.

Between the two of them, they got the ranger to a bedroom and deposited him on the quilt-covered iron bed. Rachel sank down on the bed's edge, surveying him. *What to do first? Clean him up?*

She jumped up, pulled off his boots, and noticed her grandfather hovering uncertainly in the doorway.

"Get me some water…soap…an'…an' a wash rag," she said distractedly. When he hesitated, she turned on him with a scowl. "Hurry!"

The old man came to himself and bustled away as fast as his cane would allow. When he returned, he handed over the old pitcher that had been in his family since the Civil War and eyed the ranger uneasily. "He don't look so good. What're we gonna do with him?"

Rachel poured water into the enamel basin on the bedside table. Dipping the washrag, she squeezed it out, and gently wiped Buck's face and neck. "Patch him up best we can, first!" she said crossly. "Then I guess we better call for his people."

"How girl? We ain't got no phone!"

Rachel threw him an exasperated look as she rinsed the cloth and squeezed it out. "That never stopped ya b'fore." She nodded toward the old shotgun resting against a corner.

Old Hendrickson followed her glance. "Hmmph." He shuffled off, muttering to himself.

Rachel dismissed him with a shake of her head and turned back to work. Laying the washrag aside, she hesitated, then gingerly went about unbuttoning the ranger's shirtfront. To take her mind off her nerves, she murmured to herself, pretending to scold him, "What'd you get yerself inta, fella? Look like ya fell off a cliff—"

A hand rose, gripping her wrist. Startled, her eyes flew to his face. No recognition still in those slits beneath mud-caked brows. The hand slid away, limp, leaving her to wonder at the urgency in that grasp. She caught a glimpse of flecks of blood on the upper calf of his trouser leg. Something in the pattern made her blood run cold, sending her scurrying for the old sewing shears.

Cutting away the material to expose the skin beneath, her fears were realized. Two small, neat puncture marks had torn the flesh there. Dried rivulets of blood ran from the puffy, reddened site. Her eyes travelled up, locking on the ranger's sweat-streaked face and glazed eyes.

Her lips began to move silently, reciting a verse of remedy Granny Hendrickson had taught her since she was knee-high to a grasshopper:

> *Bee balm for the monthlies,*
> *Witch hazel births th' babies,*
> *Willow bark for tooth that aches,*
> *Coneflower for bite of snakes....*

She sprang from the bed, ran into the kitchen and out the screen door into the dry heat of the afternoon sun, bare feet slapping on the wooden steps. She headed back up to slip on some old Keds lying by the door and trotted into the yard, staring about herself, grasping fistfuls of her hair in frustration. Where was it she'd seen that plant? Seemed like yesterday...or was it the day before?

Remembrance came to her.... Granny had told her she'd transplanted some as a young bride, hoping to protect her husband and children to come.... Rachel scurried down toward the springhouse and the little creek that ran beside it. There, along the bank, near the shade of a mulberry, with jewelweed, and sumac nearby, she found a patch of the purple flowers.

Dropping to her knees, she proceeded to yank them up by the root. With a sizeable bunch gathered, she hurried back to the cabin. In the kitchen, she pumped water into the sink, filled a teakettle, and set it to boil while she washed the plants in a colander, then crushed the roots with an old chipped mortar and pestle. Some she left in the bowl to form a poultice. The rest she put into a teacup and poured simmering water over it.

Hurrying back to the bedroom, she plopped down on the bed's edge, scooped up the mash with a spoon, and spread a poultice over the fang marks. Then she attempted to spoon some of the infusion into his parted lips.

He reacted with a feverish toss of the head. As he did so, one of his arms fell to the side of the bed, dangling there. His clenched fist opened, exposing a sweaty palm covered in coarse dark hair. She blinked, taking a closer look. At first, she thought it might be bear fur. Grabbing the washrag, she wiped it all into a wad and held it up to the light, studying it—and bit back a gasp.

She'd seen that shade of hair before. Trying to slow her panicked breathing, she hurried over to the old oak dresser. From its top drawer, she pulled out an old envelope, slipped the tuft of hair into it and shut it back up in the drawer.

Her eyes traveled back, haunted, to the ranger lying near death on her bed. The shattering blast of a gunshot jolted her from her thoughts.

* * * *

Shane wiped the sweat from his forehead and replaced his cap, eyeing the approach of two rangers. Ben Morgan and John Gage looked grave.

"Nothing?" he called to them.

Both men shook their heads. "Pat radioed he found some trampled bushes off Little Brier Gap Trail. Could've been caused by a bear or one of those wild hogs but he's checkin' it out," Ben offered. The three turned as one to eye the sun, sharing the same thought. Shadows lengthened early in the mountains. Even in summer, twilight crept into the campgrounds and trails soon after four o'clock. And here it was September. It was three o'clock now.

"If anyone can track him, Arrowsmith can…" Shane trailed off. He rubbed his chin, trying to come up with a new tactic.

A Jeep bounced down the rutted road toward them, dust billowing in its wake.

Rob Johnson, the aquatic biologist, burst from the vehicle, breathless. "Susie just took a call. Someone complaining about gunshots going off in Wear Cove. Said it sounded like relay volleys. Harv Witherspoon was visiting and he said it could be signal shots, like they used in the old days—"

Shane jerked a nod. "That settles it. Let's go."

*   *   *   *

"Let me get this straight…you get bushwhacked, fall off a cliff, *and* snakebit? Buckley, nobody's that unlucky."

District Chief MacLeod shook his head in wonder. But staring down at the wan, battered face of the young ranger who lay on the quilt, under the amber glow of a hurricane lamp, along with his bandaged ribs, left no doubt he'd encountered more than his quota of trouble for one day…maybe several seasons' worth.

Buck rubbed his head, taking in the four rangers who stood around the bed with their arms crossed. Amusement had taken over their initial looks of concern. "Maybe you're right…" Buck mumbled. "I'm not sure, myself, anymore. But there was that penned otter, I know! I let him go! Maybe there's still some sign of the pen." He glanced up hopefully. The bruises around his eyes lent a pathetic air.

A smile touched Shane's eyes. "I promise to send someone to look. We'd better be on our way and let you rest." He looked to Doctor Alston. She seemed satisfied enough to be packing up her medical bag.

"You don't know how lucky you were, stumbling into help when you did." She looked to the young woman who'd retreated to a rocking chair in the corner. "I've seldom had faith in those folk remedies but the Echinacea seems to have helped—though I suspect it had a lot to do with our Virginian's hardy constitution."

Doc Lillian wagged a bony finger at Buck. "Three days' strict bedrest, understand? Plenty of fluids. That antivenin I administered should put you out of the woods, but any more swelling,

265

burning, or numbness, you call me first thing. I'll check back in tomorrow morning."

Pat Arrowsmith wore that inscrutable smile of his as the rangers filed out after the doctor, leaving Buck to the ministrations of his gentle caregiver.

Out on the porch, the rangers communed. Shane shoved his hands in his pockets, ruminating.

"What do you think?" he asked his colleagues.

Ben shrugged. "Anything's possible."

Shane threw him an exasperated look. "Knew you'd say that." He turned to Gage, down the steps from him. "John?"

The big ranger wagged his head as he pulled off his cap to swipe his forehead. "I don't know, Shane. Snakebite's crazy stuff. The one I got had me believin' I was married t' three women at the same time—till my fever broke. Weird...makes you lose all sense of time in the middle of all that throwing up and twitching and t'other stuff."

Behind him, Morgan cocked an eyebrow, casting a glance back toward the room where MacIntyre lay recovering. Shane ignored him and turned his attention back to Gage.

"If it's evidence you're talkin' 'bout," John went on, "that gully-washer this evenin' likely erased any sign of a struggle—or trap for that matter. I'll be glad to look, though."

"Me, too," Ben offered.

"I'd be glad to, but I got that trip to Nantahala in the morning," Arrowsmith put in.

Shane extended his hand. "No problem. Appreciate your help this afternoon, Pat." The sturdy Cherokee shook hands with him, nodding solemnly. "Don't mention it."

Big John leaned in, lowering his voice. "If you ask me, I think Buck just plain fell off a heap of crumbling rock, got bit, and hallucinated the rest. I ain't seen any traps around here in years."

Ben frowned. "There was that bear a while back, remember?"

Gage eyed him askance and snorted. "Yeah...I remember. Gall bladder, my foot!" He spat dismissively and lumbered toward his truck.

Ben shrugged ruefully and followed the others down the steps. Pat Arrowsmith nudged his shoulder. "I believe you."

They were surprised to see Gage, rather than get in, pull his rifle from the gun rack inside the cab. "But if it makes you ladies feel any better, I'll plop myself on that porch overnight and keep a watch."

"You sure?" Shane asked.

"Yeah…my long, tall Sally over t' Chilhowee Grill is out of town this week visiting her sister. Got nothin' better to do."

"Thanks, John. Take care now. Come on, Ben, let's get Buck's truck back from Greenbrier."

He walked off with Morgan, noticing he was unusually quiet, lost in thought or disgruntled or both. Shane opened the Blazer's door and paused. "Tell you what…you can help me make some calls in the morning…Nantahala…Cherokee…."

Ben looked up quizzically.

Shane shrugged. "At this point, I'm not discountin' anything. I just know…if we've got somebody out there jumpin' people, I want 'em found—quick."

Three mornings later, Buck was retrieved by Ben Morgan, who appeared at the Hendricksons' door with a carton of barbecue from a local favorite, along with sides of hushpuppies, slaw, and a peach pie meant as a thank-you. Buck felt self-conscious, knowing he looked as wan as he felt. Not up to conversation yet either. As Morgan slid behind the wheel of the Jeep, he paused to survey Buck before turning the key.

"You all right to be home on your own?"

"Yeah…I'll follow Doc Lillian's advice and rest another two days before reporting in."

"Any more memories of what happened?"

"Not yet…I guess the guys were right. It probably *was* the snakebite that made me think those things…the ambush and so forth. I mean, I was having all kinds of delusions…." He trailed off, cheeks warming.

267

Morgan wouldn't let *that* go. "Like what?"

Buck swallowed hard, mortified. "A-At least...I *think* it was a hallucination...or a dream...." A battery of vivid sensations invaded his head...the press of a gauze-draped breast as she leaned across him to bandage his wounds...soft, warm breath caressing his cheek...the sweet, sensuous lure of honeysuckle...amber lamp glow glinting off silken strands that pooled with intimate abandon across his chest.... He could swear his lips had brushed her cheek, only to find her willing mouth on his in answer....

He jumped when the engine came to life.

Morgan was grinning like a monkey. "Buck! Have you gone and gotten yourself into a ro-man-tic en-tangle-ment?"

Buck swiveled sore eyes up to meet his. "Maybe it was just the snakebite."

The rogue's smile turned devilish. "Maybe. Only one way to tell."

Buck winced, sensing, once again, he was setting himself up. "What's that?"

"Go back to the girl and find out."

Buck settled back in his seat uneasily. He said nothing else the rest of the way. Didn't want to. For some reason, was a little bit afraid to. Afraid he might spill something...about that other thing....

He still wasn't feeling quite himself the night before, when Rachel stole into his room and shook him awake. He struggled to rise up when he saw her sitting there on the bed's edge, a finger to her lips.

"What is it?" he'd whispered hoarsely.

"You gotta come with me, Buck. Now!" she whispered back.

He rose with difficulty. She braced him as he swung his legs over the bedside and went to stand. Wobbly at best. His first steps were shuffles. She led him over to the wardrobe. He raised his eyebrows when she drew back the door, pushed aside the clothes hanging within, unfastened some sort of latch at the back, and reached for his hand.

"Come on! Mind yer head!" she breathed.

Rachel helped shield his head as they bent double to fit through the small opening in the wall. Sure enough, there was a secret doorway there. The next thing he knew, they were out under the stars, hidden from view by an old althea bush.

She glanced back, catching the look on his face. "From boot-leggin' days."

Buck heard voices inside, strained to gauge their import, but Rachel tugged once again on his arm. "Follow me!"

He stumbled as he trotted along, trying to keep up with her through the dark cornfield, the waxing moon overhead the only light. "Where…are…we…going?" he panted between gulps for air that stung his weakened insides.

"Moonbow Cave!" she answered without looking back.

It seemed silly to him now, his response: "I thought…that…was…in Kentucky—"

"A lot they know," she tossed over her shoulder. "Probably never been near this place." She pressed on purposefully through a field of knee-high broom straw. A field mouse skittered across Buck's sock feet, startling him. In the distance, a saw-whet owl hooted.

They were nearing the woods now. Buck could make out the silhouettes of the trees. He came to an abrupt halt, doing his best to yank her back. "Rachel!" He bent over, clasping his knees and puffing hard as he peered up at her. "What aren't you telling me?"

She shifted restlessly in the tall grass, fumbling for his hand again. Buck could feel it trembling. "Please…don't make me tell…not yet anyways. I got t' figure it all out first." Her eyes pleaded with him. He held her in that gaze a moment longer before surrendering a nod. Straightening slowly, he let her lead him the rest of the way. Whatever this craziness was about, she seemed to think it crucial for them to stay together.

They huddled in a little grotto just beyond a gentle cascade for what seemed half the night. He was surprised to see the provisions on hand there…candles…a plastic bin of matches…old quilts folded up on a rocky ledge…ceramic cup and bowl…a knife and spoon…even a pail filled with books under a sheet of plastic. He distinctly remembered drowsing several hours against her shoulder under cover of one of those quilts, lulled to sleep by the ripple of the stream outside and the soft, warm body next to him.

They stole back later before dawn. Buck was startled by the appearance of the old man at the back door, ushering them in. Granddaughter and grandfather looked at each other but neither spoke a word. He was settled back to bed with care but no explanation for the evening's strange excursion. Only a hurried whisper, "Don't tell nobody my hidin' place!"

As he drifted off to sleep, he tried to make out the conversation in the adjoining room but caught only snatches.

"—left an hour ago."

"Did ya tell him I was havin' my monthlies? That usually scares him away."

"He didn't look in. Don't think he s'pected a thing."

Buck fell asleep after that, brow puckered. The next morning nothing was said of the incident. He began to question whether it had happened at all.

Maybe that, too, had been the snakebite.

. 21 .

Autumn worked its way through the Smokies, bringing with it a precarious time, when one day promised more Indian summer, another day hinted of the season to come. As October progressed into its last week, the fall foliage crowds began to thin. Signs of winter's approach appeared, attesting to nature's insistence to progress with the seasons, devoid of human control.

Half the jewel-toned foliage had been swept from the trees, prey to the gusty rainstorms that were intermission to stretches of sun-splashed days. On the mountainsides, fall was indeed giving way to its sister season…the tops of tulip poplar, oak, and hickory were bare, sweetgums the stubborn holdouts.

Roadsides and trails were still brilliant with goldenrod, aster, and sumac, just beginning to succumb to the grayed hues of dormancy. And broom straw's burnt-orange stalks still basked in sunlight beneath a sky of turquoise. To the casual observer, it was hard to accept that winter would show itself on the landscape any time soon.

But the rangers knew better….

"Any of you guys seen Andie?"

Ben's entrance disrupted a rare period of quiet in the Cades Cove Center. Susannah and Melba looked up from the map they were studying.

"Uh—no, Ben," Susannah returned. "Was she supposed to come by here?"

He approached the counter, took off his cap, and scratched his head. "Nahh…not necessarily. It's just…Shane asked me to look

271

in on her and the kids while he's in Washington. She wasn't home and didn't answer her cell. Just keep missing her, I guess."

One of the new rangers, a red-haired, freckle-faced boy who looked barely out of school, emerged from the back offices. "Did you say Andie MacLeod?" His face brightened, his voice taking on a note of familiarity. "I saw her this morning at the Cove stables. Said she was heading out to take some pictures. Following up on one of those stories Harvey told her, she said."

Behind Ben, Melba clucked her tongue. "She's got no business going off like that with a tiny baby!"

Susannah shrugged it off. "Probably just wanted a chance to get some fresh air. I know my sister felt cooped up after her baby came."

Ben gave both women a distracted glance but turned back to the young fellow. "Where was she headed, do you know?"

The young ranger shook his head. "No...but—"

"Was she alone?"

"Well, she had the little guy on her back—Adam? And she was gettin' on that big Appaloosa."

Ben glowered. "You let them go off like that? I'll talk to *you* later." He stalked out the door leaving the shaken young ranger and the others to stare after him.

Andie zipped up her jacket and searched a pocket for the knit baby cap. Was it her imagination or was there a nip in that breeze all of a sudden? She frowned and took another look at the crumpled hand-drawn map. So close...the abandoned village site couldn't be more than a quarter mile away. It would be a waste to turn around now.

She pulled up on the reins to consider a moment. The Appaloosa pawed the gravel path. Her slack on the reins spelled indecision. Being in limbo was not a state the horse was used to. Andie looked back the way she came, then turned resolutely forward. Heck, there was plenty of light left, a good two or three hours, right? Doubt began to gnaw at the pit of her stomach. Then she caught sight of the bridge in the distance—her final landmark. A smile smoothed away the wrinkle in her brow.

"There now! Am I a good navigator or what?" she exclaimed, half to herself, half to the tiny boy who rode contentedly in his sling before her. She grasped the pommel and carefully slid her way to the ground. The baby's added weight affected her balance, so she took each movement slowly, one hand always against the sturdy Appaloosa. It was like having a part of Shane with her. The scent of the horse was part of his smell—mixed with leather and balsam, the combination caused a wave of security to wash over her. She walked the Appaloosa across the wooden bridge, taking childish delight in the clop-clop of each hoof on the planks. Water swirled and wriggled between the river rocks below, gurgling peacefully. The hooves plodded softly again as they reached the other bank.

The sound of scraping gravel on the trail ahead reminded her, however, they were in fact, alone. That deceptive sense of security evaporated as the horse pricked up his ears. Friend or foe? More yet—human or animal?

In the year and a half she had lived in the park, she'd seen only four bears...two of those cubs. If you didn't smell like food and didn't come between a mother and her cubs, there was generally no threat. *Just give 'em space*, Shane said. She was about to mount up again and turn back when the outline of a man became visible through the trees. She breathed a sigh of relief—but caught it short.

This was no casual hiker or tourist—nor a ranger for that matter—coming toward her. Something about his appearance made her skin crawl. She wasn't exactly sure what that was. Maybe it was his clothes...the faded plaid flannel shirt worn loose, white T-shirt exposing the paunch beneath, faded jeans slung low...scuffed rubber boots that looked like farmyard wear...or hunter's. Not really all that unusual. Maybe just one of those gone-fishing-for-a-week-with-no-bath kind of camper. Half a week's growth of beard. Pale blue eyes glared beneath craggy black brows.

He stopped twenty feet before her, demanding, "Who are you?"

Andie leaned into the side of the horse, stroking its neck like a protective amulet. The guy was trying to intimidate her. People like that irritated her no end. Anger overcame fright. She stepped away from the horse and jangled the bridle, eyebrow arched.

"Who're *you*?"

The man cocked his head to one side. "I seen that horse before."

Andie jerked her chin up. "He belongs to my husband...District Chief MacLeod."

A snort issued from him. "Ranger's woman, huh?"

Andie started to say something but thought better of it. She clucked to the Appaloosa and tugged it forward, keeping her eyes trained on the ground, the way one confronted a dog defending its turf.

"Excuse me, we need to be on my way. We have someone to meet."

The man remained rooted to his spot, even as she passed by, close enough to feel the warmth of his breath. It reeked of onions. *Fried ramps*, she surmised. Fortunately, her jacket sleeves hid the goosebumps prickling the length of her arms.

He let her pass but called over his shoulder. "I heard o' you...seen you over t' gen'ral store in Townsend. Yer that sassy California gal, ain't cha? The one cain't keep her tongue to herself. Good thing for you MacLeod's got a long arm 'round here."

Andie's eyes narrowed, but she didn't look up, wouldn't meet his eyes. She kept walking, leading the Appaloosa. When she reached what felt a safe distance, she called back over her shoulder, "Tell Ranger Evans hello for me when you pass him, would you?"

She walked on, brisk and resolute, not letting herself look back. Farther on, she allowed herself to slow, a surreptitious slide of her hand into a pocket to pull out her cellphone.

No signal.

Crap.

She sighed, working the stiffness out of her shoulders.

Okay. Shake it off.

She started to head on, but a *CRASH* from behind made her jump. The unmistakable sound of wood creaking and splintering coupled with the roar of water spilling over a dam. Heart in her throat, she tethered the Appaloosa to a tree and trotted back down the trail, trying not to jostle Adam more than necessary. Rounding a bend, she came in sight of the riverbank and froze, staring in disbelief....

Ben's first stop was by the Oliver cabin, a place she was known to frequent. The old place was half-hidden from the road by tall grass. Getting out, he stomped about, calling out her name, even stepping inside, but found no sign she'd ever been there.

Hopping back in the Jeep, he followed the loop road another half a mile, coming upon a lean figure leaning on a fencepost by the side of the road. Pulling closer, he recognized Harvey Witherspoon, the retired ranger, puffing away on his pipe as he gazed across the Cove valley. Legend had it he'd been involved in a tragic romance with a Cove girl many years ago and came out here from time to time to commune with her. Not wanting to disturb the man's musings, Ben nonetheless slowed and leaned his head out the Jeep window.

"Hey, Harv! You seen Andie MacLeod?"

The old man's eyes lost their faraway look and he broke into a grin of recognition that curled around his pipe. Removing it, he nodded slowly, ambling to the Jeep's side. "Yep, she was by here a while back, maybe an hour ago. Somethin' wrong?"

Ben squinted up at him. "No—just trying to keep up with her while Shane's gone."

Harv chuckled. "That gal's a handful, ain't she?"

Ben raised his eyebrows, trying to keep the testiness out of his voice. "You can say that again."

The old ranger frowned as he popped the pipe back in his mouth, chewing on it pensively. "You might try over Abrams Falls way. Looked like she was headed that way. I told her t' watch out for those bridges. Some are gettin' mighty old."

Their eyes met, sharing the same concern.

"Yeah, I know."

Harv straightened, giving the door a pat. "Good luck, son. You let me know if you need a hand."

Ben left him with a wave and the Jeep rolled on.

At the Abrams Falls trailhead, Ben parked his vehicle, got out, and started sorting through his gear in the back compartment, pausing only long enough to question two hikers on the way to their car. Both shook their heads. They hadn't seen anyone fitting Andie's description. She could've taken the other fork, they pointed out. Ben nodded his thanks and went back to his rummaging.

Over his radio, an all-points weather bulletin repeated: All park stations alert...*report out of Cumberland Gap, Kentucky states high winds with scattered flurries, accumulation expected in higher elevations tonight. Expected to reach Smokies early evening. Please advise all backcountry hikers—*

"Yeah...yeah...heard that already," Ben groused and switched it off. He emerged from the compartment with his heavier parka and overnight trail pack, fully stocked. Slinging it onto his back, he swung down the rear window, locked up the Jeep, and headed off.

Ben came to the split in the trail about a quarter mile in and considered the hikers' words. Did she head for Abrams Falls? His heart thudded. Though it was only twenty feet or so high, there was a deep, treacherous, pool at its base with slick rocks surrounding the area. A picturesque draw for hikers, it had a hazardous history. Some had dared to swim there and twenty-nine deaths had been recorded on this trail, many more injured.

Then he spied hoof prints. Thankfully, they branched off to Wet Bottom Trail, away from the falls.

He knelt to study them, touching one imprint in the gravelly mud. The impressions had begun to dry around the edges, but the interiors were still quite damp. Probably no more than a couple of hours old. He rose and hurried on.

Coming to the first of the trail's bridges, he trod to the middle of it and stopped to look around. On each side of the wooden plank crossing, the terrain sloped upwards. Here, hemlock and rhododendron edged the creek. Decaying leaves, brown, red, and black, lay scattered across the bridge and floated on the water below, drifting down from the ridges, where oak and pine dominated. The sweet maple syrup smell mingled with the rankness of algae-covered rocks in the stream, making his nose twitch. He recalled that the creek and waterfall were named for a Cherokee chief, his village somewhere downstream long ago. How far? Could that have been what Andie was looking for?

He called on his animal senses now—honing their attention to the smallest of details. His eyes narrowed. Not a soul around, but the rushing water masked any sound of footsteps—or cries for help, for that matter. Squinting up at the patch of sky visible in the small clearing overhead, he noted more substantial clouds rolling in, confirming the reports he'd heard since noon. The wind picked up. He frowned, tugged at his pack's shoulder straps, and hurried on.

Another split-off, another decision....

This time Ben chose the southern route, the less rocky, more passable one for a person on horseback. A hundred yards up the way, he spied something in the leaves by the side of the trail and squatted down to take a look. It was the torn corner of a piece of notebook paper. A direction was written on it—*North*—followed by an arrow, two squiggly lines, presumably to represent a creek crossing, and some boxes drawn in with dotted lines labeled *Abram's Village?* It could pass for Andie's handwriting, he thought, and it clicked with what the kid had said back at the Cove station. She was out here looking for something. But it seemed like too long a trip for a pair like them, alone. He stuffed the paper in his shirt pocket and headed on.

His thoughts turned to wondering if Andie had made any enemies lately. A smile twitched at the corners of his mouth. She had a way of invoking strong feelings. People seemed to either find her brazen, exasperating, or captivating—in any case, memorable.

Just the other day, he had been at the Townsend General Store grabbing a quick lunch when Andie walked in. At first she had gone about her business shopping, babe in arms. But when she waited at the counter, she honed in on a conversation by some local men shooting the breeze at the pool table. It had something to do with logging in the national forests surrounding the park.

Andie eyed them over her shoulder and voiced her opinion on the conservation side of the issue, which caused the men to stare, struck dumb at first. Then a couple had snickered. "Nuthin' t' worry your head about, gal," one said. "Run along now."

The others laughed in agreement. One had the audacity to let his cue stick trail, snagging the hem of Andie's shorts. She whirled around, disengaged herself, and shot him a glare.

"Sorry!" he shrugged with a gap-tooth smile. His pals shot each other uneasy glances before joining him in a chuckle.

Over in the corner, Ben had braced himself to step in if necessary. But true to nature, Andie handled the situation herself. Grabbing up her sack and shifting Adam on her hip, she tossed a retort over her shoulder on her way out. "Maybe if you throwbacks thought with your brains instead of your pants, you'd have a clue what's really going on."

The men gaped after her, Ben fighting hard to hold in a laugh. None of the pool players had a sufficient reply till after she left. Ben was heading for the door when one of the men recognized his uniform. "You better talk to the new chief about that woman of his. One day she's gonna go too far."

Ben had laid a five on the counter, nodded to the elderly storekeeper, and turned around, zeroing in on the speaker. "That wouldn't be a threat you're making, would it?"

The man's gaze faltered. "Don't want no trouble," he mumbled.

Ben stared him down a few seconds more before taking a last swig of his Coke and setting it in the bottle crate at the end of the old, wooden counter.

"That's good. Trouble is, she's got a point," he added as he went out the door.

Yeah...maybe she *had* made some waves since her arrival...but she had friends, too. It was unlikely anyone would dare to mess with a ranger's family. It could bring down the whole ranger community on them. Like a police precinct, they disciplined their own and looked after their own. The vast majority of the people he'd encountered in these mountains he'd come to like, even admire. But these woods were big. A lot could happen in them, made to look like an accident. He hurried on.

Half a mile up, he came to another, wider creek crossing, but this time, his heart caught in his throat. He came to an abrupt halt, staring before him, his worries realized.

No manmade threat here but one at the hand of nature, sometimes a tougher adversary. The wooden bridge that had stood there since the fifties lay crushed beneath an old sycamore. Its roots had given way in the eroded bank, sending it plunging into the stream.

The water was a foot or more above normal, rushing now instead of its usual placid ripple. Ben scanned the area, surveying his options. The fallen tree lay on its side, tilted against the demolished bridge. And there, at his feet, he spied the same track of hoof prints in the soft mud. They led right up to the first splintered bridge plank....

At first, he could only stand there, chest heaving in alarm. His breaths came shallower, quicker.

"Andieee!" he belted out.

He stomped through brush along the bank, peering through the woods on the opposite side, and cupped his hands to his mouth.

"An-dieee!"

His eye caught movement among the bushes on the other bank and he froze, breath caught in his throat.

Arms flailed against the tangled undergrowth.

And then she appeared, breathless and staggering, bent over by the weight of the baby on her back...but in one piece.

For a minute, they just stood staring at each other across the torrent of water that separated them. Ben found his breath, and voice, first.

"Are you crazy?" His face contorted with the effort.

She grimaced back at him, but cupped her mouth to reply.

"How was I to know the bridge would wipe out like that?"

Ben flung his arms in frustration. "What're you doing out here anyway? With the baby for Christsakes! You shoulda told somebody!"

"I told Tawnee I was going out. She's keeping Marcie after school! I don't have to tell you everything, do I?" she yelled back.

That caught Ben up short, but just for a moment. He hadn't thought to ask Tawnee. Still, her tone grated him no end.

"Fine!" he yelled back. "Maybe I should just leave you here!" He threw up his hands and made to stalk off.

"You do that! I'll find my own way back!" She shot him a disgusted look and turned to disappear back into the woods.

Ben's irritation turned to alarm. It may have been just a bluff—there had been a catch in her voice—but around here, one false step could spell disaster.

"Andie!"

She turned back halfway. Ben waited. Her shoulders slumped and she faced him fully. Both took steadying breaths.

Ben shoved his hands in his pockets and cocked his head to one side. "Look—you gotta be tired. You want my help or not?"

Andie dipped her chin onto her chest, nodding finally. She threw out her hands. "That's your *job,* isn't it?"

"Yeah…but no ground rules say how smooth I have to make it for you!" he snapped back.

Andie opened her mouth but stopped short. Time to diffuse the situation. Enough sniping. She watched him look from her to the bundle on her back to the water barrier between them. When he began to shake his head, she bit her lip.

"There's no way we can get you two back here without soaking both of you," he called over. "That water's freezing…too dangerous for *him*." He nodded in Adam's direction.

Andie looked over her shoulder to check on her son. He remained cozy and dry, contentedly looking about with those deep blue eyes. He really appeared to take after his father in temperament so far. Wisps of dark hair stuck out from the baby cap, blowing in the chill breeze.

She looked back to Ben, who was studying that fallen sycamore and tried to follow his line of thought.

"You're not thinking of—"

Ben planted his hands on his hips. "Well, if I can't get you two back over here, then I guess the only thing left is for me to come over there with you," he called back.

Andie winced. "Now hold on a minute. Can't we just wait a while for the water to go back down?"

He eyed the torrent of rushing water. "I wish. But we've got a storm coming, maybe snow, due in a few hours."

Andie felt a twinge of remorse. "Sorry...I didn't listen to the weather report this morning before heading out. It looked fine. Guess I should have."

Ben dropped his backpack and stepped out on the fallen tree trunk, testing several branches. "That's part of our job—keeping up with the weather—" He grunted as he tugged on a sycamore limb as big around as his thigh. Looking satisfied, he began his ascent. Andie watched in amazement as he wedged one foot in a fork here, another in a crook there, and worked his way across. At one point, where the crown of the tree had spread out into smaller and smaller branches and the trunk tapered in, he shocked her by pivoting to slide, hand over hand, upside down, across that raging creek. The wind picked up. Andie winced as the limb Ben hung from began to sway. He paused. "I haven't done this sort of thing since I was fourteen, you realize—"

Andie's teeth dug into her lip. "I think *you're* the crazy one!"

"Maybe...so..." Ben grunted as he commenced inching her way. "But...if you've got a...better...idea...I'd be...happy to hear it...right now."

Andie had nothing to offer. She took off the carrier and propped it against a tree so she could be ready to assist. But she could only stand there, frozen, watching his painfully slow progress as Ben scooted his six-foot frame grasp by grasp along the limb above. Time and again, a knot on the limb or a small branch would snag at his pants leg or a sleeve. Ben would pause and cautiously shake his ankle or rub the fabric back and forth along the branch until it came free.

Things were going guardedly well…till something fell out of his pocket. It landed with a *ka-plooch* in the water below and was carried swiftly away by the current.

"Damn—"

Andie cupped her hands to her mouth. "What was that?"

"My radio!" Ben yelled over his shoulder. He shook his head in disgust then continued his hard-fought progression. A couple more scoots and he was at a crucial juncture. Somehow, he had to let go with one hand long enough to grasp the next branch strong enough to hold him—hopefully without dunking himself in the freezing water. Hand flailing, he took hold, sliding up the second hand at the same time to minimize the sway.

Andie cringed, rubbing her hands together nervously.

He seemed to be on the downhill slope now—but his grip began to slide, sanding off small branches and clumps of dry leaves. He opted to make a jump for it, swinging his weight best he could toward the bank. Andie teetered below him, hoping to somehow block his fall—that is, until he yelled, "Out of the way!" and slid in the rest of the way as if on a zip line. He landed hard in a crouch, staggering to a stand with a grin of triumph, and began brushing himself off.

"Are you alright?" she gasped, resting a hand against his shirtfront.

His grin revealed a trace of exhilaration. "Sure! That wasn't so bad. Just don't ask me to do it again any time soon."

Andie saw then where she'd planted her hand and removed it. "Well…thanks. It does feel better to have you with us." She looked about them. "What do we do now?"

Ben surveyed the mountains in the distance. Andie followed his gaze. Above the ridgeline, a bank of clouds was growing in the north, likely the front itself.

"I'll head us toward the Abrams Falls station. There's no one there this time of day, but we can call from it. About a mile that way." He pointed to the west. "I think we can make it there before the bottom drops out of this. It's uphill, but we'll take it slow. Can you make it?" He eyed her as she strapped the baby carrier back on.

Andie shifted her shoulders with an air of nonchalance. "Sure. Let's go."

Ben turned back to her with a frown. "Where's Trampas?"

She pointed ahead of them on the inclined path. "I tied him to a tree up there when I heard the bridge go."

Andie led the way up the gravel-strewn trail. Ben followed, casting one more backward glance at the creek.

Fifty feet up the trail, they found the Appaloosa waiting patiently. Ben untied it from the oak trunk and took the lead, checking behind him frequently. The sure-footed Appaloosa plodded along dutifully.

Ben paused for mother and child to catch up at the top of a slope. He offered a hand down to her, a pang in his heart—a glimpse, perhaps, of what might have been. There had, after all, been a time when all their old college cronies expected it. He blinked out of that reverie with haste. It was safer to stay combative.

"What got into you, anyway?" he asked as they trudged up yet another rise.

Andie adjusted the straps of the baby pack and frowned up at him. "What? Just because I had a baby you expect me to spend the rest of my life sitting around the house?"

"No, but...you know what? This is just like you were in college!"

"What d' you mean?"

"Always wanting to keep up with the boys but not quite up to it."

Andie stopped dead in her tracks. Ben plodded on some thirty feet before realizing she no longer followed. He pulled on the horse's halter and turned.

She'd planted herself in the middle of the trail, hands on hips, blinking back tears.

"Damn you!"

Executing as abrupt a turn as she could manage, she headed back the way they'd come.

Ben stayed in place, jangling the Appaloosa's reins. The horse nickered in confusion. After a moment, he shook his head, muttering under his breath.

"Okay! I'm sorry!" he called after her. "It just burst out. I don't know why." He cocked his head, squinting. She hadn't stopped, not even slowed down, about to become a dot in the distance.

Alright…if that was the way she wanted it. She would come to her senses soon enough…realize she didn't want to be out here alone. He'd just take it nice and slow and steady. She'd come trotting up in a little while. Up the path another thirty feet, around a bend on a downslope, he stopped.

A dip in the trail lay before him, some fifteen feet across, that didn't look right. It was dry now, but Ben guessed it was the victim of a washout from a previous storm. The bank to the left showed signs of erosion. No one had mentioned any such damage in recent reports. But then, maybe they hadn't been travelling with a horse. It probably was still passable for a sure-footed hiker, but there was no way to tell from where he stood whether the ground beneath was sound.

He scanned the area to each side of the trail. The bank looked uncomfortably steep both above and below. In fact, there was a rock face to his left higher than his head. He stood there in a quandary before coming to a decision. Walking the Appaloosa over to a tree at trailside, he looped the reins there and set out.

He made it across a third of the way when he felt the path collapse beneath him—

Andie turned at the sound. It had been more a rush of breath than a word—but the sound carried in the gust of wind that blew in her face, whipping tendrils of hair loose from her hood. She pulled a strand out of her eyes and listened again, frowning. The clattering of rock mingled with the unmistakable thud of dirt clumps tumbling downslope. The connection seemed clear. She broke into a trot, mindful of Adam's jostling on her back.

At first, when she reached the site of the depression, there was no sign of Ben, only a crumbled, gaping hole. Already breathing heavy, the gasp of fright yanked from her sent her nearly to her knees. Her head swam, too stunned to be of help.

Then she heard a grunt, followed by the rustling of leaves. Dirt-caked fingertips appeared at the top, grasping for a hold.

"Ben!"

She dropped to a sitting position, knees bent, and braced her feet against a chunk of rock, reaching to him. All Andie could see was the top of his head. Her fingers pried at his, trying to gain a hold.

One of his hands flailed in the air and clamped onto her forearm. Andie panicked, sure her arm was going to be pulled from its socket, but he let up just in time. He must have been thinking the same thing, grasping just long enough to haul himself up to his elbows on the edge of the pit. Ben's chest heaved as their eyes locked.

She still held onto his hand—a good thing. The edge he rested against started to crumble and he started sliding back.

"Unhhh!"

"Oh no you don't!" Andie threw herself forward, grabbed hold of his forearms, and pulled with all her might. Below, Ben's boots scrambled and must have found purchase. He started pushing up, relieving the strain on her quivering arms. He suddenly shot forward and she lost her grip, sending her sprawling backwards into the rock face.

Flat on his stomach, Ben flung out an arm in alarm.

"The baby!"

Andie threw herself to one side, half-rolled, and lay there, panting. Ben hauled himself to his knees and crawled to her. He helped her sit up and slid the carrier off her shoulders.

She wiped a grimy hand across her nose, arms trembling as she reached for the child Ben handed her. Adam wriggled vigorously but his cries were more irritable than pained. Together, they looked him over. Other than some debris in his hair and a tiny scrape on one hand, he was sound.

Nonetheless, Andie choked back tears. "I'm a terrible mother!"

Ben tossed an arm around her, pulling her to him. "No you're not. See? He's fine." He kissed the top of her head, his eyes squeezed tight. "Sorry 'bout back there. Don't know what got into me. I knew better."

She nodded, cheek pressed against his jacket front.

"You okay?"

"Yeah...."

They huddled a little longer, catching their breath, before Ben slipped his arm from her shoulder. He sighed, eyeing the gaping hole before them, and looked back the way they had come.

Andie sniffed. "I saw a split-off back there."

He squinted. "Uphill, right?"

Andie nodded, her mouth twisted.

Ben looked over at Trampas, waiting calmly amid the trials of his human companions, and shrugged. "It'll be tougher going, but I think we can handle it. I know of a house, other side of the ridge. I've met the guy. He spends half the year in the Caribbean, I think. Asked me to keep an eye on the place for him." He stood, dusted off, and offered a hand to pull her to her feet.

"Didn't you say there was a station around here somewhere?" she asked.

"Yeah...that way." He nodded in the direction that the now-demolished trail led.

She followed his gaze and swallowed. "Never mind."

While Ben went to untether the horse, Andie settled Adam back into his carrier. Somewhere, downhill from them, came the sound of a muffled *mmmpfff*. The hairs on the back of her neck prickled as she rose to scan their surroundings. She hadn't heard that sound in the wild before, but instinct told her it was a bear. How close or what direction, it was hard to say. She saw Ben straighten, his hand drift back to finger the snap on his Glock's holster. She scurried over to join him.

Ben unwound the reins with a snap of the wrist and jerked his head. "Let's get moving."

Half an hour later, they rounded a crest and the vision of a contemporary jewel box, nestled into a mountainside, came into view.

"*That's* the place you've been watching?"

"Yep." Ben didn't sound impressed.

"But...how...I mean, isn't that on park property?"

"Actually, it's right at the boundary. That's how he got away with it."

Andie stopped and cocked her head, taking a good, long look. She'd heard from Shane about the ongoing battles between developers and conservationists trying to preserve the Smokies' ridgelines outside the park. It was hard to find a mountainside *not* dotted with vacation chalets nowadays. And not all were content to blend in with the nature they were presumably here to admire. Some builders had the audacity to build on the very crest of a ridge. She recalled something from her design classes...Frank Lloyd Wright, a proponent of organic architecture, advocated building *of the hill* not *on the hill*. At least this structure before them was set on the brow of the hill, as he might have approved, the impact of its glass window walls filtered by a generous shielding of evergreen and hardwoods. But did it have to face the park lands?

"It's beautiful, I suppose..." she mused aloud.

"I guess." Ben paused to consider it with a critical eye, then took hold of her hand and gave it a tug. "Come on, let's get up there before this gets any worse."

Andie pulled the hood of her parka closer against the swirl of snowflakes. "Agreed."

Both were breathing hard by the time they reached the steep site. Only the Appaloosa seemed to weather the climb well.

"How…do you propose…we get in?" Andie asked between puffs. Ben stretched his back and heaved a sigh as he surveyed the imposing façade. "Wait here a second."

He was back in two minutes, a tight look on his face. "There's one window that's accessible, not too high. I think I can break in there, unlock the front door, and you two can waltz right in. Come on, I'll show you."

Andie followed him around the corner and saw what he had in mind. About eight feet up on the west face of the structure was a recessed window in the rock wall base. Ben pointed to it. "Seems like the least damage if I go in there. The front doors had some kind of bronze plating. Looked like Fort Knox. And I sure don't want to break any of those panoramic windows on the back. Those would cost a fortune to replace."

She eyed the little window dubiously. "I don't know about this…."

But Ben was already climbing up the rock wall. Wedging the toes of his boots into the grooves of the mortar-set stone, he hoisted himself with the know-how of someone who went rock climbing as a teenager. Just the same, Andie found herself holding her breath till he scrunched himself into the three-by-four-foot recess and reached for the butt of his Glock to smash in one of the panes. He half-expected to hear an alarm go off, but oddly, there was no sound. Gingerly twisting his arm, he reached in to undo the latch at the base.

Ben retrieved his arm and shook the ache out of it. He then put all his weight into his arms, shoving the sash upwards. With a grunt, he forced the opening wide enough to squeeze through.

From the ground below, Andie called up, "Be careful!"

The sound of muttered curses came from inside. "Too late."

Andie winced. "Are you okay?" she shouted up even as the security alarm was tripped.

There was a pause before Ben's head reappeared in the window. "Yeah…kinda. Hang on a sec while I cut this thing off. Meet me around front and I'll let you in."

She hurried to meet him. Seconds later, she and Adam were being ushered in to the warm, dry interior.

The first thing Andie noticed upon entering, however, was Ben's right hand rather than the opulent surroundings. He cradled it in his other hand, trying not to make much of it, but she could tell it hurt.

"First we see to that."

Ben looked about them, grimacing. "Just trying not to bleed all over the expensive stuff."

She took hold of him and led him to a bench in the entryway. "Here, take a seat and I'll go find something to bandage you up with." She found a safe resting place for little Adam in his carrier, then scurried down the hall in search of a bathroom and, hopefully, a medicine cabinet.

Ben watched her go then settled back, eyeing his surroundings. On the walls were trophy mounted heads…elk…wolf…. His brow hardened. A little too close to home…. His gut said something wasn't right here. Then the contemporary crystal sculpture beside the bench caught his eye. He squinted and cocked his head sideways. He suspected it was supposed to be something erotic but couldn't for the life of him figure it out.

Andie came back in the room, catching him. "Not exactly your taste?" She smirked.

Ben tore his gaze away, feeling his face warm. "Place looks like a damn museum."

"Mmmhm," Andie returned absently as she knelt before him and tugged his injured hand toward her.

Ben winced. "You don't have to do this—"

Andie pried open his fist and reached aside for the medical kit. She held up a wicked-looking pair of surgical scissors and cocked an eyebrow. "Ef you cooperate, eet vill go better vor you," she warned, mimicking a malevolent Russian accent.

He relaxed with her teasing and behaved for her. When she finished, he flexed his hand appreciatively. "Not bad."

Andie sighed as she scrounged up the remnants of her first aid ministrations. "I'm really sorry about all this."

Ben stood and reached down with his good hand to give her an assist. "It's alright. Like they say, *it's not just a job, it's an adventure.*"

He pivoted on his heel, suddenly all business. "Let's see if we can find a landline around here somewhere."

Andie unlatched Adam from his carrier, gathered him up, and ventured into the elegant, white living room that beckoned beyond.

"Come on, little man. Let's check out this castle and find you a place for a diaper change...."

They met back in that same room after a thorough inspection of the interior and outlying buildings. Ben tramped in, brushing snow off his jacket. "Damn cellular phones. Nobody's got a plug-in anymore. This place is weird. All these locked doors! And some rooms are furnished, others still under construction. But not a jack to be seen. At least I was able to find some shelter for Trampas. I put him in the garage. It was completely empty. Spotless too. Really strange."

Andie stood before the great expanse of glass that looked out over Hatcher Mountain. She hugged Adam closer but said nothing as Ben took off his parka and joined her. Outside, it was now snowing heavily.

"Does that mean we're stuck here?" she asked softly.

Ben shoved his hands in his back pockets. "For the time being, looks like...."

. 22 .

District Chief MacLeod wasn't back within park boundaries five minutes before getting word that something was amiss. As soon as he stepped into Sugarlands, he was accosted by a volunteer at the information desk. "Got a message for you, sir. The Cove wanted to see you as soon as you got in."

Shane frowned, reached for the phone at the counter, and punched in the station's number.

"MacLeod here. What's up?"

Susannah's voice came over the line. "Just wanted to check with you sir. Has…your wife been in touch with you yet?"

"No, I just got in. Why?"

"Well…she—uh—went out on horseback this afternoon. With the weather coming in, Ben Morgan decided to go after her. Trouble is, we haven't heard back from either of them yet. There's no answer at your house."

"Where's Marcie?"

"She's with Tawnee Morgan. She hasn't heard anything either."

Shane's eyes flicked away from the phone. Outside the window, the flurries had begun to thicken. He worked the ache out of his shoulders, still stiff from the flight out of D.C., and tried to get his mind back in gear. With military precision, a plan of action took form in his head.

"All right…when and where were each last seen?"

Susannah knew the drill. "Andie was last seen about one o'clock, sir, heading away from the John Oliver Cabin. Ben, about three, at the Cove stables. That's all we know so far."

"Was Adam with her?"

"Yes, sir."

Shane digested this. "Call Cal Evans and have him meet me at the Cove stables. We'll start from there."

Not knowing what else to do, Ben planted himself by the window wall, peering out at the storm. It had picked up strength. The swirling flakes were hit by a gust of wind, obliterating any view of the slope below. He turned to eye Andie, curled up with little Adam in an oversized white leather chair.

"You got food for him, too?" he asked brusquely.

She looked up, meeting his eyes. "A little."

Ben turned back to the window. "You nursin'?"

"What?"

"Are you nursin'?" he pressed. He shifted his shoulders, awkwardness hanging in the air.

"No. Tried for a couple of weeks but it didn't work out. I was a milk dud, okay?" She snorted with bitter humor, though she sounded more torn between embarrassment and exasperation. "Not everything in this world works like clockwork." She looked past him to the snow scene outside and he followed her example, grateful for its comforting barrier.

After a while, he ducked his chin on his chest and sighed, considering her out of the corner of his eye. The poor kid's nerves were no doubt raw by now, and he wasn't helping a bit.

He walked over to her chair and knelt down. "Sorry…it's not your fault, Hon. Just would've made things easier." He brushed wisps of the baby's dark hair with his fingers.

She rearranged her face, sniffed, and nodded. Ben rose, giving her shoulder a rub. "I bet we can find something around here for a four-month-old. Maybe us too. Let's case out that kitchen."

The lights from the dash of the NPS Blazer illuminated the faces of Shane and Cal. The windshield wipers worked furiously against the flurries. Cal cast a sideways glance Shane's way. "I've alerted Look Rock and Chilhowee."

"How about Abrams Creek?" Shane shot back.

Cal grimaced. "It's only bein' staffed part-time, what with the season cut-backs. There's no one there on Mondays through Wednesdays."

Shane was silent a moment. "Y'think Morgan's aware of that?"

Cal shrugged. "Possibly. Not for certain. Look, if she's with Ben, you know she's in good hands. He's a pro at backcountry."

Shane shook his head. "I keep tellin' myself that. The guy was *first* in his orienteering class in college, cut his teeth at Rocky Mountain and Glacier. What more could you ask for in a search and rescue man? Still…it's awful strange neither of 'em's called in."

A pucker formed along Cal's brow as he turned to look out the window, searching for something of encouragement to say. Thoughts jumbled up in his mind, bumping into each other, jockeying for position to form a coherent picture. It wasn't a comforting one…that exchange he had with Ben after the wedding reception…the stark fright in his eyes the day Andie collapsed…the occasions when the two had looked more than casual friends…. *Maybe they didn't want to be found.*

He felt a twinge of disloyalty just thinking it. But Shane could well be thinking the same. "Maybe his walkie conked out on him…or fell out. And you know cellphones are unpredictable in that area," he said aloud.

Shane shot him a grim look. "Yeah…or maybe they're *both* hurt."

Cal turned away, keeping his peace.

* * * *

After downing a mug of tomato soup, Andie had nodded off in the cushy leather chair, curled up within the confines of its comforting expanse. Ben quietly retrieved the tumbler about to fall from her hand. As he turned to put the glass beside his on the end table, baby Adam started making restless cries in his makeshift bed, a nest of blankets in a very expensive-looking beanbag chair. Ben bent over and picked him up.

"Shhhh…come on, little guy. Don't wake your mama. Let's you and me take this bottle of yours and go for a walk." He hefted the little boy securely into the crook of his arm and strolled down the hall and back.

He returned to find Andie stirring. She sat up, yawning.

"Guess I just zonked out. Sorry."

"Don't be. You needed it. That was a pretty tough trek."

"Don't say *for a girl* or I'll have to slug you."

Ben shook his head and smiled, not rising to the bait.

Her expression softened, watching the two of them. "You seem to have the situation well in hand."

Ben hoisted the little boy playfully. "Oh yeah, we're fast friends." Adam's soulful dark blue eyes crinkled as he broke into a smile, making him look like a mischievous elf. Others had remarked that when the child was serious or sleeping, he looked like Shane, and when he smiled, took on his mother's sparkle. Ben saw both…Shane's concentration in the way the child manipulated those tiny fingers; his mother's roguish grin when delighted. "Maybe he senses a kindred spirit. We both have big appetites, for one thing."

Andie stood and stretched. "I'm not going to touch that one. What time is it?"

He glanced down at his field watch. "Going on seven." Adam started to squirm, face reddening. Ben made a face and handed the baby over. "Looks like you woke up just in time. I think he needs a change."

Andie sighed as she breezed off with her son to see to his needs. "Just like a man."

After returning Adam to his bed, Andie came to join Ben by the fire he'd built in the state-of-the-art fireplace. She grabbed a fistful of blue corn chips from the bowl on the cocktail table and sat down on the floor across from him, stretching out jean-clad legs that matched his, inch for inch.

"Almost like old times," she murmured.

He flicked a smile her way before returning his attention to the fire. "Almost...."

She found herself studying him, a twinge of poignancy hitting her. The firelight glanced off the planes of his face, accentuating the familiar profile, with the changes time had brought to it—the more serious set to the jaw, the lines etched deeper now around his mouth and eyes. He was more the man now, no longer the boy. She knew the same smile was there, the same roguish sparkle in the eyes, but they came less often now....

Ben broke her reverie. "I heard from Terry Wyss other day. He said they're setting up plans for a reunion back at Colorado State. You planning to go?"

Andie wriggled back against the sofa front. "I doubt it.... You know I don't suck up to that sort of thing. I mean, heck, I can't even walk in heels anymore. I couldn't pull off that image stuff. It's like everyone goes back to those things wanting to beat their chests—*Look at me, how successful I am!* You're either some big male tycoon or a female attorney in a man's suit...or show up hanging on the arm of some sugar daddy, looking like an expensive accessory."

Ben cocked his head thoughtfully. "I know that's always been *my* dream—"

Andie grabbed a pillow, threatening to clobber him. He fended off her blow with a chuckle. "And then there are the lost causes like me," he added.

Andie shot him an exasperated look and tossed the pillow aside. "Don't be silly...." She trailed off, but then she brightened.

"Remember that time we sneaked in, all dressed up, and joined Terry in the marching band?"

Ben snorted. "You always did have a thing for drums...but you could've picked a better game—*Homecoming?* Seriously?"

Andie conceded with a grimace. Fragments of memory came back to her from that day...the frantic attempts to keep in formation...dirty looks from the other band members...those hot, itchy wool uniforms…sweat rolling down Ben's face beneath that cap as he shot her a look that said *How'd you talk me into this mess!?*

"You're probably right…" she giggled, yielding a sigh of nostalgia.

Ben smiled down at the glass in his lap. "Guess that was always one of your best traits…you were one of the guys…only a lot prettier…." His expression said it came out before he'd had time to think. Their eyes locked for too long. Both turned away.

In the heavy silence that followed, Adam stirred. Andie rose abruptly and went to her tiny son, picking him up and rubbing noses with him. "What's wrong with you now?" she scolded playfully. "Hungry again already? You're getting insatiable, know that?"

She turned back to Ben. "I should probably give him a bedtime snack and settle him down for the night. But where?" She took in the opulent surroundings…Persian rugs, pristine ivory sofa and chairs…mahogany cabinets and rosewood tables…hardly any place for an infant.

Ben craned his neck to look around and shrugged. "Around here, I'd say one room's as good as another. Might as well make yourself comfortable. Why not the master suite?" The ghost of a grin was there, but something was still tight about him. Andie noticed but let it go.

She shifted the baby on her hip. "Feels kind of weird, sleeping in someone else's satin sheets, but hey—seems just as crazy sleeping on the floor in a place like this. Where are you gonna sleep?"

Ben stood and stretched. "Oh, I'll probably sack out here in a little while." He gestured offhand in the sofa's direction.

Andie couldn't resist going over to give him a quick hug. "Oh, all right. Good night, hero…and thanks again." Brushing his cheek with a kiss, she turned to go before he had time to return the embrace.

Ben stood staring after them long after they'd gone, aware that he was suddenly struck with a twinge of *something.* It grew into a surge of some powerful but nameless emotion. Something about seeing her, just then, with the baby…something like *possessiveness* came over him. They made a fetching pair.

God, she was beautiful….

If anything, becoming a mother had made her more so, adding a whole new dimension, a softer side to her…but she hadn't lost the spunk he remembered. This afternoon, when she'd hauled him out of that pit, bare-handed, she had shown a new fierceness …a tigress ready to risk all to protect those she loved….

He shook his head to clear it and walked resolutely to the window. Peering out but a moment, he moved with a restlessness to the bookcase, scanned it briefly, and pulled out a book on South American jungle fauna. Taking it to the sofa, he plopped down, ostensibly to read, anything to distract from these disturbing thoughts….

An hour later, Ben stretched stiff muscles and swung his legs to the floor. He sauntered once more to the panoramic window. The blizzard had subsided, but intermittent gusts flung flurries that swirled out of the darkness against the glass. Here and there in the sky were clear patches where stars winked, teasing, behind wisps of cloud. Pale moonlight reflected against the white ground. At the edge of the woods, a pair of deer emerged, venturing with caution across the back lawn, and leaving a trail of prints behind them.

The scuff of bare footsteps startled him and he swung around to see Andie there. "Hi," he said solemnly.

"Hi," she returned. Her hair had an endearing tumbled-ness to it and her eyes, though pinched with fatigue, held a glittering alertness.

"Couldn't sleep. You?" Her voice was soft but hoarse.

Ben found himself clearing his throat for her. He shook his head, mouth firmed. "Me, neither."

She looked toward the kitchen. "I think I saw some packets of hot chocolate in the pantry. That might help."

Ben nodded tightly, returning his attention to the scene outside. Out of the corner of his eye, he thought he caught some movement down the slope. Or maybe it was just tired eyes playing tricks on him.

In the kitchen, Andie found her hands fumbling as she pulled down cups from the cabinet shelves.

Minutes later, she re-entered the living room and paused, a steaming cup in each hand. Taking a deep breath, she let it out slowly. That first glimpse of Ben was in stark contrast to the college boy she had known so well. The ranger uniform, of course, was the most striking difference. It gave him an air of responsibility that hadn't been there before. His back and shoulders were broader now...no longer the lanky boy...more commanding....

She treaded up behind him, put down her cup, and placed a hand, palm-first, against his back. He turned sharply, eyeing the cup she held out to him before taking it. He looked so tense....

"Thanks." He turned his gaze back to the window, eyes haunted. Her gaze followed his, mouth parted in wonder. "It's still snowing? Isn't it early for such a heavy snowfall?"

"It's not unheard of at this elevation."

His manner struck her as brusque. *He's just worried over the trouble this will cause,* she told herself, and thought again, with a twinge, what Shane must be wondering. Surely he would know they were together...but what if he didn't? The thought made her shudder. The sudden need for closeness came over her, to be held and reassured that everything would turn out all right...that this mess would all be over in the morning, soon to be a distant memory.

Seldom in her life had she felt this need so acutely as right now. In a gesture born of old habit, she rested her head against Ben's back, reaching up to rub it, as much for his comfort as for her own.

"Don't."

Andie backed away. "What?"

"Just...don't, Andie."

Stunned, she stared up at him, fumbling for words. "What do you—?"

"You know what I mean," he shot back, heatedly. But there was something vulnerable there, too. He jerked his head, impatient. "I should have seen this coming."

"I-I'm sorry if I—"

"No—I don't mean you. I mean me."

She blinked dumbly. He'd been the perfect gentleman...the consummate professional all afternoon. What in the world was he worried about?

"It's my penance I guess. I had it coming."

She shook her head in bewilderment. "Penance?"

He finally dared to turn, meeting her eye to eye. "For leaving you." He shook his head with a hint of resignation. "You never forgave me, did you?"

Andie froze, taking it all in.

"So...it's finally come." She exhaled sharply and crossed her arms, ready for battle. "All right...good...it doesn't have to be ignored anymore...swept under the rug...." She made an expansive sweep with her arms. "Don't have to pretend all that hurt never happened." She narrowed her eyes. "No, I guess I never *did* really forgive you. For a while there I think I even hated you. Hated you for being so selfish...for hurting me so bad I thought I'd rather die than believe I would never be with you again!" Her voice broke and she swallowed, hard.

Ben's eyes darted up to meet hers, pinched with their own pain.

But she gathered her strength and went on. "I finally came to terms with all that, over the years. I came to accept how you could've gotten wrapped up in that other life. You were in another world up there...so far from everything else...so far from everything that used to be us...."

"What were you waiting for? You could've come. But you didn't." Ben's voice was the one to crack this time.

Andie found her throat too dry to speak at first. "I thought you were done with me. I...I don't think I knew *what* I wanted...back then."

He'd gone into his head now, not hearing her. "You weren't there...you don't know what it was like. You can't imagine...."

Struck by the transformation in his face, she took hold of him by the arms, anger forming a ball of ache in her throat. "Then tell me what happened," she managed.

Ben shook his head, trying to pull loose. "Things I'd rather forget."

Her grip tightened on his arms. "I think I have the right to know!"

He swung back on her, eyes sparked with such anger she thought he might strike her…but the moment passed. His shoulder slumped. "The constant, grinding poverty…the insults…the sickness…the cold…drunken brawls…dying children…everyday life on a reservation. I got in over my head one night soon after getting there, caught up in a scuffle that got out of hand. Probably would've died if Tawnee and some others hadn't patched me up, let me stay there to heal. They took me in when I didn't feel like I had anywhere else to go." His eyes focused on her, frightening in their intensity. "Do you know what that's like?"

She almost forgot her own pain during his outburst…but it came back in a rush. "You could've come back to me!"

"Crawled back, you mean?"

"I wouldn't have seen it like that and you know it."

He let out a sigh. "I—I know. But I was still finding myself. You knew I was a mess."

"You always did throw yourself into things whole-hearted or not at all." She blinked back tears. "But you could have said good-bye! We were…we were *part* of each other…." Her accusation trailed off, a choked whisper.

Ben winced and looked away. "What scares me is…I think we still are."

His face was a battlefield, struggling to harden, even as his hand rose to brush a strand of her hair. "I thought all this old junk was over."

Andie's lips parted. This about-face from combative to tender threw her off balance. Her heart broke into a gallop. What she— what *they*—were feeling right now could end up wiping away a carefully reconstructed world. She backed away, bumping into the grand piano there, and froze, hardly daring to breathe. Then he had to go and take that fatal step toward her, so close she could feel the warmth of him.

Challenge....

That twinge of guilt stung again. She should do...say...something.

She should've said *stop* but her throat closed on the word. Already, it was too late. Ben cupped her cheek and she closed her eyes, yielding to the pure joy of that hand's touch again.

Acceptance....

Tears spilled from the corners of her eyes.

His voice came in a breath, soft and warm against her hair, "It's not your fault...." He lifted her onto the piano and planted his mouth on hers.

When she dared open her eyes...seeing him there, leaning over her, those green eyes sparked with a dangerous energy, she lost her grip on reality...on right and wrong....

It was unbearable to *not* give in. She'd never wanted anything so badly in her life. Before the moment was lost, she had to feel that chest again, the one she remembered...from her dreams...from so long ago....

Her hands flailed free, fumbling at the shirt buttons. Yes...there it was...her fingers tingled at first touch. But it was different now...broader...hairier...the peachy down from his early twenties turned a dusky blond. Only a streak here and there in the sandy hair hinted at the sun-splashed boy of years ago. And flecks of silver testified to the passage of years. She swallowed back the groan that rose in her throat. *So many years apart....*

"God, I missed you, Boy!" She squeezed her eyes shut against the agonizing ache. *Fifteen years....*

But their bodies still knew one another, pressing from instinct into all the old hollows. He wedged between her thighs and nuzzled her neck deliciously. Her breath caught, legs entwining his. Lips locked with his, she hardly noticed him lift her and lower them both to the floor....

* * * *

Andie awoke, wondering why she was on the floor, cushioned mid the fluffy white spikes of a bearskin rug. *Where in the world?*

She squinted and things gradually came into focus. *The underbelly of a piano...of all places....*

She rose on her elbows, twisting to look at the fireplace. It still blazed, but much lower now. Warmth still issued from it. Staring into those flames, an image—memory?—flashed before her eyes. She could only recall snatches, as from a feverish dream. Some of those visions seemed unbelievable...like watching another person. The two of them, backlit by fire...arching her back as he descended for another kiss...that sharp shuddery cry, half hunger/half despair...so many emotions hitting her at once.

Then a soft nothingness...no thoughts left...only the faraway sound of Ben's soft panting...and the sensation of strong arms pulling her close...holding her safe....

Still drowsy, she dragged an arm across her forehead then sat up the rest of the way. In the next room, her son slept on contentedly, a nest of pillows covered with a ranger's parka for his crib. Ben's arm slid across her side. She twisted to see him there resting on an elbow. Their eyes met.

"Oh crap...that wasn't a dream, was it?" Her voice was hoarse. Every muscle in her ached. "I don't feel so good."

"You're not gonna tell me I'm too much for you now, are you?"

His eyes crinkled but his mouth, she noticed, remained solemn. So he, too, had mixed feelings.

Andie went to stand up, found herself wobbly, and plopped back down. "What's wrong with me?"

Ben slid up close, bracing her, and she found herself leaning into him. His voice came, gentle, in her ear. "Take it easy. You've got good reason to be wiped out. The rest is just nerves."

They nestled for a time, staring into space, until Andie ventured, "I guess we should...you know...."

Ben looked on soberly as she rose, wrapping herself in a throw from the couch. He hoisted himself up and slipped on his pants. Together, they padded in the direction of the master suite, shoulder to shoulder. At one point they bumped, Ben's arm sliding down automatically to catch her at the waist. A self-conscious chuckle escaped them both.

On the way to the master suite, they took a wrong turn and came to a stop, their attention drawn to something at the end of another hall...something blue-green and shimmering. Curiosity being a trait they shared, neither could resist trotting down to check it out.

Both stared at the scene before them, mouths ajar. A beguiling, jewel-like expanse of turquoise water spread, beckoning, in a marble-tiled solarium, surrounded on three sides by walls of glass that kept the cold at bay. In the middle, water poured out of an elaborate terraced fountain of river rock. Underwater lights at pool's edge added an irresistibly romantic glow.

For a moment, neither spoke. Then, in a voice hollow with memory, Andie whispered, "Remember that jungle pool at Tucumai Falls?"

Ben's eyes remained glued on the mesmerizing view before them. "Uh-huh...." He blinked back to the present. "You ever learn how to swim?"

Andie shrugged. "Yeah...well...kind of."

He cocked his head. "Looks as good a time as any."

Andie backed up, eyeing first him, then the pool. "It's probably ice-cold."

Ben stepped to the water's edge and bent down, testing it. "Nope, it's plenty warm." He stood back up, studying the rafters. "Looks like he installed solar panels for back-up, too. State of the art." He turned back to her. "Well?"

"I don't have a suit."

He grinned, "That never stopped you before."

They floated dreamily along the surface of the water, a comforting glow emanating from the pool's edge. Ben executed a lazy backstroke as she glided alongside him, arms crossed upon his chest. With a drowsy smile, she rested her chin, floating along in utmost serenity.

Ben's eyes fixed upon her, intense...unwavering...beginning to spark with that look of want again. All was silent, save for the gentle rippling of the water. As they neared the center, Ben pulled up, pressing her to him. Their heads melted together, mahogany against blond....

Out on the snowy slope below, an ATV stopped at the edge of the forest, its heavy-set, goggled rider peering up at the house. More lights than usual appeared to be on. He sat there a moment longer, considering, then turned the vehicle around. Looked like something he should report in....

. 23 .

Shane rested his forehead against the steering wheel, taking a moment's respite to close his eyes and offer up a silent prayer.

He was dog-tired after a day that had taken him from a congressional hearing to traffic snarls to a flight home delayed by a storm front…only to face this. A tap at the Blazer's window brought him 'round. He turned to find Buck MacIntyre standing outside and rolled down the window.

"Chief? I think you'll want to hear this."

Harvey Witherspoon approached, cap in hand and looking agitated. "What's all this I hear 'bout those two goin' missin'? Why didn't anybody tell me b'fore now? I coulda helped—"

Shane opened his mouth, a sharp retort on his lips. They'd been through this before. Harv had trouble accepting retirement. Sometimes Shane could work with that. This was not one of those times. He turned away. "Not now, Harv."

But the old man was insistent. "Dadburn it, if anybody'd bothered t' ask, I coulda told 'em where they went."

Shane swung back, attention arrested.

"You know?"

"Hell, yes! Ran into Ben yesterday afternoon, lookin' for your girlie and her baby. Sent him off Abrams Creek way. They musta got stuck in the storm. Came up pretty sudden. Prob'ly sat it out in one of those old field study shacks. There's some new construction goin' up, too, other side of Hatcher Mountain. Several places up there they coulda gone for shelter."

Shane started up the Blazer's engine. Buck tugged on the old ranger's arm, pulling him back to his truck. "Come on, Harv, you're with me."

Shane stuck his head out the window. "Thanks, Harv. I owe you one."

The old ranger shrugged with that twinkle of a squint. "Like I said, all you had t' do was ask."

* * * *

Night dissolved into daybreak....

Stars gave way to the first pink rays of dawn. Brilliant light rimmed the ridge tops, spilling over mountain tops, onto the roof of the secluded hillside retreat.

Andie stirred beneath the satin coverlet, opening her eyes to see Ben beside her, awake and alert, staring out the window at the dawn landscape. He appeared calm, even stoic.

She could guess what he was thinking. It had all finally struck him, like a cold slap of reality. She laid her head against his chest...for what might be the last time...and stared out with him.

"What have we done?"

He didn't shy away from the answer. "Broken a cardinal rule...or two. Maybe the most important one."

Her eyes started to tear up. "The last thing I'd ever want to do is hurt Shane."

Ben squeezed his own eyes shut, nodding. The arm he draped about her shoulders gently caressed her skin. "I know...." The old stirrings rose to the surface yet again. She stroked his chest...out of habit...out of need. He drew closer at the touch, betraying that he, too, was still held captive by old desires.

Andie's hand clenched, claw-like, against him. "I'm just so damn confused! I love *both* of you too much. It's not allowed for a woman to love two men at the same time...but it seems almost crazy that it's not! It happened so naturally to me...but...if I have to choose...I can't give up what I have with Shane. It's too, too precious...." Her voice broke, but she struggled on. "This might sound corny...childish, even...but...he really *is* my hero...."

Ben smiled down at her, his fingers brushing back the russet hair. "There's nothing silly about that. He *is* one...a true one." His gaze drew inward. "Crazy thing is...I love Tawnee, too. We've been through some rough times…awful times. I know I couldn't have gotten through them without her. You take it for granted, having someone there who knows you to the core…has seen you at your worst but still puts up with you. Someone you've got this storehouse of experiences with, good and bad. It keeps you grounded. Keeps you sane…God, I love her…."

Andie plucked at the hairs on his chest, pensive. "Maybe…maybe we don't have to tell either of them. What they don't know won't hurt them…."

Ben winced as she pulled a little too hard in her distraction.

"Sorry!" She rubbed the sore spot and planted a kiss there.

Ben shook his head. "Who're you kidding? That look Shane can plant on a person will drag the truth out every time. We'd crack. They're the stable ones, remember? We're the nut cases. Nah…there's gonna be hell to pay for this, one way or another." His expression went grim. "We're just gonna have to face up to it." He paused, giving a humorless snort.

Andie raised her head. "What?"

Ben nestled back against the pillows. "I was just remembering…last night, for two cents, I would've taken off with both of you…somewhere…anywhere…." His eyes drifted to the baby boy stirring in his makeshift cradle at the foot of the bed.

The child had barely broken into his first waking cry when Andie threw back the covers and went to him. Gathering him up, she disappeared down the hall and returned, equipped with his breakfast. Bottle firmly entrenched, Adam sucked away.

She settled back languidly on the bed. Ben found himself reaching over to brush the boy's dark wisps of hair…entertaining thoughts of *what if*….

The sound of helicopter blades flying low overhead shattered their peace.

Ben bolted to his feet, threw on his pants, and rushed to the window. Andie sat up straight, the bottle shaking in her hand.

"What is it?"

He turned back to her, mouth grim. "We've got company."

Ben reached for his shirt, throwing it on as he trotted into the hall. He got no further than the living room when he came face to face with the new arrivals. Three men stood before him, assault rifles aimed at his chest. Through their midst, a fourth man approached, serene, dapper, slicked black hair, aquiline nose…. He recognized him immediately. Louis Delacroix, the urbane businessman who had asked him to watch this very house. Ben froze, grasping the implications.

Delacroix waved off his men in heavily accented English. "Ah, Ranger Morgan, it is *you*! An associate informed me that I had visitors."

Ben licked dry lips. "There-uh-was an emergency situation last night. We were forced to break in to weather the storm. We'll pay for the damages."

There was the sound of rustling behind him as Andie attempted to slide discreetly out of bed back in the master suite. He flinched, wishing he could signal her to be quiet. But the others heard as well. Delacroix shouldered past him to take a look. A sly smile spread across his smug features.

"Well! What have we here?" His eyes scanned Andie a little too appreciatively, Ben thought. She'd managed to throw on her flannel shirt and jeans but the bed was still in disarray, as was her hair. Her indignant stare didn't help matters. Delacroix looked back, noting the unbuttoned ranger shirt and bare feet. Ben tensed.

Delacroix executed a mock bow in Andie's direction. "A thousand pardons for this rude interruption, madame."

Her eyes slid past him, taking in the automatic rifles, and her eyes shot daggers.

Delacroix straightened. "Ahh…Mrs. MacLeod, is it not?" He then noticed the infant squirming in protest in his nest of blankets on the floor. "What a predicament we have here. Interesting…."

Delacroix's eyes met the ranger's with an oily smile. "Your tawdry little escapades are your business, but *really*, Morgan, must you use my home for them?"

Ben bristled but did not respond. Inside, he was sick at heart, and it showed in the look he threw Andie. She, on the other hand, was seething. With that temper of hers, she could burst out with something they'd both regret.

He maneuvered himself between her and Delacroix. The guns of his henchmen came up, but Delacroix signaled them at ease again. He knew as well as Ben did, a ranger wouldn't risk endangering those under his protection. The two men locked eyes, Ben speaking with deliberate care.

"I'm sorry about the window. I'll see to it personally it gets fixed. Along with any other damages we caused. Now, if you'll excuse us, we'll get ready to leave. There's a station, next ridge over. We can call for assistance there."

From the corner of his eye, he could see Andie frown and open her mouth. He flicked a hand behind his back to silence her.

Equally formal, Delacroix responded, as though the two of them were executing a delicate negotiation. In essence, they were. *Our silence for his silence,* Ben thought, even as things started clicking into place. *What is he hiding?*

"Very well. That would be appreciated."

At least that was his response on the surface. Who knew if he might decide to let his guards shoot them in the back as they left?

Once they were alone, Ben whirled into action, grabbing up all their gear. Andie took his lead, casting him worried glances. She hurriedly secured Adam into his carrier.

"Want me to carry him?" Ben asked, forcing gentleness into his voice.

"No, thanks, I can manage."

"You sure?" He reached up to stroke her cheek and she gave him a tight smile. He could see the pulse at her throat throbbing rapidly. With a last, lingering caress, he turned to lead them out.

"Let's get outta here."

They paused in the living room to take leave of Delacroix and company. "Thank you again for the shelter last night," Ben said rigidly. Delacroix dipped his head ever so slightly, crossing his arms before his chest.

They turned to make their exit out the front door. But just as they reached the threshold, Andie reached into her pocket and came up empty.

"His cap! Wait!"

She turned abruptly, heading back toward the kitchen before Ben could stop her. He threw up his hands and charged after her.

"Sorry! Just a second—"

Delacroix maintained his stance, drumming fingers on the sleeve of that expensive jacket, and rolled his eyes.

Ben entered the kitchen to find Andie rummaging through the cabinets. "I know I left it in here somewhere!"

He grabbed her by the arm. "We don't have time for this!"

"But I have to find it! Shane's mother made it for Adam! I can't just leave it! Wait—I think I laid it down on a shelf in the pantry. Now which door was it...." Faced with two paneled doors opposite one another, she chose the wrong one.

Throwing it open, she found not canned goods but a strange assortment of jars. They appeared to contain the pickled remains of animals...or parts of them. Andie stared at the macabre collection, horror and fascination battling on her face. What's more, on the bottom were plastic baggies. Closer inspection revealed them to contain plant material...roots...and wrapped bricks of some substance....

Ben pushed her out of the way, rushing to shut the door.

Behind them came Delacroix's voice. "Is this what you were looking for?"

They straightened slowly and turned around. The three automatic rifles were now leveled at them in earnest. Delacroix was twirling a tiny blue and white knit cap on his finger. "What an unfortunate development...."

One muzzle gestured at Ben. "Hands please."

He lifted them slowly, flinching as one of the henchmen came forward and removed the Glock from the holster at his hip. The rifle gestured again and they were ushered into the entryway.

Ben glared over his shoulder at Delacroix. "Let them go. They're not part of this."

The Frenchman broke into a grim smile. "Oh, I'm afraid they are now. A ranger, a ranger's wife...it makes little difference when it comes to causing trouble."

Ben and Andie chanced a look each other's way. Ben swallowed hard. One of the hired guns turned to his boss. "What do you want us to do with them?"

Delacroix tapped his fingers against his chin. "Let me think...yessss.... Take them down to Abrams Falls. A blow to the head and dumping into the water there should suffice. Make it look like a botched rescue attempt." He looked up cheerily. "Sorry if that sullies your sterling reputation, Ranger Morgan."

"What about that damn horse?" another of his henchmen asked.

Delacroix shrugged. "Set it loose."

There was no holding back the look of dismay on Andie's face. Their inhospitable host flicked his hand. "Take them away."

As they were escorted out, Ben barked over his shoulder, "They'll be looking for us, Delacroix!"

"Not soon enough, my friend. Not soon enough...."

. 24 .

Shoved out the door and prodded down the steps by Delacroix's gunmen, Ben threw his thoughts into high gear. He glanced over at Andie, walking with her head bowed, and wondered what she might be thinking—and wished for God's sake that she'd look up, at least giving them a chance to communicate. Under different circumstances, he would be tempted to make a break for it, but he dared no fancy maneuvers for fear of harm to her or Adam. But that could be a moot point soon....

Andie, though quick-witted enough when it came to hatching schemes, was hampered by carrying the baby right now.

But as they cleared sight of the house, Andie dropped to her knees, gasping for breath. The man with her froze, unsure what to do. Ben read the ploy for what it was. *Good girl.*

His thoughts sparked to action. He swung on his guard.

The man was quick, ducking as he spun around. Ben thought he'd made his last mistake. As if in slow motion, he saw the rifle waver out of range then level pointblank at his sternum.

Behind him, Andie's breathless cry.

There was nothing he could do....

His outstretched arms flung back at the shoulders...some vain attempt to back out of the way.... A gasp burst from his lungs as mind and body registered he was about to die.

To his ears came the incongruous sound of baying dogs...*my last sound?* He almost snorted a laugh....

At first faint, then filling up the cold, still air, the noise spilled over the ridge. All heads turned.

Five men in ranger winter gear appeared, silhouetted on the ridgeline, tramping toward them in the knee-deep drifts. Shane was at their head.

312

In defiant glee, Ben waved his arms above his head, turning to cast the gunman a look of challenge. But when he looked back, the gunman was nowhere in sight.

For a moment, he was disoriented, unsure which was more real…the terror of imminent death or the unbelievable lightness of deliverance.

But then, Delacroix's voice rasped in his ear, "Just remember, my friend, we each have a little something on the other now." He slid a sideways glance in Andie's direction and backed away.

Ben whirled around to catch a glimpse of Andie. She'd risen with a look of rapture.

"Shane!"

Her knees buckled and she nearly collapsed. Ben plowed to her through the snow, grabbing on to steady her, then looked behind himself.

Delacroix had vanished. Ben was still looking about in distraction when Shane reached them. He pulled himself together, holding out his hand. "It's good to see you," he greeted him, heartfelt.

Shane grasped his hand. Still breathing hard from the climb, he broke into a shaky laugh. "I'd call that an understatement! You had us worried there. Everyone all right?" He turned to Andie, the anxiety of the past night showing full in his eyes. The second he held out an arm, she plunged into his embrace, burying her face in his parka. He gave her a tight squeeze and kissed the top of her head, reaching around to rub his baby son's head. Andie broke into a laugh that was half sob and wiped her eyes.

Ben's throat tightened and he looked away. He must have wavered on his feet. Shane's steady hand was there in an instant, pressed against his jacket front. "Whoa there, sure you're all right?"

"Definitely," Ben was quick to answer, but sounded tight even to himself.

The two men locked eyes. District Chief MacLeod was back now, no longer just the worried friend, husband, and father. There was that squint, the one in the left eye.

Ben forced the muscles of his face to relax into a smile, if faint. Shane's level gaze drifted away, letting him off the hook. For now, it was enough that they were all safe.

"We got a scare when we found your backpack by that collapsed bridge, then found Trampas runnin' loose. We hoped to find you three close by."

Andie glanced at Ben. "I'm so sorry. He took off when the garage door was opened. That was where we kept him overnight. I gave him a couple of carrots yesterday evening, but the poor thing must be famished."

"Cal took him in hand. Said he'd get one of the boys from the stables up here with a trailer for him."

Andie swallowed hard. "I feel really terrible about all this trouble."

Shane tugged her close again. "We're just glad everyone's safe and accounted for. Come on—let's head over to that meadow. The copter should be showin' up any time now."

Even as he spoke, the sound of whirring blades came overhead. All three squinted into the sun to catch the direction of the aircraft's path. It headed for a clearing upslope. They started off. Shane slung an arm about Andie's shoulders and clapped Ben on the back. "Now you two can tell me how all this started...."

Ben settled himself down on the seating ledge of the helicopter's passenger bay and looked around himself uncomfortably. He almost jumped when Shane stopped before him, holding out a capped cup of coffee. He took it with a solemn nod and took a swig.

With a sharp jiggle, followed by a jerk and the rattle of metal vibrating, the craft lifted off. An old hand at riding in the contraptions, Shane was well-equipped to keep his balance while standing, but grabbed a hand strap just the same. "Wasn't somebody with you two when we came up the slope?" he yelled over the blades' roar.

Ben chanced a sideways glance at Andie. "Yeah…the owner of the place showed up this morning to check on things. He thought there might be some damage."

"Was there?"

"Only where we had to break in. One window pane. Told him I'd see that it got fixed." Ben paused to take another gulp of coffee and looked up at him, eyes pinched. "Sorry we couldn't contact you. Wasn't a single landline phone in the place."

Shane nodded easily enough, before shooting him a look of scrutiny. "What about your radio?"

Ben grimaced, bracing himself for a reprimand. "At the bottom of Abrams Creek. Lost it on my way over to join them."

That drew a wry grin out of him, not the reaction he expected.

"Glad to hear it. 'Cause if I heard you'd gone out without it, I'd have t' cite you for it. Even if you had it, though, this weather can play havoc with 'em. Andie said her cellphone was useless." He clapped Ben on the shoulder and headed up to the cockpit.

Only a short time later, the helicopter began its rattle-y descent, everyone onboard reaching up for the hand straps. All braced for the jolting bounce that meant touchdown. After a wait for the whir of the blades overhead to slow, they stood.

The door was pulled back by a Guardsman. A blast of frigid air and blazing sunlight hit them. Equally jarring was the sight of the crowd waiting there on the snow-covered lawn of Park Headquarters. Cal, standing in the hatchway, chuckled at the look on Ben's face. "You didn't think that one of our own—and the Chief's wife—could just disappear without there being a fuss now, did ya?"

Ben shot him a sick look and climbed out on unsteady legs behind Shane and Andie.

A round of cheers burst out at their appearance. They continued as the three made their way through the throng, amid pats on the back for returnees as well as the rescue team.

Beside Park Head Tom Jeffries, visiting Assistant Director Bill Hayes watched with satisfaction. "MacLeod always accomplishes what he sets out to do. Looks like his streak held with him."

Jeffries nodded. "He's well thought of here, already. From everything I hear, his crew feels they're in good hands."

Down the line, Melba Davis was talking aside with old friend Sylvie Myers from the park's accounting department. "I knew those two would be trouble the day each of them showed up. Oh, that gal's popular enough with the younger set, but completely wrong for the wife of a district head." She paused to catch her breath. "And then that Ben Morgan shows up, looking like a renegade. Chief MacLeod whipped him into shape and he started to look more presentable. But then he started turning heads right and left. There's not a woman in the office who doesn't blush when he flashes that smile of his. And he can finagle whatever he wants out of them, regulations be hanged!"

Sylvia shook her head sympathetically. Both eyed the disheveled Mrs. MacLeod as she approached.

"What on earth could've been going through that good, sane man's head to marry that woman? They're different as night and day!" Melba sputtered.

Doc Lillian nudged her from behind. "Honey, what's between them has nothing to do with heads."

The women put on pleasant smiles as the returnees passed by. But Melba couldn't resist one more aside. "I'd lay odds those two have been up to no good...."

Ben caught the tail end of the exchange and blanched. Shane was caught up, at the moment, responding to Marcie's monster bear hug. Ben came out of his daze in time to see Tawnee pushing her way toward him. Shoving all thoughts aside, he met her in a fierce embrace.

* * * *

Sunday was a habitual gathering night for some of the ranger families at a local hangout, a pizza joint with a tavern atmosphere and a jukebox stocked with both top forties and old favorites.

For the time being, Ben had resolved to go about his routine as though nothing was wrong. Maybe nothing was. He'd begun to convince himself that he had control over the situation. If he acted as though nothing were wrong, nothing *would* be. For once in his life, he was going to stare down deception and manipulate it rather than run from it. Sometimes the truth *did* do more harm, didn't it? More often than not in his past, he hadn't been able to hide it. But this time he could...and he would.

But as he and Tawnee passed by other booths on the way to their customary corner, he honed in on snatches of conversation. Two burly men from the maintenance division sat across from each other, idly playing at dominoes.

"If it was *your* wife, what would *you* do? I'll bet you a day's pay that guy's put in for transfer—*soon.*"

Ben shoved past quickly. Tawnee, ahead of him, had been waylaid by another ranger's wife, wishing her well. He sighed when they finally reached their own booth and slid in. His attention was drawn to the couples on the dance floor. In the background, a song called "Faithful" was playing.

Tawnee's eyes were upon him, troubled. "Is something wrong?"

"No...just tired." He frowned and looked back out onto the floor. "Wanna dance?"

She looked surprised but nodded. "All right." She rose, placing her hand lightly in the one he offered her.

As he led her into the crowd's midst, Ben could feel stares on his back...felt, too, the tightness between his shoulder blades, and tried to shrug it off. He spun her around to face him, slid his arm about her waist, and clasped her hand to his chest. She dipped her chin and looked away. Hiding her eyes or did he imagine it?

The next song that started up was about good intentions, broken dreams, and a love that kept a man goin'....

Ben fought down the urge to bolt, then and there, pulling Tawnee closer and pressing his cheek against her soft auburn hair.

At home that night, Ben rested his forehead against the cold, slick tile of the shower and let the hot water pour down the back of his neck, praying for some sense to be made of the jumbled thoughts overtaking his brain. Eventually, he turned with a sigh, staring up at the ceiling as the torrent ran down his back. The answers would not come to him here, no matter how long he stayed.

He stepped out to find Tawnee curled crossways on the quilt-covered bed, reading. She looked up as he entered the softly lit bedroom. At first he just stood there, staring back, unmindful of the towel threatening to unfasten at his hip.

"You know...don't you...." His voice was husky.

She nodded...almost imperceptibly.

Ben's eyes filled. It was several moments before he found his voice again. When it came, there was a hollowness to it.

"I'm sorry...."

She swallowed and sat up in bed, cross-legged. Head bowed, her soft voice drifted up. "I...knew the kind of man you were...when we met...what...made you 'trouble'...put you in more...dangerous spots than I dared to remember. And I've often wondered...how I ever thought we were possible...." She trailed off a moment and looked away, swallowing again. "But then I realized...that was what made me want you as well."

She raised a face full of heartache—yet this hungry glow came into her eyes as she took in the sight of him. Her smile held heartache, as well. "How else is it that even now...after all we've gone through...you can stand there in the firelight and still take my breath away?"

Ben's eyes flickered unsurely, a twitch in his lower lip. "You saying you still want me?"

Tawnee hung her head, squeezing her eyes shut, then raised her tear-stained face, nodding.

Before she'd fully risen to her knees, he lunged into her arms, grabbing her to him and nuzzling her hair. "I don't deserve you," he whispered.

They sank to the bed together....

* * * *

Across the park, in the darkened den of the MacLeod lodge, Shane reached for a mug from the coffee table. Remnants of a late supper were strewn about. He stood, stretched out his back, and gazed down at Andie, curled up asleep on the couch. Leaning over, he pulled up an afghan to her shoulder and planted a kiss in her hair before heading for the other end of the house, alone.

In the dark, Andie's eyes opened, staring into the dying embers of the fire, and traveled to the playpen and the infant boy who lay there, stirring restlessly in his sleep.

. 25 .

Andie pulled up in the black Blazer, cut the engine, and got out, pausing in the open door. Shielding her eyes from the morning sun, she studied the figure bent over at the far end of the corral, repairing a plank. Mouth firmed, she sauntered over but stopped while still a little ways off and shoved her hands in her pockets.

"Hi."

The man in jeans and a T-shirt looked up from his work. It was indeed Ben. The smile he gave her was a guarded one.

"Hi."

His eyes took her in at a glance. He straightened and cocked his head. "You look tired."

She nodded in response but couldn't meet his eyes for long. She knew she looked haggard but didn't want to lose her resolve. One word from him and she might crumble right now.

But whatever it was she had come to say, he beat her to the punch. Pausing to rest against one of the corral posts, he fixed her with a look both gentle and direct. "I…don't think we'll ever do that again…if that's any help."

Andie's eyes flicked up to meet his, brimming, but she managed a nod. "I couldn't bring myself to tell Shane yet. Sorry…I know I shouldn't be here. I just had to talk with you one more time before this breaks all of us apart."

Ben looked away, scanning the far ridgeline across the Cove. She watched him force a slow grin and recognized it…the same soft, indulgent, inclusive smile that had always drawn her close before…only this time, it was the smile of a friend, not a lover.

"I'll be your friend, a protector, a shoulder to lean on…a teammate when you need one…but I won't make love to you again. It hurts too many now."

Andie stared at the ground, hugging herself. "Agreed." Her voice was shaky.

Ben pulled his eyes away and returned his attention to the corral, testing the new post with a sound shake. "I'm gonna go talk to Shane when I finish here. The sooner this is handled the better."

She looked up, eyes wide. "Shouldn't I go with you?"

He considered this a moment. "No. Let me go first. I...owe it to him. It'll be better this way."

That afternoon, Ben stepped into the Cades Cove Center. It was quiet, no one there except a volunteer, a retired man Ben vaguely recognized. He went up to the counter, drumming his knuckles on it as he eyed the closed door marked *North District Field Office*.

"Shane in?" he asked.

The volunteer looked up from his paperwork. "No, he got called away sudden-like, to some conference in Knoxville. Seems he had to take the place of Hank Stone."

Ben's mouth twisted at this piece of news. "Know how long he'll be gone?"

The older man shrugged. "Not sure. Somethin' somebody else can help you with?"

"Nah...it'll just have to wait. Thanks." He walked back out, distracted. The burden would have to go on a little longer.

* * * *

"Thanks, son. I 'preciate this." Harvey Witherspoon climbed out of Ben's park Jeep. "Guess that old truck of mine finally bit the dust."

"No problem, Harv."

Free for the afternoon, Ben had offered to take Harv into Townsend for supplies. Jess came along, too, enjoying the old-timer's tales and a chance to run amok in the candy aisle. As the three entered the general store, however, Ben's smile faded.

Two faces he distinctly recognized from that morning at Delacroix's caught his eye. He tried to ignore them, turning away to peer inside the glass-top counter at some Swiss Army knives that Jess found fascinating. But his thoughts were reeling as he struggled to focus on what his son was saying.

"That one, you say?"

"No Dad! You're not listenin'!" His son stared up at him dolefully, adding guilt to his inner turmoil.

He swallowed down the urge to snap back. "I'm sorry," he sighed. "Tell me again."

Jesse knelt before the antique showcase and pressed his face against the glass. There was an unmistakable look of reverence in his face as he pointed. "The *green* one there, see?"

As Ben squatted alongside him, he was bumped into from behind. Glaring up, he spied the back of one of Delacroix's henchmen on his way to the door. The guy swaggered out of the store with a nasty laugh.

Ben started to swear under his breath, thought of Jess, and turned back to the counter, muttering, "Things are gettin' way too crowded around here."

The bewhiskered proprietor, Sam Watson, joined them, his jovial face creased with concern as he watched a slouched figure in plaid flannel depart with the others. The squat storekeep leaned in toward Ben across the counter, whispering, "That Stoke Hendrickson is gettin' too big for his britches! Got no business gettin' tangled up with that foreign rabble. Lord knows his pap would never allow it if he was still alive."

Ben looked up sharply. "Did you say Hendrickson? Any relation to—?"

"Wiley's nephew. He 'n that sweet grandbaby of Wiley's— Rachel—is cousins. Hard t' figure, huh?"

Ben shook his head, staring out at the hulking figure headed for a new Land Rover. "Incredible...." He thought suddenly of Buck. That attraction of his to Rachel could prove hazardous to his health. Or maybe it already had...? Ben made a mental note to mention it next time they met.

Later, as he was loading up the back of the Jeep, a truck pulled alongside. Ben swung around to find one of the gunmen sticking his head out the window. "Nice looking boy you have there." He snickered and roared off. Ben was left to stare after them, eyes narrowed. But where he was hot with fury before, this time there was a cold stab of fear in his belly. His hand clamped onto the shoulder of the eight-year-old, tugging him close. Jesse looked up at him curiously.

"Troublemakers?" asked Harvey behind him. The old man squinted after the car.

"Nothing I can't handle." Ben finished loading and opened the rear door to let Jesse in. "Maybe you and your mom and Mary should go visit the Averys in Asheville a few days. I can drive you over tomorrow."

The next afternoon, Ben stood in the dark-paneled entryway of the parsonage. He crossed, uncrossed, and re-crossed his arms as he waited, looking about himself.

"I'll be right with you. Please make yourself at home," John Matthews called from the other end of the house.

Ben turned to find himself staring into a shelf of books, scanning the odd assortment of titles: *Voluntary Simplicity...Ecotopia...The Zen of Motorcycle Maintenance....* The guy was a philosopher and anthropologist as much as a minister, looked like.

On the next shelf was a stack of *National Geographics* topped with a Moody Blues CD. Beside a book on chess he saw one on alternative housebuilding. It was a photograph, however, that really grabbed his attention...the reverend as a young man, flanked by an older couple, in a jungle setting.

"My parents," John Matthews' voice came behind him. Ben turned with a start. The reverend took the picture from him with a smile. "My father was an anthropologist and my mother a medical missionary." He put it back and slung on his vest. He looked most un-pastor-like this morning in an old plaid shirt, orange fishing vest, and, crowning it all off, a crumpled fishing hat with half a dozen lures dangling from it. A pair of binoculars hung from his neck. Ben couldn't help a smile.

Matthews cocked his head at the ranger. "I understand you were in South America, yourself, several years back."

"Yeah, 'bout twelve years ago, I guess. Peace Corp. How'd you know that?"

"The delightful Mrs. MacLeod told me. I suspect we may have more in common than you think." He picked up a fishing pole that stood by the door. "I want to thank you for responding so expediently to my call."

"What seems to be the problem?"

"It's Harv Witherspoon. I've tried to call him all morning to see about our bird watching expedition but there's no answer. I doubt he would've forgotten. We do this once a season. Normally, he really looks forward to it. And with his truck broken down, I wouldn't expect him to be out much. I realize that between his arthritis and that heart of his, he's been known to get bedridden and be too stubborn to call anyone. Just thought it might be prudent to check up on the old gent—and have one of you fellows along, just in case."

Ben nodded gravely. "Sure. Let's go." He held the door for the reverend, gesturing for him to go first. As Ben went to follow, however, his attention was drawn to a plaque on the wall that read:

> *Finally, Beloved,*
> *Whatsoever is True*
> *Whatsoever is Honorable*
> *Whatsoever is Just*
> *Whatsoever is Pure*
> *Whatsoever is Commendable—*
> *If there is any Excellence*
> *And if there is anything worthy of Praise*
> *Think on these Things.*
> *- Philippians 4:8*

Tearing his gaze away, he shut the door behind him....

The first thing both men noticed was the absence of the old green and white Ford as they got out of the NPS Jeep and approached the secluded old cabin.

John Matthews adjusted his fishing hat, looking flummoxed. "He must've gotten that truck towed in. Perhaps he just forgot our plans and rode into town with the driver. I'm sorry if I caused you to come out here for nothing."

"That's okay." Ben was distracted by something in the grass. He squatted down, examining where the broom straw had been matted down. "Looks like just *his* tire tracks, though." The reverend walked over to join him.

"How can you tell?"

"Tow trucks have tandem tires on the back. These are single."

"Good eye. How—"

"Friend of mine back in Wind River owned one he was real proud of. Used to ride with him some." Ben pointed to the line of muddy tracks on the road. "And that's not the direction to town. Harv must've gotten it running on his own and gone elsewhere." He lifted his chin abruptly to the west, nose twitching. "Do you smell something?"

The minister sniffed the air. "Smoke?"

Their eyes met.

Ben started back for the Jeep. "Let's head down that way." Without a word, Matthews hurried behind him. The Jeep took off with a flurry of gravel.

As they rounded the bend on Wear Cove Road, they saw it— a thin column of gray smoke rising into the sky. John Matthews leaned forward, gripping the dashboard.

"That's the direction of the Hendrickson place."

Ben reached for the dash comm, fingers fumbling, found the switch, and flicked it on. "Emergency…Emergency…assistance requested. Wear Cove Road. Possible house fire in progress. Over." He screwed up his face, still not comfortable with the lingo. Especially when he was trying to drive fast at the same time.

No immediate response. He began to wonder if he'd bungled it, then Sheree's voice came over the speakers, calm and clear.

"Roger. Request received. Please identify yourself and present location. Over."

Oh yeah...thought I'd forgotten something. Mouth tight, eyes glued to the road, he flicked the radio back on, trying to mimic what he'd seen Shane do. "Morgan here. John Matthews with me. Heading northeast on 321 from Tuckaleechee Cove toward Wear Cove. Over and out."

He untangled himself from the coiled line and flung the mike into the console compartment without looking, glad to be rid of the thing.

Fortunately, the reverend had the good sense not to say anything the rest of the way.

Minutes later, they peeled into the brushy two-track leading up to the Hendrickson farmstead. They appeared to be the first on the scene. Smoke billowed from the back of the house. No damage was yet visible from the front.

Ben did not stand on ceremony this visit. He jumped out and cupped his hands to his mouth. "Anybody home?"

No answer. John Matthews emerged from the Jeep, pointing toward the crumbling barn. "There's Harv's truck."

"*Stay in the car,*" Ben ordered. His tone did not allow for debate.

Heart racing, he unsnapped the holster at his belt and rested his hand across the back of the Glock's grip. His fingers tingled.

Stories flashed before his mind of gunslingers with itchy trigger fingers. But this was no childhood fantasy. Not trotting toward an unknown danger.

Something cold and clammy churned in the pit of his stomach. Thoughts of Buck's ambush came to mind.

Venturing onto the front porch with a cautious sidestep, he crept to the window, and peered in. All was dark inside.

He scrambled off to the side then and searched for the outside spigot, hidden behind the withered remains of a hydrangea bush. The hose was still connected. He'd just managed to spray back a tongue of flame licking through a side window when the reverend showed up beside him.

"Go on! I'll clear a path for you! Just be careful!" Matthews took the hose and gave him a dousing for good measure.

Ben ran to the front and kicked open the old door. It fell back on its rusty hinges his first try. He entered, but the smoke pushed him back. Coughing, Ben reached for the faded red bandana he kept in a back pocket. Covering his nose and mouth, he fanned a pathway for himself. Spray from Matthews' hosing made its way through broken panes.

The place looked trashed. He'd only been in it a couple of times, but enough to remember it had been spare but neat. Someone definitely had been at work here.

No sign of anyone in the front room. He edged his way to the hallway. The smoke was thicker here, the heat stifling. Even so, there was a cold thud in his chest when he remembered that most of these old places had a tank of heating oil sitting right outside along a side wall. If there was one, he could be just about adjacent to it now....

Should the fire reach that, the whole place could go up like a rocket—

Sweat ran into his eyes, in rivulets down his shirt. Ben pushed forward through the haze, groping for the doorway to the kitchen. He could hear water splashing onto the linoleum floor through a window. Through stinging eyes, he made out two forms on the floor.

Dark...still....

He stepped over to them, slip-sliding on the wet floor.

Two bodies....

He knelt beside them, but could tell at a glance there was no need to check for a pulse. Both were face down, but there were shriveled, charred patches on the scalps and hands.

Clenching his teeth, he forced himself to turn one of them face up. One glimpse of that gruesome death mask was all it took. A dizzying wave of nausea hit him. The searing, noxious air only made it worse.

The floor seemed to buckle, rising to meet him. He felt a yank on his collar just before he blacked out....

Ben came to on the grass in front of the old place. The face hovering over him came into blurry focus. His head was resting in John Matthews' lap, a washcloth draped across his forehead. Something plastic covered the lower half of his face. For an instant, he panicked, trying to shove it off.

"He's coming to. Give him space," someone ordered. The oxygen mask was lifted. Ben started coughing.

"Someone get him some water!" a voice yelled.

A canteen was shoved in his face. He gulped greedily, soothing his parched throat. The canteen was pulled gently away.

"Take it easy now."

They were all strangers' voices. Ben lifted his head, looking about in wonder. People were scurrying in every direction.

"You had us worried there, Morgan. Lucky for you, the reverend got a grip on you and hauled you out."

The ranger bending over him wasn't one Ben recognized. His fuzzy mind tried to comprehend how the man could know his name...*oh yeah...nameplate....* Head waggling, he looked down, seeing that it was tarnished with soot like the rest of his clothing. He was wet, too, beneath the blanket, from water as well as sweat.

He scooted up with help from the reverend and looked about more, still in a daze...still taking inventory. His eyes and nose stung, as well as his windpipe, all the way to his lungs, it felt like. For a second he wondered what permanent damage might be there but put that thought aside.

"Did you...did you identify...the bodies?" he rasped.

The ranger who stood over him hunched down. His nameplate read *T. Sterling*. The man nodded gravely. "Yes. Afraid so. One was that retired ranger...Witherspoon. The other was the old man who lived here. Henderson was it? No, Hendrickson. I understand Witherspoon was a friend of yours. Sorry...."

Ben stared past him, lost in thought...long enough for the ranger to comment aside. "I think he's getting shocky. Get that IV handy."

Ben waved them aside. "No...I'm fine."

Something was dogging his brain...something missing here. His brain was still too foggy to put his finger on it.

"Better keep an eye on him," Sterling was saying to the reverend. "We can get his statement later. The Knoxville authorities have been notified."

"I'll see to him," John Matthews responded. He helped Ben to his feet. Ben nodded his thanks but waved him off. He would make it to the Jeep under his own power. But once at the vehicle, he handed over the keys to the minister without protest. His mind was clear enough to know he was in no shape to drive.

He was silent on the ride back into park territory. Ben could feel the reverend's glances aside at him from time to time. The man probably thought he was traumatized but he was really trying to place that missing piece to the puzzle. Then it came to him.

"The girl!"

"What?" Matthews jerked upright, jolted by Ben's outburst.

"Where's the girl?" Ben turned a grim, soot-streaked face to him. Latching on to the reverend's arm with an iron grip, he looked downright dangerous.

Stark realization registered on Matthews' face. *"Rachel!"* He sounded as though the wind had been knocked out of him. "Why didn't I think—!"

"Turn around!"

"What?"

"You heard me! Turn around!" Ben grabbed for the wheel.

John Matthews slammed on the brakes, the Jeep screeching to a halt. "Now hold on a doggone minute! We've got to get you seen to first! Then I promise to search for the girl."

Ben's flick of motion was met with a powerful hold on his wrist. "Don't fight me on this, boy! I outweigh you by a good forty pounds. Most people don't know I lettered in boxing before seminary—and I'm not afraid to use it in a righteous cause!"

Ben stared from the red marks on his wrist to the big man with the gentle face gone hard. If he wasn't in shock before, he was now. The two of them froze in place, eyeing one another like wary combatants.

"Then hand me that radio, will ya?" he asked, subdued. "I'll call it in."

A flash of movement ahead at the edge of the woods brought them both around.

"What was that?" the reverend asked hoarsely.

Ben shook his head, not quite trusting his vision yet.

There it was again. A flash of white in the bushes.

Matthews followed his gaze, hand loosening on Ben's wrist. "A deer possibly?" But apprehension was in his face. He, too, was showing the effects of the day's events. Ben's anger dissolved into something like empathy.

But both men gasped when the figure in white burst into view...two-legged and staggering. In the second that Matthews' grip slid away, Ben tore loose and sprang out the door. He made for the person at a trot, his legs more sound than he expected.

It was Rachel.

The girl wavered, falling into his arms. She was shaking... from exhaustion or fright he couldn't tell...and unable to speak. Ben braced to keep them both from falling. He turned to see that John Matthews had pulled off the road and brought the Jeep alongside, shoving open the door. With a grateful nod, Ben pulled the limp girl onto the back seat with him, cradling her in his lap.

"Where should we take her?" The reverend, for once, looked overwhelmed himself.

Ben was alert now, back in gear. "I have an idea...."

* * * *

Buck MacIntyre shuffled, yawning, to answer the rapid-fire knocking at his front door. What was all the racket about? He opened it a crack to find Ben Morgan standing there on the front porch of his cedar-shake bungalow. The guy looked a mess, uniform wrinkled, water-stained...was that soot smeared all over him as well?

Beside him, gripped by the arm, stood Rachel Hendrickson, looking as though she'd been raked through the briars. Arms wrapped about herself, she kept her eyes firmly planted on the floor slats of the porch. And she was trembling.

He flung the door open wide.

Before he could say anything, Morgan handed her over to him. "Present," he quipped and turned back to his Jeep.

Buck broke from his stupor. It was then that he realized he was standing on his front porch clad only in a pair of plaid boxer shorts and an old Virginia Tech T-shirt.

"Hey! Wait!" Almost giving himself whiplash looking from the ranger to the girl and back again, he trotted after Morgan to the truck. He got a fistful of shirt, spinning his fellow ranger around.

"What's going on?"

"Fill you in later." Ben nodded toward the shivering girl on the porch. "Better have Doc Alston check her out." Lowering his voice, he added, "She's pretty shook up. Might have been assaulted."

Buck let go of Ben's shirt, staring numbly as the ranger got in. Even stranger, the reverend was with him, in the driver's seat at that. Morgan hung his head out the window before they headed off. "Keep an eye out for her cousin—big, dumb, ugly guy—or anybody you don't recognize."

Buck nodded, dazed, and back-stepped up the porch, bumping into Rachel. He swallowed, putting out a tentative hand, and tried to peer into her downcast face.

"You wanna come inside?"

The girl's eyes slid unsurely toward the open door and the warm interior waiting beyond.

"It's okay," he coaxed.

She let him lead her to the oak frame futon in the small sitting room. He went back to his bedroom, snatching a flannel bathrobe off the wall peg. Grabbing the quilt from the foot of his bed, he brought it to her, spreading it gently across her lap. She sat there as though in a trance. Buck sat across from her, not quite sure what to do. He chewed on his lip, then remembered his mom's time-honored recipe for dealing with crisis situations.

"Um—how 'bout I make you a cup of tea, or—or a cup of soup? Then you can tell me what this is all about…."

Just holding the steaming cup seemed to anchor her, coaxing the young woman out of her shell. After the first couple of sips, her trembling stopped and she looked about more, eyeing her surroundings with a degree of interest. So far, Buck saw no evidence of serious injury, though that fading bruise on her left cheek concerned him.

"Is...Is this your place?" Her voice came soft and sweet but hoarse, catching him off guard after her long silence.

"Uh, yes...yes, it is." His cheeks burned. Had he known he was going to have a female visitor over, he would've straightened up the place. She probably was seeing him at his worst. Still, the look in her eyes bordered on fascination as she looked about his modest bachelor pad.

It was time to get down to business. Buck ventured to take her hand, rubbing it in both of his to warm it up.

"Rachel...tell me what's going on."

She met his eyes with a start. For a moment, he was afraid she would retreat into her shell, but she steadied herself with a deep breath. Her lower lip trembled, but she bit it to stop, and commenced.

"H-Harvey Witherspoon come by—said he and Ranger Morgan ran inta Cousin Stoke and his cronies over th' gen'ral store. He came to speak t' Granddeddy 'bout him." She looked up from twisting her fingers in her lap.

Buck nodded. "Go on."

"Then Stoke busts in, all drunk 'n mad—says he found out 'bout us harborin' you when you was hurt. I heard 'em fussin' from my room. Granddeddy motioned for me t' git. Somethin' tole me t' grab this and I took it with me." She reached into her pocket, pulling out a wrinkled white envelope, and laid it in her lap.

Buck stared at it in confusion. "What's this?"

She opened it up, drew out a strange wad that looked like fur, and put it in his palm. The girl stared as though mesmerized by the dark, fuzzy mass. "I knowed that hank a hair you had in your fist when I first saw it, that afternoon you stumbled outta the woods t' our place. Thought it was bear fur at first…but you'd a been clawed up somethin' fierce if that was what you tangled with. Only one person I know gots hair like that…."

Buck stared at the delicate face gone hard before him, a thousand realizations coming to him at once. The feverish flashbacks had been real after all…. The reason she'd hauled him to that dank hiding place in the middle of the night?

"I had this strange feelin' it might be useful…for evidence."

Her eyes went dark…cold.

A cold tingling trickled down Buck's spine. He took her by the arms. "Rachel…what's Stoke done?"

Her eyes rose, unseeing. "I lit outta there like Grandeddy said. Didn't look back till I was on the next ridge. Then I seen smoke comin' from the house. At first I couldn't believe it…then I did…."

The girl's deadened gaze came back to earth and focused on him. "Stoke's gone mad…like a dog. He'll do anythin' now."

Buck swallowed. "I better call Headquarters."

He got up to find his phone but was startled by a rap at the door. Both turned with a start. Buck padded over to peek through the blinds. "It's Doc Alston," he said over his shoulder and ushered the doctor in. "How did you—?"

"John Matthews and Ben Morgan stopped by—insisted on accompanying me back here." She nodded over her shoulder and Buck saw the two men in the Park Jeep on his driveway. He trotted down the steps to them.

Ben Morgan leaned across to peer out the driver's window. "Any word out of her yet?"

"Yeah…says her cousin Stoke's gone 'mad dog.' That's the way she put it," he said grimly.

"I'll say." Morgan's fatigue showed in his terse manner. "Harv and Old Man Hendrickson are dead. The Hendrickson place was gutted. It was not an accident. I found them both inside."

The two rangers' eyes met.

"Park-wide alert issued yet?" Buck asked quietly.

"Shane's on his way back from Knoxville, working on it now. Cal's been alerted, Tom Jeffries, and Hank Stone."

"What can I—"

"You just worry about getting back to that girl. She needs you right now."

"Amen to that," John Matthews seconded.

Buck nodded without blushing this time.

"We'll get another ranger over here for added protection. In the meantime, keep an eye out. Take care of yourself."

"You, too."

Ben backed the Jeep up. Buck waved solemnly, returning to his porch, though he paused to eye the woods beyond the confines of the cabin's neat little yard.

He went inside to find Doc Alston beside Rachel on the couch. The girl looked up at him unsurely. Buck knelt beside her. "She's just here to give you a look-over, make sure you're okay."

Lillian Alston stood and extended her hand to the girl in that no-nonsense way of hers that invoked both trust and obedience.

"Come along, dear."

Rachel rose unsteadily from the futon. The doctor wrapped an arm around her shoulders and led her back to the bedroom. "You're with friends now. You don't have to be afraid any-more...."

Buck sat, stood, paced the length of the small living room, and sat again as he waited out the examination. When the door knob to his bedroom clicked open again, he met the doctor halfway.

Doc Lillian shushed him and drew out into the sitting room. "She's fine. We had a long talk as well. There's no evidence of assault and no history...just some clumsy attempts, she says, by that low-life cousin of hers that she was able to avoid. She swears the only man she's been with...is you."

Buck went from looking supremely confused to red-faced in the space of two heartbeats. "But I never—" He shut his mouth, but still looked bewildered.

"Don't be too alarmed. In mountain parlance, that could pos-sibly just mean a little heavy-handed kissing...or...?" She patted his cheek as she stepped past. Buck continued to stare toward the bedroom in shock. *So that wasn't the snakebite either....*

The doctor gave him a nudge from behind. "You can go on in. I gave her a sedative so she'll be a little sleepy."

Buck stepped in, and approached the bed, planting himself tentatively on the edge. "Rachel?"

She turned her head on the pillow. The bruise on her cheekbone shone a sickly yellow-green in the lamplight. Apparently, she must have overheard their conversation. "You...don't remember?" she asked in a plaintive voice.

He might be in shock but he knew a delicate moment when he saw one. "I...I thought it was just a dream.... A *very pleasant* dream."

Out in the sitting room, the physician smiled to herself as she packed up her bag. Their bashful Virginia farm boy had a hot streak after all....

Later that night, as Buck made up his bed for his houseguest, he caught her staring out at the night sky, a haunted look on her face. She rubbed her arms, giving him a big-eyed stare as he joined her at the window.

"What is it, Rachel?"

"There's a bad moon out t'night."

Buck fought down the prickling sensation on his arms at that. He had enough country boy still in him to give credence to such omens. But what else could he say to anyone? He had nothing concrete to offer. He'd already passed along the hair samples. His duty was to stay here. Still, he'd feel better if he checked in with the Chief.

The next night was Halloween, and while the dark events in Wear Cove cast a pall on the festivities, the Smokies communities were determined to let them go on, with heightened security.

The residents of Wear Cove and Townsend, in particular, were warned to keep an eye out and beefed up patrols scanned the area. While locals may once have been inclined to harbor a fugitive who had crossed authorities, an individual who killed family would be branded an outcast.

Jack o' lanterns winked their wicked grins in windows and along rock walls on main street Gatlinburg as merchants dressed up and handed out candy. Tourists strolled the streets blithely unaware and school carnivals went on as scheduled in the area, all while rangers and local police kept a watch out for suspicious characters.

Putting worries aside for a couple of hours, Shane kept his promise to Marcie to take her to the Haunted Mansion in Gatlinburg where all the big kids—that is, fifth graders—were planning to converge, followed by a candy run down the main drag. One block only, he dictated.

"Both sides?" she wheedled.

Shane sighed, "All right...."

Cal and son Ty accompanied them on the excursion into town. He was kind of surprised that Andie didn't join them, she was such a big kid at heart. But she'd been subdued lately...due in part to Harvey's death, most likely.

And anyway, Adam was too young for all the hubbub, so she chose to stay home tonight. Said she'd introduce him to some old Disney classics tonight.

Revelry aside, both rangers packed shoulder holsters under their jackets, keeping an eye out for trouble.

As the fathers waited on their children to emerge from yet another candy raid, they looked about at the parade of outlandish and frightful costumes passing by, everything from fairy ballerinas to gruesome ghouls. Shane thought he spied a fellow from Maintenance Division dressed in a steampunk outfit and escorting a pint-sized dinosaur.

He shook his head, gaze drifting to the backdrop of dark mountains beyond. "It's Halloween alright...there's a monster loose in those hills tonight."

Meanwhile, back at Buck's cabin, Rachel kept vigil by the fireplace, despite the young ranger's attempts to distract her with popcorn, caramel apples, and some rented movies. Something light and goofy, he thought, classics like *Hocus Pocus* or *Beetlejuice. Practical Magic*, while a favorite of his, he judged too dark. But he miscalculated. Other than casting a jaundiced eye at the images romping across his TV screen, the girl kept that shawl from Doc Lillian wrapped tight about her and brooded by the hearth. Maybe something like *Cinderella* would have gone over better, he wondered.

After a last-ditch effort of hot chocolate and cinnamon donuts, Buck gave up, seeing her off to bed before returning to catch a late showing of *Young Frankenstein,* his Glock near for good measure.

An hour later, he looked up to see an apparition in white standing in the doorway. His heart skipped a beat before realizing it was Rachel. And she looked like she'd seen a ghost for real.

He stood, on guard. "What?"

The girl blinked solemnly from her daze. "Granny just spoke t' me. There's gonna be death on the mountain."

* * * *

The little white frame church in the Cove was packed this day with mourners, come to pay their respects to the elder statesman of the ranger corps.

Harvey Witherspoon's uniformed colleagues—those overlapping his era along with youngsters just come into the ranks—were scattered throughout the crowd.

Andie sat in one of the front pews, looking dazed. Beside her, Shane sat, face solemn. He raised his chin and turned a narrowed gaze out the window. Somewhere beyond the confines of the churchyard, a mourning dove made its hollow, lonely call.

Along the outer aisles, the rank and file of the Smokies' rangers stood, Ben among them. The lines of his face were stoic but his eyes betrayed outrage.

The congregation rose and six rangers—Shane, Ben, Cal, John, Pat, and Head Ranger Hank Stone—came forward to act as pallbearers. Six honorary ones joined them, Harv's retired comrades spanning five decades of National Park service.

As they passed down the middle aisle, in procession toward the door, Ben's eyes flicked to Andie. Their faces echoed each other's thoughts.

The casket bearing Harvey Witherspoon made its way down the front steps, accompanied by the twelve rangers and followed by six more, then the rest of the mourners. Issuing from the open doors came the strains of a familiar old hymn:

> *Give heed, oh saints of God!*
> *Creation cries in pain....*

The procession continued into the centuries-old cemetery. Andie hung back, stopping under the spreading arms of an ancient white oak. She found Doc Lillian at her side. Andie sniffed, looking after the others. "I bet he was a lot like Shane when he was younger."

The doctor scoffed. "Don't you believe it for one second, girl. That man was a rascal to the core—though a darn handsome one years ago, I'll admit. More like that Ben Morgan there...." She turned to leave, eyeing Andie as she went.

Andie stared after her, lips parted.

Out at the gravesite, the service ended. Shane's steely gaze rose, catching sight of the other fresh grave across the way... Wiley Hendrickson's.

He turned to address the four rangers who snapped to attention.

"As of *now*, all patrols in *pairs*."

. 26 .

The afternoon following Harvey's funeral, Ben pulled up in front of the Cades Cove Visitor Center and went inside. Susannah was putting up equipment from her morning's lecture on mushrooms at a local school and turned to see him.

"Shane in?" Ben asked with a grim look. Susannah nodded and thumbed in the direction of the District Chief's office. With a curt nod, he stepped on back. The young woman eyed him curiously as he passed by. Ben's knock on the half-open door was answered immediately.

"Come in."

Shane looked up from his desk. The flicker of a frown crossed his face as he watched Ben make a point of closing the door behind him, something he didn't usually bother with. He didn't take a seat, either—not unusual, given his restless nature—but the guy did seem more restless than normal.

"What's up?"

Ben's gaze flitted everywhere before settling on a point somewhere on the desk before him. Mouth firmed, he pulled the badge from his shirt pocket, stepped forward, and tossed it onto the blotter. "This has got to be the hardest thing I've ever done."

District Chief MacLeod looked from the badge lying there to the man who stood before him.

"Morgan, what're you doin'?" Ben's face was as stoic as Shane had ever seen it, but the eyes were a dead giveaway to the turmoil within.

"Consider that my resignation."

Shane squinted up at him. "Harv's death makin' you do this?"

"Among other things." Ben shoved his hands in his pockets and looked away. Again, the furtive eyes.

Shane swiveled sideways in his chair and toyed with a pen on the desk. "You let all those rumors flyin' around get to you, didn't you? You can't let 'em do that."

Ben swallowed hard. His eyes slid up to meet Shane's.

"They weren't rumors."

Shane's eyes hardened. *"What are you sayin'?"*

Ben looked as if he wanted to answer but couldn't find the words. He ended up meeting that steely gaze with a tormented one of his own. "Do I have to spell it out for you?"

Shane took a measured swallow. Shock and nausea battled for equal space on the weather-beaten face.

It was a look Ben had only seen on his friend once in all the years he'd known him. That was four years ago…. Ben squeezed his eyes shut to block it out.

"I'm sorry," he croaked.

Shane ignored him at first, turning to stare out the window. His chest rose and fell several times in the silence that followed. "At least you had the guts to come forward. There's just one problem. I can't spare any men right now."

"What?" Ben stared down at him.

Shane jerked around to face him. *"You heard me."*

About this time, the tone in the two men's voices was becoming evident to those in the reception area. One by one, the people working there stopped to look at each other uneasily. But no one dared creep toward the door for a better listen.

Back inside Shane's office, Ben was supremely confused. "But…this is too big a…a…."

Shane stared him down. "There are bigger things than us going on right now." He turned away to stare at the floor a moment, gave the desk a resounding *whack* with the palm of his hand, and surged to his feet. Crossing to the window, he plopped down in the chair there, raking his hands through his hair. "Damn it, Ben!

I've put up with a lot of junk over the years. And I can forgive a lot. But *this*!"

Ben sagged against the adjacent wall, looking like he wanted to cave in on himself. "I know…I swear…it wasn't planned. And it won't happen again."

Shane cocked his head. "You forget. I've seen you in action, remember?" His voice was acid.

Ben's head whipped up. "*That* time wasn't my fault! You said yourself it was a downright criminal seduction!" He jabbed a finger at Shane. "Then you and Stevens went and spied on me!"

"If we hadn't come after you, you'd prob'ly still be rottin' in some Mexican prison!" Shane shot back.

"Maybe. Or *you'd* be lyin' on a desert highway with a knife in your ribs if I hadn't stopped that day to begin with!"

They stared one another down. Ben broke off, settling back against the wall. Shane stood up, casting about for what to say next. His voice, when it came, had a dulled edge to it.

"So why didn't she tell me herself?"

Ben's chin came off his chest and he looked out of the tops of his eyes. "I told her to let me talk to you first. She doesn't have to know about the resignation till after I'm gone. I've…got a few things to wrap up first." He pushed off the wall. "Look, I don't know exactly what she feels for me right now, but one thing I *do* know…the way she feels about you borders on worship."

Shane's eyes crept up to meet his, unflinching. But he yielded a sigh. "You make a good speech, don't you?"

The door burst open upon them. Andie stood there, breathless, looking from one man to the other.

Shane crossed his arms. "Good timing. Join the party."

She closed the door carefully behind her, flicking a tense glance Ben's way.

Shane caught the look and leveled his best intimidating gaze at both of them. "Alright, I want the *whole* story this time. How long have you two known each other?"

"Fifteen years."

"How long were you…involved?"

Ben and Andie exchanged glances. The barest of nods from her and he turned back to Shane. "Six years?"

"My God...you two were practically married...."

"That was a long time ago, Shane," Ben said from the corner. "We slipped up once...it won't happen again. Don't take it out on her. It wasn't her fault."

Andie opened her mouth at that but Shane was focused on Ben. "Things are never simple with you, are they?" He pressed his palms to his temples, rubbing there. A humorless snort escaped him. "Funny the people life throws your way. What're the odds of me gettin' tangled up with both you head cases? Why didn't ya just go and get hitched in the first place 'stead of screwin' up other people's lives?"

Andie sank into an old vinyl-padded armchair. "We would've fought like tigers."

"Tigers in heat," Shane muttered. He stopped to assess them. "You're both temperamental, that's for sure." His eyes widened. "In fact...you're just plain two-of-a-kind...aren't you?" That was an unsettling thought. How come the same tendencies he once admired in Ben...spontaneity...individualism...that near-rapacious appetite for life—the ones he now had to rein in on the job—were the same ones possessed by the woman who'd stolen his heart? He drew a shaky breath.

Ben chanced a look up. "For what it's worth...we discovered something else that day...that we're both really in love with other people. The ones we're married to."

Shane shot an unsure glance from him to Andie.

Her eyes were wistful. "You always did underestimate your own appeal, Shane. Why else would I want so badly to stay with you?"

"I *don't* know. *Why?*"

Over in the corner, where Ben had wedged himself, he squirmed.

Andie flinched at Shane's bark but steeled herself to answer. "*Because*...you're the most one-of-a-kind...independent...fearless...selfless...kindest...wisest man I've ever known...*and* the best lover," she added for good measure. The catch in her voice rang genuine.

Shane looked disgruntled despite the glowing accolades. He flicked a sour glance in Ben's direction. *"Right."*

"I never loved Ben *more*," Andie pressed, "just…differently. I…I swear I'd lay claim to both of you if I could! And don't think I couldn't handle you both!"

The two men glanced guardedly each other's way.

Andie plowed on. "Look—I was crazy for Ben almost fifteen years. I thought there wasn't any man who could take his place. Then I saw you and got the shock of my life. There actually *was* someone who could make me forget him. I didn't know they still made men like you."

She paused for a shaky breath and jabbed a finger in Shane's direction. "You knocked my socks off, Mister! Don't you ever forget that!"

She snatched up her jacket and stormed out of the office, flinging the door back on its hinges.

For a moment, both men just stood there, staring after her. Shane was the first to come out of his daze. He scowled Ben's way. "This stays between us, *understood?*"

Ben swallowed, nodding readily.

Shane went to close the door, only to find his entire staff standing there, dumbfounded.

"What're you all lookin' at?"

Melba appeared the only one who would take him on. Arms crossed before her ample bosom, she challenged him eye to eye. "Just waiting to see which one of you heroes is going after her." She pointedly kept her gaze planted on the Chief.

Shane made an agitated sound deep in his throat. He whipped around, pushed past Ben to yank his jacket off its hook, and stalked out. Ben ducked his head and tried to make as clean an exit as possible—only to bump into Shane, storming back in. Shane sidled past him with a frown.

"Anyone see which way that crazy wife of mine went?" he barked to no one in particular, then muttered, "She took my truck…."

Ben bit back a grin.

Melba cocked an eyebrow. "If you're referring to that Blazer that just went charging up the hill...." The Chief had obviously forgotten that his wife dropped him off after the funeral. She went to a cabinet, unlocked it, and pulled out a set of keys. "These are to the spare Jeep parked out back."

Shane snatched them from her with a mumbled, "Thanks," and bolted out the door.

* * * *

Andie sat hugging her knees, staring across the lake. The sound of a vehicle stopping on the road above made her turn. She was surprised to see that it was a Jeep that looked like Ben's. Turning back around, she shook her head, eyes squeezed shut. The sound of footsteps drew nearer. She didn't look up, afraid who she might find standing there. But then, low and quiet came the distinctive voice that gave her visitor away.

"Andrea...."

Tears welled in her eyes. She turned to look up at the man who stood there, her mouth working its way into a crooked smile at the lanky cowboy stance.

Shane squatted down a few feet away and stared out over the water.

Andie brushed at her eyes. "Have to admit, I wondered which one of you might show up—if either of you would."

Shane plucked loose a blade of grass, toyed with it, and tossed it aside. "You sure know how to mess up the minds of a couple of otherwise decent guys, know that?"

Her mouth twitched. "I'm glad you realize that—that you're both decent, I mean. You know he loves you like a brother. He'd cut off his right arm for you."

"Don't tempt me. Right now, I'd be inclined t' let him."

He took in a long breath and let it out. "Trouble is...I still want this t' work out, for some reason. I just don't know how long it's gonna take me t' handle it—if I ever can." Those eyes, so often sparked with decisiveness in the past, now held a lost look.

Her heart ached for him...for herself...for all of them. She started to speak but was interrupted.

"Cove Station to Chief MacLeod...Cove to Chief Mac-Leod..." crackled the radio at his belt. Shane eyed her a moment longer, gathering his wits before snatching it up. "MacLeod here."

"We've got a missing hiker, sir—" came Susannah Corbin's voice. *"Hank Stone is gathering a team at the Cooper Road trail-head right now. Over."*

Shane did some quick calculating and glanced at his watch. "Alright. I can be there in twenty minutes. Over and out." He rose to his feet, hooked the radio back on, and regarded Andie.

"Gotta run."

Andie raised wistful eyes. "I know. That's part of what made me fall for you in the first place."

He started to reach down to finger back a wayward tendril from her forehead but stopped short, not there yet. He backed away. "I may be late gettin' in."

Back at his truck, Shane got on the radio again. "Sue? Shane here. Listen...try to get hold of Morgan, too. Tell him I expect to see him there as well. Over."

"Yes, sir."

* * * *

Shane knelt streamside, overseeing the grim task of recovering the missing hiker's body. Battery-powered lamps and miners' helmets were being used to illuminate the site in the dwindling light of a cold dusk. He rose with a nod, and three rangers lifted the limp form of a bearded young man onto a plastic sheet, wrapped it over him, and carried him to a litter. Shane turned to find Ben at his side.

"You wanted to see me?" Morgan asked, subdued.

MacLeod spared him only a glance. "You're back on duty till I say so."

The veteran rangers proceeded up the bank. Morgan followed without argument, though he reacted with a grimace at first sight of the hapless hiker's body.

In that fleeting second, Shane realized that his time in the military had steeled him for such sights, more than he cared to admit. It had gotten to the point where he had trouble remembering to show emotion at all in these situations anymore. Except when it came to children. Still, his analytical mind took over.

"Something doesn't look right here," he muttered, brow creasing. "I saw the marks when they pulled him out. There were more than just rock injuries, looked like to me. No one else seemed to think so, or even question it. The report's gonna say he died from slipping and drowning."

Ben swallowed hard and looked after the group carrying the litter back up the trail. "You think it could be tied to Hendrickson?"

Shane gave a weary shake of his head. "We've got two men posted on every trail, in every campground, and every road out of here...everything short of shutting the park down. Knoxville and Asheville airports as well as the highway patrol are on watch. Reports come in sighting him as far away as Newfound Gap then a call comes in about suspicious activity over on Twenty Mile Trail. We have to check out every hint of a lead, even if it's a dead end."

"Or a misdirection," Ben ventured.

"Either he's craftier than we gave him credit for or—"

"He's got help," Ben interjected.

Shane's eyes locked on his, searching.

A haunted look stole over Ben's face. "We need to talk."

It was late when the two rangers emerged from the darkened Cove station and walked out together to their vehicles. Stopping between the two Jeeps, Shane peered through the darkness.

"Why didn't you tell me all this Delacroix mess before?"

Morgan shifted uncomfortably. "It seemed best to lay low at the time. Besides, I knew it didn't look good, what with me agreeing to watch the place for the guy. He would try to implicate me in a heartbeat. At least no money changed hands yet."

Shane looked away, considering. "I guess I can…appreciate… the situation that put you in."

Clearing his throat, Ben turned to load the rest of his gear into his Jeep. "Anyway, I went up there later, by myself, to scout around, but there was nothing, not a shred of evidence left behind. Not a damn thing…" He stopped to meet Shane's eyes. "You probably just think I'm concocting that story to distract you from…the other business." His gaze slipped.

Shane blinked twice. "I believe you."

"You do?"

"I didn't say you were back in my good graces," Shane muttered. "I said I *believed* you. That never changed."

Ben's mouth twitched, almost a smile. "It's a start."

Shane left him to go around to the driver's side of his borrowed Jeep, but paused. "Get your horse and meet us, first light, back here. We're gonna take us a nice routine patrol through the area." He climbed in behind the wheel.

Ben nodded and stepped away from the Jeep. *Or could this be Shane's way of getting him somewhere remote and disposing of him? He wouldn't do that, would he?*

The key turned with a barely audible click and Shane stepped quietly into the darkened lodge. He let the backcountry pack slide off his shoulder and plopped it down by the door. Stretching out the soreness in his back, he bent over to untie his shoes. He slipped them off and padded down the hall, looking in, first, on the sleeping children, before proceeding to the master bedroom. Andie was not there as he expected. Alarm bells went off in his head before another thought came to him.

Padding back quickly to the living room, he found her deep in slumber on the couch. Something she'd been doing a lot lately, come to think of it. From the looks of things, she had tried to stay up as long as she could for him, judging from the empty coffee mug resting on the desk, and the way she lay, as though she'd keeled over in exhaustion, like so many of them this day. Her breathing was so peaceful, he couldn't bring himself to wake her. He gazed down at her for several moments before turning to go.

An hour later, Shane was still at his desk, poring over maps in the guest room that doubled as his field office. Even a long, hot shower wasn't enough to wash this day away. He paused to rub his eyes and glanced at the clock. Almost one-thirty. A flicker of movement in the doorway made him look up sharply.

Andie stood in the shadows, melted against the jamb, her arms wrapped about herself. Long and leggy, in that drape of white gauze that spilled over each round and curve with equal abandon, she caused his pulse to quicken. God, she had the most beautiful eyes....

Andie bit her lip wondering whether to enter or not. He was peering up at her through those metal-rim glasses, his one concession to the passing years. Something intimidating yet calming was encompassed in that look...the look of a captain, ready to mete out reprimand, but with gentleness. All those images she'd treasured of him in the past...the good and fair commander, protector, father-figure, husband, lover—swam in her head all at once. She wasn't sure which she wanted most right now...perhaps all of them...but knew she deserved none of them.

Still, she ventured forward. He had a cautious expression on his face, but said nothing. That steady gaze drew her in when her will might otherwise have failed. His expression turned to one of consternation when she came right up to him, then sank in a pool of white at his feet, resting her head despondently against his knee.

Seeing her curled up like a repentant child, tears wordlessly rolling down her cheeks, his own eyes began to sting. His hand wanted to caress those dark tresses with the mahogany glint he loved so well, though a voice inside warned *distance yourself.*

Despite the ache in his throat, he held back. "What do you want, Andrea? I'm not your father. I'm not gonna pat you on the head, give you a hug, and tell you all will be forgiven. I'm your husband. Different expectations. Boundaries have been crossed."

He could feel the shudder that ran through her body, making it all the harder to steel himself.

She blinked up at him through her tears. "I know. I'm so sorry. I know I don't deserve you…I can only pray you'll give me a second chance."

He swallowed, considering a response. The next few words could determine their future, if there was one. The silence dragged on. Then he uttered his decree. "If we do move forward, there will be some changes."

Her head nodded against his knee. A sniff and she wiped at an eye. "Why is it…the closer we get to heaven, the more things try to pull us away?"

That struck a chord. *Don't I know it, Girl.*

Her plaintive tone tugged at his heart…more than he could bear this time. His hand travelled down to cup one of those wet cheeks. "I don't know, Baby…."

Resistance crumbling, he slid down alongside her on the floor and gathered her into his arms. "I keep askin' myself…was it somethin' I did? Did I leave you alone too much?"

She nestled against him, a faraway look in her eyes. "It wasn't you…." She swallowed hard. "I had this perfect life here with you…all I dreamed it could be…then I went and messed it all up…." Her brows knit together. "I've got this dark side that pulls me into trouble. I'd tear it out of me if I could. The last thing I ever want to do is hurt you…of all people."

Shane felt her body shiver again. He rubbed his chin against her hair, thinking back to his exchange with Ben. Perhaps they had each suffered in their own way…a misstep of mangled feelings all around. Certainly, they had their moment…moments entwined… the image seared into his mind.

But now he could see, appreciate, that their pain had come, just as surely. Maybe more slowly, more ache than burn, but just as relentless as his own. He'd lit the match, bringing Morgan here, throwing them together again…not knowing she'd carried a torch for the guy since she was a girl. They *had* grown up together…. And she had known *him* first. Fifteen years didn't go away like that. What was he thinking?

Without realizing it, he squeezed her hard against him. Still holding on. Not ready to give up yet.

It almost hurt, but Andie didn't mind. There was something fiercely possessive in his hold yet comforting, infusing her with a sense of security she desperately needed right now.

"All I know is…I'd be lost without you, Shane. You're my anchor."

A shuddery sigh escaped him. "I never set out t' be anybody's anchor…but it seems I keep gettin' thrown into that job."

She raised her head from his shirtfront and sniffed. "You just don't realize what a turn-on that is." Her attempt at a smile went askew. "Would it be wrong for me to say I want you…really bad…right now?"

Shane hesitated. But then the faintest smile twitched at the corner of his mouth. "Guess I was just waitin' for you t' say so."

He pushed her back firmly onto the rug….

. 27 .

Three rangers sat astride horses in a highland meadow, scanning the surrounding countryside. At this elevation, beech, maple, buckeye, and basswood interspersed with spruce and fir. Some of the deciduous trees had begun to lose their leaves. No sign of activity anywhere, just the gentle sway of broom straw and dried wildflowers at their feet. Nothing out of the ordinary. Shane, Buck, and Ben lowered their binoculars and looked each other's way, shaking their heads. The men shifted in their saddles, sore from the long morning of combing the region, high country and lowland alike.

District Chief MacLeod pulled his Appaloosa around, gauging where to try next. "Let's try toward Ace Gap. I've got a hunch."

Ranger Morgan had been about to indulge in a yawn when a glint from the woods caught his eye. He had no time to think, only to yell, *"Look out!"*

He lunged from the saddle, taking Shane with him. Shots rang out as the rangers hit the ground hard. Both lay stunned in the thick, high grass. Grimacing, Shane rolled over. His eyes met Ben's, who threw him an exasperated look.

"Next time, you have a hunch, remind me to duck!"

"Sometimes you just have t' draw 'em out."

Over a ways, hidden by grass, came MacIntyre's plaintive voice. "Wait...you guys came out here planning to make yourselves targets? I missed that memo." His quip sounded edged with pain.

"You hurt, Buck?" Shane bellowed out.

"I'm okay...just a graze."

Shane cursed under his breath. "Sounds more 'n that. Stay put. I'm comin' over." He turned back to Ben. "Cover me."

Ben rolled his eyes. "That goes without saying."

Shane started crawling on his belly toward Buck. Grass stubble poked through the canvas of his jacket front and pants as he inched forward, keeping an eye out for a repeat performance. He paused for a second, nose twitching. The horses had scattered but he could smell them. One of them nickered softly, not far off. Spitting out pieces of dry grass, he reached MacIntyre.

Keeping his head down, he tore back the sleeve from Buck's left forearm.

"How bad is it?" Ben called over. He tossed off his cap to venture a peek above the grass line. Another bullet whizzed by and all three rangers flinched. "Does the term *sitting ducks* sound about right?"

"This is startin' t' get me riled," Shane muttered. He reached 'round for his radio. "HQ...HQ...this is MacLeod. Morgan and MacIntyre with me. One ranger with surface wound. Pinned down under sniper fire on east face of Hatcher Mountain. Seal off surrounding area...repeat...seal off area. Request air extraction with rifle posted—"

A fourth bullet sang overhead.

"*Now* would be a good time! Over."

The dispatcher's voice crackled back, *"Roger, Chief. Got you loud and clear. Chopper scrambling. ETA eight minutes. Hang in there. Over and out."*

Shane lowered the walkie with a sigh. "Remind me to teach you kids some combat tactics." He looked over his shoulder at Buck, lying in the grass. "First of all, you don't turn full-frontal like that when you hear a noise. Makes you a bigger target. Tuck and drop. Fold in on yourself. Don't spread your shoulders wide f' God's sake!"

Buck grimaced. "Sorry. Reflex."

Ben looked from him to Shane sourly. Even in pain, MacIntyre was polite. But he was still fuming himself. "Don't worry about it, Buck. We can work on that." He turned his wrath on

Shane. "It was your idea to ride up this damn hill. If that's not making yourself a target, I don't know what is."

Shane locked eyes with him. "Good point. But there was no reason to think they'd be reckless enough to attack in the open."

"Or stupid enough," Ben growled.

Shane's gaze lingered on him before sliding away to scan the horizon. "Now we know what we're dealing with…."

Twenty minutes later, the helicopter bearing Shane, Buck, and Ben touched down on the front lawn of Park Headquarters. The three scurried out from under the copter blades, Buck cradling his bandaged arm. Superintendent Jeffries and Chief Ranger Hank Stone rushed out to meet them. With a handful of other park officials, they hurried inside.

The three rangers emerged later from the hastily arranged conference. Before the doors had even closed behind them, Ben was grousing about the consensus reached.

"I don't see why the FBI has to be called in on this. It's a local matter. We can handle it just fine, ourselves."

Shane was unruffled by the call. "Yeah…well…when a national park's involved, it can become a federal issue. But they're still gonna need us. With nine hundred miles of backcountry trails, there's no way they can find their way around without a substantial amount of help."

"So we get to be glorified trail guides?"

"If that's the job. Sometimes you have to swallow it, lick your wounds, and go home."

"Sorry. I never was very good at that," Ben snapped.

Shane shot a glance at their injured companion. "We know."

Buck clapped Ben on the shoulder as the three proceeded down the hall.

* * * *

That afternoon, Andie was finishing up her weekly excursion to the Townsend General Store, a favorite outing for her and little Adam. While standing in line, she noticed two government cars pull in the gravel parking lot outside. A big *Federal Bureau of Investigation* shield was plastered on the doors in no uncertain terms. Two men in suits and sunglasses got out and approached the front steps.

"Look like they stepped out of some dadburn movie!" Sam Watson grumbled. The storekeeper shook his head. "Wonder what they're convergin' here for?"

She cocked an eyebrow, ears honed as the strangers came up to the counter.

"Could you tell us the most direct route to Cades Cove?" one asked.

Sam put on the same friendly smile he gave all his customers. "Why sure…go straight on 321 past the Wear Cove turn-off and head for Tremont. When you intersect Laurel Creek Road, turn right. It'll feed you right into the Cove Loop Road. The signs'll guide you there."

"Thanks." With terse nods, the agents turned to go. One almost bumped into Andie. He looked down, scanning her with fathomless black lenses. "Sorry, ma'am."

Andie's response was a fixed stare. She watched their exit, mouth firmed. At mention of the Cove, the bottom fell out of her stomach. This had to involve Shane…or Ben…or both.

"Miz MacLeod?"

"Huh?" She broke from her daze.

Sam was regarding her with his head cocked. "You all right?"

"Oh—yes. Sure. I'm sorry." Still, she had trouble tearing her gaze away from the activity outside. Two other agents from the second car met up with the ones who had come inside. All four were now holding a powwow, heads together.

"Now that was strange…" Sam pondered aloud. "Those fellas have cell phones and all that GPS stuff these days. Why would they bother with askin' directions?"

Andie shook her head, not moving her gaze. "I think that was just a cover. They were casing out the place, looked like to me. Maybe to set up a field post. Don't be surprised."

Sam peered over his spectacles at her. "Cades Cove...that where your man is stationed?"

"Uh-huh...." She strained to watch the two cars disappear up the road. *Toward home.*

* * * *

After negotiating her way through a park police road stop, Andie pulled into the Cove Visitor Center and looked about in wonder. It was chaos, bustling with strangers, their attendant vehicles, and gear. Some were law enforcement personnel from the surrounding towns, others wore badges labeling them as Feds. Cables ran everywhere, supporting additional electronic equipment.

On the sidewalk, she passed Superintendent Jeffries, fielding questions from a cluster of reporters who had managed to work their way into the center of things.

"...Yes, the man we're looking for is a foreign national, French with ties to the Caribbean. He has an international record for dealing in contraband, including operations uncovered in several national forests and parks in this country. Bottom line, he's a drug smuggler, poacher, and weapons runner. We have reason to believe he's tied in with some locals, one of whom is a suspect in the murders in Wear Cove. The rash of recent violence—including a hiker's death last night and potshots at some rangers this morning—are thought to be diversions while they clear out their base of operations, which we're still in the process of pinpointing. Okay, folks...I'll have to ask you to leave the premises now. We don't want to tangle up the lines or get in the way of the people doing the real work here. Facilities are being set up for you at Sugarlands. We'll keep you posted there."

Jeffries looked up as Andie, Adam in hand, squeezed through the crowd. She pointed toward the back offices. He hesitated for a moment, then nodded before turning aside, leaving the herding of the media to his assistant.

At first, Andie had trouble recognizing anyone inside, but then she spotted Melba's harried-looking face and maneuvered her way over, shielding Adam as best she could. Grabbing hold of Melba's arm, she shouted to be heard over the noisy crowd.

"What's going on?"

Melba bent toward her ear. "They're trying to catch some contraband dealer hiding in the mountains west of here. They think he's connected with the death of that hiker last night. Maybe Harvey's and Wiley Hendrickson's too."

Something cold took hold of her heart and squeezed. "Where's Shane?"

Melba nodded toward the offices. Andie started that way but was blocked by the older woman. "I wouldn't go back there, honey. You'd just get in the way and the two of you trampled in the process. Go on home. We'll keep you posted."

Andie turned on her, teeth clenched. "I want to see my husband!"

Just then she spied Tawnee coming through the back entrance. The young woman was looking about herself, clearly overwhelmed. Clutching little Mary Rose Bear on her hip, she turned to say something to Jesse at her side. The boy wore an angry expression but it turned to bewilderment at sight of the strangers milling about the center. He looked lost.

Andie's heart went out to him even as a sense of dread washed over her. She wanted to go to him, hold him, but that wouldn't do right now. First, she had to find Shane.

He emerged from the back hallway with another ranger. Catching sight of Tawnee, he excused himself and went to her straightaway, laying a hand on her arm. Andie watched as the young woman put down her daughter and began to talk low and rapidly to Shane. He responded with a frown and shook his head, mouth drawn into a thin line. He then nodded, taking leave of her with some apparent word of reassurance, and walked back to the front counter, coming within Andie's reach.

She grabbed his arm, heart in her throat. "Shane...*where's Ben?*"

Shane turned, registering surprise. He hesitated a moment before directing crisply, "Come with me—but stay back."

She nodded and followed him down the hall to his office. It was already full to capacity. Cal and Buck sat at a side table looking over aerial maps while two federal agents looked over their shoulders. All of them looked up when Shane entered.

"Morgan's gone and jumped the gun on us," he announced. "Went off the radar sometime this afternoon. I'm guessin' he lit out, figurin' to take care of this personally. His wife just came in. She thinks one of your agents shadowed him when he left after lunch."

One of the FBI agents heaved a sigh and snapped, "Can't you control your men better than that, MacLeod?"

Shane's eyes came up and locked on the man. Andie felt the hairs rise on the back of her neck. But instead of the barrage she expected, he returned coolly, "Are all your men accounted for, Agent Hatfield?"

The Field Head whipped around, scanned the office, and glanced at the other agents. The only response among them was raised eyebrows. Shane and the agent stared one another down, broken by the signal of an incoming call over the radio. The operator looked to Shane.

He lunged across her to snatch up the receiver.

. 28 .

Ben crept through the tangled brown undergrowth, dry leaves, and shriveled vines crunching underfoot. He winced and looked up, following the nearest tree trunks up to the canopy of bare branches above. Here and there a massive old cedar or shortleaf pine lent dense shade to the sun-speckled woods.

These were the areas most attractive to drug growers, a secluded boundary of the park yet within reach of the Foothills Parkway. In the Smokies, as in hundreds of other parks and national forests across the country, there was often a clearing to be found just a few hundred feet from the road, invisible to the casual passerby. Clearings could range in size from a plantation-style, wholesale production of a thousand plants to an individual's plot of a few dozen plants, scattered carefully at the edge of an abandoned pasture to get sunlight yet blend with the surrounding foliage. At over a thousand dollars per stalk, it was considered worth the risk. In summer, the bigger fields could be detected by helicopter overhead, discernible by their telltale blue-green hue. The small operators were much harder to root out, but equally dangerous to bust.

Those individuals in the surrounding area who felt cut off from the local tourist economy, or were laid off by the aluminum mill or disenfranchised by the fall in tobacco production, could be easily lured by the prospect of big money peddled by a suave, well-dressed foreigner with a sympathetic air. To the down-on-their-luck, it invoked a romantic image—contemporary bootleggers.

Ben was working on a hunch, something Harv had told him a while back. It had to do with those old field study cabins. It might not be the right time of year to catch a marijuana field in peak production, but Delacroix's other pursuits might have a stash site hereabouts. The fact that the chalet had turned up clean meant he must have interim storage elsewhere, maybe not too far away.

And here, on the back end of the park, away from rest stops, ranger stations, or even trails for that matter, seemed a perfect spot.

Ben and the young Federal agent spied the cluster of cabins at the same time. Vine-covered and fallen into disrepair, they looked as though no one had been near them for years. A perfect hiding place….

He stopped to scan them first before venturing closer. The boy-agent who had been dogging him all morning stopped alongside him, clearly impatient. "What?"

Ben couldn't help throwing him a sour look. *Damn fool kid could get us both killed.* He'd been near furious when he discovered the young Fed in coat and tie trailing him this morning, then dismissed him. *Fine. If they want to kill off one of their own guys in the name of bureaucracy, let 'em. The minute he can't keep up, he's on his own. And don't even think about getting in my way.*

Ben's scrutiny of the dilapidated cluster of buildings finally clicked with Agent Mercer. "You think this is a stash site?"

The kid trotted ahead and started peeling away vines from the half-rotten log walls. Brushing aside the piles of accumulated pine straw and dead leaves, he uncovered a window, amazingly intact.

He wiped one dusty pane with the back of his jacket sleeve and peered in, letting loose with a low whistle. "You were right, there's a whole table of something that looks like cannabis bricks under camouflage nets—and—and jars of stuff on a shelf along the opposite wall. You think he's got cabins like this one all through the mountains? You're probably looking at several hundred thousand, street value, right here!"

Ben was looking elsewhere. "Watch your step. I've heard enough tales about booby-traps around these sites. There's gotta be some in here somewhere."

Something akin to a sixth sense set the gooseflesh prickling the length of his spine. He stiffened, eyes swiveling to scan the undergrowth around them, then up into the trees.

"For all we know, they could have—"

He signaled Mercer to freeze.

It was worse than he thought. Beneath the swish of gently swaying underbrush, he made out the sound, ever so faint, of approaching footsteps. The agent headed around the corner of the cabin.

"Down!" Ben forced under his breath. He dove for a gully, catching a glimpse of Mercer as he whirled about, question on his face, hand reaching inside his coat for his gun. A single muffled shot felled him instantly. Ben wedged himself under the tiny overhang of rock and froze, holding his breath as the footsteps came over the lip of the gully. He heard the sound of something being kicked in the dry leaves. Had only Mercer been seen? He held his breath, sweat breaking out on his upper lip, as he remained frozen, not even daring to reach for his Glock.

A dismissive grunt and the footsteps moved on.

Ben rose to peer over the edge of the gully and sank back down, chest pounding even as he calculated wildly. He counted three of them…too many to take on alone. But he could follow at a distance, discover their base, and radio in for help. But for now, that radio remained off.

He emerged and stepped over to where Mercer lay on the ground. He lay at a skewed angle on his back, a circle of red spreading across the center of his white shirt. *Don't they give these guys bullet-proof vests?*

At the same moment, he realized he did not have one on, either. Budgets made some lives expendable…. He knelt, feeling for a pulse at the neck, but the young man's eyes were wide and staring, the pupils fixed. Already too late. *Poor kid. At least it was quick.*

He rose, skirted the rest of the cabin site, and broke into a trot. But he hadn't steered clear enough. All he heard was a soft whipping sound before the sensation of a thousand stinging needles dug into his flesh. Hard put to stifle a cry of pain, he collapsed to the forest floor. He lay there in a crumpled heap until his senses returned to him. Finally, he dared to look down, eyeing the strand of barbed concertina wire that had embedded itself in his chest, arm, and thigh. A stinging sensation near his right eye told him a glancing blow must have struck there as well. The sight of the myriad red spots spreading across his shirt and pants made his head swim. He squeezed his eyes shut, fighting off nausea with slow, determined breaths. Head lolling back, he stared up into the spaces between the branches overhead, the deceptively calm, blue sky beyond…knowing what he had to do…waiting for the next wave of nausea to pass. And for courage to return to him. Teeth clenched, he reached down, hand trembling, to pluck, one by one, the torturous barbs from his flesh. It proved to be an agonizingly slow process…too much so. He came to the raw-nerved conclusion he couldn't stand it any longer.

Bracing, he forced himself to peel off the remaining wire in one quick yank. A sickening, zipper-like sensation, and Ben felt himself come free of the hellish entanglement. Afterward, he just lay there, panting, for several minutes, unable to summon the strength to do more.

Eventually, he forced himself to rise up and look about.

The patrol was long gone. But he might still be able to follow their path if he kept in the same direction he'd last seen them headed.

Part of him began to wonder why in the world he was continuing on this foolhardy chase. He thought, then, of Mercer with a pang of guilt, and of the hapless hiker who'd strayed too close to their operation…not to mention Harv and Wiley. He owed it to them to stop this before others became victims. It was unconscionable to think otherwise….

Ben's hand brushed against the radio at his belt. With a wince, he squatted down and hauled the radio to his mouth. He flicked the transmitter, then froze. A rustling in the surrounding brush made his free hand drift toward the semi-automatic at his hip. He peered through the laurel thicket. The rustling in the leaves grew louder…closer. He could hear breathing…fast…shallow. Whoever it was had come alone.

Deciding he'd rather be the discoverer than the discovered, Ben forced himself to surge to his feet, Glock trained.

A breath of surprise burst forth from the boy who froze before him. Ben's brow twitched. No more than thirteen or fourteen, the shaggy-haired youngster in camouflage fatigues was poised for flight. Ben surveyed him with caution. He was unarmed.

There was no way to tell if the kid was even involved with the operation, but Ben couldn't take the chance of losing his only possible lead.

"Just…hold it…right there," he said, wavering.

The boy stared back, wide-eyed, taking in the sight of the disheveled and bloodied ranger aiming at him pointblank.

"No one'll get hurt if you just answer a few que—"

The boy dove into a crevice among the boulders and scampered down into the next ravine. Ben was left to stare after him, stunned. Gathering his wits, he scrambled in pursuit. He wasn't about to shoot a youngster, but he wasn't going to lose him either.

The young devil was quite familiar with these woods. He seemed to know every depression in the rock, every low-lying branch, every stream crossing, and every drop-off. When his quarry succeeded in disappearing completely from sight, Ben sagged against a moss-covered boulder and pulled out the comm once more. Even he knew when it was time for reinforcements.

"Cove Leader…Cove Leader, this is Ranger Six…repeat…this is Ranger Six. Requesting back-up on west side of Hatcher Mountain near Cane Creek Trail…over."

Tense seconds ticked by in his head before the dispatcher's voice crackled back: *Roger, Six. We read you. Where is your partner? Repeat…where is Agent Mercer? Over.*

Ben hesitated but this was no time for formalities. He let out a sigh, then clipped, "I'm afraid he's dead…."

He could sense the shocked silence spreading across the room at the other end. A background buzz of reaction followed, at first a jumble of chaotic noise. With a surge of relief, he recognized Shane's voice taking over the mike, calm but firm. *What's your condition, Morgan? Over.*

Ben looked down, surveying the damage, and couldn't hold in a grimace. "Look out for some nasty boobytraps. Concertina wire…spring-loaded. Got on the losing end but I can manage. Can you get a fix on me? Over." His voice sounded thin even to his own ears. He must be more winded...or weaker...than he thought.

A pause and Shane's voice came back: *Affirmative. Keep your comm open. Over.*

Ben opened his mouth to answer but felt a cold steel tip nudge his shoulder. He whirled around. Louis Delacroix stood on the bank above, flanked by two men kneeling with rifles.

"Good work, Lyle. Your uncle would be proud of you." The boy stood behind him, breathing heavy.

Ben's eyes swiveled to study the boy...red-haired, freckled...he didn't look kin to Hendrickson. Must be another one of the locals in training.

Morgan, are you there? crackled the radio in Ben's hand.

One of Delacroix's guards reached down to retrieve it, handing it to Delacroix. The Frenchman raised it to his mouth, lips curling into a sneer.

"That makes one down, one as yet to be determined...."

At the Cove Center, the Chief of Ranger Activities lurched forward to take the mike. Shane waved off his superior. This was getting more and more personal. He knew now who he had to deal with. "What do you want, Delacroix?"

There was a pause on the other end before the response came back: *We will speak again.*

The radio switched off. Ben's radio. The only link they had to finding him with any amount of expedience. Now they would have to wait....

. 29 .

Over two hours had elapsed since the last communication from Delacroix.

Andie shifted on the thinly padded vinyl seating in the lobby and glanced out the window, noting the setting sun. She sat alongside Tawnee Morgan, each of them cradling the head of a sleeping child. Mary Rose Bear dozed on in her mother's lap, thumb in her mouth, peacefully unaware of the measured undertones of tension around her.

Andie gazed down at Jesse and ran her fingers through the dark blond hair so disturbingly like his father's.

The wait was becoming unbearable. Gently, she slid out from under the sleeping boy and turned to tuck Shane's parka more securely about her own small son to keep him from rolling off the seat. She made her way over to the front counter. It took her a couple of minutes to catch Shane's attention. He extracted himself from the crowd of strangers bunched together and met her there.

"What's going on?" she whispered. "Why is it taking so long? It looks like nobody's doing anything!"

Shane nodded. "I know, I know. But there's nothing we can do at the moment. The fact that they've taken a hostage means they want to negotiate. Otherwise—" He stopped, their eyes meeting. He cleared his throat and went on, "Alive, he's their ticket out of here. We've got men positioned in the area but don't want to jeopardize Ben's chances by too hasty a move. What we're waiting on now is the call stating their terms. Then we make our plans accordingly."

As if in answer, came the beep of an incoming call. Shane turned and trotted over to the dispatcher's desk, plucking the transmitter out of her hands.

"MacLeod here."

Shane frowned as a Federal agent flicked on the speaker. The entire room listened as the oily voice of Louis Delacroix spilled forth:

"...Perhaps there will be enough left of him by the time you agree to our terms...."

Shane jerked around to face the wall. "I want to speak to him *now*." He swung back, making a cutting motion, but the agent did not comply. Shane shot him a dangerous look before turning back to the wall. "Morgan? Is that you?"

The barely distinguishable voice of the captive ranger came over the intercom. The tone was labored...morose...chilling to those who knew him.

"Shane...."

The District Chief looked up to see the stunned eyes of those around him and swallowed. "This is gonna work out, Ben. We're gonna get you out of there."

The voice on the other end did not share his optimism. Evidence of brutal treatment showed in Morgan's savage response:

"Take 'em out, Shane. Take 'em all out—Unnhh!"

The sound of a vicious punch preceded that grunt of pain.

Shane squeezed his eyes shut. He opened them to look in Tawnee's direction. The young woman sat, statue-like, staring into space as she ran her hand through the hair of her sleeping son.

Andie turned from her to Shane with a look that said *do something.*

Delacroix's voice came back over the radio. *"I suggest if you want this one alive by tomorrow morning, you respond quickly to my terms. There will be no further communication—and no compromises. I wish to finalize my negotiations with the Park Superintendent now, please...not one of his lackeys."*

A hard sigh of restraint and Shane handed over the mike to Tom Jeffries, trading places with him. Sympathetic gazes followed District Chief MacLeod as he walked wearily to his wife, infant son, and the family of his colleague. "I gotta get outta here awhile. Come on. I'm takin' you all home."

A respectful silence ensued as the six went out the door, but soon after, the bustle in the room resumed. Two pairs of eyes, however, followed the group intently.

Shane took the whole crew back to his place. They picked up Marcie from the Evans's cottage to rejoin the family. But no sooner had he gotten them settled, grabbed some supper—and instructed them to stay put—when he headed for the door again.

Andie waylaid him in the entry. "You're going after him, aren't you?"

He said nothing, only turned and went out the door. But Andie would not give up so easily. She caught up with him at the Blazer. "Let me help! I need to do something!"

He leveled that gaze at her. "You *are*, by stayin' here."

"Don't give me that Old West hero crap! I—"

Both of them turned as the headlights of an NPS truck appeared, pulling into the drive. Shane's face fought to rearrange itself. "What're you two doin' here?"

Calvin Evans stepped out, crossing a pair of well-muscled black arms before his barrel chest. "Figured you had somethin' up your sleeve when you lit out of there so fast."

"We weren't about to let you go by yourself," Buckley MacIntyre added.

Shane narrowed his eyes. "Thanks, but this doesn't have to involve you two."

Cal cocked his head. "We figured it does. He's a good man and deserves better 'n what he's got into."

Buck shoved his hands into his pockets, coloring a bit. "He's one of us. We look after our own, don't we?"

Shane turned on MacIntyre. "*You* shouldn't even be out."

"You mean *this*?" Buck waggled his left arm, still wrapped in bandaging. "Heck, this is nuthin'! My granddaddy once plowed twenty acres with a broken collarbone."

Shane rolled his eyes. "God save us from Virginia farm boys." He turned back to Andie. Her eyes were damp. He threw her a look of exasperation. "*Now* will you let me go in peace?"

She bowed her head, looking away. When her eyes came up to meet his again, she wore a lop-sided smile. "I guess I have to. Is this where I'm supposed to say something like *you better come back safe or I'll kill you*?"

Shane almost gave in to a smile. "Yeah...somethin' like that." He jerked his chin at her. "C'mere." Pulling her to him, he laid a kiss on her lips that was devoid of his usual reserve. With a parting squeeze, he let go, flashing her a no-nonsense glare. "Listen, I gave John Gage a call. He's comin' over to help you keep an eye on things. And you know where that Colt is if you need it. Now git yerself back in there so I have somethin' t' come home to." He gave her a swat on the backside that was more than playful.

She backed away, shooting him a look of challenge that softened into a twisted smile. Rubbing her sore spot, she waved them on their way, watching until the truck disappeared from sight. Her smile faded as she turned and walked slowly back into the lodge.

As the park Jeep bearing Shane, Cal, and Buck pulled in silently, lights off, and rolled to a stop at the Ace Gap trailhead, Shane tried to prepare his companions for what lay ahead. "If my instincts are right, they didn't return to Delacroix's place. They could be holed up in one of those old field study cabins over in this vicinity—" He pointed on the map before him. "I figure to lay low and keep a watch on that side of the mountain—an ear on the radio as well. If we see any indication of lights up there, we can start moving in for a closer look." Shane paused. His glance included Buck in the backseat. "Once we do reach Morgan I don't know how easy it'll be to get him out of there fast. We don't know if he'll be able to walk or even stand. We may have to carry him out." His eyes met Cal's.

The big ranger gave him a knowing nod. "From the sound of things, it's gotten ugly up there. If he's hurt bad, guys can get crazy, try t' resist help when we need him t' be quiet. I've seen it before."

Shane nodded in agreement.

Buck leaned forward from the back seat, eyes widening. "In which case—?"

Shane turned back to him. MacIntyre looked younger than usual, scared but eager. It struck him that this youngster had no combat experience, no real background for being here—just a willing heart and spotty target practice. *What am I getting him into?*

Sure, the fella was packing a .40 caliber sidearm but he was a field scientist by nature, for God's sake! Still, he could hardly shame him by sending him back alone. Shane stared into the wide blue eyes and forced down his reservations with a swallow.

"In which case, knock Morgan out if necessary and drag him the hell outta there."

MacIntyre nodded, looking like he was hanging onto his every word like the God's truth. That disturbed Shane no end.

The senior ranger shook it off and lifted his binoculars to scan the mountainside. It loomed dark and ominous, the half-moon above doing little to light the night. The chill in the air would only get worse. Shane shifted that tingle of apprehension from between his shoulder blades and reached for the satchel of night vision goggles that Buck had brought.

From the backseat came MacIntyre's voice, subdued. "Shouldn't we check in with Stone first?"

Cal shared a look with Shane. "Guess you missed that. Stone gave him the go-ahead nod on the way out. Let them make their negotiations. We're the cavalry."

"Don't worry," their chief added, "I won't rush us into anything before the chances are good of doin' this right. Sometimes the hardest thing is waiting."

An hour later, Shane lowered his binoculars. "Got those canisters of tear gas?"

Cal nodded coolly and reached behind him. "Right here."

"Good. Keep 'em handy. Let's go take a look."

. 30 .

Ben awoke to a throbbing head and double vision that took several minutes to clear. His throat was so parched it was on the verge of closing up. Swallowing with difficulty, he tried to focus on his surroundings.

Dark, rough-hewn walls, lit by the blue-white light of a battery-powered lantern. His nose twitched at the mustiness of disuse...decades? He'd smelled that before...old toolsheds.... That was it. He must be in one of those old field study cabins from the thirties or forties.

He tried to shift, found himself hampered. Craning his neck to the side with a painful ratcheting, he saw that his wrists had been bound...his ankles as well. He couldn't remember how he came to be on this old cot...a rusty contraption with ancient ticking that smelled mildewed. They must've thrown him here after that last, ill-worded communiqué to Shane.

A flicker of movement caught his eye and he squinted at the window. He could swear he'd caught a glimpse of someone there. His eyes must still be playing tricks on him.

Since his capture, he'd been kicked, punched, signed by a sadist with a cigarette butt—and knocked senseless twice. Small wonder if his brain should start deceiving him. Just hoping against hope....

He'd seen enough in the past day into night—or was it two?—to conclude these people would think nothing of double-crossing any negotiators and ending his life at a moment's notice....

Ben curled himself into a ball, holding on to pain-wracked sides, and wrapped himself in delusions of rescue.

His hallucination returned to taunt him. He rose jerkily to his elbows but sank back breathing hard. A spark of hope surged when he made out the face of Cal Evans, then Shane's, peering over the window sill. He wanted to call to them, but didn't dare. Wanted to assist, but he was of little use in this state.

Ben looked on helplessly as Shane raised the sash a few inches and maneuvered his lean frame through the opening. He headed straight for the bed but was stopped short by the sound of the doorknob turning. Shane stole into a corner, wedging into a space between an old cabinet and the log wall.

Ben pretended to be asleep but kept slit eyes trained on Shane. One of the gunman, a heavy-set one with thinning red hair, sat down in a creaky, rush-bottom chair near the bed and began to pick at his teeth. A swell of frustration rose in Ben's throat.

He glanced back at Shane and their eyes met. Shane nodded once. They would have to work together on this, and time it perfectly.

Ben groaned, pretending to loll in his sleep. He rolled to his side, draping his bound hands over the bed's edge. He let slip the elaborately carved Arapaho wedding band that had been on his finger for nearly ten years. The silver ring landed with a clatter on the plank floor. True to expectation, the scavenger instincts of his guard rose to the occasion. The thug couldn't resist bending down to snatch it up.

Ben summoned all his strength, including some he didn't know he had. He reared up, flung his upper body forward in an arc, and came down with bound fists on the back of the man's neck.

Shane rushed over, delivering a blow to the man's head with the butt of his Glock, to finish the job. At the same time, he managed to break Ben's fall. Ben sagged against the side of the bed, panting.

But Shane could not allow him the luxury of rest. He whipped out his pocketknife and cut him loose, then grabbed him under the arms. "Come on! This place is gonna fill with tear gas any second!"

Sounds of coughing came from the front room of the cabin. Wisps of vapor were already stealing under the closed door as the two struggled out the window together. They stumbled to the cluster of boulders where Cal and Buck awaited them.

Cal kept his rifle trained on the cabin door. Two men ran out of the cabin, coughing and shooting their handguns wildly.

Buck dove into the first aid pack, coming up first with the canteen. Ben grabbed it out of his hands and drank from it greedily.

Bullets began to hit closer, glancing off the rocks. Cal traded shots with the gunmen. Shane swiveled around, scrunched low, and joined Cal in the exchange of fire.

Delacroix's men broke off, sprinting with purpose in the opposite direction. Shane rose cautiously, peering through the trees. The sound of rotors whirring up to speed startled them all.

Shane's face contorted. "He's got a damn chopper hidden in there!" Piles of camouflage netting were strewn in the clearing.

Cal made to head after them but Shane yanked him back. "No! Wait! If we hit the fuel tank, we'll have a blaze in no time with *us* in the middle. Let 'em go—I'll call for an intercept."

As the bird lifted off, the rangers dove for cover. Bullets rained down as a parting shot. Shane grimaced in the middle of his call. He thought he got a crackly response but couldn't make it out. Shane rose, trying to determine the flight path, but then the copter veered back toward them. "What now?" He scowled.

The four rangers watched in disbelief as one of the gunmen tossed bottle after bottle trailing flaming rags from the aircraft into the surrounding forest. Majestic pines and hemlocks turned into gigantic torches as the canisters made contact. Bursts of flame exploded all around them as the rangers fought to gather their wits.

"Wh-What's that?" Buck cried, incredulous.

Ben turned on him with a snarl even as the next fiery missile hit the treetops. "Never seen a firebomb before?"

Shane reached for his long-range rifle. "Enough of this."

Raising the sights to his eye, he squinted, finger ready on the trigger. But a noise across the clearing drew his attention away.

Pink rays of dawn rising behind him, Louis Delacroix appeared at the crest of the hill, running up a path. Abandoned by his own henchmen, he shook his fist at the copter, yelling for their return. The craft banked to leave the area. Delacroix raised his rifle, taking aim at the fuselage. A spray of bullets hit its side. The craft appeared unscathed—then burst into a ball of flame that disintegrated into hundreds of pieces flying in all directions. Shock waves shook the ground below. Delacroix screamed, throwing up his arms at the rain of flaming shrapnel.

"Down!" Shane yelled. The rangers dropped into fetal positions behind the shield of boulders. Metal fragments glanced off, shooting sparks. All four men flattened themselves against the rock, pressing into any crevice they could find. The smell of singed fabric and burning fuel stung their noses.

Gradually, the shower of debris subsided, leaving behind an eerie quiet, punctuated by cracking and popping. Shane was first to regain his wits, peering over the boulders.

Destruction lay everywhere. Blackened, smoking fragments of the helicopter lay twisted and scattered amid a gray, powdery silt that covered the clearing.

"My sentiments exactly," he said grim-faced.

One by one, the other rangers rose and looked about, meeting each other's eyes with silence.

Their attention was redirected to scanning the surroundings for the best way out. Pockets of fire now dotted the mountainside. There wasn't time for debate.

"We better split up. You two go on, try the north trail," Shane directed Cal. "We'll take the east." He slid an arm under Ben's shoulder. "Try to meet down at Rich Mountain Road. Call into the Cove soon as there's no interference." He turned back to Ben. "Can you walk with help?"

Ben managed a haggard smile. "I'll be caught tryin'."

As Shane bent to retrieve his rifle, Buck helped steady Ben, who eyed the bandaged arm. "Kinda surprised to see you here." His mouth twitched. "Where's Rachel?"

Devoid of his usual bashfulness, MacIntyre threw him a tight look. "Where she *should* be."

Morgan's smile softened. "Glad to hear it."

Shane nudged MacIntyre's shoulder. "Let's get out of here. Last one back buys the steaks."

Cal and Buck headed down through the trees.

Shane and Ben tried out a couple of halting steps across the rocky terrain, but Shane pivoted back, catching what he thought was the faint sound of moaning. It seemed to come from the splintered heap of logs and rubble that used to be the field cabin. He squinted at the smoking ruin. "Did you hear somethin'?"

"What?"

Shane shook his head. "Not sure." They looked at each other, then after Cal and Buck, almost too far away now to call back.

"You want me to—?"

"Nah…let 'em go." He stared back at the cabin, pondering the situation. "Here, stay put—unless it starts gettin' hot." He eased Ben down onto a stump, eyeing the smoldering treetops. The wind seemed to be heading away from them for the time being at least.

He pulled his Glock from its holster and approached the debris-laden site with measured steps. The roof of the cabin still blazed. One corner was left standing, the rest blown down by the explosion. He headed over for a final sweep of the area, convinced now his ears must have tricked him. Perhaps it had been the wind in the trees.

As he rounded the corner, something hard banged against his hand, jarring the Glock from his grasp. With a grunt of pain, he fell back, cradling his wrist. A blur rushed at him. Shane made out the splintered plank poised overhead and dropped, rolling out of the way. As he lay there panting, he got his first good look at his assailant.

It was Delacroix. Somehow, he had managed to survive the hellfire of debris. Face blackened, half his hair singed away, bloodied and furious at being left behind by his own men, he stood over Shane ready to take out that fury on the ranger. Delacroix bent down unsteadily to retrieve Shane's handgun, a grim smile of triumph on his face. Shane's gaze travelled to the Frenchman's side. A charred hole in his expensive jacket testified to a grave wound there still smoking. His breaths were ragged wheezes.

Shane found himself gauging how long the guy could last, much less stand in such a condition. Maybe long enough.

The gun wavered, but kept its aim on his chest.

"So...MacLeod...at least...I have...the satisfaction...of gaining...the upper hand...on you...once more." Delacroix attempted to cock his head, but it had more the effect of a sag. "I believe...that makes...*twice*...now?"

Shane kept his eyes trained on the Glock. Surely it couldn't be long now before he collapsed. But the gun could discharge when he went. Delacroix wouldn't give up, wouldn't let go.

"I'd be...glad to fill you in...on the details...of how I found...Morgan and...your wife. How does it feel...to be played...for the fool? Or does it...affect you...at all? No...a man...such as yourself...wouldn't let it...interfere...or does it?"

Shane's face drained of color but he said nothing. But the slime-bag's venom had touched a nerve.

From behind them came Ben's voice. "You're the fool, Delacroix—"

Both men swiveled to find the other ranger standing on the hill of debris above them, rifle poised at his hip like a lanky gunslinger. Shane wondered how Morgan managed to look so steady, masking the extent of his injuries. Brutal red stripes crisscrossed the Park Service uniform.

Shane turned back to Delacroix. "Some things are worth not givin' up on."

Ben's eyes flicked to Shane for the barest second but turned back to Delacroix, keeping his rifle trained on him.

A popping noise came from a shed some fifty yards away. All three turned to look—just before the explosion that blew out the structure from within. Splinters rocketed into the air even as the men were knocked off their feet.

Ben found himself sprawled, face down, in the spongy peat of the forest floor. Grunting with the effort, he rolled onto his elbows, spitting dirt, and sat up in the smoky air, staring about in confusion. Shielding his eyes, he squinted into the haze. No sign of the other two among the smoking ruins. Forgetting his injuries, Ben bolted to his feet and staggered, face ashen.

"Shane!"

. 31 .

Back at Cades Cove Visitor Center, the helicopter's explosion had been clearly audible. Park staff and media alike ran out to witness the trailing cloud of debris and smoke in the sky to the northwest. Immediately, Hank Stone dispatched several rangers in vehicles. FBI agents scrambled for their cars. The USPP helicopter, on standby, zoomed overhead, veering toward the smoking mountainside. The sound of sirens dispersed in all directions.

Up the road, everyone at the lodge was awakened by these sounds of an emergency. Jess and Marcie were the first to run outside, the first to see the mysterious plume in the sky to the northwest.

Before anyone could have a chance to react, Andie took command.

"Come on! Pile in!"

Herding everyone into the Blazer, she handed off Adam to Marcie and sped in the direction of the ominous smoke column.

* * * *

On the mountainside, Cal and Buck were picking their way down a steep incline, knee-deep in fallen leaves. The trail had almost been obliterated by the last snowstorm. Recent winds had stripped the remaining foliage and deposited it along with a number of branches across these remote, less-traveled paths.

Cal pointed to the pebble-strewn, half-dry ravine that ran alongside. "Might be easier to follow that streambed down."

Buck studied it a moment then glanced at the sky. Rangers knew there was always the threat of flash floods upstream to be considered, but that was less likely to occur in November than spring and summer months. He nodded.

"Okay, let's give it a go."

Cal jumped down into the gully first. The bank was about head high above the streambed. Buck followed stiffly, wincing. He was feeling the aftereffects of his sniper encounter more after all their hiking. Aside from the grazed arm, he now wondered if he'd bruised some ribs. He'd definitely twisted a shoulder. But he tried to put all that out of his mind for now, eager to get down the mountain. Hopefully, there would be a squad gathered there by now.

An exchange with Morgan was still dogging him. *Where's Rachel? Where she should be.* Just where you'd expect her to be....

The question was, where was Stoke Hendrickson?

Buck licked dry lips and called up to Cal trudging ahead of him. "You didn't see Hendrickson up there in all that mess, did you?"

"Naw. Sure didn't." Cal went another few steps, slowed to a stop, and turned around. The two rangers' eyes met.

"Which means one of two things." Buck lowered his voice. "He's either still loose in these woods or—" They scanned the ghostly gray, empty forest around them.

At least it seemed empty. There were plenty of outcroppings, gullies, even caves to hide in. Still, he'd rather face a madman out here in the open than contemplate Hendrickson holed up back home with Rachel held hostage.

"I gotta get back to my place quick."

Cal nodded solemnly and picked up the pace. "Let's take this fork. It's a steeper incline but more direct—if you can manage it."

The streambed widened, flattening out in the middle, but the ledge above remained high. Cal tried to make contact on his radio but still got only static. They'd gone another hundred yards, when

Buck, bringing up the rear, thought he heard rustling coming from the bank. *From inside.* He glanced back, slowing, hand reaching for his sidearm. Nothing looked out of the ordinary at first. Then he spied the hole in the bank. Hidden by a tangle of twisted gray vines like witch's hair dangling across a great, black maw.

Big enough to hold a bear...or a man....

He trained his Glock on the opening. "Step out. Step out with your hands up."

At first, nothing. Buck began to doubt himself. For good measure, he called out again, "Come out now or I'll riddle this bank with bullets till it looks like Swiss cheese."

Rustling sounded inside the blackness. Buck braced himself, realizing at the same time there was the distinct possibility that he had just threatened a bear trying to hibernate in peace. The figure became dimly visible...dark, bear-shaped enough....

The shaggy head raised. *Sure enough.*

Buck took in his breath. Cal was now at his side, gun poised in backup. Buck kept his eyes glued on Stoke Hendrickson, consternation churning in his stomach. How to handle this new complication?

Hair matted, clothes torn, scraggly growth of beard the color charcoal...Hendrickson must have been hiding out in the woods the whole of the past week. Maybe since the fire.... Those glittering eyes spoke of a death wish. He straightened from the crouch that made him look like a cornered animal.

"What's the matter, ranger? 'Fraid t' pull th' trigger?" he snarled.

Cal eyed Buck from the side, watched his Adam's apple bob. Once. Twice. There was something in MacIntyre's face he didn't recognize. Something that made him uneasy.

"Buck—"

The mountainside suddenly heaved under them, rocking with an explosion that sent the three men reeling. Cal fell hard into Buck. Both rangers struggled to keep their balance, hanging onto each other. They flashed a look of alarm each other's way.

MacLeod...Morgan....

377

Buck whirled around to see Hendrickson scrambling down the streambed fifty feet away.

"No!"

MacIntyre charged after him.

"Buck! Wait!" Cal clambered after him, catching an uneasy glance over his shoulder at the mountainside above. "God help you, fellas, you're on your own," he said under his breath. *Gotta catch that boy before he does something he'll regret....*

He caught up with Buck another hundred feet down, where the bank sloped even with the streambed. MacIntyre was leveling his Glock at Hendrickson's head, eerily calm.

The bear-like fugitive was panting but eyed the tousled young ranger coldly, almost detached. Maybe his thoughts traveled to anticipation of the wool blanket on that jail bed and his first warm meal in days—ignorant of what Cal sensed in his colleague, the air of a man pushed over the edge.

"You don't have to do this, buddy," Evans said carefully.

Buck's voice was hard-edged. "I know. I just want to."

The ranger walked straight over to Hendrickson and pressed the muzzle of the semi-automatic at the precise center of that craggy forehead. MacIntyre's eyes looked as though his soul had left his body, turned hard as steel, pinpoints of focus in deadly earnest.

Cal froze, wavering whether it was his duty to shoot a fellow ranger to protect a felon or let events take their course.

The shadow passed.

"Walk, you son of a bitch," Buck growled.

*   *   *   *

As the Blazer drew near the vicinity of the smoke plumes, Andie saw they had been preceded by a dozen Park Service trucks and emergency vehicles, along with several FBI cars and a water tank truck. All had converged at the northwest end of the Cades Cove Loop.

Andie was first to jump from the truck as soon as it stopped. "Stay in the car!" she barked. "I'll get word."

Jess Morgan pulled on the door handle to follow but his mother yanked him back.

Andie ran toward the crowd, searching for a familiar face, anyone who could tell her the status of the situation. She pushed her way through the sea of strangers. Catching sight of Cal Evans sitting on the back bumper of an EMT truck, she ran to him. Buck MacIntyre sat beside him, coughing, his arm being treated by a paramedic. Both rangers were soot-covered.

Breathless, Andie grabbed Cal by the arm. "Have you seen them?"

The ranger reached up to touch her arm, face solemn. "No, Baby...I wish I could tell you."

A shout went up. A young ranger, standing atop a park truck, focused his binoculars on the mountainside. "I see 'em! No... wait.... It looks like one...."

Andie backed away, shaking her head in disbelief. Hands pulled her out of the way as a team of firefighters barreled through. She looked up to find the calm, towering presence of John Matthews at her back, bracing her.

"I came as soon as I heard...."

She pulled free and staggered away in a fog, hugging herself tight. The ground seemed to pitch beneath her. She groped for the tailgate of the truck behind her and sank onto it. A hundred terrible visions, each more terrifying than the last, swam through her head.

What if one didn't make it?

Who can I live without?

Shane? Never to come under the spell of that steady, all-knowing gaze again...that low, deep laugh he shared with few but gave willingly to her...that smell of leather and horses mixed with balsam that was uniquely his...the patient, kind hands...weathered, gnarled from war wounds yet still strong, that reached to help when hers were flustered...that gently guided a daughter's hands in learning a new skill.... Would they have a chance to teach his son?

Ben? That infuriating charismatic grin…those magnetic green eyes that could go from impish to irresistible in a heartbeat….. They had only gotten better with age. Thought she'd found the ultimate cure for getting over him…only to rediscover that part of her that still belonged to him. Those eyes couldn't be gone! That grin couldn't be gone!

A wail welled in her throat.

A cry went up. *"I see two! It's both of them!"*

Andie lunged forward, shoving people out of her way, wrestling aside the sea of shoulders that blocked her view. For one dizzying second, she wasn't sure which one she would run to in her relief and joy. But her legs propelled her onward.

She tore through the crowd, some realizing who she was and making way.

They were in her sights now…two worn-looking, sooty men hobbling down the trail, hanging onto each other for dear life. They sagged against a boulder near the trailhead.

Both rangers looked up at the same moment, spotting her. Both seemed to have the same question written on their faces as she approached them at a dead run. Each man braced himself.

Cal Evans and John Matthews eyed one another uncomfortably, Melba and Susannah watched with apprehension as Andie ran into the arms of the one man while the other had to look on….

It was Tawnee, breaking through the crowd, who broke the spell. Chest heaving, she reached the front lines and spied Ben. It took him a moment to pull his eyes away from the pair beside him and look up to see her standing there. Her eyes took him in ravenously.

Ben surged to his feet, unmindful of the dirt and smoke, the blood-stained uniform, and gathered her in. She vented her frustration with a hearty pounding on his chest but he just grinned sheepishly.

A cheer went up, but neither ranger seemed aware of it, locked tight in their embraces, neither about to let go.

*   *   *   *

Later, as Ben sat in the back of a paramedic truck having his injuries tended alongside Cal and Buck, Shane ambled by, an arm slung around Andie's shoulders, something casual but possessive in the gesture. Little Adam dozed on his mother's shoulder, oblivious to the world now that the commotion had died down. Big sister Marcie clung to her dad's hand as if afraid to let go.

Shane looked over to where Stoke Hendrickson was being escorted into an FBI vehicle and nodded to Cal.

"Good work."

Cal nodded to his partner. "It was all Buck's doin'."

The Virginia farm boy-turned-ranger blushed pink. But all the praise he really needed was in the eyes of the young mountain woman lingering at his side. "Thank you for bringing her," he said to the white-haired woman smiling behind Rachel.

"We look after our own," Doc Lillian returned.

A familiar voice called out from behind Shane. He turned with a lop-sided grin and thumbed over his shoulder. "Oh, yeah, look who I ran into."

Ben squinted past him. "Oh, no…."

Phillip Stevens bounded toward them, camera cases flying off his shoulders.

"Don't jostle your equipment," Ben cracked.

"Good to see you, too," Phillip puffed. He flashed an exhilarated smile. That usually meant trouble.

Ben eyed him warily. "What're you up to?"

Stevens proudly tugged at the badge dangling from his lanyard. "Photographer! UPI Services. Heard you guys were wrapped up in this story and convinced my new boss to let me have a go at it. Told him I had inside connections with the Park Service."

Ben and Shane eyed each other.

"And?" Shane prompted.

"I got this epic shot of you guys—" Phillip formed a frame with his hands. Thought I'd title it *Singed Heroes Save the Smokies*. Like it?"

Shane looked to Ben. "I liked him better as a dentist…stuck in San Diego."

Ben wagged his head. "At least we were less likely to run into him then."

"S'cuse me guys. Gotta run! See ya in the newspapers!" Phillip bounded off like a gleeful teenager. An attractive blonde with a press badge was signaling him from the back of a camera van.

Bemused, they watched him go.

Shane turned back, planting a look of assessment on Ben. He scratched his jaw. "I suppose you can come in a little late in th' mornin'. Just don't make a habit of it."

District Chief MacLeod limped away, the ghost of a smile on his face.

Ranger Morgan stared after him, breaking into a slow grin of his own.

*   *   *   *

The Blazer wound along the Cove Loop Road beneath a thinning canopy of leaves, slowing to a stop adjacent a spread of open meadow. The window rolled down on the driver's side.

Andie MacLeod's face appeared, staring pensively across the fence at a figure on horseback. Pulling onto the shoulder, she got out, eyes wistful.

The rider, now discernible as a ranger, looked up and headed her way. Andie swallowed, leaning on the split rail fence. Still, a smile tugged at her mouth as the man approached on that showstopper of a Palomino. The last sweetgum leaves blew free, showering horse and rider with stars of gold. She bit back the urge to laugh. *Of course….*

The ranger stopped across the fence from her with a tight smile.

Andie squinted up at him, shielding her eyes against the morning sun. "I heard you're taking a transfer."

Ben's face crinkled into a mischievous grin. "Yeah…to Oconaluftee…*South* District."

"Oh...." Andie's eyes widened in surprise. She frowned, digesting this piece of news. "So...we'll still be like...neighbors, huh...."

Ben cocked an eyebrow. "Yeah...like neighbors."

Andie's eyes flickered before rising to meet his with a smile of understanding.

EPILOGUE

The ongoing march of seasons is evident in the trees and along the roadsides. Now in late spring, the park, along with the rangers, prepares to meet the onslaught of visitors for yet another busy year....

Not far from the Oconaluftee Visitor Center, groundhogs scamper across open fields. Beneath a dogwood resplendent in white blossoms, Ben and Tawnee Morgan sit quietly on a rock wall. The ranger looks about with the air of a man at peace with himself.

A quartet of college girls dressed in hiking gear passes by. His gaze wanders after them until Tawnee reaches out a finger to turn the chin of her well-intentioned but easily distracted husband. She presents him with a little kiss of reminder. Ben grins sheepishly, throwing an arm about her, and answers with an exuberant kiss of his own.

Fortunately, there are no passersby to see the two lose their balance and fall unceremoniously backwards into the underbrush. Nor does anyone catch Ben's contrite voice grouse softly, "Aww...geez...poison ivy, wouldn't you know it...."

Across the park, District Chief MacLeod is just arriving home. He pulls into the drive, gets out, and saunters down to meet his wife, returning from the mailbox.

At sight of that cascade of russet hair swirling as she turns to greet him, there's an undeniable surge in his chest. The light come into her eyes tells him he made the right choice to hang on for dear life to this exasperating, distracting, but intoxicating creature he allowed to run rampant over his heart.

She gives him that teasing look that always keeps him guessing. "It's good to have you home early."

"It's good to *be* home."

She takes his hand, tugging him toward the lodge.

He follows at his own steady pace.

"So how did the visit with Marcie's teacher go?" she asks over her shoulder.

The ranger groans. "Turns out she's smart. Just my luck...."

His young wife looks at him askance. "But we knew *that*."

"Yeah...it's just...now they're talkin' special classes. And then there's college...."

She loops her arm through his. "Not to worry. I'm guessing she'll get all kinds of scholarships when the time comes. Besides, I may have come up with an idea today that could help."

"What's that?"

"I had a revelation today! I think I've finally figured out what to do with myself!"

"This should be good." He stops, breaking into an indulgent smile. "Okay, give."

"I'm going to write that book about rangers! Really!" Her eyes sparkle at the declaration.

Shane stands there, blinking, before a slow, warm grin breaks across his lean face. He reaches around to steal a hand into her back pocket drawing her close.

"I don't know...seems like last time you said that, all hell broke loose...."

She bumps him with her hip and slides her hand into *his* back pocket as they stroll, together, up to the lodge.

* * * *

A family of early morning hikers looks up the trail to see two rangers on horseback leisurely approaching. One of the rangers touches his cap in greeting and turns back to his partner, continuing their conversation. The children in the group look over their shoulders to watch the rangers amble down the tree-canopied lane—remnants of another era, ever vigilant, on patrol....

~ ~ ~ ~ ~ ~ ~

RANGERS continues:

Reckoning and Redemption

Two individuals battle with guilt and the difficulties of moving on in the continuation of the RANGERS saga.

Ranger Ben Morgan struggles to regain his footing after tragedy strikes his family. A chance meeting with a fascinating stranger throws him into a tailspin, shaken to the core. Not even his stalwart friends can get him out of this mess. He's on his own.

And a young hiker from the North arrives in the Smokies after an arduous trek down the Appalachian Trail. His dark journey of soul-searching lands him on the remote side of the Smokies, finding a new identity—and new crises to face.

Both will face challenges that test their character, loyalties, and their very survival in an unforgiving wilderness....

REFERENCES

Special thanks to the following men and women of Great Smoky Mountains National Park for their correspondence, assistance, and informative interviews over the years:

George Minnigh, Law Enforcement/Visitor Protection
Bob Miller, HQ, Management Assistant
Nancy Gray, HQ of Public Affairs
Carey Jones, Interpretive/Visitor Services Division
Carroll Schell, Resource Management/Wildlife Division.
Babette Callavos, HQ Office of the Superintendent
Randall R. Pope, Superintendent of Great Smoky Mountains National Park 1987-93

Smokies Life Magazine National Parks Centennial Issue, Volume 10 #1, Great Smoky Mountains Association, Steve Kemp contributing editor. www.SmokiesInformation.org

Friends of the Smokies www.friendsofthesmokies.org

Bruce Bytnar, Retired National Park Ranger, author of *A Park Rangers Life*. www.aparkrangerslife.blogspot

National Park Service: The Story Behind the Scenery by Horace M. Albright, Russell E. Dickenson, and William Penn Mott, Jr.

Great Smoky Mountains: The Splendor of the Southern Appalachians by Steven L. Walker

Yosemite: The Story Behind the Scenery by William R. Jones, KC Publications

Park Ranger Guide to Wildlife by Arthur P. Miller, Jr.

www.bioimages.vanderbilt.edu "Trees of the Great Smoky Mountains"

Smokies Guide official newspaper of GSMNP

Great Smoky Mountains National Park Map by National Park Service, Dept. of the Interior

Cades Cove Guide publication by GSM Natural History Association

Great Smoky Mountains National Park American Park Network

www.plants.usda.gov *Echinacea purpurea* (purple coneflower)

Our Southern Highlanders Horace Kephart

Philippians 4:8 Quote: Bible, New Revised Standard Version

Historical Note:

Great Smoky Mountains National Park established 1934.
Yosemite National Park established 1890.